WESTMORELAND
NIGHTS
BY
BRENDA JACKSON

AND

SCANDALISING
THE CEO
BY
KATHERINE GARBERA

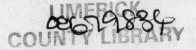

MILLS
BOON

"When I get around to kissing you, I'll feel better knowing your mouth doesn't belong to any other man. Legally or otherwise."

She didn't say anything for a moment. Then she opened her mouth, probably to tell him just where he could take his own mouth—legally or otherwise—but instead of saying anything right then, she just clamped her lips together.

He chuckled. "Tightening those lips shut won't keep me from a kiss, if that's what I want to do, Chloe."

Chloe folded her arms across her chest. "Is there a reason for this madness?"

"Is that what this is? Madness?" he asked.

She lifted her chin and glared at him. "You got another name for it?"

"What about *hunger?*"

HOT WESTMORELAND NIGHTS

BY
BRENDA JACKSON

Published in Great Britain 2011
by Mills & Boon, an imprint of Harlequin (UK) Limited,
Eton House, 18-24 Paradise Road, Richmond, Surrey TW9 1SR

© Brenda Streater Jackson 2010

ISBN: 978 0 263 88211 7

51-0411

Harlequin (UK) policy is to use papers that are natural, renewable and
recyclable products and made from wood grown in sustainable forests. The
logging and manufacturing processes conform to the legal environmental
regulations of the country of origin.

Printed and bound in Spain
by Blackprint CPI, Barcelona

Brenda Jackson is a die "heart" romantic who married
her childhood sweetheart and still proudly wears the
"going steady" ring he gave her when she was fifteen.
Because she's always believed in the power of love,
Brenda's stories always have happy endings. In her real-
life love story, Brenda and her husband of thirty-six
years live in Jacksonville, Florida, and have two sons.

A *New York Times* bestselling author of more than fifty
romance titles, Brenda is a recent retiree who worked
thirty-seven years in management at a major insurance
company. She divides her time between family, writing
and traveling with Gerald. You may write to Brenda at
PO Box 28267, Jacksonville, Florida 32226, USA, by
e-mail at WriterBJackson@aol.com or visit her website
at www.brendajackson.net.

Dear Reader,

Family is important to me and I love writing about the love and escapades that go on within a family structure. Can you imagine being in your middle twenties and helping a cousin barely a year older than you to raise your other young family members—all thirteen of them?

You've met Dillon Westmoreland in *Westmoreland's Way*. The second oldest of the Denver clan is Ramsey, a man who doesn't have marriage or love on his mind. Ramsey's only ambition is to make his sheep-ranching business a success. At least that was his only ambition until he met Chloe Burton. Now he's faced with something he thought could not happen to him, and that was the possibility of falling in love.

And Chloe has her own agenda, which doesn't include a serious involvement with Ramsey. She's done the serious thing with a man and it left her deciding it wasn't worth the trouble. Ramsey becomes a challenge to her peace of mind.

I hope that you find Ramsey and Chloe's story a very special one, and in the coming months I look forward to venturing into the lives of those other Westmorelands, as well.

Happy reading!

Brenda Jackson

Prologue

Chloe Burton pressed her face to the windowpane as she watched the man sprint across the street. Her heart began pounding in her chest. He had to be, without a doubt, the most handsome man she'd ever seen.

She stared as he stopped to talk to another man in front of a feed store. He was tall, dark and every inch of sexy from the Stetson he wore on his head to the well-worn leather boots on his feet. And from the way his jeans and western shirt fit his body, it was quite obvious he possessed powerful legs, strong arms, taut abs, tight buns and broad muscular shoulders. He had everything it took to separate the men from the boys.

And when he pushed back his hat, she saw dark eyes and a medium skin tone. Then she looked at his mouth and she couldn't help licking her lips at the sight of his. His lips were full, firm and luscious. She could imagine those lips and his mouth doing other things.

Just looking at him was enough to corrupt a woman's mind, she thought. Even from this distance, her body felt flushed, hot and unsettled. Nothing like this had ever happened to her while ogling a man in all her twenty-eight years.

Actually, over the past year the only male who had gotten her time and attention had been her *e-mail*. And that was mainly because her last relationship with Daren Fulbright had been totally unsatisfying, a complete waste of the year she'd put into it, and she was in no hurry to get into another. No doubt there were some who thought she'd given up on love much too quickly, and perhaps that was true since these days she much preferred curling up with a good book during her free time than with someone of the opposite sex. And now, here she was practically drooling at just the sight of a man. He might be major eye candy, but the man was a complete stranger to her. Even so, the way he was standing with both hands in his jeans pockets, legs braced apart, was a pose she would carry to her dreams.

And he was smiling, evidently enjoying his conversation. He had dimples, incredibly sexy dimples in not one but both cheeks.

"What are you staring at, Clo?"

Chloe nearly jumped. She'd forgotten she had a lunch date. In fact she had forgotten everything once her sights had landed on the sexy man across the street. She glanced over the table at her best friend from college, Lucia Conyers.

"Take a look at that man across the street in the blue shirt, Lucia, and tell me what you see. Would he not be perfect for Denver's first issue of *Simply Irresistible* or what?" Chloe asked with so much excitement in her voice she almost couldn't stand it.

Chloe was the owner of *Simply Irresistible,* a magazine for today's up-and-coming woman. The magazine had started out as a regional publication in the southeast, but had expanded to a national audience during the past few years. By far the magazine's most popular edition was the annual "Irresistible Man" issue. The feature included a cover shoot and an in-depth story on a man who the magazine felt deserved the honor because he was simply irresistible. As the magazine had expanded, Chloe had convinced Lucia to come on board to manage its Denver office.

When Lucia didn't say anything, Chloe's smile widened. "Well?"

Lucia glanced across the booth at her. "Since you asked, I'll tell you what I see. I see one of the Westmorelands, and in this case it's Ramsey Westmoreland. And to answer your other question as to whether he would be perfect for the cover man on *Simply Irresistible,* my answer would be a resounding yes, but he won't do it."

Chloe raised a brow. "I take it that you know him," she said watching her friend closely.

Lucia smiled. "Yes, but not as well as I know the younger Westmorelands. There's a lot of them and he's one of the oldest. I went to school with his younger siblings and cousins. He has several brothers and male cousins who look just as good. Maybe one of them will agree to do it, but you can forget Ramsey."

Chloe glanced back out the window and knew two things. First, there was no way that she could forget him. Second, from the sound of things it seemed that Lucia was interested in one of those "younger" male Westmorelands. She could hear the wistfulness in her friend's voice.

"He's the one I want, Lucia," she said with both determination and conviction in her voice. "And since you know him, then just ask him. He might surprise you and not turn you down. Of course he'll get paid for his services."

Lucia laughed and shook her head. "Getting paid isn't the issue, Clo. Ramsey is one of the wealthiest sheep ranchers in this part of Colorado. But everyone knows what a private person he is. Trust me, he won't do it."

Chloe hoped she was wrong. "But you will ask him?"

"Yes, but I suggest you move on and find another man."

Chloe glanced back out the window. The man was the epitome of what she was looking for in her "Irresistible Man" issue and she was determined to have him.

"Um, I don't like that look on your face, Chloe. I've seen it before and know exactly what it means."

Chloe couldn't help but smile. She could only blame her smile on her father, Senator Jamison Burton of Florida, the man who'd raised her alone after her mother died of cervical cancer when Chloe was three. Her father was the one man she most admired and he'd always taught her that if people wanted something bad enough, they wouldn't give up until they got it.

She glanced out the window and watched as Ramsey Westmoreland ended his conversation and entered the feed store with a swagger that almost made her breathless. She *would* be seeing him again.

One

"I can't believe you're not posing for the cover of that magazine, Ram."

Ramsey Westmoreland didn't bother to look up from arranging a bale of straw in the lambing stall. He'd figured his youngest sister Bailey would show up sooner or later, because news traveled pretty fast within the Westmoreland family. And of course, Bailey made it her life's work to know everything about her five brothers, down to their every heartbeat.

"I'm not going away, Ramsey, until you tell me what I want to know."

He couldn't help but smile at the threat because he knew if he gave her an order to leave that she *would* follow it. She might like to express her emotions and display her defiance every once in a while, and God help him when she did, but when it was all said and done, Bailey knew how far to take things with him. He would be the first to admit that she had tested his limits plenty, especially during those years when she and their cousin Bane had been almost inseparable. The two thought getting into trouble was a way of life.

Since then Bailey had finished high school and was now attending college, and Bane had surprised everyone with his decision last month to join the military with the goal of becoming a Navy Seal. All was quiet on the Westmoreland front and Ramsey would be the first to admit, but only to himself, things had been a little boring.

"There's nothing to tell," he decided to respond. "I was contacted about doing that cover and I turned them down."

"Just like that?"

"Just like that." He figured she was probably glaring at him right now.

"Why, Ram? Just think of the exposure."

He finally decided to look up and the gaze that sharpened on Bailey was so keen, had it been anyone else they would have had the good sense to take a step back. But not twenty-one-year-old Bailey Joleen Westmoreland. Of his three sisters—Megan, who was almost twenty-five and Gemma, who was twenty-three—Bailey was the boldest and could test the patience of Job, so to try the patience of her oldest brother was a piece of cake.

"I don't want exposure, Bailey. I think the Westmorelands got enough exposure all those years when we had to deal with the trouble you, Bane and the twins got into."

Not an ounce of regret flared in her eyes. "That was then. This is now. And this would have been good exposure."

He almost laughed at that one. "Good exposure for who exactly?" he asked, getting to his feet.

He had a lot to do and little time for chitchat. Nellie, who'd had the responsibility of preparing the meals for him and the ranch hands for the past two years, had to leave suddenly yesterday when she'd gotten word that her only sister back in Kansas had emergency surgery for a ruptured appendix. She intended to stay and help out and it would be at least two weeks before she returned.

Ramsey understood and supported her decision, although Nellie's absence left him in a bind. Today was the start of shearing and with over twenty or so men involved, he was in desperate need of a cook to take Nellie's place. He had placed a call to one of these temporary employment agencies yesterday afternoon and was told they had just the person who would be perfect as a fill-in and the woman was to show up this morning.

"It would be good exposure for you and the ranch. It could put you in the public eye and let everyone know how successful you are as a sheep rancher."

Ramsey shook his head. Being in the public eye was something he could definitely pass on. He was close to his family, but when it came to outsiders he was basically a loner and preferred things that way. Everyone knew how much he enjoyed his privacy. Bailey knew it too, so he wondered, why was she harassing him?

"The ranch doesn't need *that* kind of exposure. I was asked to pose for some girly magazine, Bail." He had never read a copy of *Simply Irresistible,* but the name alone made his jaw twitch. He could just imagine the articles that were between the covers.

"You should be flattered they want you on the cover, Ram."

He rolled his eyes. "Whatever." He then checked his watch for two reasons. This was Monday and he knew Bailey had a

class at the university this morning *and* his temporary cook
was ten minutes late.

"I wish you would reconsider."

He glanced back at her. "No," he said firmly. "And shouldn't
you be in class about now?" He moved out of the barn and
walked back toward the sprawling home he had finished
building the previous year.

Bailey followed, right on his heels. He couldn't help but
recall that she used to do that same thing when he took over
the responsibility of raising her when she was seven and he
was twenty-one. They'd lost both parents and a beloved aunt
and uncle in an airplane accident. During that time she would
rarely let him out of her sight. He fought back a smile at the
fond memory.

"Yes, I have a class this morning, but I thought I'd drop by
to talk some sense into you," he heard her say.

He turned around, placed his hands in his pockets. At that
moment he couldn't stop the smile that touched his lips. "Fine.
You've tried and failed. Goodbye, Bailey."

He watched her place her hands on her hips and lift her chin.
No one had to warn him about Westmoreland stubbornness.
Hers could be more lethal than most, but over the past twenty-
one years he'd learned to deal with it.

"I think you're making a mistake. I subscribe to that
magazine and I think you'd be surprised," she was saying. "It's
not just a 'girly' magazine. It has a number of good articles
for women, including some on health issues. However, once a
year they feature a man on the cover. They try to find a man
who's every woman's fantasy lover."

A woman's fantasy lover? Now that was a laugh, Ramsey
thought. He was nothing more than a hardworking Colorado
sheep rancher and since he'd doubled the size of his herd this

past year, he couldn't recall the last time he'd been intimately involved with a woman. Working sunup to sundown, seven days a week had become a way of life for him.

"It will be my mistake to make, brat. I'll survive and so will you. Now scat."

A half-hour later he was alone and standing in his kitchen and clicking off his cell phone after talking to Colin Lawrence, a member of his shearing crew. Because of a snowstorm that had hit the area a few weeks ago, they were already behind in shearing and needed to get that done within the next two weeks in time for lambing to begin. Starting today everything would be moving rather fast to stay on schedule.

Colin had called to say a few of the pregnant ewes had somehow gotten out of the shearing pen and begun to wander. The dogs were having a hard time getting them back in the pen without stressing out the pregnant sheep. The last thing he needed was for any more shearing time to be lost, which meant that he had to get to the shearing plant on the north range as soon as possible.

He headed toward the door when he heard a car pull up outside. He glanced at his watch, agitated. It was about time the cook showed up. The woman was almost an hour late and that was not acceptable. And he intended to let her know about his displeasure.

Chloe brought the car to a stop in front of a huge two-story ranch-style structure and drew in a deep breath. She simply refused to take no for an answer regardless of what Ramsey Westmoreland had told Lucia. His refusal to be the cover story for her magazine was the reason she had ended a much-deserved vacation in the Bahamas to fly directly here. She intended to try to convince the man herself.

As she checked her GPS while traveling farther and farther

away from Denver's city limits and heading into a rural area the locals referred to as Westmoreland Country, she had asked herself why on earth would anyone want to live so far from civilization. That in itself was a mystery to her. She hadn't passed a single shopping mall along the way.

Looking out the car's window, she couldn't get out of her mind the man she had seen that day a couple of weeks ago. That was why she refused to move on and select someone else. The bottom line was that she didn't want anyone else. Ramsey Westmoreland was not only the man made for the title of *Simply Irresistible,* but he *was* simply irresistible.

Once she had turned off the main road, she saw the huge wooden marker that proudly proclaimed The Shady Tree Ranch. Beside it another smaller marker read *This is Westmoreland Country.* Lucia had said each of the fifteen Westmorelands owned a hundred acres of land where they had established their private residences. The main house sat on three hundred acres.

Once she turned off the main road, there had been several turnoffs, each denoted by smaller brick makers that indicated which Westmoreland the private driveway belonged to. She had traveled past Jason's Place, Zane's Hideout, Canyon's Bluff and Derringer's Dungeon before finally reaching Ramsey's Web.

She had done her research and knew everything she needed to know about Ramsey Westmoreland for now. He was thirty-six. A graduate of Tuskegee University's agricultural economics program, and had been in the sheep ranching business for about five years. Before that he and his cousin Dillon, who was older than Ramsey by only seven months, had run Blue Ridge Land Development, a multimillion-dollar company started by their fathers. Once the company had become successful Ramsey had turned the management of Blue Ridge over to Dillon to become the rancher he'd always wanted to be.

She also knew about the death of his parents and aunt and uncle in a car crash while Ramsey was in his final year of college. For the last fifteen years, Ramsey and Dillon had been responsible for their younger siblings. Dillon had gotten married three months ago, and he and his wife Pamela split their time between Dillon's home here and Pamela's home in a small town in Wyoming.

As far as Chloe was concerned, Ramsey Westmoreland was a success story and the type of man that women not only would want to fantasize about, but also one they would want to get to know in the article that would appear in her magazine.

She couldn't stop the fluttering in her stomach thinking that she was on property he owned and she would be seeing him again. If he had the ability to wreck her senses weeks after first setting eyes on him, she could just imagine what seeing him again would do. But she intended to handle herself as the professional that she was, while at the same time trying to convince him that sheep produced wool that eventually got weaved into articles of clothing—dresses, coats, jackets and such—that were mainly purchased by women.

She took another deep breath and opened the car door and got out at the same time the front door was slung opened and the man who'd tormented her dreams for the past couple of weeks stepped out on the porch with a scowl on his face, and said in a firm voice, "You are late."

Ramsey tried not to stare at the woman but couldn't help it. And this was supposed to be his temporary cook? She looked more like a model than a damn cook. There was no doubt in his mind that she would be able to generate plenty of heat in the kitchen or any other room she set foot in.

She was definitely a beauty with dark brown curly hair that flowed to her shoulders, dark brown eyes that looked seductive rather than contrite and a perfectly shaped mouth. And seeing her dressed in a pair of jeans that hugged her hips and pink blouse beneath a black leather jacket, made her look ultra-feminine and made him blatantly aware of his sexuality, while reminding him of just how long it had been since he'd been with a woman.

Ramsey hadn't expected this gut-stirring lust. He didn't need the attraction nor did he want it. It would be best for all concerned if she just got back in her car and returned to wherever she'd come from. But that wasn't possible. He had over twenty men to feed come lunchtime. He had managed to get through breakfast and thank goodness no one had complained. They had understood Nellie's emergency and had tolerated the slightly burned biscuits, scorched eggs and the overly crisp bacon. He had promised them a better meal for lunch. When they saw this woman they would definitely think *she* was a delicious treat.

"Excuse me. What did you say?"

He glanced across the yard where she was still standing by her car. Feeling frustrated as hell and fighting for control he walked down the steps, not taking his eyes off her. "I said you are late and your pay will be docked accordingly. The agency said you would be here at eight and it's now after nine. I have twenty men you'll need to feed at lunchtime. I hope there won't be a problem because I have plenty to do this morning and the agency assured me that you knew your way around a kitchen."

Chloe resisted the urge to ask what he was talking about.

Instead she spoke up and said, "Yes, I know my way around a kitchen."

"Then get to it. I'll be back for lunch and we can talk then, but I can tell you now that one of my pet peeves is tardiness," he said, moving toward his truck.

From what Chloe gathered he was expecting a cook who evidently was late in arriving. She should speak up now and explain to him that she was not the cook but he seemed to be in such a hurry. "Wait!"

He paused, turned sensual dark eyes on her and she felt a heated sensation rush up her spine at the same time she felt the tenderness in the nipples pressed against her blouse. "Look, lady, I don't have time to wait. I'm needed over at the shearing plant as we speak. You'll find everything you need in the kitchen."

His voice was hard, yet at the same time it sounded sexy. And she couldn't believe it when he hopped into his truck and pulled off. She couldn't do anything but stand there and watch him leave.

So much for having her say to convince him to do the magazine cover. For crying out loud, he thought she was a cook of all things. What she should do was to just get into her car and leave and come back another time, she thought. But where was this cook he was expecting? And did she hear him correctly when he said that come lunchtime there would twenty men to feed?

Chloe rubbed her hands down her face. Surely there was someone she could call who had his cell—who could get word to him of the grave mistake he'd made.

She turned toward the front door. He had left it wide open on the assumption that she would go inside, and at the moment she didn't have the common sense not to do so. If nothing else she could call Lucia. There was a chance Lucia knew how to contact a family member who would get word to him.

As Chloe walked up the steps it was easy to tell with the fresh-looking paint around the trim, white siding and brick sides that this was a relatively new house. There were a lot of windows facing the front, which provided a good view of the mountains and that were perfectly positioned to take advantage of the sunlight whenever it did appear, which wasn't too often this time of year. The porch wrapped around the front of the house, and the rocking chair and swing looked inviting enough to sit in the afternoons and just relax, even now in March when the weather was still cold.

And speaking of March weather, she tightened her jacket around her and walked into the living room, closed the door behind her and turned around. The place was huge and in the midst of the room, a spiral staircase led to the upstairs. There wasn't a whole lot of furniture in the room, but what was there looked rugged and sturdy. Few pictures hung on the wall and they were classic Norman Rockwell. The floor was hardwood with several area rugs scattered about.

She was about to walk through the living room to where she figured the kitchen was located when the phone rang. She quickly moved toward it, hoping it was either Ramsey Westmoreland or someone who knew how to reach him.

"Hello."

"This is Marie Dodson at the employment agency. May I speak with Mr. Ramsey Westmoreland, please?"

"He isn't here."

"Oh. Then please let him know there was a mix-up and the woman who was supposed to show up at his place this morning as a live-in cook for two weeks was sent somewhere else."

Chloe nodded and tapped her perfectly painted nail against the pad beside the phone. "All right, I'll be sure to tell him."

"He told me that his regular cook had to leave town unexpectedly due to a family emergency. I do hate leaving him in a bind like this with so many men to feed," the woman said with regret in her voice.

"I'm sure he will understand," was the only response Chloe felt she could make. "As a matter of fact, I think he's made other arrangements," Chloe added.

Moments later she was hanging up the phone, hoping that Ramsey Westmoreland *would* understand. But with what she guessed would be twenty hungry men come lunchtime, she wasn't so sure.

At that moment an idea flowed through her mind. Although her father had spoiled her rotten, he was a person who never forgot where he came from and believed in helping those less fortunate. That had been the main reason why she had spent her summers while home from college working at the homeless shelters. And since she enjoyed cooking, for three full summers while all her friends had spent time on the Florida beaches, she had volunteered her time helping out in the shelter's kitchens where large amounts of foods had to be cooked and served.

Mama Francine, who had worked as a cook at the shelter for years, had taught her all she needed to know, regardless of whether Chloe had wanted the education. Now it seemed all Mama Francine's cooking instructions about how to prepare food for a large group hadn't gone to waste.

Chloe tapped her finger to her chin. Maybe if she helped Ramsey Westmoreland out of this bind with lunch today, he just might be grateful enough to return the favor by doing her, cover story. Especially if she made sure he felt he owed her big time. She smiled, liking the thought of that.

After glancing at her watch she took off her jacket and rolled up her sleeves as she headed toward the kitchen. One good favor deserved another and she was counting on Ramsey Westmoreland seeing things that way.

Two

Ramsey's jaw tightened as he slowed his truck to a stop. He had been in such a hurry to get out of the woman's presence that he hadn't taken time to even ask for her name. All he could think about was how his testosterone level had suddenly kicked into gear and that a sexual hunger, unlike any he'd ever experienced before, had begun sliding up his spine.

And the woman was his cook? A live-in cook for two weeks? How in the hell was he supposed to handle something like that? He couldn't imagine sharing space of any kind with her. There was something about her that drew him, made him think of things he hadn't thought of in a long time, had no business thinking about now. Lustful things.

Crap!

He slid the truck into gear to start moving again. What he should do is to turn around, go back and tell her as nicely as he could that she wouldn't work out. Then he'd call the employment agency and request that they send out a replacement.

He checked his watch, wondering how much time it would take to get another cook out to his place. Would the agency be able to find someone else right away? At least in time for lunch? Probably not, which meant he was stuck with the woman at least through today. But what if the agency couldn't find anyone else by tomorrow? What then?

He brought the truck to another stop and rubbed his hand down his face. This wasn't good. The shearers had been at it since six that morning after eating the pitiful breakfast that he had prepared. And he of all people knew his men worked hard and expected a good meal at lunch to keep going until the end of the day. And as their employer it was his job to make sure they got it.

As he turned his truck toward the area where the shearing plant was located he set his jaw in determination as he thought about the challenges that lay ahead with his new cook. He grabbed his cell phone off the seat beside him and figured that maybe he should call the house and check on her, make sure things were running smoothly, and then he quickly decided against it. Although he hadn't given the woman time to say much of anything, he had liked the sound that had flowed from her lips with the few words that she'd spoken.

She looked young, maybe a year or two older than his sister Megan who would be turning twenty-five in a few months. Why would a woman that young want to be a ranch cook? The scowl on his face deepened. Sniffing behind any woman was something he hadn't done in a long time and was something he wouldn't be doing now.

A satisfied smile touched Chloe's face as she glanced around the huge kitchen thinking she had somehow pulled it off. Granted she'd had to call Mama Francine and the older woman had walked her through the peach cobbler recipe, but once Chloe had begun moving around, getting familiar with her surroundings, she had felt within her element. She had made herself at home. She enjoyed cooking, although she would prefer not doing so on a constant basis for a small army.

Ramsey Westmoreland had a well-equipped kitchen with beautiful granite countertops and a number of shining stainless steel pots hanging from a rack. There was an industrial-size refrigerator, a large stove and a spacious walk-in pantry filled to capacity and in neat order. She had been able to find everything she had needed without any problems.

She had glanced through the cook's log that was kept on the kitchen counter. She saw that on most Mondays the men were fed chicken and dumplings, string beans and bread pudding for lunch. To Chloe's way of thinking that menu sounded bland and she had a mind to fix something different. She'd decided on lasagna, a tossed salad and Texas toast. For dessert she figured the peach cobbler would do the trick.

And she had set the table differently. Although she figured when it was time to eat a hungry man didn't care how the table looked, she decided to spruce things up with a different tablecloth, a springy yellow instead of the plaid one that had been on the table and appeared to have seen better days.

It seems that knowing he would always feed a huge work crew, Mr. Westmoreland had built a spacious banquet-size dining room off from the eat-in kitchen with tables and chairs to comfortably accommodate around fifty people. To her way of thinking, it was a smart move and showed just how much he cared for his employees. They would feel important enough to eat under the boss's roof instead of them being relegated to eating in the bunkhouse. To her that said a lot about the kind of employer he was.

She checked her watch. With less than fifteen minutes left she figured it was time to place the serving dishes on the table when she heard a vehicle pull up outside. She glanced out the window and saw it was the truck Ramsey Westmoreland had been driving that morning.

She stiffened, then drew in a deep breath, fighting for control and refusing to come unglued. No matter how handsome the man was, the only thing she wanted was for him to agree to do her magazine cover. She glanced out the window and saw he hadn't gotten out the truck yet and figured because he had arrived that his men were probably not too far behind.

With that thought in mind she moved to the stove to go about getting everything prepared.

Ramsey leaned back in the leather seat and stared at his house, not sure if he was ready to get out of the truck and go inside. He sniffed the air and then out of curiosity he rolled down the window.

Was that something Italian? He inhaled sharply thinking that it certainly smelled like it. When was the last time he and his men had something besides chicken and dumplings on Monday? Nellie was a fantastic cook, but she detested change. When it came to lunch his men could expect chicken and dumplings on Monday, shepherd's pie on Tuesday, chili on Wednesday, beef stew on Thursday and baked chicken on Friday. Nellie was known to keep things simple.

Deciding he couldn't sit in his truck forever, he opened the door to get out. By the time he rounded the front of his truck his front door opened. He stopped walking, literally froze in his tracks as he stared at the woman who stepped out on the porch.

His eyes hadn't played tricks on him that morning. She was a pleasant sight for the sorest of eyes and so stunningly beautiful that he felt every male hormone inside his body shift into overdrive. He struggled, unsuccessfully, to control the attraction he felt toward her. But when a knot twisted in his stomach, he knew he had to get her gone and off his property as soon as reasonably possible. Her being here for any amount of time was not going to work.

Chloe was going through her own issues as she studied the fierce frown on Ramsey Westmoreland's face. She wondered what had him so uptight. She had been the one who'd spent the last two hours in the kitchen over a hot stove, so she saw no reason for what she perceived as an unpleasant demeanor. If he knew the real deal and how she had helped him out of a sticky situation he would be kissing her feet.

And speaking of kissing her feet...

Her mind paused, got stuck on that thought as a vision played out in her head of his actually kissing her feet before his mouth traveled upward to tackle other parts of her body. The very idea made her tighten her hands into fists at her sides at the same time a wave of heated desire suffused her senses.

Jeez. She had been dealing with all kinds of emotions and sensations since entering the man's home, and for her misery he owed her big time.

Yet at the moment, Ramsey Westmoreland was more than a little intimidating. Chloe wasn't sure if she wanted this man indebted to her in any way. He had the look of a man who shared humor only when it suited him. A man who wouldn't hesitate to offer his opinions and not necessarily in a tactful way. He would tell you exactly what he thought. And she had a feeling that he was not a man who made foolish mistakes, or one who could easily be led around by a woman. The latter perversely bothered her because she was used to being in total control of any relationships she got involved in. But then, she and this man were not involved.

Deciding they had wasted enough time sizing up each other, she spoke up. "You were in such a hurry to leave this morning that I didn't get a chance to introduce myself. I'm Chloe Burton."

"You were late this morning."

She couldn't help the frown that settled on her face. Was he thinking of reminding her of it at every turn? Evidently he had very little tolerance for certain things. "No one told me that once I left Denver's city limits that I would be headed for the boondocks, away from normal civilization. You're lucky I made it here at all. So the way I see it is you really should be counting your blessings, Mr. Westmoreland."

Chloe could tell by the way his brow lifted that he was somewhat surprised by her flippant tone. She noted his rigid stance and drew in a fortifying breath, thinking he really shouldn't be so uptight. Life was serious, but there was no reason to take it to the edge. Her father had been that way until a heart attack brought on by stress had nearly done him in a few years ago.

"So when can I expect the other men? I made a feast," she said, deciding to change the subject.

His gaze narrowed at her with shimmering intensity. "They'll finish up and should be here any minute, so we need to talk before they arrive."

Chloe decided then and there that she didn't want to talk. His voice was just like the rest of him, sexy as hell. There was richness to his Western accent that caused a tightness in her throat. Being in his presence for the past few moments had frazzled her nerves, had blood pounding through her veins and had unceremoniously reminded her of the hormones he'd awakened since the first time she had set eyes on him. It also stirred warm emotions, confusing feelings she hadn't felt in a while…if ever. That was not good.

"What do we have to talk about? You've made it clear I was late and my pay would be docked. What else are you out for? Blood?"

Ramsey tensed. Evidently at some point the woman had forgotten that she was the employee and he the employer. Maybe her past employers found her attitude amusing, but he didn't. He opened his mouth to state such a thing, but closed it when he heard the trucks pull up, which signaled the arrival of his men.

"We'll have to wait and talk after lunch," he said tersely. And then without saying anything else, he turned and headed toward the bunkhouse to wash up for lunch.

Ramsey leaned back in his chair thinking he had eaten lasagna before but never this delicious. And from glancing around the room at his men, he figured they were thinking the same thing. And there had been more than enough, which was a good thing because a number of the men had asked for seconds.

And he hadn't been able not to notice that he wasn't the only one who enjoyed seeing Ms. Burton work the room as she made sure everyone had everything they needed. Initially he'd been amused when the guys first arrived and a number of them, once they'd noticed there wasn't a ring on her finger, had tried their hand at flirting. But she had maintained a degree of professionalism that had impressed him. Even Eric Boston and

Thelon Hinton, the two hard-core womanizers in the group, had pretty much backed off when it became obvious that she wasn't returning their interest. That surprised him because those two had a reputation in Denver of being sought-after ladies' men.

Another thing that had impressed him about Chloe Burton was the way she had set up the employee dining room. It was obvious she had taken the time to spruce things up a bit, changing the decor of the men's surroundings. Changing the menu had also been a plus.

He had good men who worked hard. Moreover, they would be putting in long hours during the next two weeks. Most had been with him since he'd started the operation and were family men who went home for dinner and returned for work each day. After shearing, which occurred once a year, some of his men would turn their attention to lambing, while the others would resume their roles as sheepherders.

"I see you can't keep your eyes off her either, Ram."

Ramsey shot a sharp glance over at Callum Austell. When Ramsey had decided to become a sheep rancher he had flown over to Australia to spend six months on one of the country's largest sheep ranches. It was there that he'd met the Aussie, who happened to be the youngest son of the ranch owner. Callum had agreed to come to the States to help Ramsey start his operation. Now three years later, Callum was still here with him. He was the one who'd basically taught Ramsey everything he knew about sheep. He considered Callum a good friend.

"You must be seeing things, Aussie," was Ramsey's reply, even though he knew Callum was right. Okay, so he was looking at her, but because he was her employer he needed to make sure she did her job right and that she conducted herself properly. He had twenty-five employees year round and not including Nellie, they were all men. And he was a hands-on boss, so he was familiar with everything that went on with his ranch and if needed, he could fill in for any of his men.

"I think not, but if you want to convince yourself of it, then go ahead," was Callum's comeback. "All I got to say is that you should be impressed with the way she handled Eric and Thel. I think she might have broken their hearts."

Ramsey couldn't help but snort at that. If that was true, it was about time some woman did. He glanced down at his watch. Lunch was almost over and the men, knowing his policy about punctuality, were standing to leave and were giving Chloe Burton all kinds of compliments. He stood as well, but unlike his men he had no intentions of going anywhere until he had a talk with his cook.

After grabbing his hat off the hat rack, Callum rounded the table and halted in front of Ramsey and studied his features. "I hope you don't plan on ruining things for the rest of us. We like her cooking. And we like her. We would like to keep her around, at least until Nellie comes back."

Callum had quietly spoken his words, just for Ramsey's benefit. Without glancing over at Callum, Ramsey said, "We'll see."

And for now that was all he would say on the matter. Yes, the woman had impressed him and his men with her cooking skills, and yes, she had carried herself in a professional way. But Callum had been right. Just like his men he hadn't been able to stop looking at her and that wasn't a good thing. He had been sitting at the table eating his lasagna and imagining eating her instead. His mind was so filled with lust it wasn't funny, and the flame that burned deep inside him wasn't amusing, either.

He glanced over his shoulder and saw the last of the men had gone, all but Callum, who threw him a daggered look before walking out the door and closing it behind him. Ramsey pulled in a deep, frustrated breath. The impression Chloe had already made on his men was not a good thing. Even if she stayed for two weeks she would have to leave when Nellie returned anyway.

He heard the rattling of the dishes and glanced over at Chloe, watching her as she cleared the table. His gaze slowly swept over her figure, liking the way the jeans fit across her backside. He figured her height was probably around five-eight and he would bet all the wool his sheep would be producing this year that she had long beautiful legs. The kind that would be a killer pair in a miniskirt.

He shook his head thinking about his fetish for seeing women in short skirts. He was a leg man all the way. So why was seeing this woman in jeans having basically the same effect?

Really it didn't matter because he planned to let her go as soon as he could get in a replacement. Temptation was temptation and he would hate to suddenly develop sleepwalking tendencies knowing she would be in the guest bedroom down the hall from him.

Hell, such a thought no matter how tempting, didn't sit well with him, mainly because he made the Double Creek Sheep Ranch one of the most successful in the United States. He'd done so by staying focused on what needed to be done and not by getting caught up in a woman. He didn't intend to get caught up on one now.

He leaned against the counter, deciding not to interrupt what she was doing just yet. Not when he had her within his scope. Whether he liked it, he was enjoying the view.

* * *

The man was agitated about something, Chloe could sense it, but at the moment she refused to let him get on her last nerve. She had plenty of work to do and didn't have time for a confrontation. After she was finished clearing the table she would break the news to Mr. Westmoreland that she was not his cook, that she had done him a favor and that she expected one in return.

The room was quiet, but she could hear his breathing, strong and steady. But even though she refused to look over at him, she was well aware he was looking at her, checking her out. And she knew he was paying a lot of attention to her backside, probably had his gaze locked on it real tight, which would account for the heat she actually felt on that part of her anatomy. She'd been told by more than one man that she had a nice derriere, curvy and shapely, just the way a man liked. *Whoopie,* she thought sarcastically.

But still, she would be the first to admit that just the thought that Ramsey Westmoreland's gaze was on her bottom almost made her breath catch in her throat. His eyes, whenever she looked into them, were filled with intensity and she could actually feel that intensity now focused directly on her.

Not able to stand it a minute longer, she swung around and frowned deeply. "We can talk now."

His dark eyes remained steady on her, even when he nodded and said, "All right. First I want to say you did a heck of a job with lunch today. The men were impressed and so was I."

She blinked. A compliment hadn't been what she'd been expecting. The man definitely had a way of delivering it with mixed emotions. His words were syrupy and sweet, while the texture of his voice was brooding. "Thank you, I'm glad everyone enjoyed it."

"They also enjoyed you." At the lift of her brow he clarified and said, "Enjoyed you being here I mean."

She wondered where he was about to go with that comment and figured she would know soon enough. "I enjoyed being here as well," she responded as she placed the dishes in the sink. It was time to come clean and let him know her real purpose for being there. "Mr. Westmoreland, I think that you—"

"Ramsey. I prefer you call me Ramsey. Everyone around here does. Some even call me Ram."

She couldn't help but smile at that.

"You find something amusing, Ms. Burton?"

She met his gaze and her smile widened even more. "You can call me Chloe, and what I find amusing is the fact that a ram is a male sheep and you are in the sheep business. Unique, don't you think?"

He shrugged muscular shoulders. "Never gave it much thought."

She lifted a brow. "Are you trying to tell me that no one has ever made the connection before?"

"If they did, they knew better than to mention it."

Chloe wanted to just throw her hands up in the air and give up. It was quite evident that even when they were trying to hold a civil conversation they had the ability to rub each other the wrong way. That made her wonder about him, the man she wanted to be on the cover of *Simply Irresistible*. He looked better than chocolate cake oozing with deep, rich chocolate icing—her favorite—but it was becoming quite evident he was a complex man. She couldn't help wonder what made Ramsey tick? What would it take to make him become relaxed, more laid-back? she wondered. Although she could see that around his men he was pretty mild-mannered and friendly. It was obvious they had a good working relationship while maintaining a degree of respect. That meant he was reserving his uptightness mainly for her. She wondered why.

The research she'd done indicated he dated when the mood or the urge probably hit him. Yet he didn't have any steady woman in his life. His last serious relationship had been with the woman he'd become engaged to, a woman by the name of Danielle McKay. However, she had ruined what was to have been his wedding day by stopping the minister in the middle of the wedding and walking out. That had been over ten years ago. Surely he'd gotten over that incident by now.

In addition to the cover photo for the magazine, she wanted an interview with him and had a feeling getting him to talk would be just as difficult as getting him to agree to the cover photo. Talk about pulling teeth. She had planned to send one of her seasoned reporters to talk to him and now she could clearly see that just wouldn't work.

Suddenly an idea popped into her head. She might as well go about killing two birds with one stone. She wanted him to do the magazine cover and she wanted an article on him as well. His profession intrigued her. For instance, why had he gotten into sheep ranching versus cattle or horse ranching?

An insider's view of his operation might be good reading information to her readers. And the best way to find out everything she wanted to know about him was to hang around and get to know him for herself. The man was without a doubt masculine perfection and she wondered if there was more to Ramsey Westmoreland than a handsome face and a hard, muscular body.

Chloe nibbled on her lower lip. Now was the time to come clean and tell him the truth, but something was holding her back from doing so. He owed her for lunch today and she intended to collect, but she wanted more from him than just the photo cover. She wanted to interview him for a piece in the magazine as well. Women loved wool and she could do an article informing them of the entire process of getting it off the sheep and into the stores. At lunch a number of the shearers had explained how things were done, but she wanted to hear it from Ramsey.

"What made you get into sheep ranching?" she decided to ask. There was no sense in wasting time getting the information she needed.

She glanced over at him when he didn't say anything and felt heat thrum through her body when he shifted his gaze to her face. From his expression she could tell he was surprised by her question.

"Why do you want to know?"

He was a suspicious sort and she would add that to the list of his characteristics. "I'm just curious. You have a big spread and a good number of men to help you run things. Most people around here have cattle or horses, but you have sheep. Why?"

Taking his time, Ramsey pondered Chloe's question. It was one he had asked himself many times and whenever he did he would always come up with the same answer. "Being a rancher was a dream my father and I shared from the time he took me with him to visit a friend of his in Maryland who owned a sheep farm. I couldn't have been any more than twelve at the time. In college I majored in agriculture economics, so I would know everything there was to know about farming and ranching, although my plans were to join the family's real estate business like everyone else. It was Dad's intent to one day retire and just have a small flock of sheep, but he died before he had a chance to fulfill his dream."

"I'm sorry, Ramsey."

She had spoken quietly and he saw his sorrow reflected in her eyes. He quickly wondered why he had shared that with her. He wasn't sure why he had answered her question at all. What was it about her that had made him feel comfortable enough with her to bare his soul? "Look, Chloe, what I need to talk to you about is—"

At that moment his cell phone went off. "Excuse me," he said before fishing it out of his back pocket. "Yes?"

She watched, nearly mesmerized as a huge smile touched his face, curving his lips. If she hadn't seen it, she would not have believed it. Did he reserve his frowns just for her?

"Dillon, when did you get in?" He paused. "No problem, I'm on my way."

He quickly returned the phone to his jeans pocket and glanced over at her. "I need to run. We still need to talk. I'll be back in an hour or so." He turned to move toward the back door.

"I'll be gone by then."

He stopped and pivoted around and lifted a questioning brow while staring at her. "Gone where?"

There were those intense eyes again and she drew a breath. "Back to town."

He leaned back against the counter again. "Did the agency not tell you that I hired you as a live-in cook? The men will be expecting another meal in the morning around five."

"Five!"

"Yes."

She looked at him suspiciously. "Did your other cook live here?"

"No. But then I didn't have to worry about her getting here early enough to have breakfast ready for my men. Nellie and her husband have a house less than ten miles away. She arrived every morning at three and left in the late afternoon."

He then lifted a brow. "Just what did that employment agency tell you? This is shearing time here at the ranch and it happens only once a year. I own over three thousand sheep and have only a two-week window to get the wool off. Unlike a lot of sheep ranchers who hire a sheep shearing crew from year to year, my men are trained to do all the job duties here. That means they will work around the clock. I have to make sure they eat a hearty breakfast and are fed a good lunch. I can't wake up tomorrow morning and worry about whether you'll show up."

"I'll be back in the morning," she heard herself say. "I promise."

Ramsey frowned. Hadn't he made up his mind that they could not stay under the same roof? Wasn't it his intent to talk to her about remaining as his cook only until he'd found a replacement? So why was he making a big deal of her staying over tonight? He should be overjoyed that she was leaving.

He inwardly shrugged and figured he only cared because of his concern that she would not be here on time in the morning to feed his men. "I'm going to need you here on time, Chloe," he said in a voice that sounded pretty damn curt even to his own ears.

"I said I would be here, didn't I?" she all but snapped back in a tone that said he would get just as good as he gave.

His glare locked on her face and then he nodded stiffly. "I'm taking you at your word. Lock the door behind you when you leave and I'll see you in the morning." He then headed for the door.

He turned and met her gaze one more time and she didn't release her breath until the door had closed behind him.

Three

Three

"Please tell me you're joking, Clo."

Chloe sat her luggage down near her feet and turned to Lucia who had a worried look on her face. Chloe had decided to return to Ramsey's place tonight instead of trying to find her way there again in the early morning when it would still be dark outside. "Come on, Lou, it's not that serious. I'm doing Ramsey Westmoreland a favor and in the end he will be doing me a favor."

Lucia rolled her eyes. "He won't see things that way when he finds out what you're really about. You're not only invading his privacy, but you're also being deceitful."

"I'm not."

"You are, too, and all hell is going to break loose when he learns the truth. I live in this town, you don't. You'll be back in sunny Florida and I'll be here feeling the heat of the

Westmorelands' wrath. When it comes to anyone messing with one of them, they all stick together."

Chloe crossed her arms beneath her breasts and gave her best friend a pointed look. "And which Westmoreland are you concerned with pissing off, Lucia?"

Chloe knew she had hit the jackpot when Lucia dropped her gaze and began looking everywhere but at her. "I don't know what you're talking about."

Chloe had no intentions of believing that. "Yeah, right. You don't want to make waves with the Westmorelands for a reason, so fess up. Which one is it? Ramsey?"

"No," Lucia said quickly. "It's no one."

Chloe didn't believe that any more than she believed there was a lost colony off the California coast. "Okay, Lou, this is Clo. You can't lie straight even on your best days, so I'm going to ask you one more time, who is he and don't waste my time telling me he's not a Westmoreland."

Reluctantly, Lucia met her gaze and then in a quiet and flat voice she said, "It's Ramsey's brother, Derringer."

Chloe raised a brow. Her best friend's expression was filled with so much love it almost hurt her to look at it. "Derringer Westmoreland? When did all this take place?"

She had known Lucia since her first year of college and the man's name had never come up, yet judging by the expression on Lucia's face whatever she felt for the man ran deep and had been there a long time.

A faint smile touched Lucia's lips. "I've loved him forever."

Chloe was shocked. "Forever? And I'm just hearing about him?"

Lucia shrugged. "There was never a point. My crush began in high school, but he saw me as nothing more than one of his sister's friends. I thought I'd gotten over him when I left for college but since returning home four years ago I've discovered that isn't the case."

Lucia's face warmed when she said, "Last month I ran into him, and for the first time in years we were close enough to speak." A smile then touched her face. "And he asked me—"

"Out on a date?" Chloe asked excitedly.

"I wish. He dropped by my dad's paint store and I was working behind the counter and Derringer asked me to hand him a can of paint thinner."

Chloe couldn't help the grin that curved her lips. Evidently that little incident had made Lou's day. Just being around Ramsey Westmoreland put a spark in *her* day. Now where had that thought come from? Chloe wondered.

"Now that I know how you feel about Derringer Westmoreland, I will tell Ramsey the truth as soon as reasonably possible. I still want to make him feel indebted to me first for a while and then I'll level with him and come clean."

Lucia nodded. "I know how much having Ramsey on the cover of your magazine as well as doing that article on him means to you."

Chloe met Lucia's gaze and smiled. "Yes, I don't want you to worry about it because I believe in the end we'll both get what we want."

Ramsey looked up from the breeding charts he had spread over his desk and considered going into the kitchen to eat that last bit of peach cobbler that had been left from lunch. It had been so delicious his mouth was beginning to water just thinking about it.

And his mouth was beginning to water just thinking about

something else as well. More specifically, someone else. Chloe Burton. Talk about looking yummy. He threw his pencil down and leaned back in his chair. At that moment he couldn't help but think about snug-fitting jeans that covered a curvaceous backside and a blouse that fit perfectly over a tempting pair of breasts. He was getting aroused at the memory.

Damn.

Deciding he needed a beer more so than any peach cobbler, he got up to make his way to the kitchen. Moments later he was leaning against the counter and tipping the bottle to his lips and taking a much-needed drink. Lowering the bottle he then glanced around the room and for the first time noticed just how large and quiet his home was. Usually he welcomed the silence, but for some reason it bothered him tonight.

He studied the ceramic floor as he thought about his great-grandfather, Raphael Westmoreland, who had owned over eighteen hundred acres of land on the outskirts of Denver's city limits. When each Westmoreland reached the age of twenty-five they were given a one-hundred-acre tract of land. It was why he, his siblings and cousins all lived in close proximity to each other. As the oldest cousin, in addition to receiving his one hundred acres, Dillon had also inherited Shady Tree Ranch, the Westmoreland family home. The huge two-story dwelling sat on three hundred acres and hosted the majority of the family functions. Since Dillon had married Pamela it seemed the Westmorelands had reason to celebrate a lot. Everyone adored Dillon's wife, found her totally different from his first wife, and had welcomed Pamela and her three sisters into the family with open arms.

He lifted his head when he heard a knock at his door and glanced up at the clock on the wall. It was close to eleven, but that didn't mean a damn thing to any of his siblings or cousins. They felt they had a right to come calling at any time. He shook his head as he made it to the door, thinking it was probably his sister Megan. She was twenty-four years old and an anesthesiologist at the hospital in town.

Without bothering to ask who it was, he slung his front door open to find Chloe Burton standing on his porch and tightly gripping a piece of luggage. He was so surprised to see her that he could only stand and stare.

He could tell by the way she was nibbling on her lower lip that she was nervous, but that wasn't what held his attention, although the action caused a tightening in his gut. What had him transfixed was her outfit. She had almost ruined a saucy minidress by wearing leggings. He would have loved to see her bare legs and almost sighed in disappointment. But then he had to admit she still looked gorgeous and sexy as hell. Good enough to eat after first lapping her all over. He swallowed knowing at that moment that he was in trouble.

"I know I said I'd come back in the morning, but I figured not to take any chances getting here late. Besides, I need to get things set up, if the men eat at five. I'll need to be in the kitchen at least by four. So…here I am."

Yes, here she was, and although he wished otherwise, ideas continued to pop up in his head, literally pound his brain, regarding all the things he'd like to do to her. Even now he wished like hell he could ignore the ache that was stirring in the lower part of his body, as well as the heavy thudding doing havoc to his chest. But he couldn't.

She stared at him and he stared back at her as his insides began filling with lust of the thickest kind. He should have followed his mind earlier and contacted the employment agency to see if they could send in a replacement by morning, but he had failed to do so mainly because deep down he really hadn't wanted to. He grudgingly admitted that he had been looking forward to seeing her in the morning. But she was here now and he wasn't quite sure just how to handle her unexpected arrival.

He watched as she raised her brows. "So are you going to let me in or do I get to stand out here all night?"

At that moment he couldn't help but quirk his lips in a smile. She was almost as bad as Bailey with her sassy mouth. A mouth that at that moment snagged his gaze. Breath slammed through his lungs when she took that time to moisten her lower lip with the tip of her tongue.

He fought the heat flaring in his midsection. "Yes, I'm going to let you in," he said, reaching out and taking the luggage out of her hand and stepping back and moving aside.

"I appreciate it," she responded, stepping over the threshold.

When she walked past him every cell in Ramsey's body began throbbing as he took in her scent. Whatever perfume she was wearing was lethal and could wrap a man up in all kinds of sensuous thoughts.

She glanced over at him. "So where's my room?"

He gave her a tight smile. "Upstairs. Please follow me." A part of him wished he was leading her to his bedroom instead of the guest room. Damn, he needed another beer.

They walked up the stairs and when they reached the landing they walked down the hall. "Nice place."

He glanced over his shoulder. "I'm sure you've seen it before."

She arched her brow. "No, I haven't. Earlier today when you left your door wide open, I had no reason to snoop around up here. My job was in the kitchen area and no other part of your house."

He wondered if she could be believed, and when he glanced over his shoulder again he couldn't help but note how she was checking out several of the bedrooms they passed. Maybe she hadn't come *snooping* after all. He had five guest rooms all with their own private baths. At twenty-three, Gemma was the interior designer in the family. She had been more than happy to spend his money to lavishly decorate each of his bedrooms. And she was dying to get started on the rooms downstairs once he gave her the go-ahead. That wouldn't be for a while. He was still recovering from having her underfoot when she'd done the upstairs.

"Sorry, my mistake," he apologized by saying.

When they reached the bedroom that she would be using, he stood back to let her enter. He could tell from her expression that he had made a wise choice. She liked it, which meant she was a frilly, lacy and soft colors kind of girl. While she was standing in the middle of the room, scanning the room in awe, he placed her luggage on the bed.

His first inclination was to bid her good-night and leave her standing right there, but something about the expression on her face stopped him. She actually seemed absorbed. He somehow understood. Gemma's interior design work could do that to you. He would be one of the first to admit that his sister was good. The money used to send her to college had been well spent.

He doubted there was ever a time Gemma hadn't wanted to be an interior designer. He could vividly recall how she had made curtains for his first car—a bright red Chevy—when she was eight. To not hurt her feelings he had mounted the things in the car's rear window hoping that none of his friends saw them.

"Whoever decorated this part of your home did a fantastic job," Chloe said, as her gaze returned to Ramsey.

Chloe noted that he was looking at her again, with the same intensity that he'd looked at her earlier that day. And as she stared back his gaze never wavered, it held hers deep within its scope. Without words, with barely a breath, something was taking place between them. She wished she could dismiss her theory and believe she was just imagining things, but there was no make-believe with the heat consuming her body. Her breasts suddenly felt swollen and her nipples seemed tender against the fabric of her dress.

Her gaze moved from his face and scanned his body downward and was glad to see she was not the only one affected by the moment. He was aroused. Fully. There was no way he could hide it and he wasn't trying to. Her gaze shifted back to his face and what she saw in the depths of his eyes almost took her breath away. There were promises of hot, lusty nights, more pleasure than she could probably stand, kisses that would start at her mouth and end between her thighs and an explosion that would shatter every single thing within her. She paused for breath at the thought that those were real promises she saw in his gaze and not a figment of her imagination.

Then she also saw something else in the depths of his eyes beside those promises. She saw a warning. If she couldn't stand the heat, then she needed to stay out of the kitchen. At that moment she pulled in a wary breath. Was Ramsey Westmoreland the one man she could not handle?

"I'll leave you alone to unpack," he finally said, breaking the intense sexual tension that surrounded them. "You have your own bathroom, which I believe you'll find more than sufficient."

She nodded. Her ability to speak had escaped her.

"Good night, Chloe. I'll see you in the morning."

She could only stand and stare after him as he left the room.

There was no doubt about it. He had to get her out of his house, Ramsey thought, as he paced his bedroom hours later. What had happened in the guest room tonight was uncalled for, but still pretty much unclear. He had come within seconds of crossing that room, bending his head and taking her mouth with his to satisfy the hunger he felt. The hunger he was still feeling. The thought of his tongue mingling with hers while he held her tight against the heat of his chest caused the hot stab of arousal to nearly knock him to his knees.

And where on earth had such passion come from? It had nearly taken over him, transformed his brains into mush and had filled his mind with naughty thoughts of all the things he wanted to do to her. He pulled in a deep breath deciding he needed to analyze the situation. He needed to determine just how they had come to this point.

He would be the first to admit there had been a strong sexual attraction from the first moment he'd laid eyes on her. A rush of hot blood had shot through his veins, had hammered away at his insides, and an awareness as profound as anything he'd ever encountered before had zinged through him with the force of a volcano erupting. Every nerve, every bone and every muscle in his body had been affected.

And things hadn't gotten any better during the lunch hour when he hadn't been able to keep his eyes off her just as Callum had claimed. And he had a feeling that the reason Eric and Thel had probably backed off hadn't been because of any feeling of defeat where she was concerned. They had retreated because they'd picked up on his interest. If Callum had noticed his staring at her, then there was a strong possibility others had as well. And because doing such a thing was so unlike him, they probably figured he was being territorial. Had he been?

He rubbed his hands down his face as he uttered a frustrated curse. She was probably in her bed, sleeping peacefully between the sheets, while he was the one walking the floor with an erection that was keeping him awake. He seriously considered going into her room, getting her up and asking her to leave. How crazy was that? To even contemplate doing such a thing showed just how close to the edge he was.

Of his four brothers he was the one who could generally take a woman or leave her just where she stood. His love 'em and leave 'em attitude unnerved his siblings who thought he spent more time sleeping with his sheep than with women. Considering the time he'd done duty as a sheepherder over the past year, that accusation was not a lie. But it really wasn't any of their business. And he had been quick to point out— especially to his brothers and male cousins—that they were spending enough time chasing women without him, boosting profits for the condom industries and making it quite obvious they were men on the prowl the majority of the time. He cringed at the reputations some of them had.

And he had been quick to assure them that his decision to not bed women as often as they did had nothing to do with Danielle McKay, the woman who had walked off, leaving him standing at the altar ten years ago at a church filled with over two hundred guests. The really sad thing was that his family had liked her, until they'd discovered the truth as to why she had walked out on him in front of everyone with an "I'm sorry," instead of an "I do."

She had later confessed to having an affair that had resulted in a pregnancy. To her credit, at least she'd had the decency to not go through with the wedding instead of passing the kid off as his. But what his family hadn't known and what he'd kept hidden was that it had been a sense of obligation and not love that had driven him to ask Danielle to marry him in the first place. So in reality, her calling off the wedding had been a blessing in disguise.

He pulled in a deep breath. If anything, thoughts of Danielle should have reduced the size of his erection but they hadn't. That meant thoughts of Chloe outweighed thoughts of Danielle by a large margin. He doubted Danielle ever got him this aroused without even touching her. As far as he was concerned, this sort of physical reaction to a woman had to be cruel and unusual punishment.

Ramsey moved toward the bed, swearing with every step. He had to get up just as early as Chloe did. There were early morning chores that had to be done. Already a few of his nosy family members had called asking questions after a number of his men had bragged about his new cook and how pretty she was. News carried in Westmoreland Country and no doubt some were anticipating his next move and taking bets as to how quick he would be getting her from under his roof.

As far as he was concerned that was a no-brainer. She was definitely on her way out of there. He was determined that no matter what, he would be contacting the employment agency about finding him a replacement.

Four

When Chloe heard a sound behind her she didn't stop beating the huge bowl full of eggs because she knew who it was. She was determined that nothing about Ramsey Westmoreland was going to unnerve her today. After all, he wasn't the only man alive with a lot of sexual appeal, although he happened to be the only one who seemed to hold her interest.

She considered turning around to greet him and then decided because he was the one who'd entered the kitchen, he should be the one to make the gesture. If he didn't, it wouldn't be any sweat off her back, namely because she didn't have any sweat left after those naughty dreams last night where he'd had a starring role.

"Morning."

Okay, he'd done the proper thing and spoke first, but did he have to do so with such a deep huskiness in his voice? Such raw sexuality in his tone? It had only been one word for crying out loud. Yet the sound that had emitted from his lips was sending shudders through her body and had the potential to do other things she just didn't want to think about this early in the morning. It wasn't even four yet. And it was going to be a busy morning and an even busier noon.

Reluctantly, she turned around, deciding she would at least return his greeting. "Good—"

She swallowed the other word. And was that a moan she'd heard that had just passed her lips? Ramsey Westmoreland had the nerve, the sheer audacity to be standing in the middle of the kitchen putting on a shirt. At least now he was buttoning it up. But not before she'd caught a glimpse of his naked chest, ultra-fine biceps, sculpted shoulders and muscular arms. And it didn't help matters that his jeans were riding low on his hips and he was barefoot. It was quite obvious he had just taken a shower and had shaved. But still, he had that early-morning take-me-as-I-am look and she was tempted to do just that.

She wished she had the strength not to let her gaze hone in on such a powerful muscled body, but you could call her weak and she would answer. She was seeing firsthand why she wanted him as her *Simply Irresistible* man.

His gaze met hers when he'd noticed her looking and held on to her eyes until the last button was done. What a pity, she thought. She had enjoyed the show.

"I can't believe you beat me up," he said, now slipping a belt through the loops of his jeans.

Chloe wondered if it was the norm for him to get dressed in the middle of his kitchen. "I couldn't sleep," she decided to say. "Unfamiliar bed." There was no reason to tell him what had really kept her awake.

"But you did get enough sleep to function this morning," he stated. "The men will be hungry," he added.

She snorted, not caring how it sounded. "Mama Francine said men are always hungry. Even when their stomachs are full."

He leaned against the counter. "And who is Mama Francine?"

Too late she realized she might have said too much, but quickly decided telling him about Mama Francine wasn't giving anything away. "She's the person who taught me how to cook."

He nodded and she turned back to her eggs. She wasn't sure how many men would want their eggs scrambled, but she wanted to have the mixture ready just in case. And Mama Francine had taught her how to flip eggs, so those who didn't want their egg scrambled could tell her just how they liked it.

She heard him move, but refused to look up again. Besides, she knew he was moving toward her with a slow walk and glancing around inspecting everything while doing so. And with every step he took closer to her she felt his heat. It was even more powerful than what the stove was generating.

"I'm impressed."

She couldn't help but smile as she glanced over her shoulder. "Again?"

"Yep. You're serving both bacon and sausage."

She lifted a brow. Curious. "Something's wrong with that?"

He shrugged. "No. It's just that usually Nellie did one or the other."

She gazed him a pointed look. "Well, I'm not Nellie."

His heavy-lidded eyes raked over her. Slowly. Thoroughly. Then he said in a voice drenched with masculine awareness. "I can see that."

She didn't know what to say to that, so she said nothing at all before turning back around, placing the egg mixture aside to give attention to the pan of biscuits.

She knew he was staring at her legs and was tempted to pull her skirt down. However, doing so would give him the impression she was uncomfortable with what she was wearing. She wasn't nor should she be. It was a decent length and, therefore, it was appropriate. It hit just a little above the knee, but she was wearing leggings underneath. If he were to see her in some of the other outfits she owned, the ones that barely covered her thighs, he would probably be shocked.

"And we're getting homemade biscuits, too?"

She couldn't help the grin that touched her lips when she moved to open the oven door and slide the pan of biscuits inside. "Another abnormality?"

"Around here, yes."

That made Chloe wonder why this Nellie didn't prepare more of a variety of foods for breakfast. After closing the oven door she turned around, trying to ignore how responsive certain parts of her body were to Ramsey's nearness. He looked like he needed another five hours of sleep to do him justice, yet at the same time he looked sexy as sin. "May I ask you a question, Ramsey?"

He shrugged those massive shoulders again. "Depends on what you want to know."

She crossed her arms under her breasts and wondered if that had been a good thing when his eyes, half-asleep or not, followed the movement and seemed to be staring right through the material of her blouse to her nipples. At least the nipples thought so and were tingling at the attention they were getting. They were tingling and getting hard all at the same time.

"I want to know why this Nellie didn't offer more of a variety to the men at breakfast time."

She watched as a grin quirked his lips. "If you knew Nellie you wouldn't have to ask that question."

She rolled her eyes. "I don't know Nellie, so I'm asking it."

He tilted his head to the side, focusing those ever-so-intense eyes on her. And weakling that she was, immediately felt her body's response to his gaze. She wondered if he could detect it. It seemed so unreal that she would react to him this way when Daren couldn't get a spark of response out of her no matter how much he tried. But then, he hadn't tried too often. He'd been more interested in building his political future by parading Senator Burton's daughter out in front of those he felt he needed to impress. And when they were alone he was more into surfing the Internet for political blogs than getting into her. And those times when he had given her his attention, he might as well not have bothered. To say Daren hadn't had a romantic bone in his body was an understatement. However, the final straw came when he'd actually suggested they participate in a threesome. He claimed that kind of sexual kinkiness was a total turn on for him. For a man who couldn't even handle a twosome to fix his mouth to propose such a thing was too much. She'd sent him packing with the few items he had kept at her place and with a clear understanding not to come back.

Since then she had to focus all her energy—sexual and otherwise—into making her magazine a success and refused to think about having any type of a relationship with a man, and now, here she was, behaving like some supercharged, highly-sexed woman, ready to unzip his pants and jump his bones.

"Nellie figured that for breakfast she would give them just the basic, enough to get by so they could really be hungry by lunchtime," he interrupted her thoughts by stating.

She raised a brow. In her opinion that didn't make much sense. "Wouldn't they be hungry at lunchtime anyway?"

"Yes."

Chloe opened her mouth to say something, then snapped it shut, deciding to leave it alone. She and Nellie were two different people and the way the woman ran her kitchen was none of Chloe's business. Chloe's concern, her aim, was to make sure by the time she confessed who she was, Ramsey would feel he was irrevocably in her debt. And if offering the men who worked for him a variety at breakfast was going to get brownie points with him, then so be it. Besides, after listening to the men yesterday, it was quite obvious that most of them would like a home-cooked meal and she had no problem giving them one. Besides, being back in the kitchen had made her realize just how much she enjoyed cooking.

She heard the sound of a vehicle pulling up. "Sounds like your men are starting to arrive."

He shook his head. "No, it's Callum. He always arrives earlier than the others. He and I usually have business to discuss in the mornings."

She nodded. She had noticed the man yesterday and could tell he and Ramsey had more than just an employer-employee relationship. They seemed to be close friends. "He's from the Outback, isn't he?"

Ramsey had moved to where the coffeepot was sitting to pour a cup of coffee. He took a sip and frowned. The woman could even make damn good coffee. "Yes," he finally said, answering her question.

Few people, including some members of Ramsey's own

family, knew that Callum was a millionaire in his own right and owned a vast amount of land in Australia. He had several sheep ranches in Australia that were run by a very efficient staff. There was no need to tell her that the Aussie donated to charity the salary he earned as Ramsey's ranch manager.

Callum, at thirty-four, was the product of a wealthy white Australian father and an African American mother. His family had made billions in the sheep ranching business. Another thing she didn't need to know was that the only reason Callum was still hanging around here instead of moseying it back to Australia was because he didn't plan to leave without Gemma going with him.

Callum knew Ramsey well enough to know that when it came to his three sisters, Ramsey was a tad overprotective and would stop any advances on Megan, Gemma or Bailey cold. It had taken the Aussie a full year to convince Ramsey that his intentions toward Gemma were honorable and that he loved her and wanted to marry her. Both Ramsey and Dillon had given Callum their blessings for a marriage; however, they'd made it clear the final decision would be Gemma's. His sister had never given any indication that she was the least bit interested in Callum and was virtually clueless in regards to Callum's interest in her. As far as Ramsey was concerned maybe that was a good thing because Gemma was known to be a handful at times and would definitely have a lot to say about it; especially when she'd stated on more than one occasion that she never intended to ever give her heart to any man. That meant the Aussie had his work cut out for him if he intended to win her over.

Ramsey glanced around the kitchen before returning his gaze to Chloe. "It seems that you have everything under control."

"Sorry you thought that I wouldn't."

The mockery of her words had him frowning. Something told him that when it came to an attitude, hers was worse than his sister's. "It's not that I thought you wouldn't, Chloe. I think you more than proved your capabilities yesterday."

She lifted her chin. "Then what is it with you?"

He could pretend he had no idea what she was talking about, but he didn't. If the truth be told, he was the one with the attitude and was well aware it had probably been the pits since their initial meeting. He wasn't used to having to deal with a woman who made men pause when she walked into a room. A woman who wore her sexuality like it was a brand with her name on it. A woman who even now had blood surging through his veins.

And a woman he wanted to kiss.

His heart was racing at the very thought of locking his mouth with hers, and he knew at that moment if she stayed another night under his roof he would be doing that very thing if for no other reason than to get her out of his system. It would only be right to give her fair warning.

"How old are you, Chloe?"

From her expression he could tell she was wondering what her age had to do with anything. "I'm twenty-eight."

He nodded slowly, while his gazed continued to hold hers. "Then I would think you'd know what it is with me. But just in case you don't have a clue, I'll show you later."

Chloe felt a slow burn in her midsection followed by the feel of her heart thudding erratically in her chest. The meaning behind his words was pretty clear. If it hadn't been, then his eyes would have spelled things out for her. She could see the promises in the dark depths. Promises he wasn't trying to hide. Promises he intended to keep.

Before she could level a response the back door opened and Callum Austell walked in. He looked first at her and then at Ramsey. The smile that touched the man's lips would have been too deadly sexy if she hadn't thought Ramsey had a monopoly on sexiness.

"Ram. Chloe. Did I come at a bad time?" Callum asked in a low tone.

Chloe watched an irritated frown touch Ramsey's features and she drew in a deep breath. Lucia had warned her that he was a private person and she wasn't sure just how he felt about his friend picking up on the sexual tension flowing between them. It was tension so thick you could probably cut it with a knife and then spread it on bread. Deciding she needed to play off Callum's words, make the man think he was wrong in his assumption, she turned to Callum, opened her mouth to speak, but Ramsey beat her to it.

"No, you didn't come at a bad time. Come on, Cal, let's have that meeting." He then sat the coffee cup he'd been holding on the counter with a thud and headed out of the room. He stopped and glanced over his shoulder at Callum who had halted beside her.

"You sure look nice this morning, Chloe," Callum said in a husky tone with his deep Australian accent.

Chloe glanced up at the handsome man whom she figured was a year or two younger than Ramsey and couldn't help wondering what he was about. Had he just delivered a polite comment or a blatant flirtation?

"You're wasting my time, Cal. Are we meeting or what?" Ramsey called out in a sharp tone.

Callum looked across the room at Ramsey and smiled. "We're meeting."

And then he moved to follow Ramsey out of the room.

* * *

Ramsey clenched his jaw until he was in the office and then he all but slammed the door shut before facing Callum. The other man had the nerve, the very audacity, the damn gall, to smile. "What the hell was that about?" he asked through gritted teeth.

Callum gave him an innocent look, one Ramsey wasn't buying or selling. "I don't know what you mean, Ram."

Ramsey leaned back against his desk and frowned. "You were flirting with her."

Callum shrugged as another smile formed at the corners of his lips. "What if I was?"

Ramsey crossed his arms over his chest. "If you did it to get a rise out of me, then—"

"It worked," Callum taunted as he eased his muscular frame into a chair across from the desk. "Come on, Ram. Go ahead and admit you want the woman, which is why you're trying to get rid of her. When you know for yourself, even after eating just one meal, that she's a lot better cook than Nellie and her temperament is a vast improvement to what we're used to. I hate to say it but Nellie hasn't been missed around here and you know why."

Ramsey drew in a deep breath. Yes, he did know why. Nellie's disposition had begun deteriorating months ago after discovering her husband had been unfaithful to her. It was as if she had taken her hurt and anger out on the entire male population and his men knew it. They had tried being understanding, even sympathetic. But then after a while they'd become annoyed and just plain irritated. There was nothing worse than pissing a man off about his food.

Although Nellie's unexpected trip had placed him in a bind, he thought she needed the distance from his men for a while and vice versa. She still had a job when she returned, but the two of them would have a long talk first.

"Okay, so Nellie hasn't been missed, but when she comes back, she still has a job," he decided to speak up.

"Fine. Great. But in the meantime I think your men deserve a nice smile and friendly words every now and then, not to mention food they can eat without worrying about it being burned or overly seasoned."

Ramsey was silent.

"Look, I understand your problem with Chloe, Ram. Welcome to the club. I know how it is to want a woman so bad you ache," Callum said.

Ram frowned. He then narrowed his eyes on his friend. "You're referring to my sister," he said in a warning tone.

Callum snorted. "I'm referring to the woman I intend to marry who refuses to give me the time of day and it's getting damn near frustrating. Don't be surprised one day if you wake up and find us both gone." A smile touched Callum's lips. "I might resort to kidnapping."

Ram's frown deepened. "You'd better be joking." He then shook his head at Callum's outrageous threat. And then he couldn't help but chuckle. "Go ahead and kidnap her. I'll give you less than a week and you'll be bringing her back. Gemma will make your life a living hell if you did such a thing and I wouldn't be one to close my eyes on her if I were you. She likes getting even."

Ram smiled. Although he'd gone a little overboard he knew Callum got the picture. Of his three sisters, Gemma was the one who had a knack for not only speaking her mind but for backing up her thoughts. Callum knew this and was still in love with her. Go figure.

"Are you really thinking about letting Chloe go?" Callum

asked and Ramsey figured he was now desperate to change the subject from Gemma back to Chloe. "I think it's a sin and a shame that your men will have to suffer just because you can't control your urges," Callum said.

Ramsey knew there was really no reason to deny what Callum had just said. It was true. He was finding it hard to control his urges around Chloe. And they were urges he'd been controlling just fine before she'd shown up.

"The men are taking a bet as to how long we'll keep her." Callum grinned and said, "I bet some will be surprised to find her still here this morning."

Ramsey didn't see anything amusing. He didn't like being reminded that others had noticed his interest in her yesterday. "She's not the only good cook around these parts."

"I'm sure she isn't, but not many would want to have to live on the ranch. Most would probably have homes of their own; families they had to take care of when they left here like Nellie." Callum rubbed his chin thoughtfully. "Um, that makes me wonder."

Ramsey lifted a brow. "About what?"

"Why would a woman with her looks take a job where she'll have to live here in the middle of nowhere for two solid weeks. Doesn't she have any family?"

Ramsey considered Callum's question. To be honest Chloe's personal life hadn't crossed his mind, mainly because he hadn't intended for her to stay. In fact, he had planned to call the employment agency when it opened this morning to see how soon they could send a replacement. But Callum had posed a good question. Evidently she did have a place in town because she had returned last night with her luggage in tow.

"What if she's on the run and took the job to hide out here?"

Ramsey looked over at Callum. "On the run from what?"

"An abusive husband. A psycho fiancé. A possessive boyfriend. Hell, I don't know, Ram. But if I were you I would find out."

Ramsey's frown hardened at the thought that Chloe might be running from a demented stalker. But then when he'd mentioned to her yesterday that she was hired as a live-in cook she'd seemed surprised. And last night she claimed that she'd only returned after deciding she didn't want to risk being late this morning. What if there was more than that?

"I don't think she's married or engaged because she's not wearing a ring and there's no indentation around her finger to indicate that she's worn one in the past," he said.

Callum chuckled. "You're as bad as Eric and Thel if you noticed all of that about a woman's finger."

Ramsey shrugged his shoulders, refusing to let Callum bait him. "Whatever."

"Well, it might be *whatever* if you don't find out. If you make her leave, then you could very well be sending her to her death."

Ramsey rolled his eyes. "Spare me the dramatics."

Callum stood. "Don't say I didn't warn you if something were to happen to her." He headed for the door.

Ramsey watched him about to leave. "Hey, where are you going? We haven't had our meeting yet."

Callum smiled over at him. "And we won't. At least not this morning. I smell homemade biscuits and *both* bacon and sausage. If you're still thinking about getting rid of her, then I need to make sure I eat well this morning. No telling what we might end up with for lunch."

Ramsey had always been a man who'd prided himself on two things: strength of mind and self-control. He felt both take a flying leap when he walked into the dining area an hour later. His men were gone and Chloe was clearing off the table. She glanced over in his direction and the moment he looked into her eyes, he wanted to cross the room and pull her to him and kiss her until she was nothing more than a limp body in his arms.

"You missed breakfast, but I kept you something warming in the oven. The eggs will be made to order," she said.

He nodded, surprised she had thought of him. "Thanks." He had deliberately remained in his office, trying to concentrate on finishing reports he had failed to do last night. His men's voices had carried to his office and he could tell from their conversations that they had enjoyed breakfast and were looking forward to lunch.

"Your men were wondering why you didn't eat breakfast with them."

He glanced over at her as he poured a cup of coffee, wondering if his men had been the ones speculating or if it had been her. "Were they?"

"Yes."

When he didn't say anything but sipped his coffee while watching her, she said. "If you're ready to eat I'll get your plate out of the oven."

"Thanks. I'd appreciate it."

He moved toward the table and after sitting down he watched her and wondered if Callum's speculations were true. Was she living here at the ranch as his cook because she was on the run from someone? He sipped his coffee thinking that he was not one to overreact, but what if some of what Callum assumed was true?

"How do you want your eggs, Ramsey?"

He blinked, realizing she had asked him a question. "Excuse me? What did you say?"

"Your eggs. Do you prefer scrambled, sunny-side up or over easy?"

It was on the tip of his tongue to say he preferred them *over her* so he could lick them off, but thought better of it. She was wearing another short dress and like last night she had spoiled the effect by a pair of leggings. What was with those things? Why the hell were women wearing them under their dresses? He enjoyed seeing bare skin. Nothing was wrong with seeing a nice piece of feminine flesh on occasion. And although he'd never seen her legs, he had no reason to believe they weren't gorgeous, a real arousal-getter just like the rest of her.

The lower part of his body was already throbbing with the way her outfit fit over her bottom, showing a perfect shape. He could just imagine lying in bed with that backside curved against his front in spoon fashion, dipping his head to nibble on her neck and to place marks of passion there before moving toward…

"Ramsey?"

He blinked again. "Yes?"

"How do you want your eggs?"

"Sunny-side up will be fine."

He watched how she handled the frying pan. There was no doubt in his mind she knew what she was doing. And the way she cracked the egg was sure and precise. He couldn't help wondering about her cooking skills. Had she gone to culinary school? If so, why wasn't she working at a first-class restaurant somewhere? Why was she here on a sheep ranch on the outskirts of Denver? There was only one way to find out. He'd discovered that with some women if you got them talking they would tell you just about anything you wanted to know. It worked with Bailey, although it hadn't been a proven trick with Megan or Gemma.

As she cooked his eggs he studied her. She didn't look like a woman under any sort of duress. She seemed calm and looked cool. And she appeared to enjoy what she was doing.

His gaze moved to her face. She didn't have normal features. She was beautiful. Soft-looking brown skin, a sensual pair of eyes, a cute nose and a pair of lips he longed to taste. Her dark brown hair was shoulder length, lustrous curly strands. It didn't take much to imagine that hair spread across a pillow. His pillow. And those sensual dark eyes shimmering with arousal right as she shifted her body to spread her thighs, open her legs to fill the air with her scent while he stared down at her feminine mound, moist, ready, waiting for him to sample.

The surge of desire that swept through him at that moment was so fierce it almost took his breath away. He needed something stronger than a cup of coffee and was tempted to pull a beer out of the refrigerator. Instead he drew in a long, deep breath, shifted his gaze to look out the window. Think about something else. The bill that was soon to come due on his new tractor. The fact that Gemma was bugging him about decorating the rest of his house. Anything except making hot, carnal love to Chloe.

Trying to regain control of his libido and senses, he looked over toward her. She might know how to wield a frying pan and all that, but there was a refined air about her that disconnected her ability in the kitchen with the way she carried herself. It was as if she should be getting served instead of being the one doing the serving. "Are you married?"

She glanced over at him but only for a second. She went back to concentrating on cooking his eggs. "No."

"You sure?"

Her head lifted and she stared at him, gave him a look like he'd suddenly grown two heads or something. "Of course I'm sure." She held up her left hand. "See, no ring."

He shrugged. "That doesn't mean anything these days."

She frowned as she slid his egg from the frying pan onto the plate. "It would mean something to me."

"Okay, so you're not married. Are you involved in a serious relationship?"

She set the plate in front of him and gave him a pointed look. "Is there a reason for these questions?"

He smiled. Because she asked he might as well go ahead and tell her. She was mature enough to handle it. "Yes, there's a reason. When I get around to kissing you I'll feel better knowing your mouth doesn't belong to any other man. Legally or otherwise."

She didn't say anything for a moment. Then she opened her mouth, probably to tell him just where he could take his own mouth—legally or otherwise—but instead of saying anything right then, she just tightened her lips together.

He chuckled. "Tightening those lips shut won't keep me from prying them apart for a kiss if that's what I want to do, Chloe."

Chloe folded her arms across her chest. "Is there a reason for this madness?"

"Is that what this is? Madness?" he asked as he began eating.

She lifted her chin and glared at him. "You got another name for it?"

"What about hunger?"

She frowned. "Hunger?"

"Yes, hunger of a sexual nature. I need to get you out my

system and I figured I'll start by kissing you to see if that will work."

Chloe dropped her hands by her side. Not believing he'd said such a thing. And not believing her heart was thumping rapidly in her chest at the thought of him making good on his threat. "You're nothing like Daren."

He raised a dark brow. "Who's Daren?"

"The last guy I was involved with."

Ramsey ignored the twinge of jealousy that invaded his gut. "Is not being like Daren good or bad?"

She shrugged. "Not sure. Although, I think it would have been nice if he would have had even a fraction of that *hunger* thing."

He immediately caught on to what she'd insinuated. "I can't imagine any man hanging around you for long without wanting to gobble you alive. He must have been a real idiot."

Chloe kept herself from smiling and refused to admit she'd thought the same thing. "He had his own ideas about what down to earth lovemaking was about. He suggested that we participate in a threesome."

Ramsey frowned. He could handle the fact that her ex-boyfriend hadn't had a passionate bone in his body, but the thought that the man had actually wanted to share her with someone else was as demented as it could get. No man in his right mind would share her.

"Then he wasn't just an idiot," Ramsey spoke up to say. "He was a crazy idiot. Any man who could get it into his mind to share you evidently doesn't have the brain he was born with. There's no way I would consider doing such a thing. I would want you all to myself."

His gaze roamed over her. "It would be me and me alone who would leave a satisfied smile on your lips, Chloe."

Chloe felt a tightening in her stomach as his gaze slowly swept over her, lingering in certain places and bestowing a visual caress in others. And his deep seductive voice was stirring all kinds of sensations to life inside her.

"How long were you with this guy?"

She wondered why he wanted to know. "A year."

"And how long have the two of you been apart?"

Chloe wasn't sure why he wanted to know that, either. Why she'd even shared anything with him about Daren in the first place was a mystery to her. But she had and evidently he was curious. "Two years. Now if you will excuse me I'm about to tackle the dishes."

Ramsey watched her walk off over to the sink and, since she was doing her best to ignore him, he dug into his meal. Not surprisingly, everything was delicious and for the first time in a long while, he was enjoying his food. He was also enjoying watching Chloe while he ate. If she only knew all the things that were running through his mind while chewing on a piece of bacon and swallowing his toast.

She refused to look over at him which was probably a good thing. Instead she was trying to keep busy and continued to ignore him in the process. By the time he had finished breakfast and drained the last of his coffee, she had stacked all the dishes on the counter to load into the huge dishwasher. She wiped down the countertops until they gleamed.

Getting up from the table he crossed the kitchen to the sink to place his plate and cup in the sudsy water. And when he turned toward her she made a quick move to get out of his way. She wasn't fast enough and he reached out and took hold of her hand.

A shiver immediately rushed down Chloe's spine and she sucked in a sharp breath the instant Ramsey touched her.

She tilted her head and looked up at him. He was standing in front of her and his gaze, she noticed, was intense as ever and centered directly on her lips. Then his eyes moved slowly up her face to her eyes. He smiled and then slid his gaze back down to her lips again.

She knew at that moment he was about to make good on his threat to kiss her. Heat began formulating at the center of her thighs, and the way he was staring at her lips made her hot. Wet. Then something within her began to ache. It was a hollowed emptiness she just realized was there. He moved a step closer and his scent inflamed everything within her, pulling her into the depths of his masculinity, swirling her about and drawing her under into his sensual spell.

She studied him, became enmeshed in the starkly strong features of his face. He was a very handsome man, so much so that her senses were betraying her, refusing to let her do the right thing and demand he remove his hand from hers. Instead she felt herself easing toward him at the same time he shifted his body even closer to hers.

Chloe found herself pinned between him and the counter, felt the hardness of his erection come to rest between her thighs like it had every right to be there. For the first time in her life she felt totally in sync with a man, fully aware of who he was and what he could do. And the thought of what he could do, what he *would* do sent an intense shiver up her spine. It made her anxious to the point where she felt her nerves beginning to quiver. She swallowed deeply and when that didn't help her she took her tongue and swiped it across her lower lip.

Not a good move.

She looked into his face and saw the effect doing such a thing had on him. By no means was she trying to encourage him and when she saw heat flare in his eyes, she knew something elementally male was taking place and he had no intention of fighting it.

He leaned forward and before she could catch her next breath, he bent his head and captured her lips.

Five

Ramsey had told Chloe this wasn't madness, but at that moment he knew that quite possibly it was worse. There was no way to explain why the moment his lips touched hers he'd felt something he couldn't name or define slid up his spine. And her taste—rich, honeyed and sweet—drove him to stroke his tongue all over her mouth, sample her everywhere, taste her, and with a greed that made him groan. And when he released his hold on her wrist to place his hands at the center of her back, he shifted positions as fire spread through him.

Energy he didn't think he had, especially after a sleepless night, raced through him, gripped him hard, made his erection swell that much more. He wanted to think this was ludicrous, but he knew this was as sexual as it could get, as he took her mouth in a hot and urgent kind of way. He was determined to make her feel all the things he was feeling at that moment. And when she took hold of his tongue, he knew he'd succeeded.

The hands at her back became possessive, they lowered to cup her backside and she moaned at the same time she moved against him. They were chest to breast, hip to thigh, with mouths locked tight and tongues mingling wildly. He'd said he was sexually hungry and he was proving just how famished he was.

And the way his hands were now moving over her, as if outlining the shape of her bottom, was driving him insane. He was becoming acquainted with her curves and all her soft yielding flesh. There was no doubt in his mind that while he took her mouth with a passion, she could feel his aroused body part pressing deeply into the juncture of her legs as if that was where it belonged.

He heard the moans coming from her throat and every time one escaped he deepened the kiss that much more. He was tempted to spread her out on the kitchen table at that very moment and have his way with her. Take her with a passion until he was too weak to stand.

"We could always leave and come back later."

The heavy voice made them jump apart like kids who'd gotten caught with their hands in the cookie jar. Filled with both anger and protectiveness Ramsey moved in front of Chloe while glaring at his brothers, Zane and Derringer, and his cousin Jason.

"What the hell are the three of you doing here?"

Derringer smiled. "We had a meeting. You told us to be here at seven. Sharp. Threatened us with dire straits if we were late. Did you forget?"

He had.

"We can understand if you did forget," Zane said. He was two years younger than Ramsey and known as a smart-mouth.

"It's no big deal, Ram," Jason said. Jason was the easy-going cousin and his trademark smile was genuine. "It would be nice if you introduced us," Jason added.

"Yeah," Zane said grinning. "Any reason you're hiding her behind your back?"

Cursing quietly, Ramsey realized he was doing that very thing. He stepped aside and the moment his brothers' eyes lit on Chloe, all three gave her an appreciative male perusal. He loved every member of his family, but at that moment thoughts of doing these three in actually made him want to smile.

"Chloe, I want you to meet my brothers, Zane and Derringer, and my cousin Jason." And then to his brothers and cousin, he said. "Guys, this is Chloe Burton, my new cook."

Chloe had never been so embarrassed in her entire life and actually felt the color stain her already-dark skin. From the way the three were staring at her she could only assume that they'd never walked in on Ramsey kissing a woman before.

She extended her hand to them. "How do you do?"

Their handshakes were firm and as she locked eyes with each of them she saw a friendliness in their dark depths. And there was no doubt in her mind that when placed in the same room with a crowd anyone could easily guess they were related. They all had the same chiseled jaw, dark brown eyes, dimpled smile and creamy brown skin. They were extremely handsome men. Her gaze was momentarily drawn back to Derringer, the man who had her best friend's heart and he didn't even know it.

"Okay, so much for introductions," Ramsey broke into her thoughts and said aloud. "Let's have that meeting."

Zane, she noticed, was still holding on to her hand. He smiled, glanced over at Ramsey and said, "The three of you can have a meeting. I prefer staying here with Chloe. I hear she can whip up the best scrambled eggs this side of the Rockies."

She watched Ramsey tip his head back and sigh. He then fixed his brother a leveled stare. "Don't push things with me, Zane."

Zane drew his gaze from Ramsey and glanced down at Chloe. She thought the smile that tugged at his lips was devilish. "What about a rain check, Chloe? Tomorrow perhaps?"

She could only nod and then watched the three men follow Ramsey from the room.

"That pretty much sums things up," Jason was saying. "I talked to Durango and McKinnon yesterday and they are excited at the prospect of expanding their operation to Colorado."

Ramsey nodded. Durango Westmoreland and McKinnon Quinn were cousins of theirs, Durango by blood and McKinnon by marriage. The two lived in Montana and owned M&D, a very successful horse breeding and training operation. A few years ago they had invited another cousin, Clint Westmoreland, who lived in Texas, to join their million-dollar business. And now they were making the same offer to Zane, Derringer and Jason. The three had traveled to Bozeman and spent three weeks with Durango and McKinnon and their families, learning more about the operation and to determine if it was a business venture they wanted to become a part of. As all three were fine horsemen, Ramsey couldn't imagine their turning down the offer.

"So the three of you are really thinking about doing it?" he asked as he looked over the report. Everything was in order and M&D was doing extremely well; especially after Prince

Charming, a horse they had trained for Sheikh Jamal Yasir—another cousin by marriage—had placed in the Kentucky Derby.

"Yes, and we figured since our three properties are adjacent to each other," Jason was saying, "we can share acreage for grazing land and for future expansions. But what we don't want to do is to reduce the land you need for your sheep."

Ramsey nodded, appreciating their concern. Sheep required a lot of land and his siblings and cousins had been very generous in letting him use some of theirs for grazing purposes. At present he was satisfied with the number of sheep he owned, and other than the lambs due to be born at the end of the month, he didn't intend to increase his herd anytime soon.

"With what Dillon and I own together, there will be plenty enough," he said to the three. "And before Bane took off for the Navy he gave Dillon permission for me to use his land if there was a need. A few days ago I received a letter notifying me that the federal government has approved my use of land at Diamond Ridge, so I'll start taking part of the herd there later this year for grazing."

Ramsey glanced back down at the report. "Although I have my hands full here with the sheep, I'll be interested in becoming a silent partner with the M&D Colorado-based operation once it gets started. I think it's time that I consider diversifying. It's not good to have all your eggs in one basket."

"True," Zane nodded, casting his brother a smile. "We would love to have you on board. And speaking of eggs, you kind of got uptight when I invited myself to breakfast."

Ramsey snorted as he leaned back in his chair. "What is

it with you and Callum with your crazy games? Chloe is off limits."

Derringer, who was slouched down on the love seat, glanced over at Ramsey and asked in a belligerent tone. "Says who?"

Ramsey frowned. Derringer was younger than him by three years and enjoyed being argumentative. "Says me, Derringer. Evidently you either didn't get it or you didn't understand the message I gave Zane in the kitchen."

"So, you're saying Chloe is more than just your cook?" Jason asked, as if for clarification.

Ramsey hauled in a deep breath, irritated at the thought of having to explain anything to his relatives. But knowing them the way he did, he knew he'd better do so. There was no doubt in his mind that there would be more explaining to do to the others when word got around that these three had walked in on him kissing Chloe. Zane was probably just itching to tell everyone, especially because it had been eons since Ramsey had been involved with a woman.

"Chloe is nothing more than my cook," he said.

Now it was Zane who snorted. "I don't recall you ever kissing Nellie."

Ramsey rolled his eyes. "Nellie is a married woman."

Derringer straightened in his seat and lifted a brow. "Are you saying if she wasn't married you'd be kissing her?"

Before he could respond Zane burst out laughing while slapping his thigh. "Damn, Ramsey, we didn't know you had it in you. And all this time we figured you were living a dull and sexually inactive life."

Ramsey took a deep, calming breath. His brothers were trying to get a rise out of him and he refused to fall prey to their tactics any more than he had to Callum's earlier. He tossed the document he was holding on his desk. "Let me get something straight. The kiss the three of you walked in on was something that just happened. Chloe is my cook and nothing more. She'll be living here for two weeks until Nellie returns."

He then leaned forward to make sure they heard his next words clearly. "However, since I know how two of the three of you operate, I want to make it clear here and now that she is *not* open game. You're all welcome to breakfast, lunch or dinner at any time, as always. But that's all you're welcome to."

"Um, that sounds kind of territorial, Ram," Zane said, eyeing his brother.

Ramsey shrugged. "Think whatever you like, just make sure you heed my warning."

Later that evening Chloe went into Ramsey's living room and sat on the sofa with a glass of wine in her hand. She curled her feet beneath her as she took a sip. It felt good to relax after a tiring day.

Although she enjoyed being in the kitchen, spending her time cooking for a group of men was not how she had envisioned her month-long vacation. Especially one that had started off in the Bahamas.

But she would have to admit that just seeing the satisfied grins on Ramsey's men's faces when they had eaten breakfast that morning and lunch at noon had been worth all the time she had spent over a stove.

The men asked her to make more homemade biscuits in the morning, and they liked having a choice of bacon and sausage. She would surprise them tomorrow by going a step further and making omelets.

She had checked with her office in Florida and had spoken

briefly to her editor-in-chief. Everything was going fine, which Chloe wasn't surprised about. She had an efficient team who ran things whether she was in the office, and that's the way she wanted it. Her father had told her time and time again that to be successful as CEO of your own company, you needed a good team working for you who could handle just about anything in your absence. She had built *Simply Irresistible* to the magazine it was and was using her time expanding the market area.

Her thoughts shifted from the magazine to Ramsey and the kiss they had shared earlier that day. It was the kiss that three members of his family had witnessed. She could just imagine how Ramsey felt about it, which was probably the reason he had avoided her most of the day. He hadn't dined with his men at lunch and he hadn't returned to the ranch since she had noticed his leaving early that afternoon.

She couldn't help wondering if the kiss had worked and she was out of his system. She might be out of his, but now he was deeply embedded into hers. Never had she been kissed so thoroughly before. Never had a man explored her mouth the way he had, in such a blatantly carnal way. There had not been anything traditional about his kiss. He had delivered it with an expertise that had left her panting for hours. She had been both affected and infected by his kiss. Even now her lips were still tingling.

She would be the first to admit things were not going as she planned with him. She had been attracted to him from the first, so there was no surprise at that. But what had been a surprise, totally unexpected, was the degree of hot tension that surrounded them whenever they were in the same room. Or her to be thinking about jumping his bones whenever she saw him. In her line of business, she met plenty of good-looking men. But none had ever sparked her interest, or stimulated a deep attraction the way Ramsey had.

How was she supposed to live under his roof, breathe the same air, when sexual thoughts constantly flowed through her mind? And unfortunately that kiss had been the icing on the cake. There was no doubt in her mind that she was now addicted to his taste as well as to his masculine scent.

Chloe's thoughts shifted back to what Ramsey had said about never sharing her with anyone. There had been something about it that had touched her. She drew in a deep breath at the realization that something about Ramsey was getting to her. And she knew at that moment that he was a man in a way that Daren could never be. Ramsey was someone who could and would take care of his own. That was evident by the way he had taken on the responsibility of raising his siblings. Although he could be brusque at times, she believed he didn't have a selfish bone in his body.

And knowing that was what was endearing him to her.

She felt panic in her chest at the thought that anything about Ramsey was endearing to her, but as much as she wanted to deny it she knew it was true. There were so many things about him that reminded him of her father—especially his sense of what was right. She'd seen it in the way he treated his men and his family.

She took another sip of wine. Later she would call Lucia to let her know she'd met Derringer and thought he was definitely a cutie. Although Ramsey had given his brothers and cousin a hard time, she could easily pick up on the love and mutual respect between the four men. And all four were extremely handsome.

But still in her book, Ramsey was her choice. There was something about him that made her heart pound in her chest each and every time she saw him. Maybe the best thing would be to abandon the idea of his posing for the cover of her magazine. She should go ahead and tell him the truth tonight and be packed and ready to leave. But if she did that, it would leave him in a bind. His men were counting on her to provide them with a delicious breakfast in the morning and a tasty meal at lunch. Besides, she was not a quitter, so no matter how tough things got she would not throw in the towel.

She leaned over and placed her glass of wine on the coffee table when she heard her cell phone go off. She pulled it out of her skirt pocket and smiled when she saw the call was from her father.

"Dad, how are you?"

"I'm doing fine. Just where the heck are you, Chloe Lynn?"

She chuckled. Nobody but her father called her by her first and middle names. Only after she'd finished college and started her business did she appreciate what an outstanding man and wonderful person her father was. He had entered politics when she had been in her last year of high school and now he was in his third term as Senator and swore it was the last, but she knew better.

He had always encouraged her to do whatever it was in life that she wanted to do and not live under his shadow as the "senator's daughter." She had gone to the college she had wanted to attend and had gotten the degree in just what she'd wanted. The only thing he flexed his muscles about was his belief in helping others during her summers. In the end she'd never regretted doing so.

"I'm in Denver for now."

"And when will you be coming home?"

She raised a brow. Home for her had always been Tampa,

but for her father since becoming Senator Jamison Burton, he'd stayed in D.C. most of the time. "Not sure when I'll be back in Tampa. Why? What's going on?"

He paused and then said, "I intend to ask Stephanie to marry me tonight, and was hoping you would be here in case she said yes, so we can all celebrate."

Chloe's smile widened. Her father had been dating Circuit Court of Appeals judge Stephanie Wilcox. A fifty-something divorced mother of a son and a daughter in their twenties, her father and Stephanie had been dating for a few years and Chloe had wondered when he would consider asking the woman to share his life.

"That's wonderful, Dad. Congratulations. I'm sorry I won't be there to celebrate, but please make sure you let Stephanie know how happy I am for both of you."

Ten minutes later she was still smiling when she slipped her phone back into her skirt pocket. Finally, her father was about to commit his life to something other than politics and she was happy about it. He had remained a widower and she had often wondered why, when he would be such a good catch for someone. But she'd heard over the years from both sets of grandparents how much he'd loved her mother and he hadn't wanted to give his heart to another woman. It had taken Stephanie three years, but she had done what some would have thought as impossible.

"After all the work that went into feeding my men breakfast and lunch you have a reason to smile?"

Startled, Chloe inclined her head to glance across the room. She hadn't heard the door open and now Ramsey was standing in the doorway and looking at her.

Refusing to be rattled, she reached for her glass of wine and took a sip, not sure how she would answer his question. There was no way she could share her father's good news on the risk that he might ask questions she didn't want to answer. All he would have to do is to go on the Internet and do a search on her father to discover she was his daughter and exactly what she did for a living.

"That's not what the smile is for," she decided to say. "I just received a call from a friend to say he was asking his girl to marry him tonight. And I'm happy for both of them."

She watched as he crossed the room to sit in the chair across from the sofa. She tried not to stare and was surprised he was giving her the time of day when it was obvious he'd been avoiding her earlier, especially after their kiss.

"I guess getting married would make some folks happy," he said.

She took another sip of her wine while holding his gaze, trying not to dwell on just how good he looked while he leaned back in the chair with muscled shoulders, hard jeans-clad thighs and long legs stretched to where his booted feet touched a portion of the coffee table. She wondered if he realized he was still wearing his Stetson. "Um. But I take it that you're not one of them," she replied.

"Nope, I wouldn't be one of them. I intend to be a single man for the rest of my days."

She considered his words. "So, you're one of those men who have a problem with matrimony? Who thinks marriage isn't a big deal?"

He lifted a brow. "And you're one of those women who thinks that it is?"

"I asked you first."

Yes, she had, Ramsey thought. His first inclination was to ignore the question. Move on to something else. And a part of him wondered what the hell he was doing here, sitting across from her at all. Especially because he'd taken great pains to make sure their paths didn't cross after his brothers and cousin had left. He hadn't liked the way Zane, Derringer and Jason's thoughts had been going. He would like to think he had put their false assumptions to rest, but he knew them well enough to know that was too much to hope for.

"Take your time if you need to gather your thoughts," Chloe said.

Ramsey kept his gaze trained on her. Unwavering. He couldn't give her a forced smile even if he'd wanted to because staying single was a serious topic with him. And it wasn't that he had a problem with matrimony per se, after the last fiasco of a wedding, he figured there was not a woman alive who would be able to get him back in a church for the sole purpose of getting hitched. No, he liked his single life just fine. He would think after dealing with the likes of an ex-boyfriend like Daren, so would she.

He continued to look at her, recalled her statement about gathering his thoughts and figured she would get along with his sisters easily because she seemed to have a smart mouth like them. That thought made his gaze shift to her lips.

He then swallowed, wishing he hadn't gone there with her mouth, especially because he knew how it tasted. And then there had been her response to him. He could do bodily harm to his kinfolk for their untimely interruption.

"I don't need to gather my thoughts," he finally said. Otherwise he would be tempted to cross the room and taste her again. "Raphael Westmoreland married enough for all of us."

She lifted a brow. "Raphael Westmoreland?"

"Yes, my great-grandfather. Rather recently we discovered he had a slew of wives. We also discovered he had a twin."

Evidently that sparked her interest, and her movement on the sofa sparked his. She slid closer to the edge and when she leaned forward her blouse gaped open a little, but enough to see some cleavage, as well as the thin pink fabric of her bra. Her skin looked velvety smooth, soft and a beautiful brown. He could imagine removing her bra and then lavishing her breasts with hot kisses, then taking his tongue and—

"Well?"

He blinked, reluctantly shifted his gaze from her chest to her eyes. They were bright. Inquiring. Intrigued. Apparently stuff about long-lost relatives interested her like it did the others in his family. Once they had become acquainted with the Atlanta Westmorelands, who were descendants of his great-grandfather's twin brother Reginald, Dillon had been eager to find out all that he could. His search to uncover the truth had led him to his wife Pamela. So in a way something good had come of it.

"Well, what?" he asked, deciding to play along just for the hell of it. Irritate her a bit. He liked the way her lips curved in a frown when she was aggravated about something. In addition to that, he liked her sexy pose on the sofa and the eager look on her face to find out more. Now if he could only get her out of wearing those damn leggings.

The glare she gave him denoted she was getting impatient, downright annoyed, at the length of time it was taking for him to tell her what she wanted to know. "Tell me some more about your great-grandfather's twin," she said with barely restrained impatience.

He could and would do so if it meant keeping her mind occupied while he continued to check her out. "We discovered over a year ago that our great-grandfather Raphael had a twin by the name of Reginald."

"And none of you had any idea?"

"No. Great-Grampa Raphael led everyone to believe he'd been born the only child. One of the Atlanta Westmorelands' genealogy search provided proof that Raphael and Reginald were twins and that Raphael had been considered the black sheep of the family after running off with a married woman. He finally settled here in Denver five wives later."

Ramsey paused when he felt a rush of sensations hammer his veins when Chloe shifted her body on the sofa once again and his gaze moved to her feet. They were bare and her toes were painted a prissy pink. When had seeing painted toes on a woman become so erotic?

He found it an effort to move his gaze from her feet back to her face, especially when his eyes had to pass over her chest. Of course it lingered awhile before moving on. When he finally settled on her eyes he saw hers were narrowed. "I'm sure there is more to this story," she said.

He nodded. "Of course and maybe one day I'll tell you the rest."

He had no idea why he'd said that. There wouldn't be a "one day" where they were concerned. Although he had changed his mind about calling the agency for another cook, he needed to keep his guard up around her. Yet here he was, misleading her into thinking he would share anything else about his family with her.

He eased out of his chair, deciding he'd said enough and had stayed in here with her longer than he'd needed to. Definitely longer than he should have. It then occurred to him he was still wearing his hat. Damn.

He took it off his head thinking the woman had a way of making him not think straight and that wasn't a good thing. "I'm taking a shower and going out to grab something for dinner," he said, and then wondered why on earth was he telling her his plans. His comings and goings were really none of her business.

He moved to leave the room and head upstairs, but her words stopped him. "I prepared dinner for you, Ramsey."

He stopped, turned and looked over at her. She was only getting paid to fix breakfast and lunch because his men usually ate dinner at their own homes with their families. Usually he dined at Penney's Diner a few miles down the road or with one of his family members.

"You didn't have to do that, Chloe."

"I know, but I wanted to because I need to eat, too," she replied, as if that explained things.

"Suit yourself," he said, knowing he sounded totally nonchalant and ungrateful when he was anything but. After spending practically her entire day in the kitchen preparing breakfast and lunch for his men, she had gone out of her way to prepare him dinner when she really didn't have to do it.

He turned in the direction of the kitchen and when he got to the edge of the room, he paused and then turned back around. She was staring into space as if she was trying to figure out in her own mind what had happened next with Raphael Westmoreland. She had moved from her earlier pose and was now curled up in the corner of his sofa, and every so often after taking a sip of wine her tongue would dart out to lick her top lip as if savoring the taste. Ramsey felt his body tighten with desire as he watched her.

"Chloe?"

She looked over at him and he could tell from her expression she was surprised to see him still standing there. "Yes?"

"Thanks for dinner." He then turned and kept walking toward the kitchen.

Hours later with his jaw clamped together tight, Ramsey walked the floor in his bedroom. This would be another night where he would not be getting any sleep and there was no excuse for it, and he needed his rest. The next two weeks of shearing would be both mind- and body-consuming if today was an example of what was to come.

At least his men had been excited about breakfast and lunch and had kept a steady conversation about both most of the day. Chloe's choice of food was a big hit and at quitting time today the men had been speculating on what they would be getting tomorrow for breakfast. Chloe was a definite asset to his ranch.

Ramsey moved over to the window to look out, not liking what he was thinking. She had done it again, he thought in disgust. The dinner she'd prepared for him had been the best he'd ever eaten, so much in fact that he'd been tempted to lick the plate. He had sat in the kitchen alone, not bothering to eat at the table, but had taken a stool at the breakfast bar instead.

Consuming his meal in silence he had been well aware of the moment she had come into the kitchen to wash out her wine glass. Mumbling a good-night, she had quickly left to head up the stairs. He had watched her go. Neither of them had mentioned anything about the kiss they'd shared earlier that day, and that was fine with him because his brothers and cousin had said enough. Not surprisingly, word of the kiss had reached Dillon and Callum. At least none of his sisters knew about it. Had they been privy to such information, they would have called by now, or even worse, just showed up to introduce themselves.

Hold up. Time out. He wasn't ready for something like that to happen, especially if his sisters assumed the wrong thing like Zane, Derringer and Jason had. But knowing Megan, Gemma and Bailey like he did, there was no doubt in his mind that they would have taken things further by trying to intentionally stir interest even if there wasn't any there.

At least he could safely say from his conversation with Chloe earlier that she was not a woman on the run as Callum had speculated. Other than what she'd told him about her ex-boyfriend, he still hadn't gotten her to talk a lot about herself, although she was trying to get all in his business about good old Raphael.

He shook his head. Other than knowing she was a damn good cook, she'd had an idiot of an ex-boyfriend, and that she had a friend who was getting married, he didn't know a lot about her. But then maybe the less he knew the better. She was doing a good job at what she had been hired to do.

Although he was losing sleep in the process.

But then, his inability to sleep and walking the floors at night was not her problem. He had to be the one who garnered more control. He had to stop the flow of sexual tension between them. But how? Imagining her with a sack over her head whenever he saw her wouldn't work because he would still be able to see her body. And there was no way he could look at all those curves without a degree of lust filling his head.

Sighing deeply, he made his way back to the bed. It was close to one in the morning and if he had to lie in bed, stare at the ceiling and count sheep to get to sleep, then so be it. Hell, sheep were his life anyway.

Chloe sat up in bed and clicked on her cell phone to answer it. She smiled when she saw the call was from her dad. "Okay, Pop, it's close to one in the morning here, which means it's later than that on the east coast, so this better be good."

Senator Burton's hearty laugh came in through the phone. "It is. I have Stephanie here with me. I asked her to marry me and she accepted and we just wanted our kids to know."

Tears she couldn't hold back came into Chloe's eyes. Her father sounded happy and if anyone deserved happiness it was him. She swiped at her tears and said, "I'm happy for you and Stephanie, Dad. Congratulations. Have the two of you told Brian and Danita yet?"

Brian and Danita were Stephanie's son and daughter. Brian was twenty-six and in his last year of medical school at the University of Florida. Danita was twenty-one and attending Xavier University of Louisiana. She, Brian and Danita got along marvelously and had been more than ready for their parents to take things to the next level. There was no doubt in Chloe's mind they would be as happy for their mother as she was for her dad.

"Not yet," her father said, interrupting her thoughts. "We thought we would call our oldest child first."

She smiled. Already he was thinking of them in terms of a family. "Okay, and I hate that I'm not there to celebrate, but when I return to Florida we're going to all get together."

"And when will you be returning to Florida?"

Chloe nibbled her bottom lip. That was a good question. "Not for at least another two weeks," she said with certainty. Ramsey's regular cook should have returned by then, and hopefully she would have come clean and told him the truth. She was hoping that once she made it clear he owed her, that he would do the cover and the article, grudgingly or otherwise.

"Okay, sweetheart. Stephanie wants to talk to you."

It was at least twenty minutes later before Chloe ended the call with the woman who would become her stepmother. They talked about plans for the wedding but only briefly because Danita's input would be needed on any major decisions.

She cuddled in bed wishing her own personal life could be as happy and exciting as her dad's. She took a long breath wondering where that yearning had come from. Probably with her dad's calling and then recalling her earlier conversation this evening with Ramsey about matrimony had stirred something within her, and it was something she hadn't thought about in a long time. It was her own desire to one day settle down, marry and have children. When things had ended with her and Daren, she hadn't given up on that dream. And although such a thing was not in her immediate plans, she still had that desire tucked away somewhere. What woman didn't? Even with her determination to be successful with her magazine company, she believed once that was achieved, she would find her Mr. Right. And one thing was for certain he definitely wouldn't be some surly sheep rancher.

But then if that was the case…and she was most certain that it was, why did she go to bed thinking about him every night? And why was the last thing she saw before closing her eyes his intense, penetrating dark eyes staring at her like they could see right through to her soul.

She closed her eyes. *Like now.* There he was, in vivid color, as he had been that evening, sitting across from her on the sofa with his legs stretched out in front of him, with his Stetson still on his head and looking sexier than any man had a right to look. So much in fact that more than once she had been tempted to get up off the sofa and go to him and curl up in his lap and purr.

She slowly opened her eyes, grateful she hadn't done such a thing. She really should thank him for keeping her agitated during most of the conversation, which stopped her from making a complete fool of herself. But if the truth be told, telling her about his great-grandfather had helped to refocus her attention. She knew there was more to the story and wondered why this was her first time hearing it. If such a thing hadn't come up on one of her computer's search engines that meant it hadn't made the news. Hmm. It was definitely something she would like to share with her readers, which might prompt them to want to start looking into their own family tree.

She shifted in bed thinking she was determined to get the whole story from Ramsey. If not Ramsey, then one of his brothers or cousins would do. Before leaving today Zane Westmoreland had tipped his hat at her, given her a flirty smile and a promise that he would be showing up for breakfast in the morning.

She shook her head. The only Westmoreland she wanted to concentrate on at the moment was the one who was probably sleeping peacefully in the bed only a few doors down the hall.

Six

"Good morning."

Ramsey glanced up from reading the morning's newspaper to stare into Chloe's face and immediately wished he hadn't. Her dark eyes looked slumberous and sensuously drowsy. A part of him was tempted to suggest that she forget about preparing breakfast for his men and go back to bed...but only if she would take him with her.

The muscles in his neck tightened at the very thought and he forced out his response. "Morning."

She sniffed the air. "Great, you've made coffee!"

He watched as she quickly headed toward the coffeepot. Today she was wearing another cute short dress with a pair of leggings underneath. He frowned. Did she have a pair of those things for every day of the week? And a different color for every day?

He took a sip of his coffee and watched as she poured hers,

adding cream and sugar into the mix before leaning against the counter and taking what looked like a much-needed sip.

"Excellent," she said.

"Thanks." Was she smiling? And if she was, then what the heck for? Could a cup of coffee first thing in the morning do that to her? As far as he could recall she'd been barely speaking to him when they'd parted yesterday afternoon. And why did knowing he'd contributed to putting that smile on her face send a good feeling vibrating through him? Damn.

He gazed back down at his newspaper. To be honest, he was hoping that he would have been in and out of the kitchen this morning before she'd gotten up. He was determined more so than ever to put distance between them. Maybe then he'd be able to get a good night's sleep.

"I'm doing omelets this morning. Would you like to go ahead and place your order?"

He glanced over at her. She was opening cabinets pulling out bowls, pots and pans. Had she said omelets? The last time he'd eaten an omelet was when he'd gone on a business trip and stayed at a hotel. It had been delicious.

"Yes, please," he said, trying to keep the excitement out of his voice. "I'd like that."

"How would you like it?"

He fought back the urge not to say the first thing that came into his mind, which would have given away his lusty thoughts. Hell, it was too early to think about that kind of stuff. But then, early morning sex wasn't so bad. And he had a feeling she would be able to cook in the bedroom with just as much heat as she used in the kitchen.

It took him only a few minutes to fill her in on the ingredients he wanted in his omelet. She nodded and went right to work. He watched her as she added the onions, green peppers, tomatoes…

Ramsey's mouth began watering. For both the omelet and for her. Moving around the kitchen, she was a sight to see. And he felt the lower part of his body getting there. The huge bulge behind his zipper wasn't a joke.

"What about a glass of orange juice?"

He blinked, realized he'd been staring. "Thanks. That will work."

At the moment he couldn't think of many things that wouldn't work, especially if she were to place her hands on it. Shivers went through him when he thought of places she could place her hands…on him.

She crossed the room and placed the plate on the table, right in front of him, and a glass of OJ beside his plate. "Thanks."

She smiled. "No problem."

He began eating while thinking it might not be a problem for her, but it was definitely becoming one for him. He didn't look up when she refilled his cup of coffee. "Thanks."

"Sure."

He took his time to savor the meal which deserved all the savoring it could get. The omelet was simply delicious. He liked glancing up every once in a while to watch as she fried bacon and cooked sausage. In no time at all the smell of breakfast was all over his kitchen.

And he noted she had come out of her shoes. She had kicked them in a corner and was gliding around the kitchen in her bare feet. He smiled as he glanced down at her toes again and felt his breathing come out slow and easy.

They hadn't said a word over the past thirty minutes. He was satisfied in letting her do her thing, and evidently she had no problem in letting him eat in peace while he finished reading the newspaper.

With the newspaper read and his plate clean, he decided to strike up a conversation. There were some things about her that he needed to know. "Do you have any family around these parts, Chloe?"

Chloe kept her attention trained on what she was doing, refusing to let the sound of Ramsey's deep, throaty voice wreak havoc on her mind. It was bad enough she could inhale his masculine scent over that of the bacon frying. That might sound like a lot of bull to some, but she was convinced it was true, which was the reason her nipples felt so sensitive. Bacon would not have caused that effect.

"No. I don't have family around these parts," she said, wondering why he'd asked.

"So you relocated here?"

"Yes."

"Without knowing anyone?"

She wondered how she could answer that without telling an outright lie. "Not exactly. I have a girlfriend from college who lives here and decided to give this area a try."

He nodded. "So you're living with your girlfriend?"

Her answer to that would not be a lie. "Yes, when I'm not staying here as your cook."

He pushed his plate aside and leaned back in his chair. "So where are you from?"

She forced a smile as she glanced over at him. "Where do you think I'm from?"

"Somewhere in the South."

"Yes, I'm from Florida, more specifically Tampa."

Deciding she had answered enough questions, Chloe resolved it was her turn to ask a few. "So, what happened with Raphael and his five wives? I didn't think a divorce was that easy back in the day."

Ramsey shrugged. "During our research we discovered the first woman he ran off with was a preacher's wife. He couldn't marry her because she was already married."

Chloe lifted a brow. "Then why did he run off with her?"

"To save her from an abusive marriage. And before you ask, the second wife he took off her husband's hands, with her husband's blessing, to save a possible scandal."

Ramsey decided that was all he would tell her for now. It was just enough to keep her curious. Why he was baiting her he really wasn't sure. Maybe the reason was that he liked seeing the look of interest in her eyes.

He stood and carried his plate, coffee cup and glass over to the sink.

"You don't have to do that," she said.

"Yes, I do. I was raised to clean up after myself."

And just like yesterday, when he reached the sink she deliberately moved out of his way. Knowing she was trying to avoid his touch bothered him. He reached out and grabbed hold of her hand. She glanced over at him, startled.

"Why are you afraid of me, Chloe?" It was then that he realized he was running his fingers up and down her arm.

She lifted her chin, but did not try pulling her hand away. "What makes you think I'm afraid of you?"

"You're trying to avoid me."

She lifted a haughty brow. "I could very well say the same thing about you, Ramsey."

That was true, he thought to himself. Instead of denying it, he was silent for a moment. And when he felt a shudder pass through her from the way he was running his fingers up her arms he locked his gaze to hers.

"Why the hell do we let this keep happening to us?" he asked in a low, throaty tone.

Surprisingly, she gave him a faint smile. "Hey, you're the one who was trying to work me out of your system."

He nodded. "With yesterday's kiss," he replied.

"Yes."

Now it was his time to smile. "It didn't work."

She shrugged. "Maybe your heart just wasn't in it."

His smile quickly transformed to a frown. "Like hell. Everything I had was in it."

She seemed to consider his words for half a second. "I know," she said, and sighed in dismay.

With his free hand he took his finger and tilted her chin. "But just to be sure, I think I should at least try it again. Yesterday didn't seem to work."

He then lowered his head and caught her lips in a drugging kiss, deliberately making it hot from the start. His tongue slid into her mouth on a breathless sigh and from there it was on. He deepened the kiss, devouring her mouth with a hunger that made yesterday's kiss seem tame.

He heard her moan. He felt the way the pebbled tips of her breasts were rubbing against his chest as if he wasn't even wearing a shirt. And once again, her stance was perfect to cradle his erection, which was hard as a rock, engorged, as aroused as a male shaft could get.

And just like yesterday, she was returning his kiss, lick for lick. Feasting on his mouth with just as much greed as he was feasting on hers. What was it about her taste, her flavor, the way their mouths fit together? His tongue seemed at home wrapped around hers.

He tried doing a mental calculation in his head, trying to figure out just how many steps it would take to reach the table. There he would strip her naked and…

The clearing of multiple throats had him reluctantly breaking contact with Chloe's mouth, but not before getting one final lick of his tongue across her lips. He lifted his head to glare over at the four men standing in his kitchen doorway with smirks on their faces.

It was Callum, Zane, Derringer and Jason. Of course it was Zane who had the damn nerve to ask, "Could you explain to us why you keep kissing your cook?"

Chloe eased her body into the sudsy water. Now it was late afternoon and everyone, including Ramsey, was gone and she intended to take time for herself. And she intended to get in bed early so she could be well-rested in the morning, now that she knew the routine.

She closed her eyes and thought about the events of the day, beginning that morning when the four men had walked in on her and Ramsey. This time instead of being embarrassed by the intrusion, she had been downright annoyed. And of course Ramsey had done just what she'd expected. He had begun avoiding her again.

He hadn't shown up for lunch. Instead he had locked himself in his office. Then around two o'clock, he left and he had yet to return and it was close to six. She had prepared dinner for him again and had left it warming in the oven. She had even sat on the sofa like yesterday, anticipating his return. But when it became evident he was staying away, she decided to take a bath, make a few calls and then get into bed early.

Thinking she had remained in the bathtub long enough, she stood to dry off with the huge towel. Everything for tomorrow was taken care of, so there was no reason for her to leave her bedroom tonight. She could use her PDA to check for any messages and to call and chat with her dad.

She paused when she thought she heard a car door slam, which meant Ramsey had returned home. Slipping into her robe and tying the sash tightly around her waist, she strolled over to the window and looked out. Ramsey was getting out of his truck.

She felt her body's reaction at seeing him. And as if he felt her presence, he tipped his head back and glanced up and saw her standing at the window.

Chloe sucked in a steadying breath the moment their eyes met. For a long time they just stood there, seemingly transfixed while staring at each other. And the heat of his gaze, the intensity of his stare touched her in areas that hadn't been touched in a long time.

She actually felt her body tremble at the desire building inside her and the feelings that clawed in her stomach from his unwavering gaze. No height or distance could stop the flow of sensations that were seeping into her every pore. And as she stood there all she could do was remember how he had taken her mouth for two days straight in hard, hungry and demanding kisses.

Unable to handle the intensity of his gaze or the passion he was stirring within her any longer, she drew in a deep breath before stepping away from the window.

Chloe fought the urge to rush downstairs and meet him at the door, to throw her arms around him and lift her mouth up to him, to be bold enough to take his mouth with the same intensity that he'd taken hers with earlier that day. She shook her head knowing there was no way she could or would do such a thing.

Removing her robe, she slipped into her pj's, deciding to

stick with her original plan to remain in her room for the rest of the evening. She and Ramsey might be under the same roof, but the less time they spent together, the better. And she had a good reason for feeling that way. She was getting drawn to him in a way that was more emotional than physical. She wished she could blame what she was feeling on irrational hormones but she knew that wasn't the case. Something else was taking place and she didn't want to think what that something could possibly be.

She felt vulnerable around him, like he could be the one man who could pull her into him so much that she would forget about herself. Daren had tried and failed. But a part of her knew if Ramsey took a mind to doing so that he would be successful. He had the ability to break through all the emotional walls she'd erected since her breakup with Daren.

With Ramsey she could feel herself losing her sense of will, her sense of logic and her common sense. There was something about him that was making her think things that she shouldn't. Like a little girl with those same set of dark eyes or a son with Ramsey's smile. She would admit right then and there if she was interested in a serious involvement with a man, he would head the list. And that worried her.

Ramsey opened the door to his home and leaned against it for a moment. He was fully aroused. The last thing he had expected when he'd pulled into his yard was to get out of his truck and participate in mind sex. He had stood there staring at Chloe while his entire mind had partaken in the most erotic fantasy possible. There was no part of him that had not been stimulated.

Through the window he could tell she was wearing a robe and he figured she was naked underneath. The thought of a naked Chloe had made him hard. Desire had surged through him in a way that it had never done before. While standing there staring at her he'd actually felt every muscle in his body tighten.

He glanced up at the stairs knowing the object of his desire, his red-hot passion and his erotic fantasies was up there behind closed doors. He was tempted, boy was he tempted, to go right up those stairs, knock on her door and kiss her in a way that would make the kiss they'd shared that morning seem like child's play. And now that her taste was embedded onto his tongue, he wanted more of it, doubted he would be able to get enough.

He rubbed his hand down his face wondering what in the hell was wrong with him. He had been around beautiful women before. For a while his sisters, who felt he'd still been hurting over Danielle's betrayal, had tried their hands at matchmaking. But no woman had held his interest until now. He was finding it hard to resist her. She was temptation at its very best. And on top of everything else, he was feeling emotions that he couldn't quite identify. The woman was bewitching him.

He had remained in his office the majority of the day, but all it took was to hear the laughter and the excitement in the voices of his men when they'd arrived at lunch to know that once again Chloe had made their day. That point was proven when he'd checked the shearing records for today. More sheep than normal had been sheared. Hell, they had basically set a record. That meant there was a connection between their cheerful attitudes and the work they did. A happy employee produced more and for the past two days his men had produced. And when he had dropped by the shearing plant this evening, right before closing time, he could hear the excitement in their voices when they talked about breakfast in the morning. After the omelets their anticipation as to what tomorrow morning would bring was evident.

He drew in a deep breath and it was at that moment he picked up the smell of something delicious. Pushing away from the door, he crossed the room to the kitchen and saw that Chloe had prepared his dinner again. He lifted the pots and checked the oven. She had made baked chicken, field peas, rice and gravy, and macaroni and cheese. A real Southern meal, something a westerner like him could appreciate. He had acquired a taste for Southern cuisine after meeting the Atlanta Westmorelands.

Deciding he would wash up for dinner, he moved toward the bathroom thinking he had deliberately stayed away today. That kiss he and Chloe had shared had shredded his senses, making resisting her nearly impossible. It was already rumored by his men that he had the hots for her and he didn't want to give them any more to talk about or speculate on. So leaving here for a while had been the decision that he'd made.

And then he'd had to deal with the ribbing from his brothers, Jason and Callum. Trying to convince them that Chloe was nothing more than his cook was beginning to sound lame even to his ears. He had walked away from them when he saw they were intent on drawing their own conclusions about his and Chloe's relationship, and he'd made a point not to accept their invitation for a game of poker over at Jason's place.

Luckily for him Dillon and Pamela had returned to town for a few days for Dillon to attend a business meeting, so he'd had the chance to visit with them. The newly married couple divided their time between here and Pamela's home in Gamble, Wyoming, because one of Pamela's sisters was in her last year of high school.

Dillon seemed extremely happy as a married man and Ramsey was happy for him. From the time he could remember, he and Dillon had been closer than just cousins. In essence, they were best friends and when their parents had perished in that plane crash, he had more than supported Dillon's desire to keep the family together.

Because Dillon was the oldest by some months, he had become head of the family and guardian for everyone. But the two of them had worked hard. It hadn't been easy raising their siblings and cousins, nine of whom had been under the age of sixteen.

Now all of them were over twenty-one, either in college or working alongside Dillon at Blue Ridge Land Development, the company that the two Westmoreland brothers—his father and Dillon's—had formed many years ago. Under Dillon's guidance, Blue Ridge was now a multimillion dollar company well known in the Mountain States. It employed over a thousand people. Every family member had worked there at some point in their lives before pursuing their dreams and other ambitions.

An hour later Ramsey had finished eating and was still licking his lips. The meal had been delicious. Chloe hadn't come downstairs and in a way he hadn't expected her to. She was well aware, just like he was, that something was taking place between them and it was something neither of them wanted. So it would be best to avoid the situation by avoiding each other. The attraction between them was too strong, the passion was too thick. And she was becoming his weakness. If he didn't get things in check, the desire he felt for her would consume him and that was something he simply refused to let happen.

He shook his head as he moved toward the stairs and the

moment he lifted his leg to take a step he inhaled her scent. It was the scent of a woman he wanted. Her fragrance was emitting from behind closed doors, drenching the air, teasing his nostrils and making him even more aroused. He hadn't gotten much sleep last night and he doubted things would be any better tonight.

When he reached the landing, he worked his shoulders to relieve the tension that had built there. Drawing in a heated breath he made it down the hall, forcing one foot in front of the other, intent on passing Chloe's door without stopping.

Easier said than done. When he reached her door he couldn't help but pause. He even raised his hand to knock before snatching it back to his side.

What the hell was happening to him?

He forced himself away from her door and quickly moved down the hall toward his own. He had to formulate a plan, at least until the weekend. Hopefully, she would leave those two days to go back to her own place, get her mail, water her plants, check in with her neighbors or whatever else she needed to do. By then they would need the distance. They would need the space. The weekend was three days away and he hoped like hell that he could hold out until then.

Seven

"So what do you think of Derringer?"

Chloe couldn't stop the smile from touching her lips. This was the third time this weekend that Lucia had asked that same question. "I told you twice already, but I'll tell you again," she teased, as she pulled off her jacket. "He is a very handsome man. I like him. He, Zane and Jason come by for breakfast and lunch quite a bit. They're nice guys. Big teasers."

She saw the wistful look in Lucia's eyes. They had just returned from having dinner together after going to a movie. "You know how you can make yourself known, don't you?"

Lucia rolled her eyes. "I know how *you* would make yourself known to him, Clo. You go after whatever it is that you want. You're daring. I'm not."

Chloe placed her hands on her hips. "So what are you going to do, Lou? Wait another year or so for him to need more paint thinner and hope you're in your father's store when he does?"

Lucia dropped down on her sofa with a downhearted look on her face. "Of course not." She then looked up at Chloe. "Enough about me since I refuse to have a pity party. How close are you to getting Ramsey to do the magazine cover and interview?"

Chloe shook her head and dropped down beside Lucia, looking just as downhearted. "It's not going well. Ramsey is avoiding me like the plague."

"Why?"

Chloe smiled over at her friend. "Too much sexual chemistry in the air when we're within ten feet of each other."

"Must be nice."

Chloe leaned back against the sofa and closed her eyes thinking that in essence it *should* be nice, but it wasn't. Ramsey made an appearance only when he had to. He got up each morning for his cup of coffee while she prepared breakfast and instead of hanging around, he took his breakfast and coffee into his office, claiming he had a lot of work to do. He came out for lunch to eat with his men, said very little and only stayed long enough to eat and leave. In the evenings, although she prepared dinner for him each evening, he usually stayed away until he was sure she was in bed.

He hadn't been home when she'd left to come here for the weekend. She had left a note on the kitchen table letting him know she would be returning Sunday evening. She had left her cell number in case something came up and she needed to be reached.

A smile touched her lips. Who was she kidding? She was hoping he would contact her for any reason and that wasn't good.

"Okay, Clo, you've gotten quiet on me. Open those eyes and tell me what's going on."

Chloe slowly opened her eyes to gaze over into Lucia's curious ones. She had an idea what was going on, but to say it out loud would be speaking it into existence and she wasn't ready to do that yet. There was no way she could tell Lucia that she might not be the only woman who'd fallen for a Westmoreland man.

"Stop being a worry wart. Nothing is going on." Chloe drew in a breath thinking that Lucia had no idea just how true that was. Nothing was really going on. She was no closer to getting Ramsey to agree to that cover or an interview than before she'd shown up. Somehow, she had to get him to stop avoiding her, sexual chemistry or no sexual chemistry. And if she were to come clean now and tell him the truth, he would probably kick her off his land so fast it would make her head spin.

She stood, not ready for Lucia to question her further about anything. "It's late and I think I'll turn in early."

"I think I'll turn in as well. Mom and Dad invited us to dinner after church tomorrow and then later Aunt Pauline wants us to drop by her place."

"All right and then after that I need to return to the Westmoreland place." This would be her last week and she needed to make some kind of headway.

Later that night as Chloe lay in bed, images of Ramsey flowed through her mind. Two days ago while preparing lunch she had glanced out the window in time to see a shirtless Ramsey carrying a lamb in his arms across the yard to the barn. With jeans riding low on his hips she had stared at his physique, taking in every inch of his tight abs, strong arms and tight buns. He was the only man alive who could literally make her drool.

And if that wasn't bad enough, the following morning at breakfast when he'd sat with his men, she saw again how well he got along with them as well as his brothers and cousin.

She shifted in bed admitting she missed him. She missed the ranch. And as crazy as it sounded, she even missed preparing food for the men. They were so appreciative and complimentary.

She closed her eyes thinking of Ramsey and knowing she would be glad to see him tomorrow when she returned to the ranch.

Ramsey pushed back the curtain and looked out, something he'd done too many times over the past hour. Where was she? The note she'd left on the kitchen table said she would return Sunday evening. In his part of the world the evening time came well before ten at night. The last time he had glanced at the clock it was heading toward the eleventh hour.

She had left her phone number, but he had thrown it away, refusing to be tempted to call her and now he was worried. What if something had happened. He had no way of reaching her and had no idea just where she lived in the city.

It had rained earlier and the road off the main highway leading to Westmoreland Country was known to be slippery after a storm. He let the curtain slip back in place and began pacing the floor again. At that moment he realized just how little he knew about Chloe, other than she was the woman who aroused him to no end.

This was crazy. He'd let a woman in his house to cook for his men, sleep in his guestroom, use his washer and dryer to wash her bed linens before she'd taken off for the weekend, and all he knew about her was her name.

Okay, he knew a little bit more about her than that. He knew she was a hell of a cook and beautiful as beautiful could get. He knew she had a hell of a body, although he was yet to see her bare legs. He knew she got along with his men and had cooked a huge chocolate cake last week when Colin Lawrence had turned fifty.

He also knew what she did to him whenever she looked at him for any length of time. Truth was, although he wished like hell he didn't have to admit it, in one short week he'd discovered a taste unlike any he'd ever sampled before, and her scent was one hell of a fragrance, an aroma he could breathe into his nostrils for days. But she had managed to do something no other woman had been capable of doing in ten years.

She had ignited his passion.

He wanted to know how it felt to lose himself inside her, to feel her heat, have her body, legs and all, wrapped all around him, feel his erection swell to the fullest size possible inside her, and be as greedy for her breasts as he was for her mouth.

His hands clenched into fists at his side. He was the Westmoreland, so he'd been told, who had the least amount of charm. The one who didn't need sex as often as the rest to maintain a normal life. Yet here he was with his heart thumping like crazy in his chest as he imagined doing all kinds of naughty things to Chloe. For the first time in hell knows when, he was thinking about getting laid. Bottom line, he was horny as hell.

The unwanted direction of his thoughts no longer shocked him. Instead what it did was propel him to want to do more than think about it. He wanted to act on it and let the chips fall where they may. He wanted…

His thoughts were suddenly interrupted by the sound of a vehicle pulling up. Quickly crossing the room he glanced out the window and saw it was Chloe returning. He frowned as he dropped the curtain back in place. She was late.

He dismissed the feeling of relief knowing she was all right and was filled with anger. The least she could have done was call to let him know she would be late. Standing across the room he faced the door with his arms over his chest. She had a lot of explaining to do. The nerve of her to make him worry for nothing.

Her scent filled the air the moment the door opened, but in anger he chose to ignore it. But when she walked over his threshold wearing a white blouse and a short denim skirt—with no leggings underneath—that showed the most beautiful pair of legs he had ever seen, he gritted his teeth knowing there was no way he could ignore them.

Chloe closed the door behind her, saw Ramsey standing across the room glaring and quickly knew she was so not ready for this. In fact, she had decided to wait before returning in hopes that he would be in bed already. She tried to ignore how good he looked. The man wore a pair of jeans like they'd been made just for his body. They fit snug, showing impressive hard thighs and tight abs. Another thing she noticed was that it looked as if he hadn't shaved since she'd left. The stubble look suited him. It made him look even sexier in a sinful sort of way.

Trying to take her mind off his ultra-fine body, she stared back at him, wondering what his problem was. She had left everything in perfect order before she'd headed into town for the weekend. She had even washed and dried her bed linens, although he'd mentioned he had a housekeeper who came every Saturday morning to clean and do laundry. And why was he staring at her legs like he'd never seen a pair of legs before? Her skirt was short, but it wasn't that short. She'd worn some shorter. If he was about to tell her there was something wrong with her outfit, that it wasn't appropriate to wear on his ranch, then she would let him have it.

Deciding to just get this over with and give just as good as she got, she lifted her chin, glared back at him and asked, "Ramsey, is there a problem?"

Ramsey's gut clenched and his jaw tightened. Her legs were long and shapely. They were the kind that looked perfect in a short dress from the top of her thighs all the way down to her ankles.

"Ramsey, I asked was there a problem?" she asked testily.

His gaze moved from her legs to her face. "You're late."

What on earth did he mean by that? Chloe wondered as a confused frown covered her face. She must have heard him wrong. "Excuse me?"

"I said you're late. Your note said you would be returning Sunday evening and it's almost eleven."

She dropped her overnight bag by her feet. "And what of it? I'm not on a time clock. In fact, I am not even working for you today. As long as I'm here to prepare breakfast in the morning what business is it of yours?"

Ramsey stiffened. She had asked a good question. What business was it of his? He then said the first thing that came to his mind. "This is my house."

She seemed taken aback by that response. "Are you standing here telling me that I have a curfew?"

Was that what he was saying? He shook his head. "No, you don't have a curfew, but since you left a note saying you would be returning in the evening, at least you could have had the decency to call."

Her gaze locked on his face. *Decency?* Blood rushed through her veins as anger consumed her. He had the gall to utter such a word? She crossed the room to him. "Let's talk about decency, Ramsey. If you would have had the *decency* to be here when I left instead of avoiding me like I have the pox, I would not have had to leave that note."

Ramsey was taken aback by Chloe's anger. As far as he was concerned she didn't have a damn thing to be angry about. She hadn't been the one who'd endured sleepless nights knowing she was just down the hall from him when the need to bury himself deep inside her had nearly driven him insane. Hell, if only she knew that the reason he'd deliberately made himself scarce most of last week was because anytime he saw her he got an automatic erection that wouldn't go down.

Furthermore, he was sick and tired of finding places to go in the afternoons just so he wouldn't be tempted to make one of those erotic dreams he'd had over the past week come true. Tired of unexplainable emotions, escalated hormones and a frantic urge to make love to her until neither of them had an ounce of energy left.

He took a step closer as his anger level moved up another notch. "You don't get it do you?" he asked in a voice that was rough, close to the edge. "I stayed away to do us both a favor, Chloe. Had I been here you would never have walked out that door."

The hard, cold reality was that he was a lit piece of dynamite ready to explode, preferably inside her. Point blank, he wanted her in a way he'd never wanted any woman and with a need that was pushing him over the edge and he was determined to take her right with him.

He could tell by her expression she hadn't liked what he'd said. She took a step closer, got in his face, put her mouth just inches from his, their noses almost touched. "Ha! And just what were you going to do? Tie me up?"

A slow smile slid over his lips. If only she knew how many times such a thought had crossed his mind. He'd never been into that bondage stuff, but he could just imagine such a thing with her. "Considering the state I've been in all week, the state I happen to be in right now, tying you up would have definitely been an option."

Chloe stared at him, stunned at his admission, and at that moment she realized not only what he'd said but what he'd meant. Somewhere along the line their conversation had become sexual. Maybe for him it had always been that way, but due to her raging anger she had failed to see it. However, she was seeing it now. She could feel his heat and that heat was being passed on to her. Even the distended nipples pressing against her blouse felt like they were ready to detonate. And the area between her legs, more specifically the depths of her womb, felt hot.

"And do you know what I would have done after tying you up, Chloe?"

Nibbling on her bottom lip she held his gaze while her entire body felt like a bonfire. She'd never considered herself a fiercely passionate woman, but at that moment the raw images going through her mind, of her bound to his bed, legs spread, with him naked and crawling over her, to mate with her, had her speechless.

He didn't wait for her to respond to his question. "I would have stripped you naked and then licked you all over from head to toe."

Added to the very image flowing in her mind, she could

definitely see him doing that. A heated ache settled between her thighs and when she felt her panties get wet she tightened her legs together. Hot passion, deep desire was taking over her entire body with his words and every part of her was responding, without any restraints.

"But do you know where my mouth would have lingered, Chloe? Where it would have devoured you to the fullest, given you the most sensual pleasure?"

When she didn't say anything, he leaned in, whispered close to her ear and what he said, as well as the erotic picture his words made, had her weak in the knees. And it didn't help matters that she could feel the warmth of his breath against her neck.

"And trust me, you aren't out of the woods yet," he said in a deep, husky and sexually-laden voice. "So if you don't want me with the same intensity that I want you, with the same intensity that I plan on taking you, then I suggest you walk out that door right now, because I refuse to avoid you any longer."

Chloe swallowed tightly while admitting inwardly that she wanted him, wanted him to take her and with the same intensity he was alluding to. There was no way she could or would deny that. And she knew that standing before her was a fiercely passionate man. She had known it from the first time she had seen him that day crossing the street. There had been something about him that had sent a sensual thrill through her, had made her entirely aware of him as a woman. It had made her fantasize about him every night since then. So what he was threatening to do stimulated her more than he would ever know.

But then at the same time, he was giving her an out without having to feel guilty about leaving him in a tough spot in regard to losing a cook. She should take it. But the bottom line was that she didn't want to take it. She wanted to take him instead.

"Chloe?"

Her name flowed from his lips in a deeply throaty tone. She met his gaze. "Yes?"

"I'm waiting."

She inhaled deeply, took a couple of steps to him, flattened her hands against his chest, looked up into his eyes and then told him calmly, "So am I."

Ramsey's self-control snapped and the speed in which his mouth swept down on Chloe's had his head spinning. But the twirling stopped and was replaced by an explosion going off in his skull the moment his tongue was planted firmly in her mouth.

She tasted like the strawberry cake she had baked on Thursday and he was tempted to eat her mouth with the same greediness with which he'd consumed that slice of cake. And when his tongue began lapping her up, savoring every inch of her mouth, exploring every nook and cranny, he heard the moan that escaped from her throat. Her delicious taste consumed him, went to his head, speared every part of his body and enflamed his senses.

And he still wanted to draw her deeper into himself.

The hard throbbing of his erection was letting him know that kissing her would not be enough. His control was eroding and taking his sanity right along with it, while at the same time his hunger was being escalated. And his body, every nerve ending, every cell, was demanding to be fed. He suddenly pulled his mouth away, needing more. And needing it now.

"Ramsey?"

Her voice was soft, her breath hot, and the sound of his

name from her lips was as sweet as her taste. He knew at that moment he had to remove her clothes and the thought of taking off that skirt and getting between those legs sent a shudder through every part of him.

He knew there was no way he could make it up the stairs to his bedroom. The sofa would have to do. It was sturdy and strong which was a good thing because she was in for a hard ride. He had given her fair warning, but she hadn't taken it. Soon enough she would discover just what she had unleashed.

The air surrounding them was thick with sexual tension. The rush of sensations that were pounding through his veins and making his insides quiver, drove him to reach out and draw her back close to him. His hands began moving, roaming all over her and lifting her short skirt to touch the backside he enjoyed looking at so much.

He felt her shiver in his arms, heard her say his name again and with the sound of the hunger he heard in her voice, more than ever before, consumed him. He needed to kiss her again, let his tongue stroke inside her mouth while his hands stroked her flesh.

That wasn't enough.

Suddenly, his hands went to her blouse, his fingers gripped the fabric and with one hard tug ripped it from her body.

Chloe gasped and when she saw the intensity of desire that burned in Ramsey's eyes she knew her blouse was just the beginning. He proved her right when his hands reached for her bra. Blood surged through her veins when he opened the front clasp, freeing her breasts, but not for long.

After pulling the bra off her shoulders and tossing it aside, he took the twin mounds in his hands as if testing their softness and shaping their fullness. And then he lowered his mouth to capture a puckered nipple into his hot mouth. The moment his tongue touched the tip, sucked it deep, she dug her nails into his shoulders as sensations ripped through her. Intense pleasure trailed not far behind and caused her nipples to harden even more.

"Ramsey…" She whispered his name, barely able to stand on her feet any longer as he attacked her breasts with his mouth like a starving man.

Instead of answering, with his mouth still on her breasts, he moved his hands downward to raise her skirt. His fingers found the crotch of her panties. The moment he touched the drenched spot she moaned, but not before she heard his rough growl. He pulled back, released her breasts and gripped her skirt to pull it down her hips.

Within seconds she was standing in front of him wearing nothing more than wet panties. He took a step back to remove his shirt, popping buttons in his haste, before stripping it from his shoulders. His naked chest was perfect and she couldn't help moving, closing the distance and reaching out to rake her nails across the hard, muscled hairy chest, liking the feel beneath her fingertips.

He captured her hand and holding her gaze he began licking her fingers, one by one. His tongue felt hot against her sensitive flesh and she shuddered when sensations tore through her.

"You like that?" His voice was heavy, deep, sexy.

She could only nod.

"You enjoy my tongue on you?"

"Yes," she whispered, barely able to get out the single word.

"Good, now let's see how you enjoy my tongue *in* you."

He eased down in front of her and holding her hips he leaned forward, pressed his nose against the crotch of her panties, as if to inhale her scent. And then he flicked out his tongue and it felt blazing hot against the silky material. Pleasure eased over her and she felt on the verge of exploding.

Ramsey leaned back and looked up to hold her gaze as he began easing her panties down her legs. When she stepped out of them he could only lean farther back on his haunches and look at her up and down, fighting hard to breathe while doing so.

He was mesmerized. Her legs seemed endless. They were beautiful, shapely, alluring. They were silky smooth and should never be covered with a pair of leggings again. Unable to hold out any longer, he reached out and touched her legs, stroked them up and down, front and back, the pad of his fingers reveling in the feel of her skin. These were legs that were making him harder just looking at them. Legs he wanted wrapped around him tight, holding him inside her body while he thrust in and out of her.

But first, he had to taste her.

Leaning in closer his hands slid to her hips as he angled his mouth to her center. Instinctively, she parted her thighs and when he gently opened her up and his tongue delved inside her, she clung to him to hold on, which to him was a good thing.

His tongue swiped at her a couple of times before going for the gusto, stroking her, licking her and sucking with an intensity he felt all the way to the exquisitely painful tip of his erection. She began moving against his mouth and he gripped her hips tighter to hold her steady and then his hands shifted and went to her rump, gripping it and pushing her closer to his mouth, while at the same time he lifted her legs off the floor to wrap around his shoulders, cupping her backside in the palms of his hands for support. Keeping his mouth locked to her his tongue was having a field day, licking her into pleasure, deliberately searing her senses. She clenched her hands to the side of his head, moaned his name over and over. And then she began to shudder. He felt it. He tasted it. And he didn't intend to remove his mouth from her until he'd gotten his fill.

Moments later he pulled his mouth away, untangled her legs from around his shoulders and eased her down with him to the floor. He glanced over at her and licked his lips. "Delicious," he whispered in a throaty voice.

She had been more than delicious. She was incredible. The taste and heat of her was still on his tongue. At that moment, something inside him snapped. The need to join his body with hers was monumental.

He released a growl before he shifted his body, capturing her mouth the moment he could do so. He was going to take her, give them both pleasure, have them exploding all over the place, and his erection throbbed violently in anticipation.

He couldn't get out of his jeans quickly enough and she didn't help matters when she began nipping on his shoulders, as if branding him hers. *Hers.* A groan left his chest when she bit down and he stared at her. She gave him one hell of a naughty smile not the least regretful. "I'm going to make you pay for that," he promised in a deep voice. With that said, he kicked his jeans away and pulled her to him.

"Condom?"

"Damn." Her mention of protection made him realize just how over the edge he was and the risk he had been about to take. Looking around for his jeans he quickly found them and fumbled through the pockets until he located his wallet. He found a condom packet, not wanting to think just how long it had been in there and hoping like hell it would still be effective.

Ripping open the packet he quickly sheathed himself knowing her eyes were glued to him and watching every move he made. When he was finished, he went back to her, pulled her into his arms and kissed her deeply, hungrily and wildly.

He hadn't expected this. He hadn't expected a need erupting inside him so intense that he felt driven to make love to her in a way he hadn't ever made love to a woman before. She was demanding something from him, pulling it out effortlessly and he knew the only way he would be totally satisfied was when he was embedded deeply inside of her.

He pulled his mouth from hers, reveling in a need so intense he was goaded into immediate action. She was so responsive, filled with as much passion as he was feeling and he wanted her now. He shifted their bodies to place her beneath him, pressing her back on the rug. Ramsey spread her legs with his knee. Gripping her hips tight in his hands, he surged inside of her, going deep, all the way to the hilt.

He watched her eyes widen at the intrusion and when he began moving, thrusting inside of her, her gaze became filled with a pleasure that touched his soul and made his erection throb even more inside of her.

Her heat surrounded him. Her muscles clenched him, pulled everything out of him; made pleasure build inside of him, gather in his shaft, and he felt snug inside of her, like it was where he belonged.

He began moving harder. Going faster. Thrusting deeper. And when he called out her name the sound detonated like a bomb. He exploded at the same moment she did. Pleasure ripped through them both and he gripped her hips tighter as he drove even deeper inside of her.

"Chloe."

Her name was a guttural sound off his lips and he moved his hands from her hips to her hair as he filled her with his release. Shivers ran down his spine and he could only sigh as sensations filled him to capacity.

And when he eased up to take her mouth in his, he promised himself that sometime tonight, they would make it to the bedroom.

Eight

Sometime hours later, they made it to the bedroom. Barely. The most difficult part in getting there had been the stairs. Ramsey couldn't recall ever making love to anybody on stairs. He was a more traditional guy. But there had been nothing traditional about anything he and Chloe had done tonight, and even now as he lay flat on his back while she slept literally on top of him, he couldn't help but think about everything that had happened from the time Chloe had returned.

He'd been keyed up, part angry and part fighting an intense desire that had been eating away at him since the moment he first laid eyes on her. And when she had walked through the door tonight, and he'd seen her…and her bare legs, he had tried smothering his desire with anger by lashing out at her in a subject matter that really hadn't made any sense. That hadn't worked. And he was glad it hadn't. If she had taken the option to walk out that door, he probably would have died then and there. His need for her was so strong, so intense that even now he was getting hard all over again.

He was tempted to wake her but he would let her rest. She deserved every second that she slept. The woman was amazing and had more passion than he could ever imagine any woman having. She had met his every thrust and fueled his passion in a way that even now made him breathless. She had ridden him to the point of madness and it was only after their passion had exploded in a gigantic maelstrom that she had slumped down on top of him. She hadn't moved since.

He could only marvel at the soft body on top of him and even now their bodies were still intimately connected. He inhaled, taking in her scent. Her bare breasts pressing deep into his chest and her legs, those legs that had been his downfall earlier, were entwined in his. He closed his eyes to sleep awhile.

Ramsey wasn't sure just how long he'd slept, but when he lifted his lids it was to stare into a gorgeous pair of dark eyes. At the realization that she was awake, his body immediately became aroused. His erection jerked to life inside of her and from her expression he knew she felt it the moment he had.

He saw the rush of heat that inflamed her features and that same heat was there in the depths of the eyes staring down at him. Together they felt his shaft continue to expand inside of her, stretching her fully to accommodate him totally.

And when her muscles began clenching him, he knew it was time to start moving. But not until he was on top. She was the one who'd ridden the last go around and now it was his turn. He gritted his teeth as she continued to clench his hardness and to get control of his mind and senses. He began sliding his hand up and down her back, loving the feel of the soft texture of her skin. And then when he knew he had her absolute attention, he flipped her onto her back.

Surprise lit her eyes. "Hey! That's not fair."

Ramsey smiled, deciding he wouldn't waste time arguing with her, not when he wanted to make love to her, ride her, pump inside of her over and over again.

Automatically, she wrapped her legs around his waist and when she smiled up at him, he knew before it was all said and done, she was going to drain everything out of him. It was hard to believe they had already made love several times that night. In fact, except for the time he'd allowed her to sleep, they had made love nonstop.

When he pushed himself deeper inside of her, the groan that curled in her throat triggered something within him and he began moving, lifting up her hips to receive his strong strokes. His thrusts were fine-tuned, primitively precise and painstakingly deliberate.

"Ramsey." She moaned out his name over and over while thrashing her head back and forth against the bedcovers.

"Look at me, Chloe," he said in a guttural groan and when she did, and her eyes clashed with his, his grip tightened on her hips and what he saw in her gaze ignited something within him to the point where he felt consumed in fire, torched by desire. But he didn't stop. He continued going, moving in and out of her, needing her, wanting her and determined to consume her the way she was totally consuming him.

Chloe actually felt every muscle in her body, every single vein that ran through her, become electrified, gush with a need so extreme that she could only shiver, shudder in pleasure as Ramsey continued to drive deep and hard inside of her.

And when he leaned forward to capture her lips, she felt the sensations that started at her center, tear straight up her legs and went all the way to her toes. And like all the other times when they kissed, he took her mouth with a mastery that had her as responsive to a man as any woman could be. She wrapped her legs around him even tighter, locking him into her body.

She held tight to his shoulders, clung to him as he wrapped his tongue around hers while imitating the same rhythm of his thrusts below. She had never experienced passion this hot, this torrid, this out-of-body uncivilized. It was as if she was being sucked into a raging sea of unrestrained fervor, a heated craze that had her body literally begging for more, and she was showing him just how much more by the way she was lifting herself off the mattress to meet his every turbulent thrust.

She wanted this. She needed this. And the necessity of her desire had become essential, a crucial desperation. There was nothing trivial about the way she was feeling and when she suddenly felt herself tumbling headlong into an abyss of sensations that had her screaming his name, she shuddered straight into a climax that rocked her world. And when he finally let go of her mouth to throw his head back and let out a guttural growl, she was thrown off the edge all over again and together they went skyrocketing into another mind-blowing orgasm.

He tightened his hold on her, gripped more securely to her hips and locked their bodies into a bond of sensual fulfillment. She felt him totally and completely, and there was no part of her left untouched. Unconsumed. Not taken.

And when he leaned up to take her mouth again, she was very much aware of one major thing. He was breaking through her barriers and making her feel things that were emotional as well as physical. She had never intended for such a thing to happen. But it had, and as he continued to kiss her in a way that she felt all the way to her toes, he had proven that he *could* put a smile of satisfaction on her face all by himself.

Although he didn't plan for it to happen, Ramsey slept later than usual the next morning. It was only when he heard the sound of a man's laughter, namely his brother Zane's, that Ramsey realized he was in bed alone. He didn't recall Chloe getting out of it. Had exhaustion knocked him into a dead sleep? He'd never been a sound sleeper before and was known to be an early riser. But then he'd never had sex all night with a woman before either.

He slid out of bed. It was not his intent for Chloe to prepare breakfast alone and he had meant to help. It was the least he could do when his voracious sexual hunger had kept her up most of the night. Granted he wasn't an ace in the kitchen like she was, but he could at least follow directions.

Before heading for the bathroom for a quick shower he glanced over at the clock on the nightstand and frowned. It was just a little past four, so what the hell was Zane doing here already? And if Zane was here that meant so was Derringer and Jason because the three were thick as thieves. And he wouldn't be surprised if Callum wasn't downstairs, too. The four had shown up early one day last week. The day they had walked in on his kissing Chloe. It had been a second occurrence for his brothers and is what had prompted him to start putting distance between him and Chloe. A lot of good that did.

And as he stepped in the shower he did know one thing for certain: He wouldn't be putting distance between them any longer.

"Come on, Chloe, there's no way that brother of mine is still asleep. Ramsey wouldn't know how to sleep late even if it killed him," Zane was saying. He held his coffee cup midway to his lips, looked over at Chloe a little too long to suit her, before a smile touched his lips. "Unless…"

Instead of finishing what he was about to say, his smile widened as he took a sip of his coffee and then continued eating. Chloe was grateful for that although she wasn't sure what Zane Westmoreland was thinking at that moment. And she was grateful for the conversation going on between Jason, Derringer and Callum and the fact they hadn't heard Zane's comment. But because they knew Ramsey just as well as Zane, they had to be wondering the same thing. Why was he still in bed asleep?

She was beginning to feel uneasy. Had Zane or any of the others seen passion marks on her neck? Were they wondering why she was wearing a scarf of all things this morning? When she had eased out of bed careful to not wake Ramsey, and had gone back to her bedroom to take a shower, she had been appalled at all the marks Ramsey's stubble had made all over her body. And then there were some he had intentionally made. Specifically, the ones on her neck. It was as if he had been determined to mark her as his and the very thought of that sent shivers down her spine.

"About time you got out of bed, Ram. What are you? Sick or something?"

Chloe heard the smirk in Derringer's voice and turned to see that Ramsey had walked into the kitchen. He was wearing nothing but his jeans that hung low on his hips, and her breath stopped and her pulse leaped at the sight of his broad shoulders and bare chest. His feet were also bare and the thatch of dark hairs on his chest was damp, which indicated he'd just gotten out of the shower.

Ignoring his brothers, cousin and friend, his gaze was on

her and without acknowledging their presence he made his way to where she stood. Before she could finally release her breath, he leaned over and kissed her in front of them.

There was what seemed to be shocked silence in the room. At least she thought there was, but the only sure thing she knew at that moment was that he was kissing her in front an audience. It wasn't a long kiss, but if he'd intended to make a point, he most certainly had. And when he finally pulled his mouth away, she stared up into a face that was smiling in a way that showed both dimples.

"Good morning, Chloe."

If the kiss hadn't done her in, then his throaty and husky voice definitely would have. She forced herself to begin breathing normally and said, "Good morning, Ramsey."

With his arms still locked around her waist, he turned toward the four men sitting at his breakfast table. "Is there a reason the four of you feel you should be getting preferential treatment for breakfast? Especially when three of you aren't employed by me."

Zane smiled. "But we're family."

Ramsey nodded slowly. "Just make sure you remember that when dealing with Chloe in the future."

Derringer lifted a brow. "So that's how things are going to be from now on?"

"Yes," Ramsey said without a smile on his face. "That's how things are going to be from now on."

Chloe's eyes were glued to Ramsey as her gaze ran over him. Her attention was directed to him so much that she missed part of what he'd said to the others. All she knew was that when she glanced at the men, they were staring at her as if with new insight. Subconsciously, she reached for her scarf to adjust it around her neck, wondering if they were seeing far more than she wanted them to see.

Deciding the mood around her had turned much too serious, she pulled out of Ramsey's arms and said, "I suggest you go put on a shirt. I'm about to fry some more bacon and I'd hate for popping grease to hit you."

She saw the grin on his face and was almost taken back at how different his attitude was from last week. It was a vast improvement. Would one night of mind-blowing lovemaking do that to you? She would be one of the first to admit that whereas she should feel tired because of the brevity of sleep the night before, she felt renewed energy running through her body. Although she had to force herself out of bed, after having slept wrapped in Ramsey's arms, once she had begun moving around the kitchen she had actually felt rejuvenated.

"Thanks for the warning," he said, and leaning closer he placed a sensuous peck on her lips before strolling out of the kitchen. The swagger on his walk was enough to give any woman heart failure, while making her wonder just what he could do with that swaggering body beneath the sheets. She knew the answer to that firsthand and remnants of pleasure flowed through her body from the memory.

Pulling in a deep breath she glanced at the four men who were staring at her. They had become a bunch of regulars during breakfast and lunch, always arriving earlier than everyone to chat with her and with each other.

From their conversations she knew about the horse breeding and training business Zane, Derringer and Jason were about to embark on, as well as the fact that Callum was in no hurry to return to Australia, although she hadn't figured out why.

Clearing her throat, she asked, "Would any of you like anything else? More coffee?"

Before they could respond, she could hear vehicles pulling up in the yard. She was grateful her day was about to begin and welcomed the opportunity to stay busy.

"And you're sure without Zane, Derringer and Jason's spread that you'll still have enough land for your sheep to graze?" Dillon Westmoreland leaned back in the chair behind his desk to ask his cousin.

Ramsey didn't respond but looked as if he was lost in other thoughts. "Are you okay, Ram?"

Dillon's concerned question snapped Ramsey's attention back and he couldn't help but smile. "Yes, I'm okay."

After breakfast Ramsey decided to leave the house for a while, not to avoid Chloe, but to give her the time she needed to prepare for the noon hour. Had he remained he would have done everything he could have to get her back upstairs or better yet, he would have played his hand at enticing her into participating in a number of quickies. So trying to behave he had driven over to Shady Tree Ranch to spend time with Dillon and Pamela.

He could feel Dillon staring at him and looked up and met his gaze. "I understand things have turned somewhat serious between you and your cook, Ram."

Ramsey didn't have to wonder where Dillon had gotten that information. And today, Ramsey had no problem acknowledging that was true. Even when he had dated he'd never been into sex just for the sake of sex, which is why a casual relationship with a woman never appealed to him. And because he hadn't been in the market for a serious relationship either, he'd been satisfied to remain a loner. It was only when things with him got so bad and sexual needs got the best of him, that he would seek out female companionship for a night. But those times had been few and far between. Now he couldn't imagine not making love to Chloe on a regular basis, not waking up during the night with her beside him, their legs locked together, her delectable bottom curled up against him. His...

"Ram?"

He glanced up, realizing Dillon had caught him daydreaming again. "Yes?"

"You sure you're okay?"

Ram leaned back in his chair, deciding to be completely honest. "No, I don't know if I'm okay," he finally said. He studied Dillon thoughtfully. "I can recall the first time you mentioned to me about meeting Pamela. I could hear something in your voice."

Dillon chuckled. "Yes, and it was probably the same thing I could hear in yours that day you came over here and mentioned Chloe Burton was your temporary cook."

Ramsey was taken aback by Dillon's claim. "No way. I had just met the woman that day."

Dillon nodded. "And remember, I had just met Pam that day when I spoke to you on the phone as well."

Ramsey frowned, not sure he liked what Dillon was hinting at. He quickly stood up. "Trust me, Dillon, it's not that kind of party."

A smile curved the corners of Dillon's lips when he said, "I didn't think it was that kind of party for me either, so I can understand you wanting to be in denial. When you figure out it *is* that kind of party, make sure I'm one of the first to get an invitation."

Chloe slipped off her shoes before easing onto the sofa. Breakfast had been crazy and she needed to grab a private and quiet moment before preparing lunch. At times she wondered if she was growing men. There seemed to be more of them showing up for meals every day.

She smiled and inwardly admitted that she was becoming attached to each of them. They were good men, hardworking men, family men who often would talk about their wives and children and their love for them. Working for Ramsey was more than a way to keep food on the table. From the bits of conversations she'd been able to pick up, she knew they considered Ramsey a good employer, the best. He was fair and provided them with a means to provide for their families. She looked forward to seeing them every morning and didn't mind taking the time to prepare all the foods they liked.

To her surprise, and she was sure to his men as well, Ramsey had spent time with his men this morning. Of course they had teased him mercilessly before settling down to the huge meal she had prepared. And on the invitation and insistence from Ramsey, after everyone had been served, she had sat down with him at the table and had a cup of coffee when he conversed with his men. During that time she felt like a member of Ramsey's working-crew family. She felt as if she truly belonged. And she was learning more and more about Ramsey from those who knew him the best. It was great information she could use in the article she wanted to write on him.

The article she would not be writing now.

She breathed in deeply. She had come here with only one goal in mind and that was to convince Ramsey to pose on the cover of her magazine and to also obtain information to share with her readers. Considering everything, there was no way she could go through with doing that now. She had crossed over the line of what was professional, of what was right.

She did not want him to think she had gone to the extreme

and shared his bed only as a means to an end. Therefore, she needed to tell him the truth and would do so tonight when she had his complete attention, and somehow she would convince him not to send her away, but to let her work through the end of the week because his regular cook would return on Monday.

She didn't want to think about how he would possibly feel once he learned the truth. It hadn't been her intent for things to work out this way, but they had and now their time together was about to come to an end and she could feel her heart breaking. Things were beginning to get complicated. She was not only deceiving Ramsey, but she was deceiving his family as well, at least those she'd met. She needed to get out of dodge before drowning in her sea of lies.

She heard a quick tap and then the front door opened. She stood when three women walked in and she found herself under the intense gaze of three pairs of eyes the exact color of Ramsey's. She knew immediately these were his sisters.

Ramsey cursed under his breath when he pulled into his yard, recognizing the three vehicles haphazardly parked there. For his sisters to come calling at this time of the day and all at the same time meant curiosity had gotten the best of them and they were here to check things out for themselves.

He glanced in his rearview mirror, surprised Callum wasn't pulling up behind him. The man seemed to have some kind of built-in radar where Gemma was concerned. Whenever she showed up at his place, Callum homed in on her and would find just about any excuse to show up.

As he got out of his truck, the rich scent of something delectable cooking filled the air. This was Chloe's last week and he wondered how his men were going to readjust when Nellie returned. He had called and left a message on her cell phone letting her know they needed to talk before Monday. Chloe had raised the bar of expectations and although he knew Nellie was a darn good cook, she hadn't displayed a lot of that skill lately. And her attitude toward his men definitely needed improving.

But still, just the thought that this Friday would be Chloe's last day did something to him. He refused to believe what Dillon had hinted at earlier that he was developing feelings for her. Yes, he had enjoyed sleeping with her last night and intended to do so again, but he had no intention of progressing to anything remotely serious between them. He was a loner. He preferred things that way.

He heard the sound of feminine voices the moment he walked into his house. He paused and noted the chatter, the laughter, the downright friendliness in the conversations being shared. It seemed the four women were getting along, and for some reason that pleased him. Why it would, he wasn't sure.

Following the sound of the voices as well as the scent of food cooking, he headed toward the kitchen and then leaned in the doorway at the sight that greeted him. His sisters were sitting down at the table, sampling whatever was smelling so damn good, while Chloe stirred something in a big pot. If he didn't know better, by the way they were carrying on, he would have thought they had known each other for years.

"Forgive me if I'm interrupting anything," he said when it became obvious no one had noticed him.

Four pairs of eyes turned his way, but it was only one pair that he sought out. And the moment Chloe's gaze met his, he felt it, a deep stirring within the pit of his stomach, and it had more depth than just a sensual ache. He was tempted to do what he'd done this morning in front of Zane, Derringer,

Jason and Callum, which was to cross the room and take Chloe into his arms and kiss her, ignoring their audience. But there was no way in hell he could ignore the three sitting at the table who had huge smiles on their faces like he'd cut muster about something. And he couldn't help but notice they were watching him closely.

"You're not interrupting anything," Bailey said sweetly, smiling with too much saccharin on her lips to suit him. "We were just sitting here chatting with Chloe, trying to get to know her better."

He lifted a brow and almost asked why they saw fit to do something like that when Chloe would be leaving this Friday, but he refrained from doing so. "Suit yourself. If you will excuse me I have work to do."

He moved to walk toward his office wondering why he was doing the very thing he said he would no longer do where Chloe was concerned. But then he knew that putting any ideas into his sisters' heads would be dangerous. They wouldn't take it and run, they would take it and rush off in a mad dash. Besides, by retreating he was saving Chloe from being interrogated later, not that his nosy sisters hadn't probably tried pumping her for information already.

When he reached his office he eased down in the chair behind his desk wondering how long his visitors intended to stay. His men would be showing up in a few hours for lunch and he hadn't had any private time with Chloe since they'd last made love this morning. He at least wanted to kiss her the way he had wanted to do without an audience.

He picked up the folder on his desk. He would try to get some work done and hoped like hell his sisters would leave in a timely manner. Otherwise, he would be tempted to ask them to leave.

He smiled thinking doing something like that wouldn't go over well. He'd escorted them to the door before, but always in a teasing manner; however, today he would be dead serious. And he intended to do something about the locks on his back door where anyone thought they could just walk in whenever they wanted. That had never bothered him before but now it did.

He threw down the folder he'd been holding in his hands, not believing the way his thoughts were going. The only reason he was considering changing the damn lock was because on two different occasions he had been caught kissing Chloe. Because she would be leaving after Friday, did it really matter now?

He slumped back in his chair, finally admitting to himself that yes, it did matter. He didn't want things between them to end yet. He could ask Chloe to go out with him on occasion, he would take her to dinner and pursue some sort of a relationship with her. Nothing real serious, mind you. Was that what he really wanted? With lambing starting next week as well as some of his men returning to sheepherding, would he have the time? He knew at that moment he would do something he hadn't done in well over ten years and that is to make time for a woman.

He glanced up when he heard a knock on his door. His pulse leaped. Had his sisters left and Chloe had come looking for him? He stood and a frown settled on his face when Callum walked in. He dropped back down in the chair disappointed.

Ramsey didn't have to ask his friend why he was there. He knew. And the way Ramsey was feeling about his sisters at that moment, he was tempted to pay Callum a hefty fee to take Gemma off his hands. There was no hope for Megan and

Bailey. Megan wasn't dating anyone seriously since she had finally dumped that asshole of a doctor she'd gotten involved with last year. And lucky for him Bailey was more into her books than the opposite sex. She was determined to finish college in three years instead of four and then obtain a law degree. Although she could get on his last nerve at times, he was proud of her and her dedication to her studies.

"What are you doing here, Cal?" Ramsey couldn't resist the opportunity to tease his friend. Callum had given him enough grief over Chloe during the last couple of days to last a lifetime, so to Ramsey's way of thinking the ribbing was justified.

"What do you think?"

Ramsey rolled his eyes. Callum had been hanging around Zane too much lately. He was beginning to sound just like him. "You do know that one day you're going to have to take matters into your own hands, and I don't mean something as extreme as kidnapping," Ramsey said.

Callum didn't say anything, he just smiled. At any other point in time that smile would have made Ramsey uneasy, had him somewhat worried, but not today. He had his own problems to deal with and for once Callum and Gemma were the least of his concern.

His only concern was whether Chloe would be interested in continuing their relationship after Friday. And he intended to do whatever it took to make sure she wanted that as much as he did.

Nine

As soon as the last vehicle pulled out of Ramsey's yard, Chloe glanced over at him. He was leaning in the kitchen doorway staring at her. The men had arrived on time for lunch and Ramsey's sisters had stuck around to join them for the meal. Zane, Derringer and Jason had also shown up, and Callum had appeared out of the back with Ramsey, which meant he had been there for a while.

After everyone had been fed, Ramsey's sisters had been kind enough to help clear the table and help load the dishwasher. Ramsey had assisted with cleanup duty as well and in no time at all, the kitchen was spotless. If she didn't know any better Chloe would have thought Ramsey had pitched in to hurry off his sisters. Evidently they got the message and had taken Zane, Derringer and Jason right along with them. Callum had returned to the shearing plant with the men.

And now for the first time since waking up that morning,

she and Ramsey were alone. She held Ramsey's gaze as memories of last night flooded her mind. She instantly recalled his mouth on her body, how his lips had trailed over every inch of her, his tongue, hot, wet and greedy, had devoured her breasts and the area between her legs. She took a deep breath as she thought about how perfectly their bodies had fit and the sensations she'd felt with him moving inside of her.

He had been the most passionate of lovers, creative and imaginative all rolled into one, and she knew without a doubt that last night each and every one of her fantasies had been fulfilled. Whether he ever appeared on the cover of her magazine no longer mattered because she knew firsthand that Ramsey Westmoreland was indeed the most irresistible man that existed.

"Come here, Chloe."

His words, spoken in what sounded like a heated breath, floated across the room to her, touched her all over and in the very places, his hands, mouth, lips and tongue had traveled the night before.

And without hesitating, she crossed the room and walked straight into his arms. When he gripped her tightly to him, she lifted her face and stared into his eyes.

When he leaned down and captured her mouth in his, every part of her was stirred into action and she returned his kiss as hungrily as he gave it. Her chest settled against his and she knew he could feel the hardened tips of her breasts pressing into him. She could certainly feel his burgeoning erection that was cradled intimately between her thighs.

Moments later, their mouths broke apart and she felt her fingers flexed as they held on to his shoulders, otherwise she would have fallen to her knees. The sensations flowing through her heated her insides.

"I want to make love to you right here. Right now. But I can't risk any unexpected visitors," he murmured hotly against her lips. "It would greatly upset me if we got interrupted."

From the sound of his voice and his aroused expression, she knew he was serious. He wanted her just as much as she wanted him. "Then maybe we should go upstairs," she invited in a husky whisper.

From the darkening of his eyes she knew he'd heard every word she'd said. And before she could let out her next breath, he swept her off her feet and into his arms and headed toward the stairs.

Ramsey placed Chloe on the bed and stood back. He needed to look at her, study her, analyze how this woman had changed his life to the point where he was up here in his bedroom, about to make love to her, when it wasn't even three in the afternoon. There were forty million other things he could be doing around his ranch. Nearly half his herd was pregnant, lambing began next Monday and he needed to make sure all the lambing stalls were ready.

But at that moment nothing was more important to him than getting inside of Chloe, locking his body to hers, feeling her muscles clamp down on him, pulling him in and drawing every single thing out of him. Sensation was building in his erection, arousing him to the point where he wanted to tear off his clothes and hers. He wanted to mate with her. Stay inside her body and never come out.

Ramsey glanced over at her. He wanted her wet all over and easing onto the bed he reached out and pulled her to him, and began stroking his tongue along her lower lip. There was something about her mouth that enthralled him, made him want to keep kissing her, but first he wanted to taste her all over. He remembered all the things he had done to her last night, but was convinced that it had not been enough.

His hands moved to her blouse and within seconds he had pulled it over her head and tossed it aside. Then his gaze lowered to her chest and he saw how the nipples of her breasts had hardened to pebbles and were pressed against the lace material of her bra. And it was a pink bra that matched the color of the blouse he had removed earlier. He wondered if her panties would also be the same color. He'd noticed that about her last night. She had been wearing a light green lace bra and had been wearing matching lace panties. He found her color-coordinated lingerie downright sexy.

With eager fingers he undid the front closure of her bra and watched as it parted, exposing two of the most beautiful globes he'd ever seen. He had thought that very thing last night and it still held true in the bright sunlight. They were perfect for his hands and incredibly delicious to his mouth.

Removing the bra completely he leaned forward and captured a hard nipple between his lips and then his tongue went to work, reacquainting his taste buds with the flavor he had enjoyed last night while holding her breast firmly in his hand.

He heard her soft moans as he feasted on one breast and then another, taking his time while his tongue so effortlessly devoured her. It felt hot, inflamed as it went about licking her hungrily, sucking the tip greedily. Never before had he gotten such pleasure from such an assault on a woman's breasts.

He finally lifted his head and pulled back as a slow smile touched his lips. Without saying anything he gently eased her back while his hands went to her skirt and he gently pulled the denim material down her hips, thighs and legs, leaving her in those leggings. A pretty pink pair.

He studied the footless tights and although he much preferred seeing her legs bare as they had been last night, there was something about all those colorful leggings she wore that definitely made a statement. But at that moment he was going to enjoy peeling the damn things off her.

"You do know I really don't like these things," he said as he reached for the waistband.

She quirked a brow at him. "Why?"

He smiled and said simply. "They hide your legs."

Chloe smiled. "Leggings are part of the latest fashion trend. And they don't hide my legs, Ramsey, they accent them. Usually my dresses or skirts are rather short. Leggings work well with my outfits and with the flat shoes I normally wear it makes the perfect casual outfit."

Ramsey nodded, not believing he was actually discussing a woman's attire.

"Would you prefer I not wear leggings while I'm around your men, Ramsey?"

His answer was quick in coming. "No."

"Okay, then, rancher. You can't have it both ways."

He sort of disagreed with that. "In private I'm taking them off you because I love looking at your legs."

"Suit yourself."

And he intended to, he thought. And then his throat tightened, not allowing another word to slip through when he inched the leggings past her hips to uncover a very skimpy, very sexy pink thong.

Once he had peeled the leggings completely off her, his attention went back to that very hot-looking thong, dying to reveal what it covered and deciding not to wait.

Adjusting his body he slouched down on the bed between her open legs and lifted them on his shoulders. And just like last night, the feel of those bare legs on his shoulders, smooth and silky, rubbing against his skin made the lower part of him throb with an intensity that sent shudders through his body. And it wasn't helping matters that he was drowning in her scent. Being this intimately close to her hot mound made him crave her taste even more.

As soon as he felt he was in the right position, he leaned in and flicked his tongue across her crotch, dampening her thong in the process but getting a taste of what was behind it. She moaned and the sound went straight to his erection and made it surge.

"What are you doing to me?" she asked, in a voice that seemed strained, breathless, panting.

"What does it feel like?" He flicked his tongue across her again, wanting her to feel the strength behind it. "But if what I'm doing is bothering you, I can always stop," he said and grinned at her.

"No," she said quickly. "Please don't stop."

He glanced up at her and his response was just as quick. "I won't." The look he saw in her face, blatant need and transparent pleasure, fueled his hunger and he pulled back slightly, lifted her hips to remove the thong from her body.

He had gotten his first taste of her in this very feminine hot spot last night and had been craving more of her ever since. He hadn't known the extent of his sexual desire until he'd made love to her. When he recalled all the orgasms they had shared last night, his desperation in wanting her again was warranted.

Tossing the skimpy undergarment aside, he eased back in place between her thighs and rubbed his chin against her naked skin, liking the feel of her and the look of her Brazilian wax. Not able to hold back any longer, he began licking at her, taking his tongue and outlining her feminine mound wanting her to feel the urgency of his desire.

"Ramsey," she called out his name in a whispered tone as she tightened the legs around his shoulder.

"Yes, baby?" he asked in a deep tone.

"I—I like that."

A shiver swept through him. "I like it, too." And then he showed her just how much when he parted her feminine folds and let his tongue go to work. Her taste stirred a yearning in him that could only be appeased this particular way and by doing this precise thing. And the sound of her moans, her whimpers, the tightening of her legs around his shoulders, and the sweet liquor her body was producing, sent what seemed like an unquenchable greed through him.

He knew it was only a matter of time before she came and when that thought raced through him the pressure of his tongue inside of her increased, lapping her up like his very life depended on it. And when he felt Chloe's body jerk beneath his mouth he held on tight, knowing her spasms would soon become his.

They did. And with as much pleasure as his mental state could take, he went for the gusto, using his tongue to push her even more so over the edge while keeping his mouth locked tight to her.

Chloe was convinced her mind was splintering under the intensity of the explosion that ripped through her. She breathed in sharply and felt the lower half of her body actually being lifted off the bed, but Ramsey was there, holding on tight to her, gripping her hips, keeping her bolted to his mouth.

His tongue was assaulting her core as he continued to lap her up. She screamed out his name as spasms, as vicious as they could get, tore into her, spinning her senses out of control and into a turmoil or passion.

It was only when the last tremble passed through her that he released her and pulled back. There was nothing she could do but slump back on the bed. She felt weaker than water. She watched through partially closed lashes as he moved from the bed to remove his clothes.

She could only lay there, trying to get her breathing back to normal as she watched him lean over to take off his boots. He then straightened to unbutton his shirt and then eased it off his muscular shoulders and tossed it aside. Sliding the brass buckle belt through the loops, he lowered his zipper before pushing the jeans down his legs.

Even while lying there, with barely enough energy to breathe, Chloe watched as Ramsey removed every stitch of clothing and then he stood, fully naked and all male. Her eyes latched on his erection, big and powerful, and upon seeing it, fiery sensations swept through her, giving her renewed energy while stirring desire within her all over again.

When he reached into the nightstand to retrieve a condom packet and tore it open with his teeth, before proceeding to roll it over his swollen shaft, she felt what amounted to fire raging through her veins. She exhaled a deep breath when he came back to the bed and with gentle hands he reached out and eased her legs apart.

Moments later, in position between them, he leaned down and captured her lips in a kiss so painstakingly tender that it almost brought tears to her eyes and made her fall in love with him that much more. When he tore his lips from her to pull back, he tilted her hips up to him before surging deep within her. The pleasure she felt with his entry sent a moan from deep within her throat. And then the mating of their bodies began as he eased in and out of her, giving her the pleasure her body was aching for.

"Look at me, baby. Feel me," Ramsey said as his fingertips caressed her chin.

She did feel him. He was as deep as he could get and his need was raging just as out of control as hers. Then he picked up the tempo and she clung to him, determined to meet him on every level. Especially this one.

And when he called out her name in a guttural growl she knew that here, in bed, making love, the two of them were in the same sensual vibe. And when she cried out her pleasure, felt her body explode yet again, and knew he was following her over the edge, she could have sworn at that moment she actually felt his hot release shooting inside of her, all the way to the womb. But she knew that wasn't possible. She had watched him put on a condom. It was nothing more than her imagination at work, and when he continued to drive hard within her she knew the night was just beginning.

A long time later Chloe lay in Ramsey's arms in the position she'd discovered he liked the best: spoon style. Her backside was cushioned by his front and his muscular leg was thrown over hers. Her head was resting back on his chest and his arm was thrown over her middle.

She felt satiated, relaxed, secured. After their last lovemaking session, Ramsey had eased out of her and had gone into the bathroom to discard the condom and to put on another. He liked being ready and chances were today would not be any different than last night when they had made love, rested and made love again all through the night. However, at some point they needed to prepare something for dinner to keep up their strength.

They enjoyed each other and she couldn't see them not

making love several more times before they finally drifted off to sleep. The thought that he desired her as much as she desired him made her heart thump rapidly in her chest.

She pulled in a deep breath knowing she had to level with him. No matter how he handled things she needed to tell him the truth. She would let him know she no longer wanted him to pose for the cover, nor did she want to do an article on him.

Knowing it was best to just get it over with, she turned into his arms. She could tell the move surprised him and deciding to just tell him and not waste any time, she took a quick breath and said, "Ramsey, there's something I need to tell you."

Ramsey quickly placed a finger to Chloe's lips. Knowing his sisters and how desperate they were for him to become involved with a woman, they had probably gone overboard, shaken her up by tossing her some ideas she wasn't quite ready to catch. So she was about to bail out. Let him know that for her things weren't quite that serious. He understood, but he wasn't ready to hear her acknowledge that yet.

At the end of the week, right before she left for good, then they would talk. He would tell her of his desire to see her again when her work here ended. He wanted to take her out, make love to her, he wanted for them to continue what they had started here. He recalled what he'd said to Dillon earlier that day and knew that he *did* want it to be that kind of a party.

"Let's not get into a serious discussion about anything. Not now. We can discuss any serious topics on your last day. I need to continue to have the peace I've found with you, Chloe. Could you hold your thoughts for a while and give me that?"

She slowly nodded. "Yes, I can give you that."

"And," he continued by saying, "with shearing wrapping

up this week, the sheep that's not pregnant will be taken to pasture and—"

"You have a lot of sheep pregnant?"

He smiled. "Yes, almost half my herd."

He saw the look of surprise on her face. "How did that many sheep get pregnant at the same time?"

"It's timed that way. The female sheep, the ewes, are put out with the rams during mating season and five months later they deliver during what is call lambing. That's when the lamb is born. Luckily ewes won't deliver the same day, but typically they will all deliver within a two-week period of each other."

"Wow!"

He chuckled. In a way he was pleased with Chloe's interest in his ranch. "The rams and the wethers are—"

"Wethers?"

"Yes, castrated male sheep," he explained. "While the pregnant ewes are lambing, the rams and wethers and the ewes that aren't pregnant are taken to pasture by the sheepherders. And that is where most of them will be for the next few months out on the pasture grazing."

An idea popped into his head. "One of my men, Pete Overton, won't be able to begin sheepherding until Sunday morning, so I'm going to drive his herd out to pasture early Saturday morning and get things all set up for him. Will you come with me? We'll be back here before noon Sunday."

Chloe smiled up at Ramsey. She had wanted to come clean and tell him the truth, but he preferred they hold off and not discuss anything serious until her last day. That was fine with her because she knew that once she told him the truth he would probably be upset with her.

She leaned up and wrapped her arms around his neck. "Yes, I'd love to go with you."

Ten

Over the next few days Chloe accepted the realization that she was falling in love with Ramsey. They would share a bed each night and get up before daybreak every morning and together they would prepare breakfast for the men.

It was during those times that he would share more information about his life as a sheepherder and had begun telling her about members of his family. Five of his siblings had been under sixteen when his parents had gotten killed—Megan, Gemma, the twins by the name of Adrian and Aiden, and his sister Bailey. Zane had been a senior in high school, ready to go off to college and Derringer had been about to enter his senior year of high school. His cousin Dillon had been placed in a similar situation with four siblings under sixteen.

From what Ramsey told her, Adrian and Aiden were now in their last year of college at Harvard, as was their cousin

Stern. Another cousin by the name of Canyon was in medical school at Howard University in D.C. Brisbane was in the Navy. Micah, who was Zane's counterpart in age, was a graduate from Harvard Medical School and was an epidemiologist with the federal government.

Just listening to Ramsey share information with her about his family's turbulent years and the struggle that he and Dillon had had to endure to keep their families together, she had to admire the two men. Although she had yet to meet Dillon, she had met another one of his brothers, Riley, and found him to be just as handsome as the others.

And Ramsey had shared more information about sheepherding with her. One afternoon they had walked around his ranch. He had taken her to where the lambing stalls were and explained how next week more than a thousand of his ewes would be delivering. She had found the whole process fascinating. He had also given her a tour of the shearing plant and she was able to watch the men at work. She'd seen the dogs at work, too, and Ramsey had explained how important the sheepdogs were in managing and protecting the herds. You could definitely see that running a sheep ranch required maintaining a tight schedule and sticking to it.

Hanging the last pot back on the rack, she turned when she heard the back door open and smiled when Ramsey walked in. Closing the door behind him, and without missing a step, he crossed the kitchen floor and pulled her into his arms and kissed her.

Chloe returned the kiss, for the moment refusing to acknowledge that she was making it harder and harder to leave after this weekend, to walk away and not to look back. The thought of doing so caused her heart to ache, but that's what she would be doing. She decided she didn't want to think beyond it, so she tightened her arms around him as he deepened his kiss. His mouth slanted against hers and she could feel her knees weaken.

Moments later he broke off the kiss and pulled back slightly and whispered against her moist lips. "Why do you always taste so sweet?"

His words further eroded her sensibility. He sounded so serious like there was truly an answer for his question. There wasn't one, so she shook her head, tilted it up and smiled at him. "For the same reason you always taste so delicious."

And to show him just what she meant, she took the tip of her tongue and licked a corner of his mouth. The instant she did, his long eyelashes swept upward to reveal the depths of his darkened gaze, and she could just imagine what he was thinking now.

"Doing something like that can get you into trouble," he warned, as his arms tightened around her waist, drawing her even closer into the fit of his muscular form.

She smiled. "So you say."

"So I can prove." He took a step away from her. "But not now. First, I need to let you know that we've been invited to dinner."

She lifted a brow. "Dinner?"

"Yes, my cousin Dillon and his wife Pamela want to meet you."

Panic settled into Chloe's bones. She didn't want to pull any more of Ramsey's family members into her web of deceit. She liked all of the ones she'd met so far and from what she'd heard about the oldest Denver Westmoreland, Dillon, there was no doubt in her mind that she would like him as well.

"Why do they want to meet me?" she asked, not sure she was ready to meet the man Ramsey was so close to.

"They've heard a lot of nice things about you and want to meet you for themselves."

She didn't know what to say to that. She had heard a lot of nice things about them as well. "I bet it was Jason who told them how I could fix his eggs just the way he likes them," she said in a teasing voice, trying to make light of what Ramsey had said.

Ramsey chuckled. "Might be. Or it could have been one of my brothers or sisters. You've made quite an impression on them."

Chloe glanced down to study the floor. At any other time knowing she had impressed the family of the man she loved would have been a feather in her cap. But not now. When they found out the truth it won't just be Ramsey who'd think she'd deceived them. Lucia had been right. Chloe had been around them long enough to know the Westmorelands stuck together and if you were to hurt one, then you hurt them all.

"So, will you go to dinner with me at Dillon and Pamela's?"

A part of her wanted to come up with an excuse not to go. She should claim a headache or something, but she could not do that. Although she deserved nothing, she wanted it all. She wanted to get to know more about the man she had fallen in love with. As well as to get to know those he loved and those who loved him.

She pulled in a deep breath and then said, "Yes, I'll go to dinner with you."

Ramsey could not remember the last time he'd brought a woman to a family function. Even with the annual charity ball they sponsored each year for the Westmoreland Foundation that had been established to aid various community causes, he usually went solo. For him it had been better that way and because there had been enough eager-beaver Westmorelands who enjoyed being the center on attention with beautiful women on their arms, he was left alone.

He couldn't even recall bringing Danielle to dinner when they'd dated. He never had to bother because his mother had liked Danielle enough to invite her to dinner whenever she saw her at church most Sundays. He knew the main reason he had dated Danielle as long as he had was because his family had liked her. And then because she'd hung around waiting for him to finish college, he had felt marrying her was the least he could do.

The truth of the matter was that she hadn't been idle while she'd waited. At some point she had met someone, slept with the person and had gotten pregnant. The sad thing about it was that the man never married her and she ended up being a single mom.

He glanced around the room thinking that this was not supposed to be a family function. Dillon and Pamela had invited him and Chloe to dinner and they had accepted. He had expected to see Pamela's three younger sisters because this was spring break back in Gamble. But he hadn't expected to see his three sisters who were smiling sweetly at him at every turn. Nor had he expected to see Zane, Derringer and Jason. He saw them enough around his place for breakfast and lunch. Callum was not a surprise because the man took advantage of every opportunity to hang around Gemma. Riley wasn't a surprise either because he was known to drop in whenever and wherever there was a free meal.

"You might have disappointed me for not doing that magazine cover, but you've more than made up for it with Chloe, Ram. I like her," Bailey said.

Ramsey turned and met his baby sister's gaze. "And just

what do you like about her?" he asked, curious to hear what she had to say.

"She fits you."

Because he'd been expecting a long, drawn out discourse, he was surprised by those three words. This was definitely a night for surprises, but then he thought he would not let Bailey get off that easily. "She fits me in what way?"

Bailey shrugged. "She's pretty. You're handsome. She can cook. You can't. She's an extrovert. You're an introvert." She lifted her brow. "Need I go on?"

"No."

"Because we all know you have a tendency to stretch things out, Ram. If you are interested in her, you probably want to step up your game a notch."

Now it was his time to raise a brow. "What makes you think I'm interested in her?" he asked, glancing across the room to where Chloe sat talking to Pamela. The two women were getting along like they were old friends.

"She's here isn't she? That in itself says a lot." And without saying anything else, Bailey strolled off.

He was tempted to follow Bailey and tell her that no, nothing said it all. They were seeing things that weren't there. Seeing what they wanted to see. But when he glanced back over at Chloe, he was beginning to wonder if perhaps everything that Bailey had said just now made sense. If so, that was real scary only because it was Bailey and she never thought logically.

Not for the first time tonight Chloe quickly glanced over at Ramsey before turning her full attention back to the conversation going on around her. The topic of conversation had shifted from just how good the First Lady had looked at a nationally televised event last evening to what was happening overseas.

More than once he had caught her gaze and the smile he'd sent her way was enough to send heat escalating through every part of her body. And memories of his touch would wash over her, make her wish they were someplace else. Someplace private.

"So you're an only child, Chloe?"

Chloe glanced up at Gemma and smiled. The Westmorelands had been asking her questions about herself. Getting to know her. She had been wording her answers so they wouldn't be outright lies. "Yes, I'm an only child but not for long. My father is getting married in a few months and the person he's marrying has a son and daughter."

"And you don't have a problem with that?" Bailey asked.

Chloe chuckled. "Not at all. Dad's been single long enough. My mother died when I was two, so it's about time he tied the knot again."

The conversation shifted to Megan as she told them how her day went as an anesthesiologist. Chloe glanced back across the room at Ramsey. He was talking to Dillon. There was no mistaking the two men were related. Dillon Westmoreland was also a good-looking man.

Ramsey caught her eye and like before, the look he gave her made her heart thump erratically in her chest. And as she continued to look at him she could actually feel his heat, reaching out across the perimeters of the room and actually touch her. And then he whispered something to Dillon before walking across the room toward her.

When he reached her side he tucked her hand in his, something that wasn't missed by his sisters. "Thanks, Pamela, for a lovely dinner. It's time Chloe and I left."

Chloe glanced up at him, not surprised by what he said. It was either leave so they could go somewhere private or put on a real show for his family.

Pamela glanced at her watch. "It's early yet. Are you sure you have to go?"

Ramsey smiled. "Yes, trust us, we do."

Later that night Ramsey was wide awake as he watched Chloe sleep. They had barely made it through the front door before they began stripping out of their clothes. They hadn't thought about making it up the stairs to the bedroom; instead they had been satisfied just to get to the sofa. By the time he had slid his body into hers, all the restraints he'd held in place over the past twelve hours came crashing down.

He had made love to her with an intensity that had even overwhelmed him. She had writhed beneath him, filled with the same turbulent need as she strained against him, meeting his strokes, his single-minded thrusts as if her very life depended on it.

She had dug her nails into his shoulders and on one or two occasions, had actually bit him. He had growled and then had increased the pace as his control and hers had continued to get shot to hell. He gave it to her hard, and at her encouragement, even harder. She had transformed into a wildcat, a woman who knew the degree of pleasure she'd wanted to experience. A woman who intended for him to give her just what she needed.

And he had. The more she'd wanted, the more he'd given. And by the time their world exploded into one hell of a combined orgasm, he was barely holding on the edge of sanity. He had known the moment pleasure had ripped his soul apart that this was not just a normal lovemaking session between two consenting adults. It was a hell of a lot more than that.

The word *normal* didn't even come close. There had been nothing ordinary about their joining. It had been the most atypical thing he'd ever experienced.

And now he knew why.

For the first time in his life he wanted to have a serious relationship with a woman. And he now knew more than ever that what he felt for Chloe wasn't just a sexual thing. Tomorrow was officially her last day at the ranch, although she had agreed to spend Friday and Saturday night with him on the range sheepherding.

He could tell from the murmurs he'd been hearing over the past couple of days from his men that she would be missed, and it wasn't just about the meals she had prepared for them. It was about the woman they had come to know. A woman who took joy in making their nourishment.

Yet she had remained professional while developing friendships with them. They looked forward to seeing her in the morning and again at noon. She not only talked to them, but she also listened. On occasion, he knew she also offered advice to a couple of the men when they'd inquired as to what to purchase their wives for birthday and anniversary gifts.

They would miss her, but none of them would miss her more than he would. In just two short weeks she had touched him, given him a bone-deep feeling of total and complete satisfaction, one he could not have explained until now.

He leaned over and brushed a kiss across her brow. Last week he could barely make sense of what was happening to him, but now he knew and accepted his fate. He loved this woman. He really loved her.

And he wanted to keep her.

He knew that might be easier said than done. She might not want to have a relationship with him, one with the potential of going somewhere. She might like her life like it was now—not seriously involved with anyone. That Daren guy had probably left a bad taste in her mouth. In that case, he would do whatever he needed to do to make her change her attitude about a serious affair.

Unfortunately he did not have Callum's patience. Starting now he would rev up his campaign to win her over, prevail in getting her love. At least his situation didn't appear to be as hopeless as Dillon's had been when he'd met Pamela. At the time she was engaged to marry someone else. But with his encouragement Dillon hadn't let that stop him.

Now was time to take some of the same advice he'd dished out to Dillon. He knew what he wanted and there was no excuse in his not getting it. He had a goal. By this time next year Chloe Burton would have a permanent place in his bed as his wife.

"Are you okay, Chloe?"

Chloe glanced over at Ramsey. No, she wasn't okay. Saying goodbye to his men had been the hardest thing she'd ever had to do. And she had fought back tears when they'd given her a going-away gift.

"Yes, I'm okay," she said, knowing she really wasn't. Ramsey had helped her to clean up the kitchen after lunch and then she had thrown a couple of items into an overnight bag. When she had stepped outside it was to find a huge RV parked in his yard. He had explained that the modern-day sheepherder believed in living out on the range with all the conveniences of home. Granted most didn't have anything this large and extravagant. The majority of them did have campers that they pulled behind their trucks and would set up residence without having to sacrifice doing without satellite television, indoor bathroom and kitchen and dining facilities.

The luxury coach Ramsey was driving was his own personal beauty and as Chloe glanced around she was impressed with just how nice it was, and how much an expert driver he was behind the wheel. This was definitely a luxury coach worth owning. It was a home away from home on wheels. His men had already taken the sheep up in the high country, a portion of Ramsey's land that connected to Dillon's. Chloe hadn't been aware of how much property the Westmorelands owned until now.

"The men are going to miss you."

She smiled. "And I'm going to miss them."

"And I'm going to miss you as well, Chloe."

Chloe thought about the words Ramsey had just spoken as she watched him kill the engine of the RV. He glanced over at her and the pull that was always there between them was tugging at her today in the worst possible way. "And I'm going to miss you, too, Ramsey."

He leaned over and she was there, meeting him halfway over the vehicle's console. And when their mouths connected she thought that nothing could get any better than this.

He pulled back, but not before taking his tongue to swipe across her lower lip. "Come on, let's get out so I can show you the rest of the property while there's still daylight."

Moments later, holding hands they walked near the area where the sheep were grazing. One of Ramsey's men, Pete Overton, smiled when they approached. "Now that you're here boss, I'll just skedaddle so I'll be on time for the party." Pete's oldest son would be graduating from the university tomorrow and his wife had planned a party in his honor. Ramsey had volunteered to tend to the sheep until Pete came back to relieve him Sunday morning.

"Sure, Pete, and give Pete Jr. my congratulations and best wishes. I know that you and Jayne are proud of him."

Pete beamed proudly. "Thanks, Ram." He then glanced at Chloe and his smile got even wider. "The guys and I meant what we said earlier today, Miss Chloe. You're going to be missed. Nobody makes homemade biscuits quite like you do."

Chloe returned his smile. "Thanks, Pete." They then turned and watched Pete get in his truck and leave.

"Pete is a person who doesn't take to people easily, but it's plain to see that he likes you," Ramsey said, wrapping his arms tightly around Chloe's waist.

She leaned into him. "I know," she murmured, resting her head back against Ramsey's chest. "I like him, too. I like all the men who work for you."

Ramsey introduced her to the four dogs that would be manning the herd and told her the animals made a sheepherder's job relatively simple. The dogs were the ones who looked after the flock, making sure none of the sheep wandered off and alerted the sheepherder to any mishaps.

After Ramsey gave her a tour of the area where the sheep would be grazing for the next few months, they returned to the travel coach and ate the sandwiches Ramsey had purchased from a deli in town.

Then when it got dark he took out folding chairs so they could sit outside under the stars. They ended up doing a lot more than just sitting under the stars. Ramsey selected a nice spot to spread a huge blanket on the ground where they made love, under the beauty of a Colorado sky. Later when the night turned chilly, they went inside the coach and after taking a shower they tumbled in bed to make love all over again.

The next morning after a breakfast they had prepared

together, they walked the area checking on the sheep. After lunch they curled up in each other's arms on the sofa and watched several video movies. Chloe could tell that neither she nor Ramsey wanted anything to intrude on their idyllic weekend.

Ramsey told her about how he'd grieved after the deaths of his parents and his beloved aunt and uncle. He explained how he'd had to put aside his grief to care for his siblings.

She was touched that he'd shared details about that heartbreaking moment in his life. She was tempted to share things with him as well. She wanted to tell him that although she was too young to remember much about her mother, what she had recalled while growing up was the sadness that always appeared in her father's eyes on her mother's birthday, their anniversary day and during the holidays. That was one of the reasons she was glad for the happiness in her father's life now. But there was no way she could tell Ramsey that without telling him everything and he'd made it known he wasn't ready for any hard-and-heavy discussions between them.

Later that night they showered again together. The moment he pulled her inside the shower with him and water began spraying down on their naked bodies, Ramsey turned her into his arms and kissed her, while pinning her back against the wall.

He reached up and turned off the water and then getting down on his knees, he spread open her thighs to get the taste he always seemed to want and was intent on getting whenever he could.

The sensations he could evoke with his tongue inside of her had Chloe moaning and it took all she could not to scream out loud. Ramsey had introduced her to lovemaking in its richest form; positions that were so erotic her knees weakened at the thought of some of them.

She did scream when his tongue delved deeper into her and she gripped tight to his shoulder. And just when she thought she couldn't take any more, he eased up, lifted her to wrap her legs around his waist and then he plunged into her.

With whipcord speed he began thrusting inside of her as another scream from her filled the shower stall. She then heard herself begging and pleading for more, for him not to stop and to do it harder. Those were words she never thought she would utter, which proved just how over the edge she was. Just how Ramsey's lovemaking had torn up her mind.

Her legs tightened around his waist even more, locked him inside of her as much as possible. He threw his head back and let out a curling snarl that sounded like pain, but the look of his face showed it was definitely one of pleasure.

His features distorted in sexual gratification were a mirror of what she was feeling. And when she felt him explode inside of her, she felt her world get rocked as he continued to pump inside of her as impassioned heat rushed all through her body. And then he leaned closer to her and captured her mouth in his.

His kiss snatched her breath and, combined with the shudders ripping through her, was almost too much. His kiss was hungrier than before, just as intense. And when he finally released her mouth, she slumped against his wet chest. Regaining strength to lift her head, she met his intense gaze and it took everything within her to hold back from telling him that she had fallen in love with him.

Pete returned to relieve Ramsey early Sunday morning. Ramsey couldn't wait to get back to the ranch so that he and Chloe could have a serious talk. If he had any doubts in his mind that he loved her, then this weekend only confirmed it. He hoped he would be able to put into words how he felt and why he wanted them to continue what they'd started.

He glanced over at her. She'd gotten quiet on him and he would allow her this private time. He'd come close twice this weekend of telling her how much he loved her. But he'd held back, not wanting to screw things up.

He drew in a deep breath when they pulled into his yard. Butterflies were going off in his stomach. He'd never been nervous around a woman before. Hell, he'd practically raised three of them. But this was different. It wasn't every day that a man poured out his heart the way he planned to do. But he had to be careful how he did it. He didn't want to run the risk of scaring her off.

"Will you be talking to Nellie before she returns tomorrow, Ramsey?"

Her question broke the silence that surrounded them in the RV. He turned off the engine and leaned back in his seat. "Yes. She's supposed to call today."

"Good."

Ramsey couldn't help but smile. He found it amusing how loyal she was to his men. He parked the RV on the side of the barn and when they got out they walked to the house holding hands. For him it seemed such a natural thing to do.

Ramsey opened the door and once inside Chloe said, "How would you like a cup of coffee?"

"I'd love one. Thanks."

At that moment the phone rang. "That's probably Nellie calling. I told her I'd return this morning around eleven."

Chloe nodded as she headed for the kitchen.

"Hello?"

"Mr. Westmoreland?"

Ramsey didn't recognize the feminine voice. "Yes?"

"This is Marie Dodson of the CDS Employment Agency and I regret we were unable to serve your needs before. However, if you're still in need of a ranch cook, I have someone who might work out for you, and she's—"

"Whoa," Ramsey said, cutting in, confused by what the woman was saying. "You did serve my needs. The woman you sent to us two weeks ago worked out perfectly and—"

"There must be some mistake. We didn't send a woman to work for you."

Now Ramsey was *really* confused. "Sure you did. Chloe Burton."

There was a slight pause and then, "There's no Chloe Burton working for us. The woman we had planned to send you was Constance Kennard. Because of a mix-up, she was sent to another job by mistake. I called myself that Monday morning around nine-thirty to inform you of what happened but was told you weren't available. The woman who answered your phone said she would make sure that you got the message about what happened."

A knot tightened in Ramsey's stomach and a frown settled between his brows. What Marie Dodson was saying didn't make sense. Chloe had shown up that morning. She'd been late but she had shown up. And there was no doubt in his mind that Chloe could cook. Every single man in his employ could attest to that. But if what Ms. Dodson was saying was true then…"

"Mr. Westmoreland?"

Ramsey pulled in a deep breath. "I'm going to have to call you back Ms. Dodson."

"Oh? Well, okay."

No sooner had Ramsey hung up the phone, Chloe walked

in with two coffee cups in her hands. Ramsey stopped her in her tracks when he asked in a fierce and angry voice. "Who the hell are you?"

Eleven

Chloe was knocked speechless by Ramsey's question. Pulling in a deep breath she thought it best to place the cups of coffee on the table before spilling them all over herself. Her hands were shaking because she had an idea why he'd asked what he had.

She exhaled a nervous breath before she spoke. "That's a crazy question, Ramsey. You know who I am. I'm Chloe Burton."

"Are you?"

"Yes."

He crossed his arms over his chest. "And you work for CDS Employment Agency?"

"No."

He lifted a brow. "No?"

She nodded. "No. I don't work for CDS."

He frowned. "Well, who do you work for then? I didn't contact any other employment agency for a cook."

"I work for myself."

She could tell her answer surprised him. "Yourself?"

"Yes, and while I'm at it, I might as well tell you that I'm not really a cook. I enjoy cooking but normally do so for pleasure."

Ramsey didn't say anything for a long time, he just stared at her with an intense look in his eyes. He was angry to a degree that she had never seen before in him. Even when they'd been at odds with each other during that first week, he hadn't been this angry.

"I'm going to ask you one more time," he said through gritted teeth. "Who are you? If the employment agency didn't send you and you're not a bona fide ranch cook, then who are you and why did you pretend to be Nellie's replacement?"

Her hands nervously clenched into fists at her side. Now she wished that she had been more insistent when she'd wanted to tell him the truth a week ago. There was no doubt in her mind that now he would think the worst of her.

She stared at him, saw the hard, cold look in his eyes and knew it was too late. She cleared her throat. "I saw you last month in downtown Denver, going into a feed store. I thought then that you would be perfect."

"Perfect for what?" he almost asked in a snarl.

She swallowed deeply. "To be on the cover of *Simply Irresistible* magazine."

She watched the expression on his face as the implications of what she'd said became clear. "Do you mean to tell me that you work for that magazine?"

She shook her head. "Not exactly."

His eyes narrowed. "Then what exactly?"

She nibbled on her bottom lip. "I don't work there exactly. I own the magazine."

The next thing Chloe thought was that if looks could kill, she would definitely be dead…but not before getting sheared first. She watched Ramsey's lips tighten, his jaw clench and the eyes that glared at her appeared to be dark orbs. "And just what were you doing here that morning?"

"I had come to talk to you about being featured in my magazine," she answered.

"Why?" he said in a tone so sharp it almost made her flinch. "I'd told the person who called I wasn't interested."

"I know, but I wanted to meet with you personally. Try to persuade you to change your mind."

He shook his head. "So instead you decided to pretend to be my cook and sleep with me?"

She did flinch at that. "No. That's not true. I tried to tell you the reason I was here, but you were in a hurry to leave that morning and you left me here with your front door wide open."

"Because I assumed you were the cook," he snapped.

"I never told you I was the cook, Ramsey. And you assumed wrong. Once I walked inside your house, the phone rang. It was the lady from the employment agency who said that the cook you were expecting wouldn't be coming. I could have left you in a hot mess, especially after you indicated you would have twenty hungry men to feed come lunchtime. But I decided to help you out."

"Why? So I could feel I owed you something and do that damn cover?"

"Initially, yes. I'd even planned to squeeze an interview out of you as well."

She could tell her answer, as honest as it could get, only

made him angrier. She saw it in his features to such a point where she actually felt her heart in her throat. "But like I said, that was at first, Ramsey. Once I got to know you—"

"Spare me. Lady, you have some nerve. Pretending to be someone else and—"

"And what? Helped you out for two weeks? I tried to tell you the truth a few days ago, but you wouldn't listen. You said we would put off any serious talk until today. So you can't hold that against me."

Ramsey snorted at that and the scowl on his face deepened. "I can hold it against you and I do. You should never have been here under false pretenses in the first place. As far as having a cook, I would have worked something out. You didn't need to do me any favors. And regardless of what you did for me, I still would not have posed on the cover of that magazine, so your plan wouldn't work."

"Once I got to know you, Ramsey, the cover didn't matter anymore," she implored, thinking she had never met a more bull-headed man.

"And you expect me to believe that?" he asked in an angry tone.

"Yes."

"Is there anything else you've failed to tell me?"

She shrugged. "My father is a senator from Florida. Senator Jamison Burton. My mother died when I was two and my father raised me by himself. My home is in Florida."

Ramsey stared at her, not believing what little he'd known about her.

"And the reason I could not deceive you any longer, the reason I wanted to tell you the truth that day after we'd made love was because I knew I was falling in love with you."

He stared at her for a long moment. "If being dishonest is

your idea of falling in love, Chloe, then you need to keep your love to yourself because I don't want any part of it."

He breathed in deeply and grabbed his Stetson off the rack. "I'm leaving and I want you packed up and out of here by the time I get back."

And then he walked out the door, slamming it shut behind him.

Ramsey's hands tightened on the steering wheel of his truck as he drew in a deep breath, not believing what had just taken place. What he had just walked away from. And just to think he'd intended to pour his heart out to Chloe, tell her how much he loved her, and all it had been for her was nothing more than a sinister plan to get him to pose on the cover of that damn magazine.

A part of him felt torn up inside, absolutely wrecked. Anger, the likes he'd never known before, was consuming him. He was driving with no particular destination in mind. It was Sunday, and most of his family had gone to church. Dillon and Pamela had left for the airport that morning to return to Gamble, and Callum and Zane had driven to see a rodeo in Oklahoma. Maybe it was for the best because he sure as hell didn't feel like socializing with anyone right now.

He pulled over to the side of the road and hit his fist against the steering wheel. How could he have been so stupid to let his guard down? Why was he always the last to know anything about a woman's trickery? It hadn't been any different with Danielle. Although he'd been relieved she'd ended the wedding, the fact still remained that she had made a fool of him.

He pulled back into the road. He'd meant what he said. Chloe had better be gone by the time he got back. And he hoped like hell that he never saw her again.

* * *

"Here, drink this," Lucia said, handing Chloe a cup of herbal tea. "It will help your headache."

Chloe glanced up at her friend, not wanting to tell her it wasn't her head that was hurting as much as her heart. "Thanks," she said, accepting the cup of hot tea.

"And now you need to go take a shower and get into bed."

Chloe rolled her eyes. "Lou, it's the middle of the day."

"Yes, but a nap might make you feel better."

Chloe shrugged. "I doubt it." She knew nothing would make her feel better unless Ramsey was to walk through that door and tell her that he believed her, that he knew she truly did love him, and that even though she had planned on making him indebted to her initially, she had discarded that plan once she'd fallen in love with him.

An hour later Chloe still sat curled up on Lucia's sofa. Lucia had finally left to go have Sunday dinner with her parents. Chloe felt she needed this time alone to go back over and over in her mind what happened earlier that day at Ramsey's house, and everything else that had transpired from the moment she'd driven onto his property over two weeks ago.

She thought of the angry words he had spoken to her before he'd left his home, ordering her to pack up and leave before he got back. A part of her had wanted to rebel and be there when he returned to have it out with him. But then there was nothing she could say that she hadn't already said.

And he hadn't believed her.

It had been a teary ride from Ramsey's ranch all the way to Lucia's home, and now she knew she couldn't remain in Denver. It was clear as the nose on her face that there was nothing here for her anymore. But a part of her refused to run.

Chances were her and Ramsey's paths would not cross anytime soon, so that would give her the time she needed to recover from a broken heart.

His men were watching him and Ramsey was well aware that they'd been watching him off and on for the past couple of weeks. Today he would do something he usually didn't do. Ignore them.

And for good reason. They wanted something he could not deliver. They wanted Chloe back. Nellie had returned and although he'd had a talk with her before allowing her back in his kitchen, after one good week she was sliding back into her old ways. The men, like him, were comparing what they had now with what they'd had for two weeks.

A part of Ramsey wanted to shout at them, to tell them that although Chloe's cooking skills were superb, she was not a cook. She had done it for fun. It had been all a part of her deliberate scheme to get him indebted to her.

His cell phone rang and he welcomed the excuse to leave the table and answer it in private. He had stepped into the living room when he spoke into his cell after checking the Caller ID. "Yes, Dillon?"

"I was asked to call and talk to you. To try and convince you to get that chip off your shoulder you've been carrying around for almost ten years but has gotten most noticeable the last two weeks."

Ramsey rubbed his hands down his face. He could imagine which one of his relatives had called Dillon. It could have been any one of them. He hadn't been in the best of moods and they all knew it. And they had no idea as to why.

"I don't need this, Dillon."

"Okay, but can I ask you one thing?"

"Yes."

"Do you love her?"

The question, to Ramsey's way of thinking, came out of the blue. It was one he definitely hadn't expected. But with Dillon he would be honest because even now, his very heart, every part of his body, knew the true answer.

"Yes, I love her."

Dillon was silent for a moment and then he said, "She might have set out to deceive you. However, you did admit that she wanted to confess all, but you talked her out of saying anything."

"Yes, but only because I assumed she wanted to talk about something else."

"Does it matter? I can't help but remember the woman who for two solid weeks got up before five o'clock every morning and cooked two meals a day for your men. She befriended them. And when you think about it, she really could have left you in a bind. Even you admitted the guys worked harder while she was there and that they broke all kinds of shearing records."

Ramsey threw his head back. "Is there a point you're trying to make, Dillon?"

"Just a suggestion."

"Which is?" Ramsey said in a hard tone.

"Basically the same one you gave me a few months back. You were the one who told me that in some things you need to know when and how to adjust your thinking, to be flexible. Especially if it's a woman you want."

"I don't want, Chloe. At least not in my life."

"You're absolutely sure about that?"

Ramsey knew that, but now, he wasn't sure. When it came

to Chloe, the woman still had him tied in knots. And he wasn't sure about anything, other than the fact that he still loved her.

He pulled in a deep breath. The truth of the matter was that he hadn't been able to adjust his thinking when it came to Chloe. It had been a while since he'd had a woman in his life and over the years he'd gotten pretty set in his ways. But what Dillon said was right. She hadn't had to hang around preparing those meals for his men for two weeks. She could have bailed after the first day. But she hadn't.

She had told him that she loved him, but he'd never told her that he loved her as well. Instead he had asked her to leave. What if she'd left town? Suddenly he didn't want to think about that possibility.

But he did. He thought about it a lot. He was still thinking about it later that evening when he and Callum got together to shoot a game of pool over at one of the local pool halls they frequented. The thought that if she were to leave Denver he would not be able to find her grated on his mind. As well as the thought that he needed to let her know that he had appreciated what she'd done for two weeks, feeding his men good food, letting them know they were appreciated. She had gone out of her way to put a little sunshine in their days.

All right, he would be the first to admit he probably did still carry around that chip on his shoulder that might have caused him to overreact. After all, she had tried telling him something that day, but he hadn't wanted to hear anything she'd had to say, fearing the worst and not wanting to deal with it. And although her original intentions might not have been honorable, she had stayed around, hung in and made a difference.

His thoughts shifted back to the possibility that she had not remained in Denver. Not being able to take not knowing any longer, he turned and handed his pool cue to Callum. "I'm going after her."

Callum accepted the cue stick and merely rolled his eyes. "About time."

Ramsey raised a brow. "And you think you can talk?"

Callum gave him a sly smile. "Yes, now that I've made up my mind about something."

Ramsey would have taken the time to inquire just what that *something* was had he not been so eager to head out the door.

Chloe pushed away from her desk and glanced out the window. It was hard to believe it had been three weeks since she had left Ramsey's ranch. Three solid weeks and this morning her suspicions had been confirmed. She was pregnant.

If she thought hard enough she figured there were a number of times they had gotten careless, like one of those times in the shower. But it really didn't matter when it happened, the fact remained that it had happened. Now she had to decide whether she would tell him before returning to Florida. He had a right to know, but whether she would tell him now or later, she just wasn't sure.

She had had lunch with Ramsey's sisters last week. Evidently, he was in rare form and they figured his less-than-desirable attitude lately had had something to do with her. Chloe was surprised he hadn't told them the entire story and fighting back tears she'd ended up telling them everything. How she had initially deceived him and then fell in love with him. Instead of taking their brother's side as she had figured they would do, they ended up crying right along with her. They were convinced she loved Ramsey and that it was a shame he couldn't see it for himself. They were convinced once he thought things through he would see the truth for himself. If only she could believe that.

Chloe stood and walked over to the window to continue to look out. Her work here in Denver was finished and Lucia would be handling things from here on out. Her east coast staff was presently looking for a new prospect for the October issue of *Simply Irresistible,* and that was fine with her. She was ready to move on.

Going back to her desk, she picked up her cell phone to call Lucia who had left that morning for Atlanta to sit in on a leadership workshop with a few of Chloe's other employees. She got Lucia's answering machine. "Lou, I'm not feeling well, so I'm going to leave early for your place. That's where I'll be if you need me for anything. Otherwise, I'll see you tomorrow when you return."

Feeling tired and sleepy, Chloe took a long nap as soon as she got home. When she awoke, she saw it had gotten dark outside and she felt hungry. Reminding herself that although her pregnancy was in the very early stages, that whenever she ate she was eating for two, she went into the kitchen and prepared a meal.

Hours later she had showered, changed into her favorite yellow sundress and had grabbed a book to read when the doorbell sounded. Chloe went to the door and glanced through the peephole. Her breath caught in her chest and she pressed a hand to her throat. Standing on Lucia's front porch was the man who'd captured her heart, the father of the baby she carried in her womb. Ramsey Westmoreland.

When Chloe opened the door, Ramsey could only stand there and stare at her. At that moment he thought the same thing he had that first morning he'd seen her: She was beautiful.

He did recall that morning. He remembered how he'd tried getting away from her once he saw how attracted he'd been to her. That was something that had not been her fault. And he had done something that morning so unlike him. He had raced off in his truck, leaving his front door open to a stranger. He had assumed she was the cook and he hadn't given her time to state otherwise.

Once he'd knocked the chip off his shoulder and had taken the time to analyze the situation, sort out the mess, he saw he had contributed to the misunderstanding. She was right in saying that although her original plans may not have been honorable, she had hung around and helped him out. He could just imagine how things would have turned out if she hadn't.

"Ramsey, what are you doing here?"

Her question brought his attention back to the present. "I'd like to talk to you, if at all possible."

He saw the wary look in her eyes before she nodded, opened the door wider and then moved aside.

When he passed her the first thing Chloe thought was that Ramsey certainly smelled good. And he looked good, too. He was wearing a pair of jeans, a western shirt and boots. He had removed the Stetson from his head once he'd entered the house.

Not asking him to sit, she turned to him. "What do you want to talk about?"

"I owe you an apology. You did try to level with me that day and I stopped you from doing so. Actually, I was afraid to let you."

Chloe lifted a brow. "Why?"

"If you recall, it was the same day my three sisters came to visit and I, of all people, know how overwhelming they can be. I thought that perhaps they may have tried boxing you into a corner about a relationship with me. I haven't been involved with a woman in a while and was afraid you might have begun feeling forced into a situation you weren't quite ready for, and I didn't want to hear you say it. Especially after I'd made plans to ask you to continue a relationship with me once your time was up at the ranch."

Chloe's reaction to his words was a total surprise. "You wanted to continue a relationship with me?"

She saw the intensity in his eyes when he said, "Yes."

Happiness swirled in her veins and the intensity was back in his eyes. But still…

She searched his face. "Why, Ramsey? Why did you want to continue a relationship with me?"

He didn't say anything for a moment, but the look on his features basically said it all. There were emotions there she hadn't seen before, emotions he'd never revealed to her until now. But still, she needed to hear him say the words.

He must have known what she needed. Placing his hat on the rack, he then walked the few feet over to her to stand in front of her. She sucked in a deep breath and lifted her face to meet his gaze when he did so.

"The reason I wanted to continue a relationship with you, Chloe, is because I had fallen in love with you."

He reached out and took her hand in his. "I know for us to be in love is not a cure-all. But at least it's a start and is more than most people have. I do love you, Chloe, and I want for us to be together. I don't want it to sound like I'm rushing things, but I want to marry you. I want to give you my babies one day. Bring you to the ranch to live with me as my wife. But

I know those have to be the things you want. I'm not asking you to give up anything for me, for our love. When you have to go away and travel for your magazine company, I'll modify my schedule to travel with you. I—"

Chloe held up her finger and placed it on his lips. "If nothing else, these past two weeks have shown me I have people capable of managing the magazine without me. Besides, I rather like the idea of living on your ranch, being your wife and the mother of your babies."

The brilliance of his smile touched her. "So you will marry me?"

"Yes."

"And if you want, we can have a long engagement," he said pulling her into his arms.

Chloe chuckled, shaking her head. "Now there's the kicker. A long engagement might not work for us, unfortunately."

He lifted a brow. "Not that I'm complaining, but why wouldn't it work?"

She paused and then she reached out and took his hand in hers and carried it to her stomach. "Already, your baby is here," she said in a whisper.

Chloe thought the look on his face at that moment was priceless. His mouth dropped open in shock. "You're pregnant."

She threw her head back and laughed. "No, *we're* pregnant."

Filled with more joy that he could stand, Ramsey didn't care how such a thing could have happened when they had used protection. It didn't matter. He wanted their baby. He pulled her closer into his arms and captured her mouth with his. The kiss was hungry, it was intense and, Chloe thought, it was full of love.

When he released her, he wrapped his arms tightly around her waist. "We're getting married as soon as it can be arranged."

She looked up at him. "We don't really have to, you know. Women have babies out of wedlock all the time and—"

"My child will be born a Westmoreland."

She chuckled. "If that's what you want."

"That's what I want. Will you go back to the ranch with me tonight so we can make plans?"

She lifted her brow. "Is that the only thing we'll make when we get there?"

Now it was Ramsey's turn to smile. He answered honestly, "No."

Chloe wrapped her arms around Ramsey's neck. "Um, I didn't think so."

When Ramsey bent his head to hers, she was ready and knew that this was just the beginning.

Epilogue

No one had asked why Ramsey and Chloe wanted a rather quick wedding. They were just happy to see Ramsey finally tying the knot. It was a beautiful day in May and all the Westmorelands came.

Chloe was overwhelmed at the huge family she'd married into. And there were several celebrities—national motorcycle superstar Thorn Westmoreland, well-known author Stone Westmoreland (a.k.a. Rock Mason), and Princess Delaney Westmoreland Yasir, wife of Sheikh Jamal Ari Yasir. Everyone welcomed her into the family with open arms. She couldn't help but smile, thinking it was a small world in that her father had already met the young, up-and-coming Senator Reginald Westmoreland at a fundraiser for a Georgia congressman last year. And Chloe was practically beaming in delight that Ramsey had also told her a few weeks ago that he would pose for the cover of her magazine.

Deciding they didn't want a huge wedding, Chloe had worn a beautiful tailored white pantsuit and with Ramsey by her side they walked around Shady Tree Ranch, where the beautiful outdoor wedding had taken place, greeting their guests. She got a chance to talk to one of Ramsey's elderly relatives, James Westmoreland. He was the one responsible for bringing the Atlanta and Denver Westmorelands together.

Chloe enjoyed talking to James and after talking with him she knew most of the story about Raphael and the mystery about the man's life that was yet to be solved.

A short while later, Ramsey took Chloe's hand in his and led her away from their guests. Even his men had come to the wedding and had brought their wives. She thought they looked good in their Sunday best.

"So, we don't know if those women were wives of Raphael or not." She noticed Ramsey was leading her farther and farther away from their guests.

Ramsey threw his head back and laughed. "I can only vouch for one of them and that's my great-grandmother Gemma. I know they got married because we have a copy of their marriage certificate. The others…we shall see."

"Is there anyone else besides Dillon even interested in finding out?"

"Yes, Megan. But she plans to do things differently. Unlike Dillon, she doesn't want to do the research herself but plans to hire a private detective to solve the mystery for her."

Ramsey stopped walking and turned to her. "I didn't bring you out here to talk about Raphael."

Chloe glanced around and saw they were a distance from the house. "And why did you bring me out here?"

He pulled her into his arms. "To say in private what I said in front of everyone today. I love you, sweetheart, and for the rest of my life I promise to show you just how much, and I will love and honor you always."

Tears sprang into Chloe's eyes. "And I love you."

The moment Ramsey had pulled her into his arms, Chloe knew that their lives would be filled with love, passion and plenty of hot Westmoreland nights.

* * * * *

"Why are you walking me out?" she asked.

"So every man in the place knows that you are with me."

"Am I with you, Steven?"

"Yes, you are."

"Just for tonight?"

"No. I want to have you by my side again."

They stepped out into the March evening. It was damp and chilly and Ainsley shivered. If they'd had a different relationship he would have wrapped his arm around her. But then he thought the hell with that. He put his arm over her shoulder and drew her against the curve of his body.

She shuddered and looked up at him.

In her eyes he read the same desire he'd been battling all night. He saw that she was thinking of him as a man—not a colleague. And he knew that he'd do anything to keep that interest alive.

SCANDALISING
THE CEO

BY
KATHERINE GARBERA

Published in Great Britain 2011
by Mills & Boon, an imprint of Harlequin (UK) Limited,
Eton House, 18-24 Paradise Road, Richmond, Surrey TW9 1SR

© Katherine Garbera 2010

ISBN: 978 0 263 88211 7

51-0411

Harlequin (UK) policy is to use papers that are natural, renewable and recyclable products and made from wood grown in sustainable forests. The logging and manufacturing processes conform to the legal environmental regulations of the country of origin.

Printed and bound in Spain
by Blackprint CPI, Barcelona

For all my readers

Katherine Garbera is a strong believer in happily-ever-after. She's written more than thirty-five books and has been nominated for career achievement awards in series fantasy and series adventure from *RT Book Reviews*. Her books have appeared on numerous bestseller lists, including the *USA TODAY* extended bestseller list. Visit Katherine on the web at www.katherinegarbera.com.

Dear Reader,

Steven Devonshire is the next illegitimate son of Malcolm Devonshire we meet in this story. He has always lived by his own rules. His mother is a Nobel Prize-winning physicist who is working on the God particle and never really had much time for anyone outside her laboratory.

Steven is very much her son. He is driven and determined to prove to the world that he is just as talented and can be more successful than both his mother and his father.

Ainsley is just as determined as Steven to prove to the world that she is more than she used to be. Steven ignored her once before, but Ainsley scarcely resembles the woman she used to be. In fact, as a powerful and very sexy magazine editor-in-chief, she has caught Steven's attention.

Steven isn't used to anyone else calling the shots, and he soon finds himself battling for control with Ainsley in a relationship neither is sure they want to commit to —even though their bodies and hearts say otherwise!

I hope you enjoy *Scandalising the CEO*!

Happy reading,

Katherine

Prologue

Steven Devonshire ignored the first two summonses from his biological father, but when his mother had called and had asked him to please attend a meeting at the Everest Group in downtown London, he relented.

Stepping into the boardroom and finding his two half brothers there was unexpected as well. His half brothers and he were referred to collectively as the "Devonshire heirs" in some circles and the "Devonshire bastards" in others. They had all been born in the same year to three different mothers.

Malcolm Devonshire freely admitted to being their father and had done his duty as far as contributing financially to their upbringing. Steven had no idea what relationship Henry and Geoff had with Malcolm, but Steven had never met the man before.

Henry, the middle brother and the son of Tiffany

Malone, seventies pop star, had grown up to be a famous rugby player. After an injury a couple of years ago, he'd given up playing and taken up doing more endorsement deals and starring in a couple of reality television shows, from what Steven had heard in the gossip rags.

"Malcolm has prepared a message for you," Edmond said. Edmond was Malcolm's solicitor. Steven had met Edmond many times and actually found the older man to be good company.

The Everest Group had always been Malcolm Devonshire's life. It didn't surprise Steven that the one time he'd thought he'd meet his father, the location was this office. Malcolm had just turned seventy and probably wanted to make sure that his life's work didn't end with his own death.

Geoff was the eldest of the three of them and the son of Princess Louisa of Strathearn, a minor royal. He and Steven had almost met before—they were both supposed to attend Eton College but Geoff never matriculated.

"Mr. Devonshire is dying," Edmond said. "He wants the legacy he worked so hard to create to live on in each of you."

"He didn't create that empire for us," Steven said. Malcolm did things for himself—not for anyone else. Malcolm had never done anything that didn't benefit the Everest Group. Steven suspected that Malcolm must want something from them now. But what?

"If you would all please sit down and allow me to explain…" Edmond said.

Steven sat down, as did the two other men. By nature he was someone who was used to having things go his way. He knew how to turn every new opportunity to his advantage and saw no reason why he wouldn't be able to do that with whatever Malcolm had in mind.

As Edmond spoke, it became apparent that Malcolm wanted them to take over his businesses. Whichever one of them was most successful—financially—would be given the chairmanship of the entire conglomerate.

Steven tried to digest everything. He didn't care about the sappy emotionality of an offer from his dying father, but he was interested in the business angle. He owned a very successful, high-end china company.

And if he won the competition with his half brothers that would be the icing on the cake. He relished the thought of winning and knew he would. He wasn't like Henry—too used to the spotlight—or like Geoff—too used to the pampered, privileged life of a royal. Steven realized he was exactly the right person to win this.

Edmond nodded to the three of them and left the room. As soon as the door closed behind Edmond, Steven stood up.

"I think we should do it," Steven said. He doubted that the deal would stand if they all weren't in on it. Whatever Malcolm's ulterior motive, Steven knew they all had to be involved.

Fortunately, each of the men agreed as well. As they all stood around the boardroom table, Steven listened to his half brothers chat. The men were strangers to him, but he was used to going it alone. He'd never been a team player, to which Steven attributed his own success. He knew what needed to be done and did it. Himself.

Henry stepped out to find Edmond so they could inform him of their decision. After the other men left, Steven lingered. He wanted to know what Malcolm's motivation was in all this.

"Why now?" he asked. Edmond's mentorship to Steven gave him an opening, and he had never hesitated to use whatever resources he had to get by in business and in life.

"As I explained, Mr. Devonshire's failing health is motivating him…" Edmond began, but Steven cut him off.

"To worry about the company he gave his life to," Steven concluded. He knew enough about the absentee father to understand what he was thinking. It was exactly what Steven had expected. The Everest Group was Malcolm Devonshire's life and now that his life was ending, the last thing he wanted was to see the company fail. Other men might try to pass on something to their offspring, but Malcolm wanted the company he'd created and nurtured to thrive long after he was gone.

"Indeed," Edmond agreed.

Steven didn't need the confirmation from Edmond. He had already figured it out himself. Malcolm had always been easy for Steven to understand because he saw a lot of his father's public traits in himself. He was able to focus on a task at hand and set aside the emotionality that often derailed others. He knew how to make sacrifices in order to achieve the results he desired.

"I'm not sure that I want a part of this," Steven noted. "This competition isn't fair. The other men don't have the experience I have in business. They can't compete with me."

"I think you'll find they have their own strengths," Edmond said.

He didn't like Edmond's inference that there were strengths to the other men that he couldn't perceive. Steven prided himself on being able to read anyone.

He would meet with them later—get to know them so he'd make sure he won. Winning wasn't something that Steven was willing to let slide.

"I'll be checking in with you over the next few months to make sure you stay on track," Edmond said.

Steven shook his head. He hated having someone looking over his shoulder and he didn't need it. "I'll send you an e-mail once a week with our numbers and updating you on my action agenda for increasing our revenue."

"I'm also available, as ever, to offer my advice should you need it. I've been at Malcolm's side since the first day he started his company."

"I guess that makes you the longest relationship of his life," Steven said.

"Too true. Business is at the heart of it…and I think we are both comfortable with that."

Steven nodded. The emotionality thing again. The key to success was to stay distanced from others. Men started making stupid decisions when they thought they had something to lose.

"Save your advice for the other men," Steven said. "I prefer to work alone."

The older man narrowed his eyes, but Steven gave him no chance to argue. He didn't answer to his father's second in command.

"Have a good day, Edmond."

Steven walked out of the boardroom and out of the office building. The Everest Mega Store, in his hands, would become the premiere shopping destination for pop culture.

When people talked about the Devonshire bastards, they

wouldn't remember just the star rugby player or the son of a royal. No, they would remember Steven and the fact that he was the best.

One

"I've got an idea," Steven said to Dinah as soon as his executive vice president at Raleighvale China answered the phone.

"The last time you said that I found myself answering some rather uncomfortable questions from the police in Rome."

He laughed. "This time you won't have to deal with the police."

"Somehow my fears still aren't eased. What's this idea of yours?"

"What do you know about pop culture?"

"Why?"

"How does a position as my executive VP sound?"

"I thought that *was* my position," she said.

"For Everest Group Mega Store. I'm calling you from my new office."

"Your father's company? You said you'd never do that. Why now?"

Steven didn't talk about his personal life. *Ever.*

"My reasons are my own. Suffice it to say that there is a huge bonus in it for you if you help me make this company the top performer at Everest Group."

"Very well. When do you need me?" Dinah asked.

"In twenty-four hours or so. I need time to acclimate and find an office for you. Bring your admin for now, but once you're settled, we'll find someone else to work in the other office."

"Twenty-four hours is pretty quick," she said.

"I'll be in touch," he said.

"Steven?"

"Yes?"

"Are you sure about this? I know you—"

"I always am," he said, hanging up the phone. No one really knew him and certainly not Dinah. She only knew the part of him he allowed her to see.

Steven had taken the china company over from his grandfather. Founded in 1780 to compete with Wedgwood, Raleighvale had succeeded in creating a truly English style of tableware. They were now the royal china makers, something that Dinah Miller spent a lot of time touting to prospective clients. She recently secured for them a bid to make Raleighvale the official dinnerware for the new president of France. He knew she'd be equally successful in her new role.

His iPhone beeped, notifying him of an incoming text message. It was from Geoff, requesting that he meet him and Henry for a drink at the Athenaeum Club. He replied in the affirmative.

Then his phone rang. "Devonshire."

"This is Hammond from the Leicester Square store. I'm sorry to bother you, sir, but we have an emergency."

"Why isn't the duty manager handling this?" Steven asked. He didn't remember seeing Hammond's name on the list of managers at that location.

"I'm a retail floor specialist. The manager isn't here, she's on her lunch break and won't answer her phone. But we can't wait until she gets back."

"What is the situation?" Steven asked.

"Someone has set up and is doing a photo shoot in the middle of the selling floor. It's Jon BonGiovanni, the rocker, and there is a crowd of people blocking the elevator. They just won't move."

"I'll be right there."

He hung up and grabbed his suit jacket before leaving to take care of the problem at the Leicester Square store. He didn't have time for waffling—the last thing he needed on his first day was some sort of retail fiasco.

Upon reaching the Leicester Square store, he took two steps and stopped, gobsmacked.

The problem with the store was obvious. A model, photographer and photographer's assistant milled about in the main retail section—just as Hammond had said. It was only as he walked closer that he saw Jon BonGiovanni, the aging rock musician from the seventies supergroup Majestica standing under the photographer's lights.

He wore a pair of skintight jeans and a barely there American flag shirt displaying his bare chest with a tattoo of a fist in the center of it.

"What's going on here?" Steven said as he approached the group.

"We are trying to do a photo shoot. One that your CEO

has already approved, but today no one seems to know what was agreed on," the photographer said.

"I'm the CEO. Steven Devonshire."

"I'm Davis Montgomery."

Steven had heard of Davis—who hadn't? The man had made a mint photographing young rockers like Bob Dylan, John Lennon, Mick Jagger and Janis Joplin in the early seventies. His open approach to photography and his subjects had changed the way rock portraits were taken and revolutionized photography.

Steven shook the man's hand. "It's a pleasure to meet you. But you can't shoot in the retail store during our busy selling time."

"Ainsley received permission for us to be here."

"Who is Ainsley?"

"I am."

The woman who walked up behind him was…exquisite. She had thick, ebony-colored hair that hung from a high ponytail at the back of her head. Her dark hair and alabaster skin first captured his attention but as his gaze skimmed down her body, he was entranced by her feminine figure. Her blouse was slim-fitting with cap sleeves and a nipped-in waist, and then the curvy hips were hugged lovingly by the black skirt. She was his dream girl come to life. The thick red belt around her waist just accentuated her gorgeous figure.

And then he caught a glimpse of her legs and the silk hose that encased them.

He nearly groaned out loud. She was a Betty Page look-alike. That classic fifties pin-up girl who had captured his teenage imagination and never let it go.

"And who are you, Ms. Ainsley?"

She seemed a bit taken aback by the question, and he

wondered if he should have known who she was without asking. But she had a distinctively American accent and she was clearly in either the fashion industry or music. But he knew he would have remembered her had they met.

"Ainsley Patterson, editor-in-chief of *British Fashion Quarterly*."

"Your name is familiar, but I don't believe we've had the pleasure of meeting before."

"That's great," Davis said. "Now you know each other and I'd like to get back to work."

"I'm sure that Mr. Devonshire will be more than happy to accommodate us. After all, we have the permission of his father's solicitor."

Steven was tired of hearing about his father. Malcolm and he were little more than strangers. Though the same could be said of his mother and him. He just had never been the kind of child who'd clung to his parents.

"That's all well and good, Ms. Patterson, but neither Malcolm nor his lawyer are here right now. Let's go up to my office and discuss what you need and find a time that will work for everyone."

Steven expected Ainsley to back down, but she didn't. He'd never met a woman who could be so sexy and so businesslike at the same time. It was a turn-on just talking to her, but somehow he knew that wasn't the route he should take.

Ainsley didn't want to spend any extra time speaking to a man who couldn't remember her. But she hadn't gotten to where she was in publishing by avoiding people who annoyed her. Davis gave her a look that said he was about to blow his top and they were going to have to deal with one of his infamous temper tantrums.

"Come on. I don't have all day to hang out here," Jon said.

"Jon, I'm sorry for this inconvenience. Why don't you take a ten-minute break and Mr. Devonshire and I will straighten this out."

"Will we?" Steven said.

He had a look that was straight out of a fashion magazine: short hair, styled to look as if he didn't care, blue eyes—Paul Newman blue. So bright and penetrating Ainsley had been mesmerized by him the first time they'd met.

Of course, back then she'd been seventy pounds heavier, five years younger and minus the self-confidence she had today.

"Yes, we will. I'm sure that there is something we can offer you that will be adequate compensation—though having your store featured in our magazine is quite a boon."

"From your perspective, perhaps," Steven said.

"What can we do to make this happen?" she asked.

"I'm thinking feature articles on the Devonshire heirs," Steven said.

"That would be interesting, but we are a women's fashion magazine," she said. Her mind going over what she knew about Steven and his half brothers. The real angle would be getting them to talk about their early years, but even then there wasn't a fashion twist. Maybe the mothers, she thought. Then she knew she had it.

"How about an interview with your mothers?" she asked. "They were all very fashionable when Malcolm was dating them."

"My mum's a physicist."

"I know, but she was also named one of the most beautiful women in Britain."

Steven's eyes narrowed.

"I don't see how an article on my mum will benefit me," he said.

"We could do a photo shoot with each of the women in the business units—the airline, the record label and the retail store. I mean Tiffany Malone would be a natural at Everest Records. I can see the spread already.

"We can have each of you in there in a smaller perspective—Henry is definitely on the cutting edge of fashion...and Geoff is very traditional."

"And I'm all business," Steven said.

Ainsley looked at him. At this man who'd dismissed her because she'd been frumpy and overweight and he'd made an offhand comment that had devastated her... "Maybe we could do a makeover with you at one of our sister magazines."

He quirked one eyebrow at her. "I'm not a makeover kind of guy. If we agreed to this, then it'd be an exclusive for you."

Ainsley thought about it. She'd have to talk to her team, but there had to be some way to make this happen. "I'm not sure we can fit you into our schedule. I mean, if I had Malcolm in the article, too...then that would be a coup."

"It would be. But I can't promise that Malcolm would do it."

"Not close to him?"

"He's dying, Ainsley," Steven said.

She felt a pang. He hadn't shown any emotion at all. She wondered if that meant that he was scared of losing his father and didn't want anyone to know.

"I'm so very sorry."

He nodded. "Back to business here. You finish your shoot with Jon and then do feature articles on all of us from the fashion angle involving our mums—which issue?"

"I have to get back to the office and double-check my schedule, but I think it will be in the fall."

"Very well," he said. "It's a deal."

"Great," she said, turning to walk away.

"Do you have time for dinner to discuss the details? You could let Davis and Jon finish their shoot."

Ainsley didn't want to have a dinner with him. She'd had a crush on him ever since she'd done that interview five years ago. Not a stalk-him-like-a-crazy-woman-and-lie-in-his-bushes crush, but a kind of obsession that involved reading every article published on him. Would it be a good idea to go to dinner with him? Their relationship would have to stay professional, she reminded herself.

But he'd changed her life. When she'd realized that to a man like Steven she'd been completely invisible, it was shattering. Not just because of her size, but because she hadn't kept control of the interview. He'd unnerved the woman she'd been five years earlier and spurred her change. And now she wanted nothing more to do with him…well, that wasn't true. She'd love to exact a measure of revenge after the way he'd dissed her.

And she had no plans for tonight other than heading back to the office, working on page proofs and approving every detail of the magazine she'd fought so hard to become the editor-in-chief of. She could squeeze out a few hours for Steven.

"Agreed," she said.

"Should we shake hands and have a contract drawn up?" he asked.

"What?"

"For our dinner. You make it sound like an all-day meeting you're dreading. I think that dinner with me will be enjoyable."

He was confident and she remembered his charm only too well. "Do you think so? Can you guarantee it?"

"Indeed I can."

Her BlackBerry buzzed crazily with text messages and e-mail notifications. She glanced down at the screen. At least three fires demanded her attention. "When and where for dinner?"

She motioned for Davis's assistant to come over.

"Nine. I'll pick you up."

"That's not necessary. I'd rather drive myself."

"I'm not sure where I can get a reservation with this late notice. Give me your address," he said.

She realized that Steven was used to getting his way, which was interesting because she was, too. She thought about digging her heels in on this issue, but time was money and they'd lost enough today waiting for someone to clean up this mess.

"Fine. You can pick me up at my office," she said, and then rattled off the address.

"See you then," he said and turned to leave. She watched him walk away, admiring the swagger in his step. He was a fine-looking man from the back, she thought, noticing the way his dress pants cupped his butt when he took a step.

"Are we okay to work?" Joanie asked. Joanie was Ainsley's age and had been working for Davis for the last ten years. She was slim and tall and her striking features made Ainsley think that Joanie could have been a model. But the other woman preferred to work behind the camera instead of in front of it.

"I believe we are."

"Great. I'll go get Jon back into makeup and let Davis know," Joanie said. "This was about to be one expensive mistake."

Ainsley needed no reminding. She waved over Danielle Bridges, the editor in charge of this article. Ainsley was here for star management and she was very glad she'd been here today. Danielle was new on their staff and Ainsley had yet to determine if she could hold her own.

"I am so sorry about this. I spoke to the manager several times to confirm the details," Danielle said.

The other woman had been apologizing all morning. "We can talk about this later. The issue has been resolved and we are going to get some great photos to go with the fabulous article you edited," Ainsley said. She believed that most people rose to challenges when they felt their superiors believed in them. And she also believed in reprimanding people in private.

"Thanks," Danielle said.

A minute later a twenty-something girl with stick-straight blond hair walked up to her. "Mr. Devonshire asked that I assist you in whatever you need. I'm Anne."

"You can work with Joanie."

Ainsley and Danielle stood off to the side, with Ainsley answering e-mails on her BlackBerry and waiting until she was sure the photo shoot was underway. Then she left the store to go back to her office.

Frederick VonHauser was waiting in her office. He was on her staff but also a trusted friend. Freddie and she had met when they'd both been attending Northwestern. Back then Freddie had been Larry Murphy. But he'd decided that he needed a new name for his new college life and had changed it their junior year.

"Everything settled?"

"Yes. Steven Devonshire was there."

"No kidding. Did he remember you?"

"Nope. Not even a flicker of recognition. Should I fire Danielle? She didn't follow up and Davis and Jon stood around for over an hour with nothing to do. It was a complete mess."

"Darling, I know you too well to let you change the subject. Are you sure he didn't recognize you?"

"Yes. And that doesn't matter. I'm having dinner with him later this evening."

"Ains, you sneaky girl. So you were going to keep that to yourself?"

"I was. Because my underling shouldn't know every detail of my life."

"Underling? I prefer esteemed colleague."

"You are. Now about Danielle…"

"She's young. And the article she wrote is one of the best I've seen in a long time. But she's not going to learn if we don't push her."

"She cost me hundreds of thousands today, Freddie. I can't keep her on."

He looked as if he wanted to argue but didn't. She put her pen down and thought about the articles she'd agreed to run in the magazine.

"I need someone who can handle sports stars and royals."

"For what?"

"A series of articles on the Devonshire heirs and their mothers. I want to showcase all three separately and then I need someone with a connection to Malcolm Devonshire. I want to do a sit-down with all three of his sons and him. I want the angle to be on mothering."

"Good luck with that. How'd you get the heirs to agree?"

"It was Steven's price for getting back to the photo shoot."

"You and Steven made all kinds of deals, didn't you?"

"Yes, I did."

"Ains, was that wise? The man left you devastated before," Freddie said.

"I have no idea, but when I realized he didn't remember me and that he was interested in me now…"

She trailed off. She couldn't say that a part of her wanted revenge. That wasn't very noble and she knew she wouldn't do anything to hurt Steven. But if they had dinner and he found himself more attracted to her, and this time if she was the one to walk away without glancing back…well, then she'd be just fine with that.

"Girl, this has disaster written all over it. You emerged from the ashes the last time as a phoenix, but that kind of transformation can't happen twice in a lifetime."

"Says who?"

He shrugged. "I guess you have to do what you think is right."

"It's not that," she said. "I'm just curious."

"Curious about a man who left you so shattered that you lost a ton of weight and had to move to another continent to recover? That kind of curiosity could be more than you can handle."

She just looked at Freddie. She wasn't going to back out of the date. She'd made up her mind that this time she'd emerge the victor from her encounter with Steven. A few minutes later Freddie left the office and she sat back in her chair. She didn't want to think too much about her deal with Steven or that it had nothing to do with this magazine and everything to do with the man—Steven Devonshire.

Two

Ainsley fidgeted nervously as she looked at herself in the bathroom mirror. Sometimes she still saw the fat girl she'd once been looking back at her. She turned to her side and stared at her stomach. That carb fest she'd indulged in at lunch had been a mistake. She was going to have to have a veggie soup for dinner.

She glanced at the slim-fitting black skirt. She was always torn when she looked at her reflection. She liked the body she saw in the mirror, but she never felt at home in it. She kept expecting the image to balloon up like one of those carnival mirrors she'd seen at the county fair growing up in Florida.

Sometimes she was really struck by how far she'd come. At times she could scarcely recall the small-town girl she had been, but at other times she felt just as awkward and out of place as ever.

The bathroom door opened, she put on her power smile and leaned in as if she'd just been checking her lipstick. It was Danielle. The other woman stared at her.

"I thought we were cool," Danielle said.

Ainsley shook her head. "I'm sorry, but that cost us a lot of money today and now I have to go in front of my bosses and get them to sign off on another idea."

"I know that I dropped the ball, but I'm just learning," Danielle said.

"When I was just learning, Danielle, I lost my job for making a mistake like you. It took me three years to get my career back on track," Ainsley said. The botched interview with Steven had cost her her job with the *Business Journal*.

"Then give me a break here. You know how hard it is to start over."

"That's right, I do. So I don't make major mistakes anymore. I'm not sure you learned from this one."

Danielle crossed her arms over her chest. "How about a probation period? Let's say six months of a trial and I'll prove myself to you. If I screw up again, I'll walk away and if I don't I get to stay on full time."

Ainsley realized that Danielle had gumption. She was an incredibly talented editor, if Ainsley was forced to admit it. "Okay, it's a deal. But don't make me regret it."

"I won't."

Ainsley walked out of the ladies' restroom to see Freddie leaning against the wall. "Did you put her up to that?"

"Yes, I did. I think we haven't seen the best of her yet and if she wanted a second chance, I told her she'd have to go and make you give her one."

She glanced over at her oldest friend. "You are so lucky I like you."

He kissed her cheek. "I know. When do you talk to New York about your idea for the Devonshire heirs story?"

Even though Ainsley was editor-in-chief for *FQ*, she still answered to her boss in New York. They were owned by the best-selling magazine consortium in the world, and her boss liked to say they were number one because he was so hands-on.

"In an hour. I had to squeeze it onto the agenda at the end of the video conference call. I would love to have some photos of the women from when they were all dating Malcolm," she said. "Do you think you can get on Corbis and find them?"

"I can and I will. What else do you need?"

"Nothing. I'll do my other research, but finding the photos would be time-consuming. I need them to be unique and glamorous..."

"I think I know what you have in mind. I'll e-mail them to you as soon as I have them."

"Thanks, Freddie," she said.

"I owe you one after I sicced Danielle on you."

"This doesn't make up for that."

"What does?"

"A jog along the Thames tomorrow morning at seven."

"Seven? That's still the middle of the night," he said.

"But you owe me, so you'll be there."

"You're right, I will be," he said. He headed down the hall to his own office and she reentered hers.

It was one thing to think of doing a story of this magnitude, but it was something else entirely to convince her publisher that it should be done. And she needed to make sure they could do the story she'd proposed.

She spent the next hour pulling up details on the women

who had been involved with Malcolm Devonshire. And Ainsley was fascinated by what she'd found. The women were all very dynamic and, from a fashion perspective, she couldn't have asked for three women whose sense of style was more distinctive and individual. There was Henry's mother, Tiffany Malone—the embodiment of a seventies hippie chick rocker. With her sexy long hair, sultry eyes and pencil-slim jeans, she was earthy and radiated sexuality. It was hard to think of her as being someone's mum.

Then there was Princess Louisa—the wild-child party girl who was a distant cousin of the current monarch. Her look was haute-couture sexiness from her stick-straight bob to her slim-fitting, low-cut tops and hip-hugging slacks. She was glamour with a capital *G*.

Then there was Lynn Grandings—Steven's mother. The physicist, who should have seemed very much like a bookworm, but instead radiated a keen intelligence and with her waist-length, thick, curly brown hair, she exuded her own brand of sexuality. The picture that Freddie had sent showed her laughing at the camera, and it was easy to see why Malcolm had been attracted to her.

The only thing the women had in common was a distinctive beauty all their own. These women were defined by their lifestyles and she was dying to know what had attracted Malcolm to them at the same time. How had he been able to juggle these relationships?

She finished making her notes and realized that talking to the sons would be the perfect accompaniment for the story because these strong women raised them.

Dinah sat across from him in the conference room. He'd ordered the financials for Everest Mega Stores from the last three years. The retail stores had suffered a setback over the last quarter but even prior to that there had been signs of decline. The pattern that emerged showed that the North American retail stores were the ones that were having the most problems.

"I think our North American retail shops should be closed," Steven said after he finished reading the financials.

"I'm not sure," Dinah said. "If we do that we stop the loss, but we aren't going to see a new revenue stream."

"If we focus our energies here," he said, gesturing to the spreadsheet for Europe and the UK, "I think we can make it up. But I'm open to ideas on how to keep North America. I don't really want to lose that market."

"Why don't I do some research? I can write a report on the analysis of closing the North American stores versus keeping them open. I'll recommend some course of action as well, if you like."

Steven glanced over at Dinah. "I like that idea. Can you have it to me by Friday?"

"Close of business?"

"If you need that long," he said.

"Yes. I might take all the time."

"I don't mind. I want to make sure we're doing the right thing."

Dinah stood up and gathered her purse and briefcase. "We will. You're known for saving companies like this one, so it should be a piece of cake."

"Exactly."

"Is that why you took this job?" she asked.

Steven shrugged. Dinah and he had worked together a long time and never had the conversations turned personal. They sometimes flirted and always talked business and market trends, but never did any conversation broach the personal areas of their lives.

"Off-limits?" she asked.

"No. This is business—pure and simple," he said. Opting for the truth as he saw it. The inheritance issues weren't a big thing for him, because he saw this as a challenge and the chance to prove himself was too great for him to pass up.

"Good. I'm going to let my phone go to voice mail tonight."

"You are? Why?"

She flushed and for the first time he realized that Dinah had a life outside the office. He always suspected she must, but they did work almost sixty hours a week so that didn't leave much time for dating.

"I have a date and he told me to turn the phone off at dinner tonight if I wanted to see him again," she said, her voice quiet and a little pensive.

"Okay, voice mail is fine. In fact, take the entire evening off. I don't want you returning calls until tomorrow."

"Does midnight count as tomorrow?"

He laughed. She was still his workaholic Dinah. "Of course it does."

Dinah left a few minutes later and Steven sat back in his chair thinking about Ainsley Patterson. There had been something familiar about her, but he would have remembered meeting her.

He made plans for dinner and then started going through his executive staff. He called them all in one at a time and wrote down his impressions afterward. He had a list of people he thought were go-getters and could move the company forward. Unfortunately, there was a list of people who saw their job here as a paycheck only. He'd have to move them around and see if that sparked some enthusiasm. Otherwise he'd have to fire them.

No matter the outcome, it was only a matter of time before he had this company running like a well-oiled machine.

He wasn't sure when it had happened—perhaps when he'd been a boy playing quietly in the sterile environment of his mother's lab—but he'd always known that he could rely on no one but himself.

Three

Steven had to detour back to the Leicester Square store to fire that duty manager. He had his secretary send a message to his half brothers that he'd be late meeting them. It was odd to think that these men he'd known about his entire life but had never met were now such an integral part of it. He wasn't too sure how he felt about that. He didn't necessarily want brothers.

He'd never yearned for a family as a child and as an adult he'd found that making his own way in the world suited him. Family just hadn't been part of his reality. His mum was always in the lab, and Aunt Lucy was busy with her life.

His cell rang and he glanced down to see that it was his aunt Lucy. Lucy was his mother's twin, the nurturer in their family. She called him once a week to just check on him.

Aunt Lucy had tried to mother him, but Steven had always known she was doing it because she didn't think his mum was. And that left Steven feeling…cold.

"Aunt Lucy."

"Hello, Steven. How are you doing, dear?"

"I'm good. How are you?"

"Fine, dear. I heard from your mother that your father had contacted you."

Steven sighed as he exited his building. He went to his car—a Vallerio roadster. He had an original 1969 model in his garage at home. The new roadster had all the earmarks of the original, but power for this new millennium.

"It was nothing. He wants me to run one of his business units."

"And the others?"

Others. That was how his mum and Aunt Lucy referred to his half brothers. Was it any wonder he'd never been close to them?

"They are each running a segment as well. Whoever outperforms the others will be made the CEO of the Everest Group."

"Sounds like your kind of challenge, dear. Will you be able to come home to Oxford on Sunday for dinner?"

He hesitated for a second. Not because he was considering it, but he wanted her to think he was. His aunt meant well and she was the only one of his relatives he talked to on a regular basis, so he always made the effort of at least seeming to want to spend time with her.

"Not this week."

"Oh, well, maybe another time. Have a good evening."

"You, too, Aunt Lucy."

He hung up and got in the car. He drove through the

congested London streets to the Athenaeum Club. The members-only club would afford them the privacy they needed to talk. To have a chance to get to know each other away from the prying eyes of the paparazzi. Steven wasn't used to the spotlight the way that Henry and Geoff were. But it didn't bother him. He was enough of a businessman to know that any publicity was good.

In this day and age anything could be spun. He had made a dinner reservation for him and Ainsley at an African restaurant that he liked. He pulled up to the front of the club and the valet came to take his keys.

"I know I'm not a member," a young woman said to the butler guarding the door. "I just need to send a message to Henry Devonshire. I know he's in here."

"I can relay a message for you," Steven said. "I'm meeting him inside."

"I just need to speak to him for a moment. Will you let him know I'm out here?"

"I sure will," Steven said, smiling at the woman as she stepped aside. "And who are you?"

"Astrid Taylor."

Steven nodded to her and then turned to the butler. "Steven Devonshire," he said.

"Of course, sir," he said. The door was opened for him and he entered the club.

The centuries-old club was decorated in a very conservative manner and it was lined with tables and chairs in discreet groupings. There was a bar at one end of the room and he spotted Henry and Geoff sitting at one of the tables toward the back.

"There's a girl asking for you up front," he said by way of greeting to Henry.

The other men and he shared little in the way of looks.

Geoff dressed like he was part of the upper crust of society, which he was. Henry always looked spot-on trendy, which made sense because he spent so much time with the people who made the trends that others followed.

"A girl?" Henry asked.

"Astrid," he said. "I told them I'd let you know."

"Thanks," Henry said. He put his glass on the table and stood up. "Sorry to miss chatting with you, Steven. I need to go."

"Do you?" Geoff asked. "Who is she?"

"My new assistant, Astrid Taylor."

Steven signaled the butler and ordered a Seagram's Seven. It was an old-fashioned drink, but one he'd always favored. The conversation went on between the other two men, talking about families and their half-siblings, and Steven felt distinctly uncomfortable. He had no family except his mum and Aunt Lucy. And he certainly didn't want to talk about them. Steven found it interesting that Henry and Geoff's mums had remarried and created families for their sons.

After Henry left, Steven sat back in his chair to assess Geoff's mood. "How's the airline business?"

"A mess. I'm not sure that this 'boon' from Malcolm is much of a gift. The airline is on shaky ground and the baggage handlers are threatening to strike. I have some ideas for turning it around, but it will be hard work. How about the retail stores?"

Steven had heard rumors about the airline within business circles. "The retail chain is healthy in Europe and here in the UK, but the North American division is faltering. I wonder how Malcolm let the business get into such bad shape?"

Geoff shrugged. "His obsession with flying around the

globe probably contributed to it. Or, as we all know, his obsession with women."

Steven couldn't help but chuckle. At the end of the day that might be what had cost Malcolm the cutting edge he'd had when he was younger. That was a mistake that Steven was determined not to make.

He liked to think he'd gotten the best skills from both his parents. From his mother, Lynn Grandings, a Nobel Prize-winning physicist, he'd learned to apply the scientific method to every aspect of his life and to be methodical about planning, but he'd also been introduced to some of his mum's crazy ideas. She always said that progress was made from ideas that others thought were…whacked. And from Malcolm he'd learned that winning at all costs was the most important thing.

"I forgot to mention to Henry that I have made arrangements for *Fashion Quarterly* to interview our mothers and us."

"What? Why would a fashion magazine be interested in us?" Geoff asked.

"Our mums were all very fashionable women in their day and the editor-in-chief thinks that you and Henry are fashion-forward now. She's going to do photo shoots of each us with our mums near something related to our business units. The editor-in-chief wants to assign a writer to interview all three of us and Malcolm. I'm not sure what his health is like, so I don't know if that will be possible."

"I'm not too keen on talking about myself and I don't know that my mum will agree, but the airline could use a boost. As long as they stick to that angle, I'll do it."

"Good. I'll have my assistant send the details. And now I have to go."

"Me, too," Geoff said. "Thanks for dropping by."

"You're welcome. I guess it's time we got to know each other."

"Past time," Geoff said.

The men walked out together and there were photographers waiting outside. Steven stayed back and watched the mayhem that surrounded Geoff. There were questions about his distant cousins, the royal princes, and questions about his mother. All of which Geoff brushed off as he walked to his own car, ignoring the photographers.

After the pack of paparazzi had left, Steven left as the valet brought his car to the front. After meeting with his half brothers, he knew he was going to win the challenge that Malcolm had thrown down, but he wondered if it would fill the empty hole in his soul.

The restaurant that Steven had chosen was classy, but had a homey atmosphere. The décor was distinctly African and the lighting was low, offering them a sense of privacy.

The details of the interviews weren't something she could talk about with him now. She had to talk to her staff writers and she wanted to see if Freddie could line up an interview with Malcolm before she made any decisions.

"Thank you for letting us go ahead with our shoot. I'm sure I don't need to tell you how much it cost us to just wait around."

"You're very welcome," Steven said. He'd ordered a bottle of white African wine to go with their dinner and lifted a glass to toast after the sommelier had brought it to them and Steven had approved it.

"To winning combinations," he said.

She nodded and tipped the bell of her glass toward him. Their glasses clinked together and she looked into his eyes as she took her first sip. He watched her the entire time, which she thought was interesting. He seemed like someone who was shallow and only concerned about his own needs, but he was definitely paying attention to her. He watched every expression on her face and she felt as if he wanted to make sure she enjoyed herself tonight. That was out of character for the man she'd met five years ago.

A bouquet of flavor erupted on her tongue as she swirled the sip of wine though her mouth. It was crisp and dry and had the subtle flavor of fruit to it. Not grapes but maybe apple, she thought.

When she returned her glass to the table, she smiled at him. "I like this wine. Thank you for recommending it."

"Well, it has a bite, so I thought it might suit you."

She had to laugh at the way he said it. She knew she came across as a man-eater when she was in business mode. But tonight she wanted to enjoy the opportunity to just get to know Steven.

"You mentioned earlier that your father was sick," she said.

"I don't like to talk about Malcolm," he said.

She made a mental note that he referred to his father as Malcolm. Were they close? Somehow she didn't think that question was appropriate. As an American in London, she'd learned quickly that some of the conversational topics she'd always thought acceptable weren't here.

"My dad had a health scare about six years ago…and it really shook me. I'd always thought of him as invincible and it was humbling to realize he wasn't."

"Yes, it can be hard," Steven said. "My mother is healthy as can be but she spends a lot of time in a sterile environment, so that's to be expected."

"What does she do?" Ainsley asked. She had done

her research on Lynn but wanted to hear about her from Steven.

A frown crossed his face so quickly that if she hadn't been watching him she would have missed it. "My mother is a physicist. She's won a few awards. Right now she's working in Switzerland."

"I guess you don't see her often," Ainsley said.

The waiter brought their dinners and they continued to discuss their families. It didn't take long for her to notice that Steven always deflected the questions she asked about his family. Not that it mattered—her writers would get to him.

"What brought you to London?" he asked as they were sipping a darkly brewed after-dinner coffee.

She wondered if he'd remember her if she mentioned the interview she'd done with him. It was that article that had ultimately cost her her job. She'd been so nervous when she'd met Steven at his office that she'd spilled her coffee all over his desk. He'd been cordial to her at the time but when she left she overheard him on the phone with Joel, her boss. Heard him say that she'd been more concerned about her coffee and sweet snack than about interviewing him. When she got back to her office, it hadn't surprised her that her boss fired her.

She'd written the article anyway and sent it out freelance to a couple of magazines, finally getting it picked up by one of the *Business Journal*'s competitors. It had appeared in *WIRED* magazine; they had been looking for articles on "young guns"—men under thirty who were changing and shaping the way businesses were being managed. That article put her on the map, so to speak, and gave her a chance to start fresh.

She was a little miffed Steven hadn't recognized her

name but remembered that back then she'd been A. J. Patterson—something she'd thought made her seem more professional.

"My job. I used to work as a freelance writer in the States. But it's hard to pay the bills with freelance gigs only, so I transitioned to an editor position at *Fashion Quarterly* in the States. While I was there, a piece I wrote on young Hollywood wowed my bosses and they offered me a full-time position as an editor. Once I started editing—which is very different than writing—I found that I loved it."

"As much as writing?" he asked.

She shrugged, but then she decided, why not tell him. "Some days but what I loved about writing was the discovery, digging deeper and asking questions that surprised the people being interviewed. Not in a bad way, but just in a way that pushed them to examine and expand their own responses. I liked that."

"Do you write anymore?" he asked.

No one ever thought to ask her that, she observed. The truth was there were times when she did miss writing but being an editor, especially one in her position, paid so much better. "No, I don't. I'm in charge of our entire magazine."

"Do you like being the boss?" he asked.

"Love it," she said, with a grin.

She hadn't realized until she'd gotten a full-time position at *FQ* that she really loved the competitive nature of her industry. It had also helped her focus on staying healthy. Working in fashion had made her very aware that she had to make her weight loss a permanent thing.

"But enough about me. You must be looking for a huge challenge to take on the Everest Mega Stores on top of running Raleighvale China. Or have you stepped down there?"

"No, I haven't stepped down. I don't think I ever will. Raleighvale is in my blood."

"How?" she asked. He was more open when she asked him about business. That was another interesting note that she mentally tucked away to examine later.

"It's my own company. I took it over when I was young and made it into the success it is today. There's a certain sense of pride of ownership that comes with that."

She nodded. "I'd heard you took over the company from your grandfather."

"Indeed. I was looking for something to do after college."

"Did you bum around Europe?" she asked. She couldn't see that. Steven didn't seem like the type of man who would be able to just drift.

"No. I spent a few years mining in Staffordshire learning about Raleighvale. When Grandfather wanted to retire, I jumped at the challenge it represented."

She thought about that. About what it said about Steven that he was the kind of man who could take a few years to do mining. That was tough work. Not the kind of job she would have expected Malcolm Devonshire's son to do.

"What did Malcolm say about that?" she asked.

"I have no idea. I didn't ask him."

She nodded. Her father hadn't wanted her to move to New York when she'd taken her first magazine job, and when she'd moved to London, he'd been upset as well. But her parents never hesitated to say what was on their mind. In the end they'd understood that she needed her career. Her mother was always asking if a man had broken her heart and Ainsley always changed the subject. Because

Steven had broken her heart, but not in a romantic way. He'd done it on a much bigger scale and it had completely changed the woman she had been.

They were small-town folks—mail carriers. Well, her mum now worked mostly at the counter in the local post office. A small branch where she knew just about everyone's name who came in there.

"I guess that's a good thing," she said.

He signaled the waiter and asked for the check. She took her platinum card from her wallet, intending to split the check, but he gave her a look that made her pull it back.

"This isn't a date," she said.

"Who said?"

Steven found that behind the slim-fitting clothes and the underlying sexuality of her Betty Page look, Ainsley was a very interesting woman. He wanted to know more about her. He wanted to spend all night talking to her and listening to the way she spoke. He liked her insights and the way she looked at him. For once, he felt as if he were a hollow shell of a man. A man who had only one dimension: business.

But with Ainsley...well, she made him wonder if he had been wrong to keep such a distance between himself and others.

Or maybe this was just the first blush of attraction—that potent combination of lust and intrigue. She was a mystery to him. A woman unlike others he'd met and seduced.

In her there was a sort of innocence—she seemed to be unaware of her appeal to the opposite sex. Men stared at her as she preceded him out of the restaurant, but she ignored their looks. He glared at one man who stared too long and then put his hand on the small of her back.

She was with him. He was glad that he'd thought to bargain for her magazine to do the articles on him and Henry and Geoff because he wanted to have a reason to keep in touch with her.

He was going to ask her out again—that was a given. He needed to have her in his bed. He wanted to see if her mysteries would be solved by making love. He'd found in the past that the appeal of a lot of the women he'd dated vanished after he'd bedded them.

That wouldn't be the same with Ainsley. And yet a part of him believed that it would be. That she'd be like every other relationship in his life. He was used to expecting nothing from them.

"Why are you helping me walk out of the restaurant?" she asked.

"So every man in the place knows that you are with me."

"Am I with you, Steven?"

"Yes, you are."

"Just for tonight?"

"No. I want to have you by my side again. I have to go to a reception for my mother next Tuesday evening at Oxford. Would you like to accompany me?"

They stepped out into the March evening. It was damp and chilly and Ainsley shivered. If they had a different kind of relationship, he would have wrapped his arm around her. But then, he thought, to hell with that. He put his arm over her shoulder and drew her against the curve of his body.

She shuddered and looked up at him.

He read the same desire in her expression that he'd been battling all night. Her deep violet eyes revealed that she was thinking of him as a man—not an interviewee—and he knew that he'd do anything to keep that interest alive.

With the gentle pressure of his arm on her shoulder, he steered her down the street to where he'd parked his car. When they got to his car, she stopped and turned, trapped between his body and his vehicle.

"What do you want from me?" she asked. Her voice was soft and low. There was none of the confident executive that he'd first met in the Everest Mega Store this afternoon. Instead, there was a woman who showed him a hint of vulnerability. And that touched him.

He brushed the softer emotions aside—he didn't like them. He touched the rounded apples of her cheeks, ran his finger over that arch down toward her ear. "Right now I want a kiss."

"Just one?" she asked. She licked her lips, a slow sensual movement of her tongue that made him groan inside. Her tongue was delicate and pink and he wanted to feel it on his skin. He wanted her to taste him the same way. And he needed to taste her in return.

With those full lips and her sexy smile… What would she taste like?

"To start," he said.

He traced the line of her neck with his fingertip and along the hairline of her high ponytail where her hair met her skin. She shivered a little and licked her lips again. Then she leaned toward him, not close enough that their bodies brushed, but closer.

He kept his light touch on her face. Just taking his time. All the best things in life took time. He'd never gone for instant gratification, but this time he was tempted to. He made himself wait, though. Patience always paid off.

He traced the vee at the top of her blouse. Her breasts were large, full and he didn't come close to touching them, but he wanted to. Instead, he contented himself with the soft tender skin of her chest, that area exposed by her blouse.

Then he leaned toward her and she tipped her head back and went up on her toes. He looked down into her upturned face. Her eyes were half closed and he had that momentary surge of lust that always assailed him when he was close to tasting a new woman.

She put her hands on his shoulders as he hesitated, drawing out the moment, and lifted herself even higher so that he felt the brush of her warm breath against his mouth. But he pulled back.

He would decide when they had their first kiss. He would set the tone and the timbre of the embrace. And he wanted to make sure that Ainsley knew he was in charge.

Starting where he'd first touched her with his finger, he followed the same path with his lips, caressing his way with nibbling kisses to her ear.

He blew gently into her ear. "Do you want me?"

"Yes…"

"Good."

Four

There was nothing she could do but Steven's bidding. She'd lost all sense of place and self as he touched her face. She knew that she'd do whatever he asked her to as long as he kept touching her. If only he'd kiss her. She wanted to feel that firm hard mouth against her own.

But he kept teasing her. When he bit her ear, she gasped his name and felt a bolt of pure desire go through her. Her breasts felt fuller, her blood raced through her veins and between her legs she felt moisture as her body readied itself for him.

Which was ridiculous—she wasn't about to sleep with Steven Devonshire. Or was she? She might, she thought. Immediately, her mind focused on the potential conflict of interest created by the article. The writer would simply mention that she and Steven…what? Slept together? She knew that would hurt the journalistic integrity of the piece, but the article was really more focused on the mothers.

Before she could ruminate on it any more, she felt his mouth on her neck. He ran a line of kisses down the length of her neck and then at the base she felt the warmth of his tongue. She shuddered again.

When she'd lost weight, she'd had a reawakening of herself as a woman, but the attention of men had been too much. Now she realized it was the wrong men who had been paying attention to her. Because in Steven's embrace she felt that she was where she was meant to be.

He whispered hot, dark words against her skin, which just served to inflame her. She reached for his shoulders, tried to draw him closer to her, but he pulled back.

"Do not touch me until I tell you to," he said.

"Why not?"

"Because I said so," he said.

She dropped her hands to her sides, but had no idea what to do with them. Letting him touch her while she couldn't touch him was exciting. She felt like this moment was all about her pleasure and all he'd done was kiss her. The wind blew down the street chilly and damp, and she realized they were standing on the side of the road.

Until that instant all she'd been focused on was his kiss. A kiss she still hadn't tasted.

"Let's get inside the car," she said.

"Not until I get my kiss," Steven said.

She started to argue but then felt his mouth against her collarbone. He'd brushed the fabric of her shirt out of his way, as he tasted her with short kisses. His mouth was warm and started a fire that raged all the way to her core.

She had the uncomfortable feeling that she might not

be able to deny him anything. His moved his mouth up the other side of her blouse and then at the base of her neck he suckled her. She shivered and moaned as an ache started at her center.

She couldn't believe that he'd turned her into a mass of needing and wanting and she didn't care. She wanted more of him. She reached up to touch him, but he lifted one eyebrow at her and she knew that if she touched him he'd stop. She moaned and put her hands back down beside her hips.

He smiled at her. "Good girl. You get a reward for that."

She smiled back at him. "Do I get to choose it?"

He shook his head and brought his mouth down on hers. His kiss was as intense as she'd expected it to be. His mouth was hard on hers and demanded everything she had to give.

His hands circled her waist and drew her against his body. She felt the hard wall of his chest against her breasts and the hot pressure of his tongue as it penetrated her mouth. She shifted in his arms, trying to get closer to him, but she could only touch him where he let her.

Her powerlessness—to her own passion and to Steven's control—was the headiest feeling she'd ever had. His mouth was delicious. His taste was addicting. She wanted so much more than this.

Everything in her called for her to be with him. She caught his lower lip in between her teeth as he drew his mouth back from hers. He moaned and then changed the embrace so that her lips were caught between his teeth. He sucked her lower lip deeper into his mouth.

One of his big hands moved up her back to the center,

right between her shoulder blades, and he held her with just that one hand and his mouth on hers.

She was completely his prisoner. Nothing mattered to her except that this moment didn't end. That his mouth stayed on hers.

And that frightened her. This embrace scared her. She was successful because she didn't let men or relationships of any kind interfere with her job. And that had always been easy for her, because no man she'd met had threatened that resolve.

Part of it she imagined was simply because no other man had felt right—the way that Steven did. He'd been the one to change her with that one overheard comment. And she'd realized that even though her parents had always told her they loved her and she was beautiful the way she was, that men saw that differently. That a chubby woman was almost invisible to most men—or rather to men like Steven.

She had to be careful, because the way she felt right now, she knew she could easily lose herself to him. In him. And the really scary part was that she wouldn't mind. She drew back from him and he slowly released her mouth.

She put her fingers over her lower lip, which was still tingling. She wasn't herself. This was surreal.

"That was…"

"Incredible?"

She shook her head. There was a lightness to his tone that she wanted to embrace but she sensed the steel underneath. "Intense."

"Surely a woman like you has been well-kissed before."

She started to shake her head but she didn't want Steven to remember the chubby girl no man had been interested in.

That was part of her past, she thought. His kiss had made her vulnerable enough. She didn't want to show him that kind of emotional vulnerability.

"Nothing like that," she said at last. She couldn't lie to him about that. She wasn't a very sophisticated woman when it came to bedroom matters. She might be able to hold her own with temperamental photographers and celebrities, but with this man she couldn't. And she wasn't going to pretend that this was an everyday occurrence, even if that would have been better for her.

Ainsley sat quietly next to him as he drove through the city to her home. She lived in the posh neighborhood of Notting Hill. "What made you choose this area to live?"

She flushed and looked over at him. "The movie with Julia Roberts and Hugh Grant. They made it look charming and quaint."

"Is that how you decided to become a magazine editor? You saw someone in a movie doing it?"

She shrugged. "There are worse ways to find a job. What about you?"

"Not so fast. You didn't tell me why you chose your profession."

"You can park there on the street." She pointed to a space halfway down the block.

He pulled into the spot and turned the car off, but he made no move to get out and neither did she. "Which movie was it?"

"*His Girl Friday*. Have you ever seen it?"

He hadn't. He wasn't much of a film buff. He'd spent his life out doing things. Trying to prove he was better than his ancestry, and most days he was sure he succeeded.

"No. What's it about?"

"A newspaper editor—Cary Grant and his ex-wife and star reporter Rosalind Russell…it's just great. They made working at a newspaper look like so much fun. I knew I wanted to be a reporter."

"But you're not," he pointed out.

"Once I graduated I found a different path. But I would never have thought of writing for a living if not for that movie."

She sparkled with passion when she talked about writing and he wondered why she'd given it up. He knew she'd said that the new job better suited her but he still couldn't believe she'd give up her passion for money.

"How old were you when you made the decision to be a writer?"

"Twelve," she said. "What about you? Did you decide early on that you wanted to rule the world?"

He laughed out loud at her wry question. "Pretty much from the womb I knew I wanted it all."

"Do you think you've gotten it?" she asked.

He tipped his head to the side to study her. She asked questions that no one else ever had—except that one reporter. The frumpy, clumsy woman had little in common with Ainsley except for her eyes and her probing questions. He remembered the woman's eyes…so similar to Ainsley's.

"Not yet, but I'm close," he said.

He tried to recall other details of the woman but he couldn't see anything but those wide violet eyes. He took his keys from the ignition and got out of the car to come around and open her door.

One thing his mother had been a stickler about was manners in a man. She said that women liked to be treated with respect and that they always deserved it.

He'd often wondered if Malcolm's betrayal with his other mistresses had wounded his mum deeply. She'd buried herself in her lab and in her research after his birth. Steven could think of no greater disrespect than finding out the man you were having an affair with was seeing two other women at the same time.

He opened her door and offered his hand. She took it, her fingers small and delicate in his bigger grasp. She turned in her seat, stretching her legs out the door first. They were slim and yet curvy, one of the first things he'd noticed about her. Once she had one foot on the sidewalk, she stepped out and stood next to him. He wanted her again. Wanted to kiss her once more, but he knew better than to move too quickly.

He wanted to savor every moment with her. To make this quasi-emotion he felt—one he knew was lust—last a little while longer before he went back to the dull, gray world he usually inhabited. The world where he just worked and concentrated on proving he was the best.

"I'll see you to your door," he said.

"That's not necessary," she said. "I think I can find it."

"I insist."

He put his hand on the small of her back again and nudged her toward her door. She tossed that high ponytail of hers as she looked back over her shoulder at him. "You don't take no for an answer, do you?"

"Not unless I have to. Men who back down usually end up losing."

"I don't like to lose, either," she said.

"If you want what I want, then we'll both win."

"Somehow I'm not sure I'll know if I really want it or if your will has made me think I do," she said.

Her words had been carefully chosen. She was trying to tell him that he overwhelmed her, or at least that was what he suspected.

"I'm not going to ask for anything you're not ready for," he said.

She studied him for a moment and he hoped she found whatever it was she was searching for. Hoped she didn't see that emptiness he always tried to mask. That spot inside him where he suspected other people had their hearts but he just had a driving impulse to succeed.

"Would you like to come in for a drink?" she asked.

"I'd love to," he walked behind her to her front door, keeping his hand on the small of her back the entire time.

Her waist was small and pronounced, her hips larger but not too big. He brought his other hand to her waist because he wanted to see what his hands looked like on her body. He really wanted to hold her like this when she was naked. To see the full curves of her bare derrière.

"What are you doing?"

"Imagining you naked," he said.

She blushed and dropped her keys. She bent to pick them up and he moaned as the fabric of her skirt was pulled taut against her buttocks. He let his hands slide down her curves, skimming along the outside of her hips until he almost reached the hem of the skirt.

She stood up, put her key in the lock and opened the door. "Don't do that."

"Why not?"

"Because we still have a business arrangement. A deal for me to publish feature articles about your family—we shouldn't have a personal relationship on top of that."

"We aren't working together, Ainsley," he said, stepping

over her threshold and forcing her to take a step back. He closed the door behind them and leaned forward to cage her against the wall.

"What we have is so much more than a business arrangement," he said.

"Really?" she asked. "Because it seems to me that you're the type of man who'll only say that until you've been in my bed."

Ainsley was seduced by everything about Steven. He was a charming dinner companion and he knew how to pay attention to a woman. He leaned in when she spoke, listened to her answers and then asked her questions that invited her to talk more deeply. It was something that no other man had done when she'd been out with him.

But this feeling was similar to ones he'd evoked in her before. And after those short few hours spent together talking, he'd left and ruined her life.

With this new body she knew that men found her attractive. It was silly to say but she still felt like the chubby girl who sat in the back of the classroom alone. She doubted that was going to change anytime soon.

Having Steven's attention wasn't going to make it easier. Yet she wanted him. She wanted to be the kind of sophisticated woman who could take him to her bed and have no regrets if he walked away in the morning.

But she wasn't. He was so close to her that she could feel his body heat. His hands were on either side of the wall next to her head. He surrounded her.

She glanced up at him, trying once again to see something in his eyes that would tell her what kind of man he was. All night long she'd asked probing questions—used her best reporter's techniques from the old days—and she'd gotten nothing from him.

A few answers to a few questions, but nothing that she could hang her hat on.

"What is going on in that head of yours?" he asked. His tone so very British that she wanted to melt. She loved the accent, so different from her soft Southern twang.

"I'm trying to gauge the measure of the man before me."

Steven didn't move, but she felt as if he'd stepped closer to her. His left hand shifted slightly on the wall and he stroked her cheekbone with his thumb.

His touch was electric. She'd realized that earlier when he'd kissed her by his car. She was powerless against it. No man had ever touched her like that before. No man had ever made her feel…sexy.

She realized then that there was no way she would turn him away. He was the first man to look at her since she'd lost all her weight and made her feel like she was a woman.

"Have I come up lacking?" he asked.

"No, Steven, you haven't," she said.

"I like the sound of my name on your lips," he said.

"Really? Why?"

His thumb moved lower on her face caressing her lower lip as he stared down at her. She was glad she'd left the light on in the living room because it cast a soft glow in the foyer.

"Your voice softens when you use my name. Otherwise, you're all business," he said.

In the quiet of her foyer she felt safe admitting the truth to him. "My job is my life."

He arched one eyebrow at her. "The same has been said of me."

"And is it true?"

He shrugged. "Many believe it is. But I have other interests."

"Like what?" she asked, hoping to learn something that she hadn't read online or in a magazine. Steven Devonshire raised privacy to an altogether new level.

"Skydiving."

That took her completely by surprise. Skydiving was a risky venture, despite the safety measures taken by everyone who participated in the sport. By the same token, she could see the appeal in the sport for Steven. He thrived on risk and excitement.

No one else would have taken on the challenge of Raleighvale China the way he had, she mused. But that was part of his personality. Ainsley knew he liked the challenge of knowing everyone expected him to fail and then shocking the hell out of them. She had first picked up on that when she'd interviewed him years ago.

"What about you, Ms. Editor-in-Chief? What do you do for fun?"

"Read," she said.

"Reading? That's not doing something, Ainsley," he said.

She shook her head. "You're wrong. I've lived adventures you've never dreamed of through the pages of my books. I've been places that I wouldn't be brave enough to travel to."

"Where?" he asked, still stroking his thumb over her face.

"Somalia. I read a book by a man who'd grown up there

and dealt with the violence and danger to the people still living there."

"I'd have to agree that Somalia is dangerous. Any other place you're interested in going to? Any place you haven't been?"

She shrugged. "Well…I haven't been to Ibiza but have a trip planned there for this summer. I did go to Madrid last summer."

He laughed. "Everyone goes there to vacation. That hardly sounds daring."

"I went to see a bullfight," she said.

"What did you like about it?"

"The pageantry, the excitement. We did a cover story about six months ago…actually it will be on the stands this month. It was about two brothers who were matadors—fifth-generation matadors. These men are rock stars in Spain.

"Does that sound ridiculous?" she asked.

"Not at all. It makes you sound like a very interesting woman. A woman whom I'm very glad to have gotten to know a little better tonight. How long have you been in the UK?" he asked.

"Almost three years," she said.

"Why did you come here?" he asked.

She struggled now. Outright lying to him might come back to bite her later, but that previous encounter had scared her and shaped her into the woman she was today and she couldn't regret that.

"For my job."

"That's pretty daring," he said. "Leaving behind your home and your family to come to another country."

The way he said it made her feel special. As if she were unique to him. And looking into his dark eyes she felt like he was seeing her. Not just her body or her position at the magazine. The fact that Steven liked her for herself—that seduced her more than anything else.

Five

Steven leaned forward and kissed her. It was a soft kiss that felt like it went on for days. He didn't touch her anywhere but where their mouths met. She felt as if they had all the time in the world, that there were only the two of them and this moment, which would never end.

She kept her eyes open at first because she wanted to see him. His eyes were closed and she felt the intensity in him. But this time it was focused all on her. She closed her own eyes because she didn't want to see his vulnerability. But even as she did so, she couldn't help but feel her heart melt a little. No matter how intense or driven Steven seemed, he still had some vulnerabilities.

Soon she didn't think about anything but the kiss. The way his mouth felt against hers. The taste of him, which was just right. She wanted to experience everything she could of Steven. She wanted to know so much more than the taste of his mouth on hers. She wanted to feel his hands around her waist again. To have him pull her closer.

He lifted his head up and she took a moment to compose herself before she opened her eyes. She didn't want to be any more vulnerable to him than she already was and she certainly didn't want him to glimpse her vulnerability.

She rested her head against the wall and opened her eyes. He was staring down at her, those hawklike eyes assessing her.

"What are you thinking?" she asked.

"That no other woman has ever tasted as good as you," he said.

She felt overwhelmed by this comment. They were traveling the same path in so many ways. This man— Steven Devonshire—could be more to her than a date… "I was thinking the same thing."

"That I kiss like a woman?" he asked.

She laughed and the intensity of the moment was broken. She knew it was for the best because it showed her exactly where Steven was in his thinking. And it kept her from thinking that this was more than it was.

They'd had dinner and now he was trying to score. At the end of the day she had to remember that this was Steven Devonshire, the man who'd left her in ruins. He was more dangerous to her than a seven-layer chocolate cake, because she could exercise off the effects of a choco-binge but she couldn't fix her battered emotions nearly as easily.

"Still want that drink?" she asked, not sure she wanted him to stay.

He shook his head. "I think I should be going."

She did, too. She ducked out from under his arms. She opened her front door, leaning back against it. The chill of the night air swept into her warm little house.

She shivered as she waited for Steven to leave. He turned and crossed the threshold. His car was parked at the curb, in front of her very old and very temperamental MG. But she loved that car despite its problems.

"Will you have dinner with me again?" he asked.

"Yes," she said. "But I'm flying to New York tomorrow for a meeting with the team for our American magazine."

"How long will you be gone?"

"Four days," she said. "But I won't be able to function until six days. Jet lag slows me down."

"Then we'll have dinner six days from now…that's next Monday. I'll pick you up here at home."

Ainsley realized that Steven was used to giving orders. "Do people always do what you say?"

"Most times," he admitted.

"You can pick me up at my office. I'm not going to be home in time for a dinner date."

"Very well. My assistant will call your office tomorrow to get all your contact information—e-mail address and so on. That way I can be in touch with you when you're in the States."

"What would you need to talk to me about?"

"The story, of course," he said.

"I have assigned a writer to the story and my boss wants the U.S. magazine to run the article as well. So we might actually have two writers working on this."

"Sounds good to me," he said.

She stood there until he got in his car and drove away. She stepped inside and closed the door, fastened the lock and leaned back against the door.

Steven Devonshire had kissed her.

She shouldn't put too much emphasis on it. It was

nothing more than a kiss from a man. A man she found interesting…oh, heck, who was she kidding? Steven had been the man that she'd been obsessed with for five long years.

After his comment and the massively embarrassing debacle at the *Business Journal,* she'd had no choice but to start over—and she had. Now she was focused on work and on herself. And her little habit of following Steven—almost cyber stalking him—had to stop. She'd kept tabs on him, hoping that someday their paths would cross again and she'd come out the victor. But tonight had shown her that she still had weaknesses as far as he was concerned.

No matter how much she'd read about him, she was just starting to realize that she didn't know everything about the man. The stuff she'd read barely scratched the surface of him. Words like *intense* conjured an image of a certain kind of man and Steven was so much more in real life.

And he'd kissed her.

"Stop building dreams," she warned herself. She walked through her house, kicking off her heels as she went along. Her mother hated that habit, but Ainsley always left a trail of shoes near her front door.

In her tiny kitchen, she opened her liquor cabinet, poured herself a splash of cognac and drank it. This was nothing.

She had her career and it was on track. She wasn't about to let Steven derail her. It would be so easy to just give in to her own desires and start thinking in terms of a real relationship with him, but she couldn't forget that behind that charming facade he was a pit bull.

Later on as she lay in her own bed staring at the ceiling, sleep eluded her. Instead, all she could think about was that she should have taken his hand and led him back to her bed. She should never have let him walk out her front door. Because she knew tomorrow she was going to start doubting that a man as handsome and sexy as Steven Devonshire could really want a girl like her.

Two days later Steven found himself in an odd predicament. He was in the middle of a meeting with the Everest Mega Store team at the Leicester Square location when he caught a glimpse of a woman on the retail floor who looked like Ainsley. He knew Ainsley was in New York and it couldn't be her, but he watched the woman for a minute just to make sure it wasn't her.

She was an obsession for him. He should have bedded her the first night they were together. Instead, he had waited because he wanted to unravel her secrets. Now he was thinking, secrets be damned. He wanted her out of his mind so he could get back to normal.

He wasn't the type of man to spend too much time thinking about a woman—any woman. But with Ainsley on his mind all the time he was starting to believe that something dangerous was happening to him.

"Mr. Devonshire?"

His secretary stood in the doorway. The woman was proving to be a good fit here.

"There is a woman downstairs asking for you," Marta said.

Was it Ainsley? He would be very surprised if it was. But if this attraction he felt was two-way, maybe she had come back early.

"Did she give a name?"

"Dinah…I can't recall her last name, sir."

Dinah. That was what came of letting a woman

preoccupy his mind. "I'll be downstairs and then back at the office. Can you finish up here, Marta?"

"Yes, sir."

"Take your lunch and then be back by two."

He walked out of the office. Dinah, his executive vice president, waited in the middle of the retail floor where a display of classic 1970s musicians was displayed. There was a full-sized cardboard cutout of Tiffany Malone—Henry's mother.

An earthy sexuality suffused her stare. Her hair was tousled and she wore a pair of skintight, faded denim jeans and a flowing top. It was a classic seventies photo, but Henry's mother made it so much more. She looked iconic standing there.

He wondered how Malcolm could have been attracted to his mother after being with someone so overtly sexual. His mum exuded none of that. She was smart and classically beautiful, but compared to Tiffany Malone…she would definitely come in second.

"Thanks for getting here so quickly," he said to Dinah.

"Not a problem. You promised me a nice bonus, so I wanted to jump in and get started on this project of yours," she said.

"Just the attitude I like. Let's discuss the details back at my office."

"Okay, but why did you have me meet you here?" she asked.

"I want you to take a look around. This is our best-performing store. What are they doing here that is different?"

"You want me to go to all the stores?"

"Not all of them, but most of them. I want to know

if it's the location or if it's the product. Should we have something different in each location? I mean in addition to the music."

"Very well," Dinah said. They walked the store. He and Dinah made notes on what they saw and then they went back to the office to discuss their findings.

Steven stayed late at the office and worked. It hadn't taken him too long to realize he could easily beat both of his half brothers in this competition. He'd had the financials from the record label and the airline sent to his office. Dinah had e-mailed her recommendations for the North American operation based on the data they had.

Someone should go to New York, he thought. They needed to see the operation there to make sure that their recommendations could be implemented.

He picked up the phone and dialed Dinah's number.

"Yes, boss?"

"How do you feel about a trip to New York?"

"Like you are a mind reader. I was composing an e-mail to that effect when you called. I'd like to take Harry from finance with me."

They discussed the details of her trip and he thought of Ainsley in Manhattan. Steven was pleased with Dinah's plan of action. She'd check in daily, but he didn't like to micromanage unless things were going poorly. He hired the best people so he didn't have to do their jobs for him.

It was midnight when he was ready to leave the office. And he took a moment to log in to his personal e-mail account. He wanted Ainsley. And he wanted her to be thinking of him.

He wanted to disturb her workday the way she had his. Because although he'd been focused on work, she'd been like a shadow in his mind making him wonder what her day was like. It was five in the morning in Manhattan and he wanted her first thought to be of him and their date.

He composed an e-mail to her. Taking his time with his words because he wanted every moment between now and the time they were face-to-face again to be a slow seduction.

I can't stop thinking about you. The feel of your lips under mine and the scent of your perfume lingers in the air around me. Be safe in New York.
Steven

He could have written more, but he preferred to be subtle. He'd learned early in life that small gestures often had a deeper impact that big, flashy ones.

He hit Send and left the office. The streets in the financial district weren't busy and he made his way easily though the traffic, which was a good thing because he found himself thinking of Ainsley next to him in his car.

The scent of her perfume hung in the air; it was almost as if she were there. He shook his head, hoping to dislodge the thoughts of her and find his peace again.

Once he got home and undressed, he lay naked in his king-size bed and groaned. He remembered the feel of her curvy body against his and the taste of her mouth under his.

Ainsley had a hard time adjusting to the time change. She'd gone to bed at six p.m. yesterday and gotten up at five. She had a lot of meetings to attend and would be getting as much work done as possible.

Freddie had accompanied her, since he was her right-hand man. They had always worked together as a team, and even though she was the boss that relationship—the closeness of it—had remained.

He kept odd hours, though, and she doubted he'd be awake now. So she called room service and ordered a pot of coffee and fiber cereal and fruit for breakfast. She wanted to order the New York cheesecake with strawberry sauce and in the old days she would have, but she forced out the word *muesli* and hung up before she could give in and order something fattening.

It was silly, but she was constantly battling with food. She had talked to her leader about it when she'd been on Weight Watchers full time and Marianne had suggested that she used food to cope with life.

Ainsley knew that was true. She'd been overweight most of her life and then at college, when she'd been on her own, she'd found comfort in doughnuts and carbs. Before she knew it, she was obese. That had helped with her studies. Had made it so much easier to focus on her education because most men weren't in the least bit interested in her.

It had been almost three months since she'd been tempted by a sweet like the cheesecake. And she knew that it was because of Steven.

He was making her feel unsure of herself, and she had always combated those feelings with food. It didn't help matters that she knew if she were fat he probably wouldn't have even noticed her. Ugh, this was making her crazy—*he* was making her crazy.

When she closed her eyes, she could still see his face as he'd kissed her. And she wanted to be a girl worthy of his attention. She wanted him not to be disappointed in her. But she was afraid that wouldn't be the case.

She had lost all her weight by dieting, not by exercising. So even though she was slim now, she still had parts that weren't as fit and toned as those of someone who hit the gym every day, twice a day.

What if he saw her naked and changed his mind about her? What if…

She'd never been this wishy-washy. Any other man she would just walk away from. But this was Steven. The man she'd always wanted.

She wasn't going to let her doubts feed her food obsession. She wasn't going to let her doubts overwhelm her or let her miss the opportunity to be with him. She wasn't going to let her doubts control her. If she'd done that, she'd still be sitting in her apartment in Chicago having never left school.

She opened her e-mail to find the very first one was from Steven. She read it and felt herself flush. She needed to be much more confident if she was going to be with him. But she had no idea how to do that. She couldn't change the fears she'd always had of her body that easily.

She walked away from her computer and stood in front of the mirror. She stared at her features. Her face was so different now that she scarcely recognized herself sometimes: her cheekbones thin and prominent, her mouth still full and pouty. The biggest change had been her figure.

No it wasn't, she reminded herself. The biggest change had come at work. She remembered when she'd been called to Maurice Sheffield's office. The owner of the Sheffield Group had taken thirty minutes out of his day to congratulate her on running the *British Fashion Quarterly* and bringing up revenue at the magazine. No one got thirty minutes with Maurice, her boss and the publisher and CEO of the consortium.

She looked at the slim woman in the reflection and wondered where she'd come from and prayed in the same breath that she'd never leave. In her heart she knew that her weight had nothing to do with her success. She'd changed on the inside and she just wished she'd stop seeing the old Ainsley when she looked in the mirror.

She shook her head. She needed to believe in herself as a person the way she believed in herself as a professional. She was capable of winning Steven's affection...was that what she wanted?

Her assistant, Cathy, had sent a note to Tiffany Malone, Lynn Grandings and Princess Louisa to see if they'd consider being interviewed. Maurice loved the idea of a retrospective fashion piece on these women, and Ainsley wasn't about to disappoint her boss.

Freddie had suggested letting Danielle do the interviews, but Ainsley wasn't about to risk giving it to someone she had placed on probation. Instead, she had assigned the story to Bert Michaels. He'd interviewed Prince Harry last year for a Mother's Day piece they'd run about how mothers influence fashion—his mother had set a standard many other women were still trying to live up to.

And she had an appointment with Malcolm's attorney to talk about interviewing him. Malcolm Devonshire was one of the most famous personalities of their time. He was legendary not just for his affairs but also for his zest for life. As much as he lived big, he'd been very private about his personal life. Only the tabloids had ever run stories about him.

If she got an interview with him in her magazine she'd

have landed a real coup. Something that her bosses wouldn't overlook. And it wasn't lost on Ainsley that meeting Steven that day in the Everest Mega Store had been fortuitous.

She showered and dressed, keeping her mind firmly on her meetings for the day, but before she left her hotel she knew she wanted to return Steven's e-mail. She just had no idea what to say to him.

Somehow *Me, too* didn't seem like the right response. Yet more than that might be making promises that she wasn't sure she could keep. When she was with Steven, it was easy to forget herself. Forget her fears and the fact that she wasn't who he thought she was.

But apart from him she could count the obstacles between them. She had too little experience and he had too much. She was a small-town girl and he was the son of a billionaire and a world-renowned scientist.

But none of that mattered when they were together. Nothing mattered except the way his hands felt on her. The way his taste lingered on her lips after he'd kissed her. The way the scent of his cologne lingered after he left.

He was just so much more than she thought he would be. And there were still so many questions she had about him. So many answers that she wasn't sure she'd ever get.

Yet she wasn't going to give up. When she'd decided to change her life and lose weight, she'd made a promise to herself to stop hiding. And she had done a good job of it until now.

Steven was the kind of man she should be going after. But first she had to figure out what to say.

She hit the Reply key on the e-mail and sat down at the chair, trying to be more comfortable.

Dear Steven

No, that sounded too businesslike.

You've haunted my dreams.

She hit Send before she could change her mind.

Six

Steven decided at the last minute to go to New York himself instead of sending Dinah and he was glad that he had. The Everest Mega Store in Times Square was a major asset, and as he walked the floor with the VP of the North American unit, Hobbs Colby, he realized that Hobbs had some great ideas on ways to capitalize on the store's potential.

"Let's go back to the office and figure out how to make the most of this store," Steven said.

Steven followed Hobbs into the conference room on the third floor. There was a radio broadcast studio built right into the store so they could do live broadcasts and this conference room overlooked the selling floor.

"I think this property is an asset we aren't exploiting to its fullest. I want to set up live broadcasts from here for all Everest recording artists," Steven said. "Let's make this place into the go-to spot for live music promotions. I want release parties and signings."

"That won't be a problem on our end. Typically I've had trouble getting Everest Records to return my calls. I know I'm new, but I worked for a concert promoter for years so I have the experience to do those kinds of events."

"Let me make a few calls. Give me a minute—I'll call right now," Steven said.

Hobbs nodded and left, and Steven got Henry on the line. Though it was about ten at night in London, he knew that Henry would still be up.

"Devonshire," Henry said.

"It's Steven. I'm in New York and I wanted to go over something with you. Can you talk?"

"Certainly. I'm in a club. Give me a minute to find someplace quiet."

Steven held the line.

"Okay, what's up?"

"I'm not sure how familiar you are with our retail stores, but some of them were set up to do live remote broadcasts for radio. This store in Times Square has the facilities not only for that but for live performances as well. My U.S. VP, Hobbs Colby, has been trying to get some artists to come here and perform."

"I haven't had a chance to call him back yet. What are you thinking?" Henry asked.

"That we use this place for exclusive North American releases of our CDs. Maybe one week early? Not sure how you feel about that. Then we need to book the groups into this store. I think this will help both of our business units."

"I agree. Let me talk to the artists and I'll get back to you."

"Thanks, Henry."

Steven spent the rest of the afternoon in meetings and on the phone working on getting the ball rolling. "What other stores do we have with these kinds of facilities?"

"Miami, LA, Vancouver, Toronto, Chicago and Orlando. We can update other facilities if you think that it would be worth our while."

Steven shook his head. "Not yet. Let's do a pilot program at these locations first. I don't want to have the same groups everywhere. I think we should brand each of the locations with a genre. Build up a strong local following. I think New York and LA would be great for any group, but in Miami we should book our Latin groups."

Hobbs nodded. "That works for me. I'll get some ideas to you."

"I'm in New York for two more days. We'll talk more in the morning," Steven said.

Hobbs left and Steven checked the e-mail on his iPhone. That one from Ainsley early this morning was still at the top of his inbox. He'd made the decision to come and see her after reading that she was haunted by him the same way he'd been haunted by her.

He hadn't wanted to wait a week to see her again and he wasn't a man who hesitated when he wanted something. He knew that pursuing Ainsley was complicated. But he didn't let that stand in his way. He'd had to work for everything he had in his life.

His phone rang while he was debating how to contact Ainsley.

"Hello, Aunt Lucy."

"Hello, Steven, how are you today?"

"I'm good. What can I do for you?" he asked.

"Are you available for dinner tomorrow night? I'm coming to London."

"I'm sorry, but I'm out of town right now," he said.

She sighed. "I wish you'd make more time for your family."

"I see you once a month," he said.

He didn't like to think about his childhood. He'd grown up alone and his aunt Lucy had been too busy with her own career as a chef then to notice him—much as his mother had been. But when he'd been a teenager, Steven had gotten into some trouble with drinking and for some reason that had made Lucy notice him.

She'd tried to force a relationship between them, but it had been too little, too late. His character had already become firmly entrenched, and that character wasn't a family guy.

"That's right, you do. You know I'm here if you need me."

"I do. I've got to go now. I'm going into a meeting."

"Goodbye, Steven. I love you."

"Bye, Aunt Lucy." He never said the L-word. He wasn't even sure that emotion existed for him.

Hanging up the phone, he called his assistant and had her find out where Ainsley was staying. He wasn't just here for business, even though he knew he should be focusing his energies on the Everest Mega Stores, he was also very interested in Ainsley Patterson.

It had been a long, exhausting day and when Ainsley got to her hotel in the middle of Times Square she wanted nothing more than to head to bed. But as she walked through the lobby she heard someone call her name. Not just anyone—Steven Devonshire.

"What are you doing here?" she asked.

She didn't want to see Steven here. Here in Manhattan was where she'd had her horrible interview and her career had gone down in flames. She mentally shook herself. She'd started over and she needed to stop thinking of Steven as her own personal Waterloo. She needed to remember that he'd made her into the woman she was today. No, that wasn't right. *She'd* made herself into the woman she was today.

"Is that any way to greet the man who haunts your dreams?"

"I knew I'd regret writing that."

"Is it true?"

"I'm not a liar," she said.

"Good. I'm in town on business and I'm free this evening."

"Aren't you lucky. I am, too," she said. "Would you like to have drinks?"

Since he was here, she decided to take control of this relationship.

"I'd love that. I know a place close by, Blue Fin."

"I need to change and then we can go."

"You look lovely," he said.

She shook her head. "Thank you, but I need a few minutes."

"Not a problem. I'll meet you back here in thirty minutes."

"Okay."

Ainsley left him in the lobby and took the glass elevator up to her suite. She changed into a pair of tight-fitting jeans and a cami top she usually wore under her suit. She undid the ponytail she typically wore at work and fluffed her hair around her shoulders. Then she put on fresh makeup and went back downstairs.

Steven was waiting where she'd left him, but typing on his iPhone when she approached. She gave him some distance to finish in private.

"You look so incredible tonight," he said.

She nodded. His compliment made her uncomfortable.

He put his hand on the small of her back as they walked out of the lobby. The foot traffic was heavy on this early spring evening. Steven kept her close to him and made sure that no one bumped into her as they were walking. They didn't talk until they were seated at a high table in the bar, Bluetinis in each of their hands. "I love the Swedish fish in the bottom," Ainsley said.

"Women always do," Steven said.

That gave her pause. "Have you taken a lot of women here?"

"No. I just meant that women like sweet things. My mum is crazy for wine gums."

Ainsley arched an eyebrow at him. "They are pretty yummy."

"That was my point."

She shook her head. "Why didn't you mention you'd be in New York when I said I was coming here?"

"I wanted to surprise you."

"You did. You are not turning out to be what I expected."

"What did you expect?" he asked, taking a sip of his drink.

"Someone a little colder," she said.

"Why?"

"I'd just heard that you can be kind of callous in business."

"That's business."

"Are you different in your personal relationships?" she asked.

He looked distinctly uncomfortable and leaned toward her to answer. "I—"

"Ainsley! What are you doing out?" Freddie asked as he approached their table. "I thought you were calling it an early evening."

Damn, she wanted to know what Steven would have said in response to her query. "I ran into Steven and we decided to have a drink. Steven, this is Frederick VonHauser. He works for me at *Fashion Quarterly*. Freddie, this is Steven Devonshire."

Freddie gave her a surprised look. "Mind if I join you? I'm meeting some friends, but I'm a little early."

Ainsley started to say no, but Steven nodded and gestured to the chair. "Have a seat."

Freddie sat down between them and Ainsley instantly wished that her friend would leave. She didn't want Freddie and Steven to talk. Didn't want to risk Freddie saying something that would remind Steven of the woman she had been.

"How long are you in town?" Freddie asked.

"Just three days. I have recently taken over the Everest Mega Stores and I'm checking out our North American operation."

"So it's just coincidence that you are here when Ainsley is?"

"Indeed. A happy one," Steven said, looking straight at her.

She knew she shouldn't read too much into that, but she

also realized he'd come to New York to see her and that meant a lot to her.

"Sounds like it," Freddie said. "I see my friends, so I'll leave you two. Enjoy your evening."

"We will," Ainsley said.

"Sorry about that," Steven said after Freddie left. "You seemed a little uncomfortable."

"I just wasn't expecting to see anyone from work."

"Is that an issue?" he asked.

"It might be. I don't want to have the journalistic integrity of the article compromised because we're seeing each other. If we're going to see each other, I need to talk to my boss."

"With the focus of the articles on the mothers of the heirs, I would think that would take care of any conflict of interest," he said.

"Would it matter so much if we didn't see each other again?" she asked. She needed to know. She wasn't about to compromise her career for a man who was simply trying to score.

"Yes, it would. I wasn't playing games with you when I sent that e-mail. I can't stop thinking about you, Ainsley, and that's very dangerous for me because I'm used to being focused only on business."

"Me, too," she admitted.

"Good. We'll figure this out."

She nodded toward him. They finished their drinks and then Steven left for his dinner appointment. She went back to her hotel.

She knew she wanted to see Steven again, and if that was going to happen then she needed to clear it with her boss. She wasn't about to lose another job because of Steven Devonshire.

* * *

The next morning Ainsley woke up to a knock on her door. There was a delivery for her—a huge bouquet of flowers. She carried them to her sitting area and then checked the card. They were from Steven.

In his scrawling handwriting was a simple note that thanked her for the evening and told her he couldn't wait to see her again.

She held the card in her hand and sat down next to the flowers. She didn't want to fall for Steven, but when he did things like this it was hard not to.

All her life she'd been a misfit. She hadn't dated in high school because she'd been a chubby bookworm. And in college she'd just sort of muddled through. She'd had a boyfriend there, but Barry hadn't been the dream lover she'd longed for, and she'd ended up pouring herself into her classes and eventually her job: working and eating and pretending that her job was enough.

But when she'd lost it because of Steven, her awakening had changed her focus, but it hadn't changed her dreams for the future. She'd never pictured herself in a long-term relationship.

She'd always been happy on her own. Now, though, she was dreaming of Steven, wanting to wake up with him—and she didn't even know what that meant. She was scared to think that she was coming to need him. She didn't want to need a man like Steven Devonshire.

She put down the card and picked up her phone. If she were going to take a chance on dating Steven, on letting him be important to her, she had to make sure that Maurice wasn't going to fire her over this.

She dialed his direct line and he answered on the third ring.

"It's Ainsley."

"Good morning, Ainsley. Did you get our Devonshire story details locked up?"

"I'm still working on that, sir. But I did need to talk to you about something."

"Yes?"

"Steven Devonshire asked me out and I'd like to go out with him. I don't want it to affect our story. However, I thought since we are going to run the article in the U.S. and UK editions, it might not be a problem. The focus of the articles is on the mothers and Malcolm."

"Let me think about this, Ainsley. I don't want to stand in the way of your personal life. As far as I know, you rarely do anything but work."

"That's true, sir. This job is my life."

"I can understand that. But having a life is important, too. I think we'll add a note that you are dating Steven if it turns out that you are and since the focus is on fashion I think we'll be okay."

"Thanks, Maurice."

"You're welcome. Now get me all the people I need for this article so it can rock."

"I will."

She hung up and realized that she had no more excuses to keep Steven at bay. She wasn't going to lose her job over him and that was reassuring, but it also took away her safe out if things got too deep, too fast. One part of her was happy about that; the other was a bit worried.

She thought she was still in control of her life. But her heart argued that it would be making the decisions when it came to Steven.

Seven

"How was your date?" Freddie asked as he joined her in the cab at the end of their third day in New York.

"What date?"

"With Steven Devonshire. We haven't had a moment to chat and I want all the details. Was it everything you thought it would be? Did birds sing? The heavens open up?"

She punched him playfully in the arm. "You make me sound like…someone who is obsessed. It was just drinks. He's a very sophisticated and charming man."

"What makes him sophisticated?"

"His choices."

"Tell me everything."

She wanted to laugh at the way he said it, but she knew that she'd never share what she felt about Steven with Freddie. It was one thing to let him know about what she'd read on the Internet, but how Steven kissed was personal and she wasn't about to share it.

"It was just a nice evening."

"A nice evening? What are you hiding? Do you like him?"

She shook her head. "It's complicated."

She wanted the taxi ride to be over. But of course it was rush hour and they'd be stuck here for at least thirty minutes. *Damn.*

"Tell me."

"I can't. I haven't figured it out yet myself," she said.

He reached over and patted her knee. "I'm here if you want to talk."

"Thanks," she said. "Isn't it funny how foreign this city feels?"

He laughed. "Yes. I think we've been in London too long."

"It's only been three years. Do you ever think of coming back?" she asked him.

"Never. I like London. And my best friend lives there."

She smiled at him and blew him an air kiss. "We'd still be BFFs if you moved."

"You say that, but life would change. Besides, I have my Maxim now and he likes our quiet neighborhood."

Maxim was Freddie's English Bulldog. And she knew he'd never move if he thought that dog would be traumatized by it. He was so attached to him that he'd set up a webcam so he could chat with the dog once a day while he was on this trip.

She made small talk until traffic started moving. Her BlackBerry pinged and she glanced down at her e-mail—she didn't know how she'd live without her BlackBerry—and saw that Tiffany Malone had accepted the invitation to do an interview.

"Yes! Just what I was hoping for. Tiffany Malone said yes to the interview."

"She's one of my faves. Her music was so earthy. It's a shame she stopped performing."

Ainsley nodded and typed an e-mail back to her assistant to finalize the details for the interview. She would use the leverage of Tiffany's agreement to secure an interview with the other women. No one had ever printed their stories and it was past time that those women had a voice.

She sent a personal note to Tiffany, telling her that one of their writers—Bert Michaels—would be in touch with her soon. Once the article was written they'd compile pictures from the past and present to round out the piece.

The rest of the day was busy, but Maurice wanted her to lock in all three of the Devonshire heirs for the interview. Cathy had tried, but her secretary hadn't been able to get the men to return her calls, so Ainsley knew she'd have to do it herself. Geoff was difficult to reach, so she had to settle for leaving a voice mail.

She called Henry's office and got his assistant, Astrid, who put her right through.

"Hello, Henry. This is Ainsley Patterson with *Fashion Quarterly*. I spoke to Steven a few days ago and he intimated that you'd be agreeable to participating in an interview with our magazine."

"I can't say no. My mum would have my head. She told me you were going to interview her."

"We are. Once I have a confirmation from Geoff, my assistant will call you and set up the times and all that. I'd love to photograph you with your mother and maybe get one with all three of you boys and Malcolm."

"Good luck with that. I'm not sure that Malcolm's health will allow it."

"If it does, will you participate?"

"I'll think about it. Probably."

"Thank you, Henry."

"No problem. According to my mum, your magazine is one of the best. She had nothing but great things to say about it."

"Thanks," she said. She ended the call a few minutes later and then dialed Steven's number.

He answered it on the third ring. "Devonshire."

"It's Ainsley." She didn't want to mention last night or the fact that they were both in New York.

"What can I do for you?"

"I need you to talk to your mother about the interview. Tiffany Malone has already agreed. If we can get your mum as well it would be a more well-rounded interview."

"I was hoping you were calling to talk about our date."

"Nope."

"That's a very American answer."

"Is it? I can't talk about that right now. I'm in a conference room with other staff members."

"So you're not alone?"

"Exactly."

"If I talk dirty to you will you blush?" he asked, his voice deepening.

"Probably," she admitted.

"I will do my best to get my mum to agree, but someone is going to have to go to Berne to interview her. Her work is entering a critical stage and I know she won't leave."

"Should I go there and ask her?"

"It might help."

"Okay. I'll work that out. I guess that's all for now."

"I suppose that is. I can't wait to kiss you again," he said.

"Me, too," she said, preparing to disconnect before he could say anything else.

"Are you available for dinner tonight?" he asked.

"No. I think we'll have to wait until we're back in London," she said.

He agreed and hung up. She thought that she'd dodged a bullet. She was cool and confident when it came to business, but the personal aspect of her relationship with Steven scared her.

Steven left a message for his mother with Roman, his mother's lab partner and assistant, to alert her that Ainsley would be calling. Roman had been working with Lynn for the last fifteen years. Steven actually liked the man; he was funny.

"How are you, Steven? Your mum mentioned that you were running Malcolm's business now."

She would put it that way. Either she didn't listen to what he'd said or she simply assumed that he'd won the competition that Malcolm had set up for all his heirs.

"It's going well. I'm not running the show yet, but I've been here less than a week."

Roman laughed. "I'll give you one more week to get everything in order."

"That should just about do it. Will you let my mum know I need to speak to her?"

"Of course I will. She's spending most of her nights in the lab, so if you try after nine, you can probably reach her there."

"Thanks," Steven said. Thinking back he realized

that he'd always learned what his mother was doing from Roman. It had been that way his entire life.

"I'll call back later."

Steven had a lot of information to go through and he spent the rest of the day running numbers. He was happy when Geoff called and invited him to join him for dinner.

Steven often wondered if his life would have been different had he and Geoff met when they were boys. Steven had used Malcolm's name to gain entrance to Eton. The prestigious school the young princes had attended was extremely hard to get into. And Geoff's mother's family had been going there for generations. But at the last moment Geoff had been sent to a school in the States.

Steven had always believed it was because of the publicity that had surrounded the enrollment of two of the Devonshire bastards. That had been the first time that he had become aware of how many people were interested in the circumstances of his birth.

It had been a bit overwhelming—he'd almost asked his mother to withdraw him, but she'd been called to a meeting in Switzerland and he'd had no choice but to go to school as scheduled.

He shook his head. He had forgotten what it had been like to be that boy. He'd been scared and had felt out of place there. He wasn't a boy with the family background of the other boys who attended Eton. And he had quickly learned to fend for himself. He'd used his wits to survive and that had been his first lesson in how to succeed in this life.

Geoff was waiting at the club when he got there. It didn't surprise him. Geoff had struck him as someone who didn't like to keep others waiting.

"Thanks for agreeing to meet me."

"No problem. What's up?"

"I wanted to talk to you about the interviews that you agreed we'd do with *Fashion Quarterly*."

"Of course. What's the problem?"

"My mum doesn't really like publicity and the editor-in-chief has called her a couple of times. She has never talked about her affair with Malcolm and she moved on when she married my stepfather…she just doesn't want to discuss the past."

"I understand that. I have no idea if my mum will agree to the interviews or not. I do know that Tiffany Malone agreed to do it. So she will be sharing her perspective on what happened."

Geoff took a long swallow of his drink. "I don't know what to do. I think that having just Tiffany's story will be a bit odd. Will they still do the interview with us?"

Steven had no idea. He suspected that Ainsley would. She wanted to talk to them. "Probably. She wants to talk to Malcolm, too."

"I wish her success with that, but he wasn't much for agreeing to things when he was healthy. I can't see him doing it now."

Steven would have concurred, except he'd seen Ainsley in action and he was willing to bet that if she got in to see Malcolm, she'd find a way to convince him to do it. She'd find an angle that he wouldn't be able to say no to.

"I'm going to try to convince my mum to do the interview. I want to hear her side of the entire affair," Steven said.

Geoff shrugged. "My mum will be harder to convince, but I'll bet if she hears that Tiffany and Lynn are doing it she'll agree as well. Of course, she'll have to coordinate with the royal family's PR department."

"I hope so. Ainsley is really hot to do this interview and I've been working the business angle. I know she wants to talk about the past, but I want each of us to talk about the new things happening in each business unit."

"Henry and I are collaborating by painting the album covers of his new artists on the side of several of our planes."

"I love that idea," Steven said. "I think we'll produce some T-shirts picturing the album covers to sell in the store. And maybe we can run a promo the first week the CD comes out to bundle the shirts with the CD."

"Yes, that'll work. I'm sure Henry will agree to it," Geoff said.

They talked more about the business and it wasn't lost on Steven that the father he'd never known had given him brothers that he had a lot in common with. As a man who'd always been on his own, it was unnerving to realize that he finally had a family.

More than his mum and Aunt Lucy anyway. He wasn't sure he liked it. But he did know that Henry and Geoff were men he'd have hired to work for him. They were driven and innovative and together the three of them were going to take the Everest Group to heights that Malcolm had only dreamed of.

Ainsley's office overlooked the Basilica at St. Peter's Cathedral. She stood at the window as dusk fell over the city and thought about the coming evening. New York had been exhausting and she'd spent too much time in the offices there. She was glad to be back home.

She wasn't sure when it had happened, but at some point

in the last three years London had become home. She'd gotten used to the sights and sounds of this city and made it her own.

Her assistant, Cathy, stood in the doorway when Ainsley turned around. "I thought you'd left."

"Not yet. I had something that I wanted to talk to you about. Geoff Devonshire wants to meet with you before he will agree to be a part of the interviews."

Ainsley thought that Steven had already gotten the approval of his half brothers so this was news to her. "Fine. When is he available?"

"Um…he's actually in the reception area. He stopped by and wouldn't take no for an answer."

Cathy guarded her office like a shark, so to hear that Geoff had somehow gotten her to put him in the reception area surprised her.

"He's charming?"

"And so very handsome," she said. "Too handsome. But I also knew you wanted this locked up so I figured I'd let him stay."

"Good thinking. Hiring you was a very smart decision," Ainsley said.

"As I remind you daily," Cathy said, turning toward the door. "I'll go get him. Do you want me to interrupt after ten minutes?"

Ainsley rarely had time in her schedule to give anyone more than ten minutes, and from the beginning she and Cathy had an agreement that the assistant would come in and stop the meeting if it ran long.

She had dinner reservations with Steven tonight. Would there be time to collect herself before he arrived?

"Yes, please."

"Okay. I have put some things for your signature in your

box. If you want to be efficient and sign them now, I can process them while you're in your meeting."

"You're getting a little too bossy, Cath."

"That's the only way I keep you in line," she said, walking out the door with a smile.

Ainsley reached for the folder that Cathy had mentioned. Inside were some mock-ups for the cover of their current issue. She made notes on three of them. None of them were that exciting. She was going to have to address this first thing in the morning at their staff meeting. She made a note for Cathy to make sure that those responsible for the cover shoot were there.

Then she moved on to the photos Davis Montgomery had taken of Jon BonGiovanni. They were perfect. She approved three of them for use before she heard her door open.

She stood up to greet Geoff Devonshire. He looked tall and elegant and, aside from the set of his eyes and his jaw, he scarcely resembled Steven.

"Hello, Mr. Devonshire. May I call you Geoff?"

"Of course," he said, taking the hand she'd extended for him to shake.

"I'm Ainsley," she said. "Please have a seat. Can I offer you something to drink?"

"I'm good," he said.

"That's all for now, Cathy," Ainsley said to her assistant, handing her the file she'd made notes in.

She walked around her office and sat behind her desk. Sinking down in the big leather chair, she took a moment to make sure he realized that she was in a position of power. That was the only way she dealt with men, she thought. That was why Steven was throwing her. He didn't see just the woman and the job—he saw the woman behind it.

"What can I do for you?" she asked.

"My family is highly private and I agree with Steven that these interviews will be great for our new careers running the Everest Group. However, I have concerns about the questions that you may ask."

She understood that. Geoff was a double-whammy publicity draw. He was a minor member of the current royal family and he was a bastard son of one of the most controversial men in the UK.

"We can draft a list of topics that are off-limits and the writer will not ask about them. If he does, then you can simply decline to answer," she said.

"That's all well and good. But I'm also going to need to approve the final draft of the article."

"I'm not in the habit of doing that, Geoff. Our articles are about the people behind their celebrity."

"I realize that, but this is a deal-breaker for me. I'll give you enough personal information to make the article interesting."

Ainsley wasn't sure he would. But from her dealings with Steven she recognized that stubborn Devonshire will when she came up against it. "You drive a hard bargain."

He smiled at her and when he did he was a breathtakingly handsome man. "So I've been told. But you must understand, my mother is adamant that she will not talk about Malcolm or the circumstances of my birth."

She'd been afraid of that. She had found no recent mention of Princess Louisa in any of the Internet databases she'd searched. The woman was a recluse and had been since the birth of Geoff. Before that she'd been a party girl and the toast of London. "I'd really like to have her in the article. We will do everything to accommodate her and keep her out of the spotlight if that's your desire."

"Yes, it is. But more than that she doesn't want to be profiled in an article with the other mistresses of Malcolm. She had enough of that when I was born. She might agree to a sidebar featuring her. I realize your magazine will probably put the articles in the same issue, but she won't do a photo shoot with the other women."

Ainsley hadn't realized how invasive her idea for the article was to those three women. How had three smart, sexy women all fallen for a man who had kept them all on a string? Her readers would eat up the answer to that question. But how would Geoff, Henry and Steven deal with seeing their mothers back in the spotlight again? That was something she'd have to figure out.

"We will be careful to keep the article within the parameters you mentioned," Ainsley said. She wasn't going to agree to not talking about the past—that made the story juicy.

"That's all I can ask for. The same circumstances apply to her interview—she'll have to approve the questions and such if she grants it. I will submit topics that are off-limits and I will approve the final draft."

Since she had no choice, Ainsley agreed. A few minutes later Geoff left. Cathy was already gone when she changed clothes in her executive bathroom and went downstairs to meet Steven.

Would reading the interview with Steven's mother give her any insight into his character and personality? She wondered if a part of her hadn't come up with this idea because she wanted to know more about the man who'd affected her so deeply. The man who'd changed her. She wanted to know what had shaped him, and the best way to do that would be to talk to his mother.

Though it had only been five days since she'd last seen

him, it seemed much longer when she stepped off the elevator and saw him waiting in the lobby. He put his hand on her shoulder and she looked up at him. Saw in his eyes a hint that maybe he'd missed her, too.

Eight

Ainsley looked as ravishing as he remembered. It ticked him off a little that the attraction he'd felt for her hadn't waned.

While he'd been away from her, he'd speculated that the attraction was driven by lust and had been intensified by his own lack of a current lover. But the moment she'd stepped out of her building he'd known that that was a lie.

"Good evening," he said.

"Hello. How have you been?" she asked. The words were banal, and he who had no patience for small talk wanted it to continue so he could keep listening to her voice.

"Good. I have a bit of a surprise for you," he said. He'd debated taking her to St. Peter's and the upper galleries. It was a beautiful and quiet destination. And it was someplace different.

There was majesty to the cathedral that was unrivaled by anything else in the world, in his opinion. Though it was late, he'd made special arrangements for them to tour the gallery by themselves.

She arched her eyebrow at him and then said, "I love surprises."

"No, you don't," he said. "I've been around you long enough to know that you like to know every detail and you like to be in charge."

"Touché! I think the same could be said of you."

"I've heard it many times. But I think you'll like this surprise."

She didn't say anything else. He held her hand, sliding their fingers together until their palms met. Then he led her out the door of her building and down the street toward St. Peter's. She wore a pair of two-inch, round-toed, patent leather shoes. So she reached his shoulder as they walked. Her thick black hair had been left down and brushed her shoulder with each step she took.

The formfitting black blouse with red decorative buttons accentuated the curves of her breasts. She had the blouse tucked into a long red skirt that ended at her calves. The skirt had a slit on the side that gave him a glimpse of her left leg with each step she took.

He wanted to draw her into a dark alley and have his way with her. Needed to taste those full lips under his. Needed to feel her curvy body pulled flush against his hard angles. Needed…her.

And he needed no one.

"About the interviews," he said, thinking it was time to get all that out of the way.

"Yes, about the interviews. Why didn't you tell me that Geoff was reluctant to be interviewed?"

"I didn't know myself until I spoke to him. But we discussed it and he'll do it."

"I know. He was in my office today. His mother might not be a part of it, which is disappointing."

"I'm sure you'll still have a fabulous story without her. Princess Louisa just doesn't like to speak in public." Ainsley nodded. Steven had never met any of the mothers of the other Devonshire bastards and he'd been curious about that when he'd been younger. But now he knew who he was and what he was trying to accomplish. The past could stay in the past as far as he was concerned.

Ainsley would play a key role in spreading the word to many people that the Everest Group was back. That Everest was the exciting company it used to be and that Everest was about to change the way the world looked at retail marketing.

He wasn't the least bit bothered by the fact that he wanted her and that their business arrangement might be affected by his desires. As they entered St. Peter's and walked up the steps, he was aware that he'd do anything to keep Ainsley by his side. And he wondered just for a moment if he'd suggested the interviews, a gross invasion of his privacy, just to stay by her side.

"St. Peter's?"

"Yes. I have arranged a private tour of the upper galleries."

"Really? I've been dying to see them, but haven't had a chance. Thank you, Steven."

She hugged him and started to pull away quickly, but he brought his hands to her waist and held her there. This was what he'd been waiting for. This was what he wanted. He needed this woman in his arms.

He thought he'd wanted to unravel her mysteries but now

he knew he just wanted her. He didn't care if he unlocked the secrets she kept unless they were secrets about what she hoped he'd do to her.

She wrapped her arms around his neck and tipped her head back to look up at him. Their gazes met and he couldn't help but feel something pass between them. Something hard to define.

"Why haven't you kissed me yet?" she asked.

He didn't answer her, just brought his head down and took her lower lip between his teeth.

Her hands tightened on his shoulders as she tried to pull herself closer to him. This was why he'd waited to kiss her. They were like flint and steel when they touched, and the sparks of the flames they generated consumed both of them.

If he wasn't careful, he'd end up taking Ainsley for the first time in some very public place. And he'd never been much for exhibitionism. She went to his head faster than his first sip of whiskey had and the results were unpredictable.

Tugging her off balance, he pulled her close and felt her settle against him—first her breasts to his chest, then her belly against his stomach. Then she canted her hips toward him so her feminine mound rested against his erection.

He cupped her bottom and held her there while he continued to thrust his tongue deep into her mouth. The sun set around the city and a cold, damp chill filled the air, but he wasn't aware of anything but the woman in his arms.

Ainsley thought of nothing but that kiss for the rest of the evening. As they walked past the crypts of monarchs and poets and through the whispering gallery, all she could think of was Steven and how much she wanted to be alone with him. He had dialed back his attraction and seemed absorbed in what the guide was saying. She tried to listen, but she couldn't help but remember the way his arms had felt against her.

The feeling of the firm grip of his hands on her waist lingered. She could taste him each time she licked her lips.

"Ainsley?"

"Hmm?"

"I was telling our guide how much we enjoyed our tour."

She'd been standing there staring at Steven with a dazed expression. "Yes, we did. Thank you so much."

Steven tipped the man and they left. It was cold outside now that night had fallen and she felt the chill settle over her. She'd left her raincoat at the office. "I forgot my coat."

"I noticed. I thought you were a hardy American."

"I am."

She didn't want him to know that he'd distracted her. While getting all the Devonshire heirs and their mothers to agree to be interviewed was a coup, she normally wouldn't have been involved in the details of a story like this. She would have delegated it. But with Maurice's interest in the story, she was reluctant to let any detail out of her hands. She wanted to be the one to make all the arrangements particularly so she would have an excuse to see Steven.

He shrugged out of his suit jacket and handed it to her. She reached for it, but he drew it out of her grasp.

"Let me help you," he said.

She did, turning to face away from him as he held his jacket up. She slipped her arms inside and was immediately surrounded by his body heat and the scent of aftershave. It was a warm and welcoming feeling, and she was unnerved because as she turned back to Steven, he seemed to know how she felt.

He took her hand in his and continued leading them back toward her office building. His car was still parked on the street and he opened the door for her to get in. "Ready for dinner?"

"Yes," she said. The feelings she had for him were starting to overwhelm her. She wanted to be alone with him. To take off his clothes and see his naked body. But she was also very afraid of that moment. Afraid he'd see past the shields she'd put in place to make the world think she was different from who she really was. Afraid that he would see her naked and turn away from her.

Then she worried that she was worrying for nothing. That he might not even want to make love to her. Her fingers were tightly knotted together, something she realized only as Steven put his hand over hers.

"Relax," he said. "What are you thinking about?"

She couldn't tell him. Couldn't tell this man who exuded sexuality that she was afraid of her own. But then she looked into his dark eyes and remembered the way he'd looked as he'd kissed her that very first time.

She could trust Steven. "I'm not sure I'm like the women you're used to."

"In what way?"

"I haven't had many lovers," she said.

"And that bothers you?"

She shrugged. "Not really. But I think it would be nice to have more experience, especially since you seem to."

He smiled at her, reaching over to stroke her face. "Don't

worry about any of that. You and I are in sync when it comes to physical desire."

"Are you sure? I'm not what you think I am," she said.

He arched one eyebrow at her. "Unless you're secretly a man, I think you are exactly what I believe you to be."

She gave a nervous laugh. "No, I'm not a man."

"Then we have no problem, do we?"

She had wanted to be smooth and confident, but instead she was showing him exactly how vulnerable she was. A part of her knew that letting him see the weakness in her gave him an advantage. She'd heard that the power in a relationship went to the person who wanted the other one less. And she knew that if that were true, she was the one with less power.

She wanted Steven in a way that was overwhelming. It made her do things she'd never done before. She was on a date on a worknight, but then the last time they'd gone out it had been a worknight, too. She always got a good night's sleep so she was sharp at work the next day. She still had e-mails to answer tonight and photos to approve for tomorrow.

But as she sat across from him in a very posh restaurant run by a celebrity chef, she didn't care. She just sat and talked about books and movies, surprised to find that Steven and she had a lot in common.

"Why are you looking at me like that?" she asked toward the end of the meal when he was staring at her mouth.

"I'm wondering how your mouth will feel against my chest," he said. "Will you kiss me there?"

"Yes," she said. The passion and the tension underlying that question brought back all her fears. A surge of electricity cascaded through her. She leaned closer to him at the table. She wanted this man and nothing, not even her own fears, was going to stop her from having him.

She thought he'd ask for the check so they could leave, but instead he took her hand in his under the table and placed it on his thigh. She felt the muscled hardness of his legs and let her fingers caress him.

Steven took a sip of his espresso and kept his hands off Ainsley. It was a struggle because she kept moving her fingers up and down his thigh. He'd taken a gamble by putting her hand there. But her earlier fears had told him that she wasn't sure of her appeal.

And he wondered how a woman as sexy and smart as Ainsley could doubt herself. She had declined dessert, but he'd never known a woman not to want sweets, so he had ordered a seven-layer chocolate cake for them both and offered her a bite.

She shook her head, but he kept the fork extended. "Please take it away, Steven."

He took the bite for himself. "Why?"

Pulling her hand from his leg, she wrapped it around her own waist. "I...I guess this is a good time to tell you. I used to be fat."

Women were always obsessing over five or ten pounds. But Ainsley was perfect. Beautiful, curvy, everything a woman should be.

"I find that very hard to believe."

"Well, it's the truth. Men rarely noticed me when I was in a room."

Again he didn't believe her. "Maybe that was your perception, but I promise you they did."

"No, they didn't."

"Well, then they were fools because I would never have forgotten you," he said.

"But you did," she said. "I interviewed you five years ago. And you don't even remember me."

Steven tried to recall…the girl with the pretty violet eyes? She had been big, he remembered, but more than that she'd been almost invisible when she hadn't been interviewing him. "I remember now. Weren't you A.J. then? You were so shy when the interview was over. Almost as if you wanted to fade into the background."

She flushed. "I did. But you didn't remember me, did you?"

"Not because of the size of your body," he said. "Because you made yourself unremarkable. You've changed. I don't think it's just weight loss. I think it has to do with your personality."

She took a sip of her espresso and then joined her hands together on the table. "A man *would* see it that way."

"Anyone would," he argued. "You used to make yourself invisible. Maybe you felt more comfortable that way. But the woman you are right now is who I'm attracted to, and it wouldn't matter what size she was."

He saw her blink and turn away. "Now I want you to try a bite of this dessert. It's delicious."

"I can't, Steven. One bite will turn into the entire cake. You have no idea what a struggle it is for me to keep from overeating."

She was too disciplined now to overeat. He could tell by the way she held herself that she wouldn't let her control slip. She just wasn't that sure of herself. He vowed that she would be. That he would show her that she was so much more than unfulfilled wanting.

"Trust me."

She looked over at him and he felt like this had become about something more than dessert. The moment sharpened until he knew this would change the course of their relationship. Either she would trust him and it would move forward or she wouldn't and he'd sleep with her and they'd never see each other again.

He wasn't sure which scenario he preferred. Because if she started to trust him, that meant he had the burden of continuing to be worthy of her trust—something he wasn't sure he could do. He'd been dead inside for so long. He'd settled for one-night stands and short-term affairs.

But as the fork was suspended between them and he watched Ainsley move slowly toward it, he knew that things were changing. Not just for her, but for him as well.

She was the first woman he'd wanted physically who had tempted him emotionally. And that scared him. He'd always been alone and he didn't want to depend on a woman whose career was so important.

She took a bite, the fork entering her pretty mouth, and when he pulled it away he noticed that she'd closed her eyes. She savored that bite of cake the way he wanted to savor her. He wanted to linger over every curve of her body, wanted to explore each inch until he knew her better than she knew herself. And he would.

If she trusted him, he'd do his best to live up to that for as long as he could. He knew himself well enough to know that eventually he'd let her down.

He'd done that most of his life when it came to relationships, but for the first time he didn't want that to happen. He wanted to be a man that she'd always be able to look up to.

"Thank you," she said. "That was delicious."

"You're welcome," he said. He put the fork down and signaled for the check.

He hadn't realized that by playing games with her, by seducing her slowly and trying to find her weaknesses, he'd find his own.

With her wide violet eyes and her full red lips, she'd drawn him into her web. And a part of him would be happy to stay there. But a bigger part of him knew that weakness lay with emotional dependency.

Not the small weaknesses that made up character flaws but the bigger ones, like needing Ainsley, that were something that could cost him the competition with Henry and Geoff. And possibly the success of the retail group.

Ainsley was dangerous.

Looking at her sitting across the table from him, it was hard to believe it, but she was. She made him want things that weren't work-related. She made him want to sit at home at night in front of a fire with her curled up by his side.

She made him want to think about the future with her and maybe having some kids. And that was a very frightening picture. Being a parent and being successful just didn't go together.

Nine

Finding herself sitting outside her house with Steven again, she had an odd sense of déjà vu. Her emotions were all in a jumble and she was worried about what she might do or say. For the first time in a long time she felt out of control. She wanted Steven and that desire was taking over every part of her.

She wanted to be smart and charming—Rosalind Russell in *His Girl Friday*. But she was afraid that if she opened her mouth, she'd come off as more unsure and awkward.

"Haven't we been here before?" she asked.

"I believe we have," he said.

He'd turned the car off and turned to face her. It was a lane dimly lit by streetlamps. The light from one of them illuminated his face but kept part of it in shadow.

He was a mystery to her. Even after all her research about him, she still couldn't figure him out. He sat with his body turned toward her and his arm resting on the steering wheel.

"Invite me in," he said at last.

She was going to, but why did he make everything he said sound like an order? "Why are you so bossy?"

"Because men who aren't don't get what they want."

"What do you want?" she asked.

"You really don't know?"

She did know what he wanted, but somehow saying it out loud would make it too real and she wasn't sure she wanted to do that. "To come inside."

"Indeed."

"Would you like a drink?"

"Would you?"

She laughed. "I think I need one. You tie me up in knots."

"Do I? I think that's a good thing," he said.

"Why?"

"You do the same thing to me," he said, reaching over to caress her face.

"Oh."

"Oh?" He leaned in. "You have the most kissable mouth."

He rubbed his lips against hers gently. The kiss was nothing like the one he'd given her earlier—so demanding and bold. This was soft and seduced her by degrees. Slowly. He kissed her as if he had all the time in the world, which he probably did. They had all night.

He pulled back, opened his door and came around to open hers. She gave him her hand and then climbed out of the low-slung sports car. She led the way up her walk to her front door. This time she didn't drop the keys. She wasn't nervous at all.

A strange calm had settled over her when he'd kissed her so softly. Steven was more than her obsession; he was a man she had come to know a little better over the last week.

She unlocked her door and stepped over the threshold. The lights were on in the living room and cast a warm, inviting glow into the foyer. Steven stepped inside, closing the door behind him. She led the way, almost kicking off her shoes in the hallway, but she remembered at the last moment that she had company and according to her mother, men didn't like messy women.

"What can I get you?"

"You," he said.

As he pulled her into his arms, she wrapped her arms around his waist and rested her head on his chest. She suspected that he wanted the embrace to be something more than this, but right now this was all she could do. She took comfort from the feel of his chest under her cheek. From the feel of her arms around his waist. From the scent of his natural musk with each inhalation.

She was tired of denying herself everything she wanted. It was one thing to resist dessert but something altogether different to deny herself the chance to be with Steven. She had fantasized about him every night since their first date.

His hands stroked her back gently. The touch was comforting at first and then the timbre changed and it became seductive. His hands swept lower each time, his fingers caressing her back with each stroke.

She tipped her head to the left and he kissed her first on the forehead and then let his lips move down the side of her face. Small, nibbling kisses that felt light, almost as if she were imagining them.

Then he reached her ear. His tongue traced the shell of her ear and she shivered as darts of awareness shot down her neck and arms. Her nipples tightened and her breasts felt fuller.

"Remember when I kissed you by my car," he said, his hot breath going directly into her ear. She shuddered with the memories of that kiss and how inflamed she'd felt.

"Yes," she said.

"I'm going to kiss you like that again, but this time I'm not stopping until I'm buried hilt-deep inside of you."

Her inner body clenched and she felt a humid warmth bloom between her legs. She shifted around until she could look him in the eyes. "Good. I want that, Steven. I want everything you have to give me."

Ainsley realized that he couldn't make promises. She might not believe him if he did. She trusted him because he didn't make promises he wouldn't keep. And she wouldn't ask him to.

For this night, she wanted only to be in his arms. She didn't need to think about the future. She'd never been one to think about forever. Losing weight and changing how she looked on the outside hadn't changed her on the inside.

"Do you want that drink?" she asked, not sure how to proceed.

"No," he said. "I don't want anything but you. But if a drink will relax you, I'll have one, too."

She hesitated. She wished she could just take him by the hand and lead him to her bedroom, but she definitely needed a drink. She pulled away. "Wine okay?"

"Yes," he said.

She left him in the living room and went into her kitchen to get the bottle she'd chilled earlier. She savored white wine. Hopefully, he liked the dry taste of pinot grigio.

He was moving around in the living room and then she heard the mellow sound of Otis Redding. She had a huge collection of old-time R&B. It was her favorite, and she was surprised that he'd chosen it. But the music relaxed her a bit more.

She poured them each a glass of wine and then took a deep breath before going back out into the living room. It would be so much easier for her if Steven Devonshire were just another man. Instead he was *the* man. Oh, my God, she thought. He was the one she wanted out of all the other men. And that made this night so important to her. A first kiss only happened once—and that had been eminently memorable. So did a first-time sharing each other's bodies. She wanted that to be perfect as well.

Steven knew he could easily push Ainsley's shyness aside by kissing her until she had no choice but to be swept down the hall and into her own bed. But he wanted her to want to be there, comfortable in her own skin.

He loosened his tie and undid the first button of his dress shirt, then walked around her living room to the Bose stereo system where music played softly. In a cabinet next to the unit were her CDs and they were all lined up in alphabetical order. She had an eclectic collection, including a lot of old rhythm and blues CDs. Otis Redding, Ray Charles, Marvin Gaye and some of the classic Italian-American singers like Louis Prima, Frank Sinatra and Dean Martin.

There was Cold Play and Green Day in there, too. And some newer artists he'd never heard of. Seeing her music collection showed him that he'd only scratched the surface of who she was. Ainsley wasn't a woman who was easy to know. He put on an Otis Redding album, turned off the larger overhead light and turned on the lamp on the side table.

The ambient light created the intimate mood he wanted. He thought about everything he knew about Ainsley, how she'd been fat, and that had virtually defined her. He'd been thinking a lot about the woman who'd interviewed him five years ago. He'd been telling her the truth when he'd said that she'd seemed invisible. But he had started to wonder if he'd done anything to contribute to that. Had he simply ignored her because she wasn't slim?

He couldn't change the past, but he intended to make sure that she knew he wanted her now. She'd have no doubts that he loved her and her body. He'd do everything in his power to make sure that she got lost in his embrace. That she didn't have time to think about her past or any of her imagined flaws.

She came back into the room and hesitated in the doorway. She held two glasses of wine and her expression was a mix of bravado and desire. Clearly, she wanted him— probably with the same intensity as he wanted her, though he found that hard to believe. No way could she want him as much as he wanted her.

He walked over to her and took one wineglass from her.

"I hope you like white wine."

"I do," he said. He put his hand on the small of her back and led her into the living room. She perched delicately on the edge of the love seat, her legs crossed demurely, and he felt as if he were back in his aunt Lucy's drawing room.

He took her hand and drew her to her feet. He might not be much of a dancer, but he could sway with the best of them. And he knew the surest way to coax Ainsley out of her reserve was by putting his arms around her.

"To a lovely evening," he said, raising his glass to hers.

She clinked her glass to his and took a sip. So did he, draining half the glass and setting it on the side table. He took hers and did the same. Then he came back behind her and pulled her into his arms. Her back against his chest.

He lowered his head next to hers and whispered sweet nothings to her, bending his knees to spoon her while they were standing there together. He wrapped his arms around her, letting his thumb and hand rest under her right breast, his other hand on her abdomen.

He swayed back and forth to the music and felt her relax against him. He put his mouth on her neck right at the base and kissed her, then let her feel the edge of his teeth.

He felt her breast jump in his hand and she shifted her hips to rub against his erection. He hardened and his blood ran heavier. Every instinct he had told him to hurry this up.

But he'd learned over time that he enjoyed his orgasm more if he drew it out. He continued swaying with her and found the buttons of her blouse with his left hand. Slowly he undid them. He left the blouse tucked into her skirt but unfastened it all the way.

Her skin was lily white and soft. So soft that he couldn't stop caressing her. He traced a path up the center of her body from where her belly button was to her rib cage to the sin-red bra that encased her full breasts. He traced his finger over the underwire that supported her. Then he skimmed the edge of the lace where it met the creamy skin of her chest. He let his forefinger dip under the fabric to caress her creamy breasts.

She rotated her shoulders, seeming to want his touch to move to her breasts, but he wasn't ready for that yet.

He nibbled on her ear and kept his finger moving slowly over that part of her breast. Then he inched his way to the velvety skin of her nipple, touching her carefully when she jerked in his arms. Her hips swiveled against his and her hands came to his wrist to grip him.

"I want to see you," she said, trying to turn in his embrace.

"Not yet."

"When?"

"When you are totally a slave to love," he said.

She tipped her head back so that their eyes met. The action thrust her breasts out and made his finger run over her nipple. She shuddered again.

"I already am," she said.

"Not like you will be," he said.

He pinched her nipple lightly, watching carefully to see if it was too much for her. But she liked it. She bit her lower lip and her hips moved against his again.

He slid his hand around to the zipper in the side of her skirt and drew it down. The skirt slid slowly over her hips and then fell to her ankles. He glanced down to see that she had on a minute pair of panties that matched her bra. But above that she had on a garter belt that held up her hose. He took a step back and pushed her blouse off her shoulders.

He walked around in front of her. She was an image straight from a wet dream. She was hot and sexy, and as she stood there in her high heels and her decadent underwear, suddenly a slow seduction seemed like a very stupid idea. All he wanted was to rip those little panties from her body and make her his. She belonged to him.

Possessiveness wasn't his style, but he wanted every inch of Ainsley, and he was going to claim it all.

* * *

Ainsley's body was on fire. Steven called to her. When he finally entered her line of vision, she was surprised that he was still dressed. She didn't feel vulnerable, as she had expected to standing in front of him, because of the lust in his eyes. He wanted her and he couldn't stop looking at her.

The bulge of his erection also made her feel feminine, sexy. Like a woman who held power over her man. And for tonight Steven was *her* man. She started to take his clothes off, but he held up his finger. "Not yet."

"Why?" she asked.

"I'm not done looking at you yet."

She felt a sliver of fear but it passed quickly and she put her hands on her waist and cocked out one hip. "Take your time."

"I will," he said. "I can't believe you're mine."

"Am I yours?" she asked. No man had claimed her before. She'd had one lover before Steven—that had been in her early twenties, and now she was thirty. The sex had been okay but she knew that Steven was the type of man who'd make her come. Sex wasn't going to just be okay. She knew she'd never look at him the same way after this.

"Yes."

He put his hands on her shoulders and held her where she was. He lowered his head and kissed her. It was the same kiss he'd given her by the car that first night but at the same time a million times more intense. He didn't let their bodies touch at all. Just used his lips and teeth and tongue to make her his and she was helpless to do anything but respond.

She reached between their bodies and took his tie off. Drawing it out of his collar and dropping it on the floor by her skirt. Then she started unbuttoning his shirt, her fingernails scraping against the wall of his chest.

He shuddered and pulled back from her. "Do that again."

She did, scraping her nails down his body all the way to his waistband. The skin on his stomach jumped as her touch went lower. She pushed his shirt from his shoulders and then realized she'd left his cuff links on. The shirt bound his hands. And he couldn't touch her.

"Now you are *my* slave," she said. "And you are one fine-looking slave."

She walked around him and stood behind him as he had positioned himself behind her. She touched him from his shoulders down the center of his back and then cupped his tight buttocks. She put one arm around his chest and drew him back against her. The other arm she put around his lean waist and then she went up on her tiptoes and bit him lightly on his neck.

She unzipped his pants and let her hand drift lower inside his underwear to caress him. She rubbed her fingers up and down his length and then massaged the crown of his erection. She felt him shiver in her arms and she smiled to herself.

She was just following what he'd done to her. She unfastened his belt, drawing it slowly from around his lean waist.

She reached into the opening of his pants, touched him through his underwear and then found the opening in his boxers and let her fingers sweep inside and stroke up and down his length. He turned in her arms and knocked her off balance, but he caught her quickly, lifting her up in his arms and going to the love seat. He set her on her feet and pushed his pants and underwear down his legs. Then he took off his cuff links and shrugged out of his shirt.

He stood before her, an Adonis of a man—perfectly formed. His erection stood out from his body and she felt a rush of pure desire as she realized that she had turned him on.

"Take your panties off," he said, his voice low and raspy.

She hesitated for a second and then kicked off her shoes. She started to undo the garter belt, but he stopped her.

"Leave that on."

"Okay." She got her panties as far as her knees when he stopped her again.

"Turn around."

"Why?"

"Because I love your behind," he said. And I want to see you when you bend over.

A shudder of awareness ripped through her at his words and she did as he asked. As soon as she bent forward she felt his hands slide over her back. Then his nails did the same down the line of her spine.

She stepped out of her panties and when she stood up, he kept the pressure on her back. "Stay like this."

She wasn't sure what he had in mind, but she did as he said.

"Are you on the Pill?"

"No. Sorry, I didn't think about protection," she said, trying to turn around and stand up.

"Don't worry, love, I did," he said. He reached for his pants and pulled a condom out of the pocket. She heard the packet rip. Then she felt the tip of his erection against her. He held her hips in his hands and leaned forward so that his chest settled against her back. He reached around her. Held her wrapped in his arms as he eased himself into her body.

Just the tip in and out until she thought she was going to die from wanting him.

He reached lower between her legs and parted her nether lips. His finger rubbed her up and down until she felt like she was going to come. She couldn't stop moving her hips. Couldn't stop trying to get more of his hardness inside of her.

"Steven, take me."

"Yes, ma'am," he said. He bit down on her neck and thrust himself deep inside her. Ripples of her climax washed over her and she was a shivery mass of nerves.

He continued to thrust into her, driving her to another orgasm, and the third time she came, he did as well.

He fell back on the couch and held her in his arms as they both came back to themselves. She curled herself into his arms, feeling more vulnerable than she ever believed she could. For the first time the girl who never thought she'd find a man to love realized that she wanted this one.

Ten

Ainsley woke up at 2:00 a.m. and knew she wasn't alone. She bolted upright in bed, jerking all the covers with her.

"Love?"

"Steven?"

"Who else would it be?"

"I don't know," she said feeling very silly. But she had never shared her bed with anyone.

Steven stroked his hand along her spine and then drew her down into his arms. He was warm and her head seemed to find the perfect spot on his shoulder. He put his arm around her shoulder and she lay quietly trying to go back to sleep. It was hard.

Way too hard to figure out how to sleep with this man...

"What are you thinking about?" he asked.

"That I've never slept with anyone," she said. An only

child, she'd never been scared of the dark and as a child her parents' bedroom had been off-limits to her.

"Never? Not even as a child?" he asked.

"Nope. My parents believed in kids in their own beds. And I wasn't very social as a child, so I didn't do sleepovers." She had been chubby even as a child, but more than that she'd simply liked being by herself. She didn't mix well with others. She'd been more interested in the world she'd created in her head. A world where she could be a princess and everyone liked her.

She hadn't thought of that in years. Thought of that painful time in her childhood.

"So I'm your first?" Steven said.

He was in so many ways. The first man she'd made love to, not the boy-man she'd had sex with before. She tipped her head up, but her room was dark. She wished she could see his expression better.

"Is that good?"

He shrugged, dislodging her from his shoulder. He didn't say anything else. What did this mean to him? What did it mean to her? She knew better than to make decisions in the middle of the night, but a part of her wanted to. She wanted to figure Steven out so she wouldn't get hurt, but a part of her was afraid that it was too late for that.

She was already falling for him.

She wasn't going to ask, but she wanted to know. Did she mean more to Steven than this one night or even a series of nights that added up to weeks before he moved on?

She had no idea what any of his behavior meant.

"Are you sleeping?" she whispered.

"With your hand stroking my belly button? No, I'm not sleeping."

She hadn't realized she was doing that, but sure enough her hand was low on his stomach. She stopped moving it.

"Don't stop. I like it."

She started moving her hand again, and noticed that his hand was caressing her arm. There was nothing overtly sexual in the touching; it was two people comforting each other, she thought.

"I haven't slept with that many people, either. I tend to go back to my place instead of sleeping over."

"Really? Why?"

"I don't like mornings. It's always awkward."

That revealed a lot to her. He didn't like to stay because though sex was okay, anything resembling a relationship made him uncomfortable. "Awkward how?"

"Normally I have work to do and have to leave early and—you don't want to hear this."

Yet she did want to. She didn't want to know the details of his past affairs, but she did want to know why he left. Or was she simply drawing a conclusion based on her perceptions of who he was? Work was one reason but she suspected that was an excuse. Steven was the CEO of a large company. If he came in late, no one was going to say a word to him.

"Work's not the reason you leave," she said. "You leave because you don't want to stay."

His hand stopped moving on her arm and she wondered if she'd said too much. Even so, she didn't care if she had. This affair with Steven was something totally new to her. She wasn't going to hedge her bets or try to play it safe. If he didn't want her once they'd slept together, she wanted to know now.

"I think you're right. I've never given it much thought.

Just got up and left when I wanted to. Work calls… My job is my life…"

"And no woman could compete with that," she finished for him.

"That's right."

She lay still next to him, knowing that she was going to ask the next question whether it was wise or not.

"What about me?"

He turned on the bed so they lay facing each other. He put both arms around her—one around her neck the other over her waist and drew her flush against his body.

"I have no clue. You aren't like anyone else."

That didn't reassure her at all and in fact raised more doubts about being with Steven. He wasn't an easy man to get close to. With each step she took toward him, he found a new way to freeze her out and keep her at arm's length.

She wanted to ask more questions, but she had a feeling that was all he'd admit to her. She closed her eyes and enjoyed being so close to him. She put her arm over his waist and tucked her head under his chin.

He held her like that until they both drifted off to sleep. Ainsley tried not to let it mean too much that he held her as tightly as she held him.

Steven woke to bright sunlight streaming in through some filmy curtains. Ainsley was curled by his side. He eased out of bed to go to the bathroom and saw his clothes where he'd left them on the overstuffed chair that sat in the corner of her bedroom.

He almost walked over and got dressed. He could leave. Nothing was keeping him here. But as he looked at Ainsley sleeping in her bed, her hand reaching out to where he'd lain, he couldn't do it.

He didn't want her to wake up alone. He had the feeling from what she'd said last night that she'd led a very solitary life.

Dammit, he cared about her. Yet he didn't want emotional entanglements. How had this happened? She was a woman who looked like she shouldn't have touched any of his emotions. But she had.

And that was the problem.

"Steven?" she called his name as she sat up in bed. She wore a pretty flower-printed nightgown and her hair was tousled around her shoulders. Her eyes were sleepy as she tried to see him. Last night he'd learned that she wore contacts—something as new to her as her weight loss.

He saw her reaching for her nightstand and the glasses she had set on the top last night.

"I'm here."

"Are you leaving?" she asked.

"Do you want me to?" he asked. It would be so much easier if she said yes. He could walk away and he'd never forget the time he'd spent with her, but this encounter would fade into a memory. Nothing more.

"I would like it if you came back to bed."

He smiled. He went back to the bed and sat down next to her.

"Happy now?"

"Yes," she said, squinting up at him.

"Put your glasses on," he said.

"No. They aren't attractive at all. I'll go put my contacts in."

That made no sense to him. "You don't have to."

He reached for her glasses and handed them to her. She held them for a minute and then put them on. "There you are," she said lightly.

"Here I am."

He leaned in and kissed her softly. "Good morning."

"Good morning," she said.

"Why didn't you want to put your glasses on?"

"I...they are part of the old me. Not this new person that you found attractive."

He crossed his arms over his chest. He was getting a picture of Ainsley as a woman who hid her true self from the world. "So who's the real Ainsley? The sexy temptress I met last night or this shy woman I'm seeing this morning."

She bit her lower lip. "I don't know. I would have said this is me, but last night I felt comfortable in my body for the first time. I'm not talking about just since I lost weight—I mean ever. I've never felt like my skin fit me. Last night, when I was in your arms, I found myself."

She shook her head. "Oh, God, I sound like a moron."

He laughed, but deep inside he knew that being with him wasn't an easy decision for Ainsley.

Hurting her was the very last thing he wanted. He had to be careful if he didn't intend to lose his heart or let his emotions overwhelm him. And the only way to protect himself was to make sure she didn't get too involved with him.

He wanted to go back to bed with her but he wasn't sure that was wise. He'd only brought two condoms with him last night. It would take a box to continue this affair with Ainsley. Twice wasn't nearly enough to get his fill of her.

Ainsley was finding her confidence as a woman in his arms. What she'd said about finding herself made sense to him. Because he'd noted that change in her. She dressed like a confident woman who knew the power of her sexuality but until last night he didn't think she really had.

"I have a meeting with Henry and Geoff in an hour," he said.

"I am actually going to be late if I don't leave in ten minutes. Freddie is never going to let me live this down."

"What does he have to say about this? I thought he worked for you."

"He does, but he's also one of my best friends."

"You're friends with a man?"

She laughed at him and punched him lightly in the shoulder. "Yes, I am. Don't you have any women friends?"

He didn't. If pressed, he might describe Dinah as a friend, but she was really more of an employee. "No, I don't. And you don't need any guy friends while you're with me. I can provide all the testosterone you need."

"Steven, I'm an independent woman and I'm not about to let you tell me who I can be friends with. I'm not going to be sleeping around, but Freddie and I are still going to stay friends."

"Fine."

This was precisely why he avoided relationships. Because he was always afraid of losing the very thing he wanted. And he hated to admit that he might need anything from Ainsley other than sex, but she was different. And he disliked this feeling of needing to be the only man in her life. It was crazy.

She looked up at him with her wide violet eyes and he was very afraid that she'd complicate his life. That his life had changed so much last night when he'd taken her in his arms.

He didn't want his life turned upside down, so he left a few minutes later when she got into the shower. He wasn't a man who was jealous or possessive, yet Ainsley awakened both emotions in him. Why?

As he drove through the early morning traffic, he had doubts. Why was Ainsley affecting him this way? He had always been able to put women in their place in his life and just keep on his path to total world domination. But she was playing with his head and he was very afraid for his heart.

He knew that he couldn't insist on crazy things, like forbidding a woman to have male friends, and he had never done that with his other girlfriends. So why with her? What made her so different?

To a man used to always having the answers, this situation was thoroughly unsettling. Until he knew why Ainsley was affecting him this deeply, he needed to keep his distance. He didn't want to end up with a messy personal life the way Malcolm Devonshire had.

Ainsley couldn't talk to Freddie about last night no matter how many times he asked. Steven had left while she was in the shower. And even though she knew he had a meeting this morning, she'd expected him to say goodbye. She knew he had things to do and she hadn't expected him to just hang out at her house all day, but leaving without a word...well, she knew he was running away.

It shouldn't matter, but it did. She'd taken a big risk last night by having sex with him and the reward had been better than she had expected. She'd never had an orgasm like that before or that many. She'd also never felt as appealing to the opposite sex as she had when she'd been in his arms.

But she'd never been as disappointed in a man as she

had been when she'd come out of the shower and realized that Steven had left.

It had been a cowardly thing to do. Frankly, she'd expected better of him. When her staff meeting ended, she stood up and left the room. Freddie followed close on her heels.

"Hold up, boss lady. We need to talk."

She shook her head.

"Nope, I'm not going to let you get away with that. We've been friends too long for you to hide things from me."

Ainsley stared at her friend. He wore his short hair spiked up this morning. He had on a pair of gabardine slacks, combat boots and a vintage Stones T-shirt. His round, horn-rimmed glasses were for show, but the expression in his eyes was sincere.

"I can't talk about it. Not yet. We can do drinks later in the week and we can talk then."

"Are you sure?"

She nodded. "I'm too raw about this. I have a magazine to run. I can't afford to let this bother me."

"What happened?"

"Nothing," she said, aware that she was making this into something bigger than it was. But she'd let Steven see the most vulnerable side of her and he'd left without saying anything.

"Fine. Drinks Friday. I'm not going to let you get away with keeping this in."

"Sounds good. Now get to work."

He hugged her and then walked away. The fact that he'd hugged her told her that she needed to get to her office before anyone else noticed that the ultra-efficient boss they'd come to know wasn't herself.

Cathy had left a stack of messages for her and there were

proof sheets that she needed to sign off on, but all she could do was think about last night. She spun her chair around to face the window, but found no solace in the spectacular view.

St. Peter's now reminded her of Steven.

She turned back to her desk, opened her e-mail account and thought for a long minute before she started writing to Steven.

Was there an emergency this morning? Leaving without saying goodbye was cowardly. I thought you were a different kind of man.

She hit Send before she gave in to her anger further and called him an ass. Twenty minutes later her cell phone rang.

She glanced at the caller ID to see Steven's name. She didn't want to talk to him, but she realized that calling him a coward and avoiding his call would make her one.

"This is Ainsley," she said as she answered her phone.

"I'm sorry about this morning. I just felt the walls closing in and I had to get out of there. It wasn't you," he said. "It was me."

"What does that mean? Walls closing in?"

Silence buzzed on the open line for a long minute. "I wanted to stay. I wanted to come into the shower with you and make love to you—to hell with the consequences. And that's not who I am."

She flushed at his words. Realized that he wanted her with the same intensity as she wanted him.

His fears mirrored her own. They were both so used to going their own way that coming together seemed like it would be an immense challenge. A challenge that might be too much for them.

"I feel the same way, Steven. But at the end of the day, you're worth the risk to me. That's why I called you on your actions. If I'm not worth the risk to you then fine—just say so and we can end this now."

"And if I think you are?" he asked.

"Then we try to figure this out. We figure out how to make this relationship work for us."

"Relationship?"

"Yes. I don't want to be one in a line of lovers you have. I have too much respect for myself to get involved with a man like you unless there is more than just sex."

"A man like me?" he asked.

She had said too much. Steven was the kind of man she could fall in love with and saying that to him would leave her feeling like she'd stripped her clothes off in the center of the office.

She thought for a moment. No risk, no reward, she thought. "I could fall for you."

"Ainsley…"

"Don't say anything else. I know you aren't the kind of man to fall in love, but I am that kind of woman. If you aren't looking for at least some kind of solid relationship, then I have to end this now."

"I don't want to see you hurt, but I have to tell you I'm not…I've never been a forever kind of guy. But I'm not ready to let you go, either."

"Is it me or any woman?"

"Damn. I can't believe we are having this conversation on the phone," he said.

"Stop stalling, Steven. Is it me?"

"Hell, no, Ainsley. It's not you. I'm not ready to let you go. So yes, I want to pursue this."

The not-loving thing she'd deal with later. It was enough for her that he wanted to keep seeing her. Because she wasn't ready to let him go, either. "Okay. That's all I wanted to know."

"Glad you're happy," he said.

"I want you to be, too," she said.

"I will be when we're together again. I have to go to Berne so I'll be out of town for a few days."

"To see your mum?"

"Yes. She's busy at the accelerator and won't answer her cell," Steven said.

"Is it an emergency?" she asked. "Something with your family?"

"No. It's you. I told you I'd get my half brothers and our mothers to talk to you and mum won't unless I go there and ask her in person."

He was doing it for her. Suddenly it didn't matter that he'd left her this morning. No matter how confident Steven seemed, this "relationship" between them was throwing him off his normal game. She wasn't sure that was a good thing. The two of them might be destined for something greater—maybe to fall in love or perhaps to destroy each other.

Eleven

Steven entered the secure facility in Berne and found Roman waiting for him. The older man hugged him and greeted him like an old friend.

"Hello, Steven. Lynn will be up here in a few minutes. How was the drive?"

"Long," he said. He could have flown, but he needed time in the car alone to try to figure out why he was doing this. He'd always been careful to give his mum space, never wanted to be too clingy to her and yet he was in Berne because Ainsley needed an answer. He'd hurt her by walking out on her.

He'd made up the excuse that his Moretti roadster was made to be driven. So he'd taken it on this cross-continent trip. But on the drive he'd had a chance to put things into perspective and had made sense of his decision to do the articles. They were for the good of his company, not just for Ainsley. Now he felt more like his old self.

Ainsley had overwhelmed him during the night they spent together, but he had decided that it was only because it had been the first time they made love that he'd reacted like that. Once he got back to London and saw her again, she'd be like all the other women he'd dated. She was hot, but she wasn't any different from any other woman he'd slept with.

"Steven," his mum said from the doorway.

"Hi, Mum," he said, walking over to her. She hugged him close and held him for a few minutes before letting go. She always did that. He didn't know why she held him for so long, but a part of him liked it. When she hugged him he felt like she was just his mum, not a brilliant physicist everyone in the world wanted a piece of.

"I'm sorry I couldn't call you," she said.

"It's okay. I needed to get in my car and drive," he said.

She laughed. His mum had changed very little over the years. She was tallish, almost five-foot-eight, and had thick, curly brown hair with streaks of deep red woven through it that she wore in a very casual bun at the back of her head. Tendrils of hair escaped it to drift around her face. She had on her lab coat and the earrings he'd given her for her last birthday.

Roman watched them both, as he always did, like an indulgent father figure. Steven suspected that Roman was Lynn's lover, but his mother had never said anything about a romantic relationship between them so he kept that thought to himself.

"Do you have time for me?" he asked his mum.

"I've got an hour, sweetheart. I'm all yours."

"Want to go for a drive?" he asked her.

"I'd love to. I haven't left this facility in days," she said. She glanced over at Roman. "Will you call me if anything happens?"

"Of course. Enjoy your time with Steven. I'll take care of everything here."

She nodded and waved three fingers at Roman before linking her arm through Steven's. "Let's go."

He led the way to his car and got her seated. Then he put down the top of the convertible.

"Why are you in Berne?" she asked as he drove the car to a park that his mother suggested.

He parked the car and they got out and walked around the grounds. His mother was always very touchy-feely when they were together and he remembered as a small boy how much he'd enjoyed the fact that when she left the lab, she'd given him her full attention.

He suspected a part of her knew that he was lonely from spending so much time by himself. He hated how weak he felt when he was with his mum. He'd always wanted to make their time together last longer but yet, eventually he'd just found a way to let her go. It had meant shutting down everything, especially the hope that she'd stop being a physicist.

"Remember when Malcolm contacted you about me?" he asked, knowing that she would need all the details before she could make a decision about doing the interview with Ainsley's magazine.

"Yes. Did that work out?"

"Well, he laid out a challenge for all three of his heirs. We're all competing to see who can make the most profit in one of the business units and I need your help," he said.

"I don't know anything about business," she said.

"Mum, is it my first day being your son?"

She laughed. "I guess not. What can I do?"

"I've arranged for *Fashion Quarterly* to do a series of articles about the Everest Group. And the editor-in-chief wants her writer to interview each of our mums. As a fashion magazine, they want to talk to the women involved."

"About Malcolm?" Lynn asked.

"I don't really know. Maybe about your work."

"Is this important to you?" she asked.

Steven thought about it. No one had been important to him, but he knew that Ainsley was. He didn't want to be the reason why her article didn't fly.

"Yes, she is."

"*She* is?"

"I meant *it*. The articles are important. They will reintroduce the world to a brand that they may think of as passé."

"Don't even try it, Steven. You said *she*. Do you like the writer who is doing the articles?"

"No, Mum. I like the editor-in-chief."

"What's she like?" Lynn asked.

"She's American."

"Oh. What's that mean?"

He wanted to laugh. "She's different. She works in publishing and she's smart and funny."

"Sounds perfect for you. Did you take her to meet Aunt Lucy?"

"No. I'm not going to, either. You know how Aunt Lucy can be."

"I know she loves us," Lynn said.

"Yes, she does. But she can be pushy. She calls me once a week."

"Me, too," his mum said with a laugh. "Poor Lucy, stuck with two workaholics as family."

"Yeah, poor Lucy," he said.

"Do you ever resent me for the way your childhood was?" she asked.

"No," he said. "Why?"

"Roman said that I compartmentalize people. And I thought about when you were little and you wanted to spend time with me but I was always in the lab."

"You were the best mum you could be."

She shrugged. "That's true, but was it enough?"

"I have no idea. You're the only mum I have."

She smiled at him. "I don't want you to feel like I ignored you because I didn't want you."

This wasn't about him at all, but something was bothering his mother. He wondered if being with Roman had made her realize that family was more important to her than she'd acknowledged. "I always knew that your job takes all your attention. And you're brilliant at what you do, so that's okay."

She leaned over and kissed his cheek. "Thank you, Steven."

"You're welcome."

Her watch alarm went off. "I have to get back."

They walked back to the car and when they got there, Steven asked her, "Will you do the interview?"

"Only if the writer e-mails me the questions."

"That's all I ask. Bye, Mum," he said, wanting to be the one who said goodbye first.

"Steven?"

"Yes?"

"I...I've been thinking that maybe I didn't do a very

good job of showing you that life is about more than work."

He didn't respond to that. "Why does that matter?"

"If you like this woman, don't make the mistakes that your father and I did. You might find yourself looking back on life with regrets."

"What do you regret?"

"Not making more time for you," she said.

"Why now?" he asked her.

"Roman asked me to marry him. And I...I've said yes."

"Good. Congratulations," he said. But inside a door was closing. His mum and Roman would have their world together. Their life would be in the lab most of the time and that was something Steven couldn't be a part of.

"Thanks, sweetheart. I want you to be happy, too, Steven. Don't wait until it's almost too late to realize that life is more than work."

He nodded. He doubted that he could change the way he was. And he wasn't too sure he'd ever be able to be with a woman like Ainsley. He already knew that she made him react with jealousy and that wasn't the thing he needed to keep a calm head and stay focused on business.

Yet at the same time he'd always been determined not to repeat the mistakes his parents had made. He was going to pursue Ainsley and see if she could be the missing link in his relationship DNA.

At this moment everything seemed easy, but he knew it wouldn't be. He didn't love her. In fact he wasn't sure he had the capacity to love. He only knew that he wanted her and it was damn hard to work when he kept thinking about her. And he thought—knew—that Ainsley felt the same way about him.

Having her officially as his own would take away the doubt and hopefully the jealousy. He called Ainsley's office and found out that she was in Milan. Good, he thought. That gave him the time he needed to plan.

His mother's engagement to Roman had planted the seeds of his own engagement. To Ainsley. As his mum had said when he'd left…don't wait until it's too late.

Ainsley flew back from a meeting in Milan and arrived at Heathrow close to midnight. She was tired and wanted nothing more than to go home and sleep in Steven's arms. But she hadn't seen him in over three weeks. The logistics of a relationship like theirs was harder to figure out than she'd expected.

Steven had gotten his mother to agree to the interview, and she was using every contact she had to try to get in to see Malcolm Devonshire. But she had almost given up. Okay, that was a lie; she wasn't going to give up on getting him until the issue was on the newsstands.

She walked down the gateway wheeling her laptop bag behind her. It was one of those with a compartment for carry-on clothing as well and she found it was perfect for the short-haul business trips she took a lot of the time. Especially in the spring when all of the fashion weeks were in full swing and she traveled every week.

She turned on her BlackBerry as soon as she was down the gateway and found a message waiting for her from Cathy, informing her that a car would be picking her up at the curb.

It was times like this when she really adored her assistant. She was too tired to even think of dealing with a cab. She walked out of the terminal building, past the barriers and saw Steven standing by his car, leaning on the hood and watching for her.

She was so happy to see him. She had forgotten how much she liked his handsome face and that half smile of his made her feel like she really was home.

"Are you my ride?" she asked.

"I am. I figured the only way we'd be able to see each other was in the middle of the night when the rest of the world doesn't need us.

"Is that the only bag you have?" he asked.

"Yes. I hate to wait for luggage, so I ship it wherever I'm going."

Steven walked beside her and a part of her liked it. He opened the door for her and she climbed inside, relaxing back against the leather bucket seats as he climbed into the car.

He was playing music by one of the newer Everest Group recording artists, Steph Cordo. "This song is so popular right now. You must be excited to have a company artist doing so well."

"No, I'm not. I'm trying to beat Henry financially," Steven said.

"You are? Is that one of the stipulations of the deal with Malcolm? I know you are all competing."

"Yes. How was Milan?"

"Busy. But it was a productive visit. We're getting ready for the fashion shows coming up in the fall."

"Do you go to them all?"

"Usually. We sponsor a runway for upcoming artists and do other events," she said.

"Do you like it?"

"Most of the time. When I get home I generally take a week off to recover."

She glanced out the window and realized that they weren't heading toward Notting Hill. They were on the A3 heading south. "Where are we going?"

"My place."

"Oh."

"Is that okay?"

"Yes," she said. "I'm going to need a ride to work tomorrow."

"No, you won't. You're taking the day off."

"I am?"

"Yes. As luck would have it I have the day off, as well. I thought we'd spend it together."

She smiled to herself. "That sounds wonderful."

Her eyes drifted closed for a minute and when he stopped the car, rousing her, she found they were in a large rustic garage.

"We are at my country house in Cobham," Steven said.

She had spent little time outside London and she wished it were daylight so she could see the Surrey countryside surrounding his house. "I slept the entire way. Sorry about that."

"You were tired," he said. He got out of the car and took her bag from the trunk. He led the way up the path from the garage to the house. It was very modern and large, especially compared to the townhomes she was used to.

They entered through a side door into the kitchen. It was outfitted with all the modern conveniences and a large restaurant-grade stove. "Do you cook?"

"It's a hobby. My aunt Lucy is a chef and she taught me when I was little."

"Did you spend a lot of time with her?" Ainsley asked. All the articles she'd read about him in magazines and on the Internet had been about his business interests and nothing had been about family.

"Yes, whenever my mum was needed in Berne. She's been working on the particle accelerator for years."

"Is she working on the God particle?"

"Mum started working on it with Peter Higgs. He found the Higgs Boson. Then she started doing her own research. It's been her life's work. I'm sure she'll talk to your writer about it, but only via e-mail."

"That will be great," she said.

He led the way through the house. She had a vague impression of dark blue hues and a very British-looking den before he led her upstairs.

"Spend a lot of time here?"

The master suite had a large king-size bed in the middle of it and an en suite bathroom. There was a flat-screen, LCD TV on the wall and a love seat in front of it with a large padded ottoman.

"It's my retreat," he admitted.

"Do you bring a lot of people here?" she asked.

"You're the first," he said.

Ainsley didn't want to read too much into that. After all, this was only the third time they'd been together, but she couldn't help but feel special.

Steven had been busy over the last three weeks but mostly he'd been aware of how much he'd missed Ainsley. She was a busy woman and though she'd made a big deal about having a relationship with him he suspected she'd gotten scared because she hadn't had a free moment since they'd slept together. He thought her actions were deliberate.

Plotting with her secretary had been his only option.

He knew she was going to keep making him work to get back into her good graces. She might not be doing it intentionally, but she was definitely avoiding him. And he'd had enough of that.

Having her here in his bedroom felt right. It was the place he thought of when he pictured her with him.

He put her tote on the padded bench at the end of the bed. "Would you like a bath?"

"Yes. I think I would."

"I'll draw you one while you open this," he said, handing her a gift-wrapped box.

He left before she opened it. The ultramodern bathroom was an oddity for the UK, but he'd seen it in a magazine and decided he wanted one. It was large, with a garden tub and a stained-glass window that overlooked the backyard. He had a glass-enclosed double shower and a steam room in the space as well. The double sinks had a marble countertop.

He drew the bath for Ainsley and added some soothing bath salts he'd had his secretary order. He turned on the heated towel racks and checked to see that the champagne he'd left chilling was still cold. He popped the cork and poured them both a glass.

When he went back into the bedroom, she was still sitting on the padded seat with the gift box on her lap.

"You didn't open it."

"I was waiting for you," she said.

"I'm here," he said.

She toyed with the white ribbon on the box. "Why did you get me a gift?"

"Not so we could play twenty questions. Are you going to open it or not?"

She ripped the paper, folded it into a neat square and put it next to her on the bench. Then she opened the shirt-sized box. She drew back the tissue paper and pulled out the La Perla negligee. She pulled it from the box and held it up in front of her.

"Thank you."

"You're welcome. I wanted to find something that was as sexy as you are, but this was as close as I could come."

She blushed. "I'm not sexy."

"Then my memories of our night together must be wrong. Because I remember a very sexy woman in heels, hose and a garter belt seducing the hell out of me. Ready for your bath?" he asked, raising one eyebrow.

"Yes." Ainsley kicked off her shoes and then stood up to follow him into the bathroom. A sigh escaped her when her bare feet hit the heated wooden floor. This bathroom—this entire house—had been designed with comfort and luxury in mind.

He turned off the taps of the tub, helped her take off her clothes and then hugged her close. "I missed you."

"Me, too," she said. The weeks apart had been long and made her realize how important Steven was to her.

He undressed and they both got in the tub, sitting behind her and drawing her into his arms and back against his chest.

She sighed again as she relaxed against him. He cupped her breasts in his hands as she let her head rest against his shoulder. Her head tipped to look up at him.

"Tell me what you've been so busy with that you couldn't see me," he said.

"Work. Seriously, that's all I've been doing. I have to go to parties and dinners and every minute of my day is claimed by someone."

"I want to be that someone. I thought you wanted a

relationship," he said. He circled his fingers around her areola.

She shifted her shoulders and the tips of her pink nipples poked up through the suds in the tub. From his perspective, her body was all creamy skin, white soap bubbles and then there were those pink nipples…

"I do want one. I just didn't anticipate both of us being so busy. What have you been doing?"

"Getting the North American unit up to speed."

"How did you do that?"

"I sent my best man to do the job—Dinah. She works for me at Raleighvale."

"Is it hard running two companies?" she asked.

"Not for me," he said.

He lifted one hand from her breast and tipped her chin up. He leaned down and kissed her long and deep. Just what he'd wanted to do ever since she'd walked out of Heathrow.

She turned in his arms until she straddled him. He hadn't had a chance to have her on top of him as they made love, and he wanted to be able to see her face above his as he took her.

He cupped the water from the tub and rinsed her breasts off. Her nipples beaded in the air as his hands left them, replacing his touch with his mouth. She pushed her fingers into his thick dark hair and drew him to her.

Steven knew he'd revealed too much of himself by bringing her here, but as she shifted on him, her warmth replacing the warmth of the water in the tub, he didn't care.

He wanted this woman. He knew he couldn't take her in the tub. He needed to put on a condom before that happened, but for now it was enough to tempt both of them.

To let the tip of him tease the entrance of her body as his mouth moved over her breasts.

She wrapped her arms around him and hugged him close to her. He needed to keep her by his side, he thought. Marriage?

"Make love to me, Steven."

"Yes," he said, standing to lift her out of the tub and carry her into his bedroom. Thoughts of marriage would wait until later.

Twelve

Steven wrapped Ainsley in one of his big bath towels and carried her to his bed. He took a minute to dry off and then reached for the box of condoms he had in the nightstand drawer. He removed one and sheathed himself before falling down next to her on the bed.

"I thought you'd want to see me in that beautiful nightgown," she said.

"Not until I've had a proper welcome home. Then you can try on whatever you want."

She laughed. "I missed this."

"Did you? Then why did you refuse my calls while you were in Milan?"

He shifted on the bed so he was lying on top of her. He braced his elbows on either side of her body to keep most of his weight from her, but probed the entrance to her body.

She twined her arms around his neck, lifted herself up

and kissed him. "I wanted to make sure that you really wanted me. And I knew if you were serious about me, then you'd still want me when I returned to London. After you left that morning, I needed to know that I was as important to you as you are to me."

"I'll show you how important you are," he said sliding into her body inch by inch, taking his time and claiming her.

"I hope you can," she said softly. She wanted to believe in Steven, yet knew she still didn't trust him with her heart.

She held tightly to his shoulders as he began to thrust into her. She stopped talking and her eyes closed as her head fell back. He wanted to draw out their lovemaking, but couldn't. It had been too long since he'd had her and he felt his orgasm coming fast.

He tried to hold back, wouldn't come before she did. He whispered hot, sexy words into her ear. Brought his hand up between their bodies and caressed her breasts, teasing her nipples until he heard her gasp and then the sound of her low moan as she climaxed.

"Come for me," he said.

He held himself still as her body pulsed around him and then he started thrusting again. He ducked his head, caught her nipple between his lips and sucked on her until he felt his orgasm explode though him. He was blinded by it as he thrust into her two, then three times, until he was completely drained.

He collapsed next to her on the bed, using a corner of her towel to wipe the moisture from between her legs. He went to wash off and then came back to bed, pulling her into his arms.

"Now that pressing matters are out of the way, what were you saying? You were testing me?"

She pinched his side. "Yes, I was. I don't want to be the only one who has something at stake here."

"And what makes you think that you are?"

"Because you left," she said. "If you'd stayed that morning...well, I would have felt more confident."

"Why don't you?" he asked. She was lying on his chest and toying with the light hair that covered him. Her lowered head hid her expression.

"You're the first man I've felt this way about," she said. "And you aren't like my magazine. I can't manage you the same way."

"Why can't you?"

She shrugged. "Because I care about you, Steven. I've really missed you."

He hugged her tight for a minute. He was glad to hear that she cared about him. It meant a hell of a lot more than he'd thought it would.

"If you hadn't been playing games, we could have enjoyed the last three weeks."

She pushed herself up on an elbow and looked down at him. "I wasn't the only one."

"No, you weren't," he admitted. At first he'd been waiting for her to make the first move. After all, she was the one who'd wanted a relationship. But it hadn't taken him long to realize what she was doing. So now he was here with her in his arms and he didn't want to let her go. He was going to ask her to be his wife.

That was dangerous thinking for a man with no roots. A man who always moved on. He wasn't looking for a permanent home. He reached over and turned off the light. He didn't want to dwell on that now.

She curled on her side and fell asleep but he stayed

awake, holding her as tightly as he wanted to because there was no one but the moon and stars to see him.

In the quiet of the night, he realized his half-hatched plan of an engagement wasn't going to work. Ainsley cared about him. She was going to want the whole shebang. She wasn't going to settle for some long-term engagement just so he could sleep with her every night.

He only knew that he wanted her by his side and he was going to have to figure out how to make that happen. He wondered if she'd stop playing games now that he'd made the first move.

He hoped so, because he wasn't going to let her retreat back into her shell. He wasn't going to let her use work as an excuse to keep him at arm's length. He was in charge of this relationship and he would set the terms.

The words were strong and he knew he could say that now in the middle of the night, but in the cold light of day... he would do whatever it took to ensure that she was in his arms every night.

She stirred in her sleep as he squeezed her tight—too tight. He soothed her and then tried to go to sleep, but he held her for a long time before drifting off. He kept watching her face. He had to figure out how to keep her from meaning too much.

Ainsley woke up alone in Steven's big bed. There was a note on the nightstand. She reached over and picked it up. She'd forgotten to remove her contacts last night so she had no problem reading it.

Steven's spidery scrawl read:

I'm in my home office on a conference call. New toothbrushes in the medicine chest. Breakfast on the deck at 10.

She climbed out of bed, surprised by her own nudity. But as she stood there in the room, she found that she wasn't uncomfortable. Steven loved her body and she was coming to like it, too. She was coming to realize that she was the woman she saw in the mirror. That wasn't a facade but who she really was.

When she got downstairs, he was still on the phone and gestured for her to wait on the deck. She brought her BlackBerry with her and checked her e-mail. Freddie had sent her one saying that Maurice, the publisher of their magazine, needed to talk to her urgently.

She dialed his number in New York and was put through immediately to his office.

"It's Ainsley," she said when he came on the line.

"Good. Did you get Malcolm Devonshire?"

"Not yet. I'm still working on it. I did get all three of the mothers."

"That's great. As I mentioned before, I'm going to use your articles here in the States, as well. The Everest Group is going to relaunch the Manhattan Mega Store through an in-store event with XSU, the new group that's just signed with Everest Records. It will be their North American CD launch."

"Great. I assigned Bert Michaels to do the interviews with the mums. I think I might have to assign someone to do a sidebar piece on XSU. That's a nice plus.

"Also, I wanted to make sure you know that Steven Devonshire and I are dating. Are you still okay with that?" she asked Maurice.

"I am. I think as long as you're circumspect and we keep the focus off Steven, we'll be fine."

"Okay. I'll have to talk to my assistant about which

writer we have available to do the XSU interview. Let me call you right back."

"Just send it via e-mail. I want to know about Malcolm by close of business tomorrow."

"No problem," she said. But she had absolutely no idea how she was going to make that happen. Malcolm wouldn't even return her calls. She knew he also had an estate in Surrey. She'd have to get Steven to take her there today—it couldn't be that far. The sooner she talked to him the better.

She called her office and gave Cathy a list of things to do today. She hung up just as she heard Steven behind her. He walked out with a tray of fruit salad and juice.

"I had my housekeeper prepare this for us. Do you want something heavier for breakfast?"

"No. This is perfect," she said. She hated eating breakfast. That was probably part of the reason she tended to overeat all day. So she'd started eating something small. But she still didn't really like breakfast.

"Do you have anything planned for us today?" she asked.

"Is there something you'd like to do?" he asked.

"Yes. I'd like to meet your biological father."

Steven shook his head. "Afraid you're on your own there."

"Why? Steven, this is important to me. My boss is going to run the interviews with your mothers in our U.S. magazine as well. This is huge. If I get Malcolm to agree—"

"Sorry, Ainsley. I don't talk to him. You can call his attorney and see if you can work something out."

She shook her head. "Did you two have a falling out?"

"I don't want to talk about this."

She stood up and walked over to him. "I do. This is important to both of us."

He shook his head. "Not to me. I don't need Malcolm Devonshire."

"Then why are you working for him?"

"So I can show him up."

She realized that she was making him angry. She didn't understand why he couldn't simply call his father...except that he always referred to Malcolm as Malcolm, not Dad.

"Do you want to talk about it?"

"Why? So you can get some juicy tidbits to add to your article? Or because you care for me?"

"I do care about you."

"Then let this go," he said.

"I can't. It might be the writer in me but I want to know more."

"What does that matter to you? Isn't it enough to talk to my mother and Malcolm's other sons about our business?"

She crossed her arms under her breasts and watched him. "This isn't about the article anymore. This is about you and me. I want to know why you're so upset."

He turned away from her. Placing the tray on the table, he stalked over to the railing. His house overlooked a beautiful plot of land, and she felt as if the rest of the world didn't exist.

But it did. There were bosses to answer to and articles to get published. She knew she should just let him be, but she couldn't.

She walked over to him, putting her hand on his back. "I'm sorry, Steven."

"For what?" he asked, glancing down at her.

"For not realizing that Malcolm was just a sperm donor and not a father to you."

He turned to face her and she wondered if she'd misjudged him. Had she said the wrong thing?

"Sperm donor? That's brilliant. I've never heard him described that way before, but you certainly pegged it."

"You may have noticed that I'm pretty good at observing people and figuring out what makes them tick." She smiled, half in relief.

"I am, too, which is why I'm so good as a CEO," he said.

"You are good as a man, too," she said.

"You might be the only one who thinks so."

She doubted that. Steven didn't let people in. She wasn't sure that she was the only one who cared for him. As she watched him look out over his property, pretending his parentage didn't matter, she suddenly realized that she loved him.

Steven knew that he'd made a mistake by bringing Ainsley here. Now that she was here, he wanted to get her back to the city. Anywhere he could put barriers between them. It was fine if they were going to have a relationship. That was something he could definitely handle. But if she was going to keep asking questions about Malcolm outside of the articles she was having written…well, then she had to go.

He never thought about the lack of a father in his life. Men like Roman had long filled the gap as father figures when he'd been a young boy. But once he'd gone off to Eton he'd been on his own. There had been men that he'd learned things from when he'd been starting out in business, but for the most part he was a loner.

That's right, he reminded himself. He was a loner. He didn't have room in his life for a woman with soft violet eyes and compassionate hugs.

The only thing he needed a woman for was sex. He and Ainsley were white-hot in bed, but that didn't mean he wanted to open his veins and bleed for her in private. The article was his public face and no one saw the private man—not even Ainsley.

"You haven't said anything in almost thirty minutes," she said.

"You haven't, either," he said. They were eating lunch on the patio at his house. He'd shown her his estate and the quiet day he'd envisioned for them hadn't turned out as he'd planned. They were both tiptoeing around each other and he knew it was past time to get back to the city and back to work.

"I was afraid of saying the wrong thing again."

"You won't," he said. Because he'd buttoned up his emotions and tucked them away. He wouldn't react as he had earlier. He just hadn't expected her to ask him questions outside of the article. If you asked most people about seeing their father, it wouldn't be a big deal. But he was a Devonshire bastard and even if Ainsley wanted to put a better spin on it, the world knew that Malcolm wasn't much of a father to the boys he'd sired.

But he'd spent his life knowing that his father hadn't wanted to have anything to do with him. That was why he'd been so reluctant to go to that meeting at the Everest Group and, conversely, why he was so determined to win the contest Malcolm had set in motion. He wanted to show the old man that he—Steven—was better at the business Malcolm had dedicated his life to.

He checked his e-mail on his iPhone and saw that

Dinah was back from the States. She'd sent a long file of recommendations and that was just what he needed—to bury himself in work at the office. He felt a twinge of regret that he wasn't going to follow through on his plan to ask her to live with him, but their awkward conversation today had reminded him what living with someone would entail.

When you were dating you didn't have to share every detail of your life, but once you moved in... Then came resentment and anger and he didn't need that. Steven Devonshire was a rock—an island—and he needed nothing.

"I have to get back to the office. A bit of an emergency has come up."

She nodded. "Let me get my bag and I'll be ready to go."

She went back into his house and he watched her go. Knew she'd never be here again. A part of him was really going to miss her. He liked Ainsley more than anyone he'd slept with in a long time. Hell, forever. He'd never met a woman who got to him the way she did.

And she would never know. *Could* never know, because if she did then she'd want things from him that he'd never be able to give her.

She came back down with her bag and he went to get the car, realizing that he'd simply been sitting there waiting for her the entire time. She did that to him—made him forget the parts of himself that he'd always taken for granted and now he wanted to be that man again. He was a man who didn't care and was always looking ahead. He would get back to being that way again, he vowed.

He pulled the car up to the front of the house and went in to get her. She was standing in the foyer, thanking his housekeeper for the breakfast she had made.

"Thank you for bringing me here," she said to him.

"No problem. Sorry we can't stay longer," he said.

"No, you aren't. You've been trying to get me out of here ever since I asked about Malcolm."

He shouldn't have been surprised that she saw right through him, but he was taken aback that she'd said anything. She had let him take the lead, let him be the one to make the bold moves, and now suddenly she was taking charge.

"I have been. I realized that I'd let a journalist into my house—into my sanctuary. I know I suggested the articles, but I invited you here for personal reasons."

"I wasn't in here snooping around and trying to find out your secrets. You and I are lovers, and I asked you for a favor. If I'd realized what your relationship with Malcolm was, I never would have asked," she said.

"What is my relationship with him?"

"Nonexistent. Right?"

"Very true," he said, opening the car door for her. "Get in."

"I'm not done talking yet," she said.

"I am."

He held the door a minute longer and she just stood there with a sullen look on her face. A part of him knew he was being unfair to her, but she was asking questions and pointing out things that he never wanted to talk about.

"I'm leaving. Are you going with me or not?"

"Of course I'm going with you. I can't believe you are letting this get so out of control."

"It's not me," he said. "It's you and your magazine article. Prying into lives of people who don't want to be pried into."

"*You* are the one who wanted some compensation for letting us shoot in your store."

"That's right, I did. Just the heirs and our businesses. You had to drag family into it. Never thinking that Malcolm Devonshire only ever had one family and it was a corporate business unit."

"I'm so sorry to hear that because then he missed out on three incredible sons," she said. She brushed past him and climbed into the car.

Thirteen

After driving the entire way in silence, Steven dropped her off at her office and then drove away. She knew that she'd pushed too hard with him. But that hadn't been her intent. She had no idea why things had gone south so quickly. There was one thing she knew and it was her job. When she was in her office, she was in control. It was the one place where she didn't have to answer to anyone but herself.

Cathy was surprised to see her when she walked in. "I thought you were taking the day off."

"I changed my mind. Maurice wants us to lock up the interview with Malcolm. I need you to find out who his attorney is and get me an appointment with him. Did you get the schedule of when we need answers for the article?"

"I did. I'm glad you're here. I was just getting ready to call you. We had a minor emergency with the photo shoot for next month's cover. The model we're using is refusing to wear the outfit the creative director picked out."

"This is the shoot we're doing here in the building, right?"

"Yes. But she's in your office with the creative director."

Ainsley pushed open her office door and saw the creative director, the model and the photographer all sitting there. "What's going on?"

"He vants me to wear this," the model said, standing up and gesturing to her outfit.

"Do I know you?"

"No."

"Then sit down. Tell me why I'm wasting money on another photo shoot," she said.

"She just did a shoot for *Cosmo* and wore an outfit similar to this."

"Really?" she asked the girl. "What's your name?"

"Paulina."

"We're trying to find something different for her to wear," the creative director said. "But everything I've pulled together isn't working. I know you were in Milan…"

"Go back to the fashion closet and find something different. Here are the sketches I brought back from Milan. Let's find something inspired by these. It's different."

"Agreed. Thanks, Ains. You're a lifesaver."

"And my head is on the chopping block if I screw up this magazine," she muttered to herself after they left.

She walked over to her desk, but didn't sit down. Instead she went into her private bathroom and washed her face. She didn't look at herself in the mirror because she didn't want to see the stranger looking back at her. Not again.

Before Steven, she had felt as if she were wearing a

costume when she looked in the mirror—that the slim and pretty woman she saw wasn't really her. But now she knew that she had started to accept who she was and if she looked in the mirror again she was going to see a woman who'd made a huge mistake.

A woman who'd trusted the wrong man and let herself get hurt. From the beginning she'd known that Steven held a part of himself back from anyone he got involved with. She might have mistaken his reactions for those of a man who was uncomfortable letting others see him. But the truth was she suspected that he didn't feel anything at all, that he played at having emotions.

Just as he'd said to her that he couldn't love. And she'd foolishly thought that he was just saying that. That he didn't want her to build castles around him, and make him into something he wasn't.

That wasn't fair, she thought. She had no idea what kind of man he was; she kept expecting him to be one way and was surprised when he wasn't. The truth was she'd allowed herself to be angry with him because she'd realized she'd overstepped her bounds.

She had taken his idea for an article about the business and the men of the Everest Group and turned it into an article about the women in Malcolm Devonshire's life, which was what it had to be for *FQ*. Had she simply been looking for a salacious angle she could use to sell magazines?

It was only now that she'd fallen in love with him that she wanted the details for herself. Not for the magazine or the world, but for her. She wanted to know what it was like for him to grow up in the shadows.

She didn't have to ask how it had affected him because she saw how guarded he was with her—with everyone. He worked all the time and was driven to prove to the world that he didn't need anyone. She knew he'd deny it, but that was what Steven Devonshire was doing.

She wondered what he'd meant by the competition and wanting to beat his brothers. She knew that Steven had left his retreat with her because she'd made him uncomfortable. How could she make amends for that? And how could he? She'd reached out to him not to hurt but to help him.

She was still thinking about that when the phone rang. "This is Ainsley."

"Hello. This is Henry Devonshire. I'm having a get-together at this weekend's London Irish Rugby game and wanted to invite you. My half brothers will be there and my mum as well. You'd have a chance to see what my life is like away from the record label."

"I'd like that, Henry. May I bring Bert Michaels along? He's the writer doing the interview."

"Yes. That's fine. I'll leave tickets at the Will Call window."

"Thanks."

She was still going to see Steven whether they were involved or not. And she didn't know how she was going to handle that.

Being professional was one thing, but seeing the man she loved and having him ignore her… She needed to talk to him before the rugby match. She needed to figure out if she'd damaged irreparably what they had. There was only one way for her to do that. She had to call him or go to his office.

She sent him an e-mail to see if he was going to respond or ignore her.

Thank you for a lovely evening. Please join me for dinner tonight.

She didn't have to wait long. A few minutes later she had a response from him.

Are you asking as a magazine editor or my lover?

She hit Reply and knew if she had to choose between the articles she was publishing and Steven, she'd pick him.

Lover.

His response came back a minute later.

Then yes. I'm done at eight. I'll pick you up.

She thought about it for a moment and realized that she wanted to do something nice for him. Something like what he'd done for her last night.

Meet me at my house. I'll have dinner for us.

She left the office early and stopped at Tesco's on her way home to pick up the ingredients for a light pasta sauce and garlic bread. She wasn't much of a cook and if his aunt was a chef, he wasn't going to be impressed by anything she made. But staying in seemed like a good idea tonight. She wanted to be alone with Steven.

She needed the chance to repair the damage she'd done when she'd let her desire to get ahead get in the way of her relationship with Steven. And she didn't want anything to come before the man she loved.

Steven had to park down the block from Ainsley's house when he got there. He had a bottle of wine in one hand and a copy of Steph Cordo's new CD in the other. He knew he'd been a bit of a bear when she'd brought up Malcolm. But he couldn't help it.

He didn't talk about his family—ever. But he'd talked about his mum and Malcolm with Ainsley and that made him wonder if he should have turned down her dinner invite. But he couldn't. He wanted to see her again.

It didn't matter that she made it hard for him to focus on work. He was drawn to her like a moth to a flame and no matter that he knew it would end the same way the moth's life did, he was still plunging ahead.

He rapped on her door and waited in the damp April evening for her to answer. She opened the door a few minutes later. She wore a Betsey Johnson apron and had bare feet. She hadn't changed out of the same jeans and T-shirt that she'd had on when they'd left his place in Surrey.

And she looked eminently kissable.

He took her in his arms as soon as he stepped over the threshold. Pulled her close and kissed her for all he was worth. He used his mouth and his lips to tell her that he was sorry for the way he'd overreacted.

When he set her on her feet, she stepped back away from him. She put her fingers on her lips and looked up at him. He saw there were tears in her eyes.

"Don't cry."

"It's just… I'm sorry I asked those questions. I was doing it because I care about you, not to get a scoop for our writers to use," she said.

"It's okay. You just found my one hot button."

She tipped her head to the side. "Do you only have one?"

He thought about it. Malcolm was the only topic that always set him off. Even as a child he'd been quick to get into fights with other kids at school when they brought up Malcolm or his bastard brothers.

"Yes, just one sets off my temper."

"But you have other hot buttons?" she asked, leading the way into her kitchen. The scent of garlic and tomatoes filled the air and he almost moaned. The combo was one he loved. She gestured for him to have a seat at the small table in the kitchen.

"I have hot buttons for sex," he said. "Do you have a corkscrew? I'll open the wine and pour us each a glass."

"I do. How can you casually mention sex and wine in the same sentence?"

"Easily," he said. "When I'm around you, sex is always on my mind."

"Is that the only reason we're together?" she asked.

He found the corkscrew and opened the bottle of merlot she had sitting by two glasses on the table. "Sex?"

"Yes," she said, "I'd like to think there is more to us than sex."

"There is," he assured her. But he didn't know what it was and he hoped she wouldn't ask him. "Do you need my help cooking?"

"Maybe. I'm not a master chef. But I think I've got the pasta and sauce. If you want to check the garlic bread that would be great."

He did and they had a nice dinner talking about nothing important. He sensed that she was on edge. It was the first time she had been that way around him since they'd become lovers.

"What's made you so nervous?" he asked her after they cleaned up the dinner dishes.

"I just realized today that you mean more to me than I

thought you did and I don't want to say anything to make you leave."

There was more vulnerability in that sentence than he'd expected and he had no idea how to respond. Her candor startled him.

"Don't build too many dreams on me, love. I'm still just one of the Devonshire bastards. A man who was born one has a hard time leaving that behind."

"You aren't a bastard with me, Steven. And I can't help having dreams of the two of us together. Even when we were apart, I thought about you."

Steven leaned back in his chair and took a long sip of his wine. He didn't want to let her know he'd missed her. She already had too much power over him. Right now he was hard just listening to her talk about the kinds of wine she liked. How much ammo should he give her?

"I'm glad to hear that. Why did you make me wait so long before you asked to see me again?"

She shrugged. The vulnerability in her eyes returned and it made his heart miss a beat. He didn't want to see her looking like that. He wanted her happy and confident.

"Tell me," he urged her when it seemed she wasn't going to say anything.

"I was afraid."

"Of what?"

"Well, I've been obsessed with you since I wrote that article five years ago. And I wasn't sure if this new thing between us was just me wanting someone I couldn't have. I mean, five years ago I was fat."

"Five years ago I was blind. Because I like you, Ainsley," he said, even though he'd had no intention of saying anything. "Your body is sexy, but it's who you are that attracts me."

She blinked, got up and walked away from the table. He followed her to find she was crying.

"What did I say?"

"Just exactly the right thing," she said, turning and throwing herself in his arms. "I love you, Steven."

He froze, his arms halfway around her. *Love.* Damn. Normally he was adept at avoiding these kinds of relationship talks, but Ainsley had knocked him off track earlier with her questions about Malcolm and tonight with her apology. And he was gobsmacked.

She was staring up at him. Her wide violet eyes beaded with her tears and he knew he had to say something. But had no idea what to say.

He cared for her; he wanted her. But love? He had no idea what that even felt like and he had no idea how he was going to find the right words for this moment.

"Thank you."

"Thank you?" Ainsley hadn't spent a lot of time thinking about what kind of response Steven would give to her profession of love, but she'd expected something more than *thank you*.

"Yes. But I'm not sure what you see that you think is worth loving," he said.

In that moment she realized that the sexy, charming man was damaged. Why hadn't she realized it earlier? His parents' abandonment had left him as vulnerable as her weight had left her.

When he looked in the mirror, he saw someone who couldn't love and when she looked in the mirror, she saw someone who was fat.

"It's okay. I see the real you," she said.

"What do you see, Ainsley?" he asked her.

She struggled to put into words what she felt for him. It was ephemeral. More emotions than tangible qualities. But she knew what he wanted. Because he'd shown her that she was sexy despite her fears.

"I see a man who is very caring and careful with me and my emotions."

He shook his head. "You see a man who wanted to get you into bed and did everything in his power to make that happen."

She looked at him and felt the first hint of doubt that Steven was the man she thought he was.

"I see a man who took time out of his busy schedule to give me a day off and to make time for us."

Again he gave her that hard look of his. One that she was coming to seriously dislike. "I needed to work from home that day. It worked out for me."

She walked away from him and then turned back to face him. "What is your problem? Why can't you see what I do?"

"I have no idea. Maybe you wanted to see something in me that wasn't there. Some kind of fantasy based on that interview you did five years ago. I'm not that man."

She pointed her finger at him. "You could be, you just don't want to. Because you're a coward."

"I've hit men for saying that."

"You're not going to hit me and we both know it."

"That's right, but I will walk out this door."

"If you do, then it will be because you're afraid. Afraid to take a chance on something good and lasting."

He walked to her and for the first time she wished she'd left her shoes on because she could use a couple of extra inches right now. She felt overweight and weak compared to him. But she knew she wasn't.

Her size had never truly defined her. She might have let it at one point, but she was smart, funny and sexy no matter what her weight was. And right now she knew that she was worth loving. She always had been. This man was going to realize at some point that he'd given up on something good.

"Love like this doesn't come along every day, Steven. And if you walk out my door, you will miss me. Tonight, tomorrow and a hundred other tomorrows, because you will end up alone."

"Thanks for the prediction, Madame Ainsley, but I don't need your second sight to tell me that. I like to be alone. You and me, we had some hot sex and that was it."

She shook her head. "You can't even see what you are throwing away." She couldn't stop the tears that burned, but she refused to let them fall. Blinked and blinked until they pooled at the bottom of her eyes.

"Don't do that. Don't look at me with those wide, wet violet eyes and try to make me feel guilty," he said.

"I'm not trying to make you feel anything. I wanted to love you, but you're too set in your own ways to understand that love isn't a trap."

He gave her a cynical look that made her shiver. "Sorry, love, but I know better. I've seen my mother trapped by her feelings for her work. And my father couldn't even leave his true love—the Everest Group—to *meet* his sons, much less spend time with them.

"I know what love is but it's not the same love that you're talking about."

She wrapped one arm around her waist and watched him. There were no words to make this okay. Not for him and certainly not for her. She knew when he had a chance to think…hell, what did she really know about him?

But she didn't know if he'd come to the realization that she was worth keeping before she moved on. Before she looked at him and was filled with apathy, not empathy.

"I think you should go," she said.

"I think so," he said, picking up his suit jacket and walking toward the door. "For what it's worth, I'm sorry. I did enjoy every minute we spent together. You are a very special lady, Ainsley."

Then he walked out the door and she stood there watching him go, watching him walk down her block away from her. A light rain fell and he didn't quicken his pace, just kept moving steadily, inexorably toward his car.

She closed the door and wrapped both arms around her waist, feeling as if she were falling apart. She had no idea how she was going to recover from this. She hadn't thought she could feel this bad from a person again. No one had ever hurt her like him. He'd hurt her badly five years ago, and she didn't want to admit he'd done it again.

She sat there for a long time, tears burning at the back of her eyes. Finally, she just drew her knees up to her chest and put her head down. She let her tears fall freely, knowing that they were going to come one way or another.

Her cell phone rang and she thought about getting up to answer it. It might have been Steven, but she knew it wasn't him. He would have come back if he'd had a change of heart.

And she would have let him in. Even though he'd said those things, she still loved him and she had a feeling she would for a long time.

Fourteen

Steven knew he'd made a mistake the first time he'd slept with Ainsley. She was a mass of contradictions and she made him care too much.

The rest of the week passed in a haze. Dinah had gone above and beyond on her recommendations for the North American operation with detailed notes for all the locations. She was turning that line of business around. He wouldn't have anything to base that on, other than his gut instinct, until the first financials came in at the end of the month, but so far each day they were improving and were way above last year's revenue at this same time.

His business unit was outperforming Henry's by a hair and Geoff was struggling, thanks to rising gas prices. But now, he didn't care about winning the competition with his half brothers anymore. All he really wanted was… Ainsley.

But he'd made damn sure that she was out of his life. He hoped she moved on quickly, but he knew the way he'd ended things would take time for her to recover from.

But as she'd sweetly listed all the reasons why she loved him, he had felt so afraid. Not for her, because she so obviously loved him, but for himself, because he felt the same way. He wanted desperately to spend the rest of his life with her.

With one person.

And that was a weakness he'd never allowed himself before this. Never even encountered. So he'd done the one thing he could think of: end things. End them in a way that would leave him no way to go back to her. Because if he'd left even a hint of an open door there, he knew he'd come back and break that door down.

And if he held her in his arms again, he was keeping her. He wasn't about to let her go. Not his Ainsley with her sweet smile and made-for-sin body, her brassy confident manner in the office and her shy sensuality in the bedroom.

He walked out of the bedroom at his apartment in London and into the living room to the bar. He pulled out a bottle of aged scotch and poured himself two fingers. He downed it and then poured himself another one.

There wasn't any amount of liquor that could drown this, however. No amount of thinking or rationalizing that was going to make the tears he saw in her eyes okay. He should never have been so brutal.

He knew from what she'd said that she'd been as lonely as he had been. And she'd tried to change her life first by losing weight and then by reaching out to him. By making love with him and then by loving him.

And he'd spurned her.

And for what?

He was a coward, just as she'd said. He was the worst kind of man. The same as his father, the man he'd never wanted anything to do with.

He picked up the phone despite the late hour and dialed her number. What was he going to say? He had no idea.

"Hello?"

Her sleepy voice made him smile and he knew he couldn't do it. He couldn't talk to her now when he was feeling like this. He needed to make sure he could be her man. And not run away the first time there was something he deemed too emotional.

He hung up without saying a word and sat back in the big leather chair of his. He found his cell and dialed Edmond's number.

The lawyer answered on the very first ring.

"This is Steven."

"Hello, Steven. What can I do for you?"

"Tell me why Malcolm even acknowledged my birth and the births of Henry and Geoff. It was clear he didn't want a family or heirs. So why did he?"

"I have no idea. At the time the Everest Group was struggling financially and he was trying very hard to get it back on track."

"Then why have heirs?"

"I think he wanted to ensure the company would live on after he died. I just don't think he knew how to focus on a woman and his business at the same time."

"Just like me."

"Indeed, sir. I've heard you are very like your father."

"In what way?" Steven asked.

"That you are a workaholic. Someone who focuses only on the bottom line."

"That doesn't make me like him. That makes me like

any other corporate shark," Steven said. "Ainsley called him a sperm donor and that's all he's been."

"I'm sorry that you feel that way. Malcolm did the best he could by you and the other heirs."

Steven thought about that for a very long time. "Have you ever—never mind. Sorry for bothering you so late."

"Not a problem, sir. Call me any time. Is there anything else?"

"Why haven't you called Ainsley back?" Steven asked.

"Malcolm doesn't talk to press."

"This isn't press. I have arranged a series of interviews with *Fashion Quarterly* magazine and I think the promo will be great for our company."

"Sounds good," Edmond said.

"It would be better with Malcolm. Will you ask him if he will answer a few questions?"

Edmond cleared his throat. "You know he—"

"Just ask him. Say it's the only thing that his son has ever asked of him."

"I will, sir."

Steven hung up—he was going to end up as Ainsley had painted him, but he hadn't realized that before this moment. He was going to end up alone with only his business partners at his deathbed.

And he didn't want that.

He wanted a different future. He wanted to have a wife and maybe a few kids with large violet eyes and pretty dark hair.

He wanted to have something to come home to and have Ainsley in his arms every night. And that was never going to happen unless he won her back.

And there was only one way to do that. He had to figure out how he could have her and not lose himself.

But after a lifetime of running away from attachments and emotions, he wasn't sure where to begin. He only knew that if he didn't he was going to end up like Malcolm Devonshire and he didn't want that.

He'd spent his entire life trying to prove to himself that he was better than his father and it was time he took the one risk that his biological father never had—love.

Ainsley didn't attend the rugby match, but sent her reporter instead with Freddie. They both had a wonderful time, which she gathered from Freddie's tweeting of the event. It got them some nice advance publicity for the articles that Bert was writing. He'd even wrapped up his piece on Henry. And she heard from him that he'd spoken to Steven and Geoff there as well.

The Devonshire heirs could be Freddie's show now. She didn't want to have to see any pictures of Steven; it was too hard. She woke up in the middle of the night missing his arms around her and that made her mad because before him she hadn't had anything to miss.

She'd spent her entire life alone, and had expected to continue it that way. But Steven had given her a glimpse—a hint—of what life could be, what it would be like to share her life with someone. And she wanted that.

She still craved his presence; she still needed him and loved him.

So when she got a DVD by special courier she wasn't sure what it was. It was marked "Devonshire Heirs," and when she opened it up and popped it into her DVD player she saw that it was a BBC One special interview with the Devonshire heirs. At first she was worried the interview would be similar to theirs, but luckily, the focus of the interview was different from the one she had Bert writing for their magazine. But the TV coverage certainly wouldn't detract from the articles they were running.

When the camera zoomed in on Steven, she was surprised to see how tired he looked. She took a few steps forward toward the screen, not even turning around when she heard her office door open.

"I think the main thing I've taken from my life was that I needed to be better than Malcolm. I wanted to make my own life—a better life. But I never realized that I was following the same path. Making the exact same mistakes," he said, looking directly into the camera.

She felt as if he were speaking directly to her.

"What mistakes have you made?" the interviewer asked.

There was a knock on her door and she paused the DVD.

"Yes?"

"It's quitting time and happy hour has come to you," Freddie said.

Cathy entered the room behind him with a pitcher of margaritas on a tray. "I'm not sure…"

"I am. This is your friend talking and you need a break."

"What are you watching?"

"An interview with the Devonshire heirs. Steven is about to talk about his mistakes."

Freddie put his arm over her shoulders without a word. He took the remote from her hand and pushed play.

"Being a workaholic and keeping everyone at arm's length. That made me successful in business, but it has left me rather isolated," Steven said.

"I'm sure there are women everywhere ready to help you fill your lonely nights."

Steven shrugged. "There's only one woman for me…if she'll still have me."

She couldn't believe what she heard. She stopped and replayed it. She watched it again and then pushed pause. "Is he talking about me?"

"I'm sure of it. You said he was going to come back to you some day," Freddie said. "It looks like that day came sooner than you thought."

"Do you think he's changed?"

Freddie lifted one shoulder. "Only you can decide."

"I'm so afraid. I still love him. How can I say no to a chance to have him in my life? It's what I've dreamed of."

"There's your answer," Freddie said.

"When did this air?" she asked. "How did I not hear about it?"

"It hasn't aired yet," Cathy said holding up the envelope it had come in. "There's a note from the producer saying that Steven asked for an advance copy to be sent to you."

"Is there a note from Steven in there?"

She shook the envelope and nothing came out. "Nope."

"What do I do?" she asked her two closest friends.

"I'd call him," Cathy said. "Whatever happened between you, it's obvious that he's sorry. His part of the interview was all about you."

She considered that but she'd made the last gesture, offered the last olive branch, and look how that had turned out. She wasn't sure she had the confidence to do it again. She just couldn't. She needed to see a sign from him.

What kind of sign?

"Freddie?"

"I'd wait, but then I'm not courageous when it comes to matters of the heart."

He wasn't and his track record was much longer than hers. Cathy and Freddie both looked at her as if they expected her to make a choice right then.

"I have to think about this. I'm scheduled to go to New York tomorrow. I'll call him when I get back. I can't jump back into that fire right now."

"Great idea. If he loves you, it doesn't come with an expiration date," Freddie said.

That's right. Was love forever? She hoped it would fade when it looked like she'd be heartbroken forever. But now? Should she jump in her MG and drive to find him? Though she missed him, she was going to have to wait until she was sure. Wait until the memory of the pain he'd inflicted on her subsided.

She worked until nine and went home to an empty house. She packed her carry-on bag and found the La Perla negligee that he'd given her still in the bag. She'd never had the chance to wear it for him. She held it up to herself and when it was time for bed she put it on.

She lay in her bed staring at the ceiling and thinking about Steven. She reached for her phone and almost called him but stopped herself. She wasn't ready.

A part of her wanted *him* to come back to *her* because he had been the one to walk away. She rolled on her side and hugged the pillow that he'd slept on to her stomach. It smelled faintly of him but the scent was fading and she knew she should probably go ahead and wash it, but she hadn't.

She'd just kept it here because she loved a man who was afraid to admit that he loved her. That interview intimated that he might have changed his mind, but she wasn't going to risk her heart on a maybe.

Steven had hoped she'd call him when she'd seen the interview, but she hadn't. He knew that he was going to have to show her that he loved her. That would take more than vague words on a taped interview. She needed and she deserved the big gesture.

He picked up his cell and called her friend Freddie.

"This is Steven Devonshire," he said when Freddie answered the phone.

"What can I do for you?" Freddie asked.

"I need your help to surprise Ainsley."

"Why? Do you just want her back in your bed or do you want her in your life for good?"

"I don't think that's any of your business," Steven said. He wasn't about to talk about his personal feelings with this guy.

"It is, because I had to pick up the pieces after you broke her heart—not once but twice. So you tell me that you aren't going to hurt her again or you can just hang up."

"I'm not going to hurt her again—you have my word."

"Okay, so what do you need from me?" Freddie said.

"I need Ainsley to come back to the Leicester Square store today at 2:00 p.m."

He hoped that Ainsley would be flattered that he remembered that the location was where they'd both met again. He wanted to go back to the beginning with her—not five years ago, but this time—and ask her to marry him.

"I'll do it. But why don't you just call her?"

"I want to surprise her," he said.

He hung up a few minutes later and realized that he was going to be very disappointed if Ainsley didn't show up. But he had a feeling she would. A woman like Ainsley didn't fall in love easily and he was counting on the fact that she did care deeply for him.

Ainsley finally spoke to Edmond, Malcolm's solicitor, and the man told her that Malcolm was too ill to be interviewed. Maurice was a little disappointed that they couldn't get Malcolm, but the articles on the mothers were so interesting that he was happy with that.

"I need to do photo shoots with the men and their mums. But otherwise I think this is wrapped up," she said to Maurice on the phone.

"I see you didn't mention a relationship with Steven in the draft of the article I received."

"We're…this is difficult, Maurice, but I'm not sure we have a relationship."

"Why not?"

"It's complicated."

"Everything in life is if you let it be. You found a way to get these articles done and kept from compromising your integrity. Why can't you figure out how to keep your relationship with him?"

"How do you know it's me?"

"I don't," Maurice said. "But you've been happier these last few weeks as we've secured the Devonshire women. I'd hate to see that end. Unless you were using him to get him to cooperate and then I might have to fire you."

"Maurice, I would never do that. I love him, but I'm not sure he loves me. I'm afraid—"

"That's all I needed to hear. I'm giving you to close of business today to resolve this issue."

"It's not an issue," she said to her boss. "It's my personal life and it's not as easy to sort out as a magazine."

"It's easier. You just have to trust your heart."

Maurice hung up and she wanted to scream. She was so afraid of letting Steven in, but she knew she had to do it; otherwise she would spend the rest of her life wondering what might have been.

Her phone rang.

"Ainsley Patterson."

"It's Freddie. Clear your calendar for this afternoon."

"Why?"

"It's a surprise."

"Freddie—"

"Don't bother asking because I'm not saying a word," he said.

"Fine. But I need to pick your brain about something."

"Okay, I'll be listening."

Steven had planned for every detail; now he just needed her to show up. His hands were sweating as he waited for her. Then suddenly she appeared. She walked into the store the way she had that first time. She wore a figure-flattering Betsey Johnson dress and walked toward him.

She stopped as she saw him. And Steven knew it was time for him to do his part. He walked forward and drew her into his arms, kissing her deeply. She tentatively held his shoulders. He held her close to him because it had been too long since he'd held her. And he needed her.

He pulled away and looked down into those wide violet eyes and he felt his heart clench.

"I'm so sorry, Ainsley. I was afraid and I never wanted to feel the same vulnerability that I saw in your eyes. I love you so much and I hope that you still love me."

He went down on one knee in front of her. "Please

say that you haven't given up on me and that you still love me."

Tears made her beautiful eyes watery and she stood there looking down at him.

"Seriously? After all the tears I've cried, I promised myself I wasn't going to cry over you again. But here I am."

"Love," he said, standing up. "I mean it. I'm not just spouting words. I love everything about you. Your curvy body, the way you smile at me in the morning. And I'm planning to spend the rest of our lives convincing you of that. I'd rather it be with you by my side but I'll keep trying to convince you no matter how long it takes," he said.

She took his hand, drew him to stand beside her, threw herself in his arms, wrapped her arms and legs around him and kissed him for all she was worth.

"I love you, Steven. I can't live without you. I'm so glad you came to your senses."

"Took me long enough," he said.

"It felt like a damn lifetime," she said.

"Will you marry me?" he asked.

"Yes, Steven, I will."

He slipped the ring on her finger and knew he'd finally found the home he'd always been searching for in this sexy woman's arms.

Epilogue

Ainsley and Steven spent the next few months living together and reassuring each other that they were meant to be together. When the articles ran in her magazine, she felt a sense of pride at the way the women came off. Malcolm Devonshire came off looking like a man who'd given up three successful women. And Ainsley felt sorry for Malcolm that he hadn't realized what he was missing.

The *Fashion Quarterly* articles on the Devonshire heirs and their mothers rocked the publishing world. Hearing the stories of the three women who'd given Malcolm Devonshire the publicity he'd needed to take the Everest Group to the next level had been publishing gold.

A few of the gossip Web sites had made a big deal of her relationship with Steven, but that had blown over and her boss, Maurice, didn't think it was anything to worry about.

"I can't believe you're getting married today," Freddie said.

"Me, either," she said.

Freddie came over and adjusted her veil. "I'm glad you finally found love."

She smiled at him. "I think it found me. What do you think?"

"Gorgeous, darling. I think that Maurice is going to regret not covering this event."

"I think he's done enough butting into my personal life," she said, remembering how her boss had pushed her to go after a life outside of work.

"Almost ready?"

"Yes. Is my dad?"

"He's outside and your mum is nervous. She said she never thought she'd see this day," Freddie said with a laugh.

She glanced out the window of the waiting room to where the wedding was taking place. The lovely rooftop garden overlooked Berne. It was decked out in flowers and twinkle lights.

"She's said the same thing to me several times," Ainsley said. "Is Steven here?"

"Of course he is," Freddie said. "I'm going out to reassure him now."

Freddie left and Ainsley sat back down on the padded bench. She'd never dreamed of a fairy-tale wedding but Steven wanted one. He wanted everything to be perfect for their special day and since his mother couldn't leave Berne and her work, they were getting married there.

He'd flown her parents to Switzerland and Freddie and

Cathy were going to be her attendants. His half brothers had attended and were standing up with him.

He'd changed from the man who was nothing but an island to a man who was surrounded by family and friends. They'd made their own family or at least the beginning of one. They were both workaholics and loved their jobs, so they'd decided not to have kids.

Neither of them had planned for children so it wasn't something they felt they'd missed. And Steven said loving her was something he was still trying to get comfortable with.

She had everything she'd never thought she'd have. When Lynn came out of the lab escorted by her fiancé, Roman, the wedding began. She'd met Lynn a few times and liked the woman. As well as her twin sister, Lucy. Both women loved Steven and though he'd always felt isolated, they'd always been there for him.

Her parents came in and hugged her.

"Your dress is exquisite," her mum said.

Ainsley had spent hours in Milan having the dress made. It was tight at the waist, low cut at the top, and fell in a straight line to the floor. There was a small train at the back of the dress.

She'd chosen a short, sassy-looking veil to wear over her glossy black hair.

"Thanks," Ainsley said. Her parents hugged her again and then went to sit down.

The wedding march started and instead of walking down the aisle with her father, she walked down by herself. Steven was waiting for her and kissed her as soon as she got to the altar. The minister went quickly through the vows and soon it was time for their first kiss as husband and wife.

It was long and sweet and everything that she had known it would be.

"I love you, Mrs. Devonshire."

"I love you, too, Mr. Devonshire."

* * * * *

Desire™

2 in 1 GREAT VALUE

THE LAST LONE WOLF by Maureen Child

When Daisy Saxon arrived at ex-Marine Jericho King's mountain lodge he took her in. But the lone wolf was in for a shock—Daisy's plan was to get pregnant with his baby!

SEDUCTION AND THE CEO by Barbara Dunlop

Melissa Warner has CEO Jared Ryder thinking about mixing a little pleasure with business. Yet even in his passion-induced haze, he suspects Melissa of hiding something…

THE TYCOON TAKES A WIFE by Catherine Mann

A year after she left him Jonah Landis discovers Eloisa is still his wife. Jonah is determined to get the answers he still needs…

HIS ROYAL PRIZE by Katherine Garbera

Amelia Munroe is the wrong woman for Geoff Devonshire can now can he claim his birthright. Will he choose power…or her?

AT THE BILLIONAIRE'S BECK AND CALL? by Rachel Bailey

Being brash billionaire Ryder Bramson's corporate pawn wasn't independent Macy's style. On the other hand, this irresistible man's passion just might win her over to his scheme…

HIGH-SOCIETY SECRET BABY by Maxine Sullivan

Dominic finally had claimed Cassandra Roth, but he could not reveal her daughter's true parentage without risking his tenuous hold on happiness…

On sale from 15th April 2011
Don't miss out!

0411/51

&🌹RIVA™

Cupcakes and Killer Heels
by Heidi Rice
Ruby Delisantro's usually in the driving seat when it comes to relationships, but after meeting Callum Westmore's bedroom eyes she's in danger of losing control and—worse—of *liking* it!

Sex, Gossip and Rock & Roll
by Nicola Marsh
Charli Chambers has *never* met someone as infuriating—or delectable!—as businessman Luca Petrelli. Can she ever get close enough to the real Luca for their fling to be more than just a one-hit wonder?

The Love Lottery
by Shirley Jump
When her name is unexpectedly drawn in the town's love lottery, uptight Sophie Watson's horrified to be matched with smug-but-sexy Harlan Jones! A week of dating him will be *terrible*—won't it?

Her Moment in the Spotlight
by Nina Harrington
Mimi Ryan's debut fashion show is her dream come true. If she's being bossy then grumpy photographer Hal Langdon will just have to live with it! It's a shame she can't get his strong arms or teasing smile out of her mind…

On sale from 6th May 2011
Don't miss out!

Available at WHSmith, Tesco, ASDA, Eason and all good bookshops

www.millsandboon.co.uk

BAD BLOOD

A POWERFUL
DYNASTY,
WHERE SECRETS
AND SCANDAL
NEVER SLEEP!

VOLUME 1 – 15th April 2011
TORTURED RAKE
by Sarah Morgan

VOLUME 2 – 6th May 2011
SHAMELESS PLAYBOY
by Caitlin Crews

VOLUME 3 – 20th May 2011
RESTLESS BILLIONAIRE
by Abby Green

VOLUME 4 – 3rd June 2011
FEARLESS MAVERICK
by Robyn Grady

8 VOLUMES IN ALL TO COLLECT!

THE

LEGACY

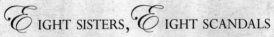

EIGHT SISTERS, EIGHT SCANDALS

VOLUME 5 – OCTOBER 2010
Zoe's Lesson
by Kate Hewitt

VOLUME 6 – NOVEMBER 2010
Annie's Secret
by Carole Mortimer

VOLUME 7 – DECEMBER 2010
Bella's Disgrace
by Sarah Morgan

VOLUME 8 – JANUARY 2011
Olivia's Awakening
by Margaret Way

8 VOLUMES IN ALL TO COLLECT!

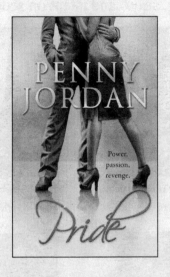

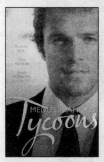

How far would you go to protect your sister?

As teenagers, Maya and Rebecca Ward witnessed their parents' murder. Now doctors, Rebecca has become the risk taker whilst her sister Maya lives a quiet life with her husband Adam, unwilling to deal with her secrets from the night her parents died.

When a hurricane hits North Carolina, Maya is feared dead. As hope fades, Adam and Rebecca face unexpected feelings. And Rebecca finds some buried secrets of her own.

One innocent child
A secret that could destroy his life

Imprisoned for a heinous crime when she was a just a
teenager, Allison Glenn is now free. Desperate for a second
chance, Allison discovers that the world has moved
on without her…

Shunned by those who once loved her, Allison is determined
to make contact with her sister. But Brynn is trapped in
her own world of regret and torment.

Their legacy of secrets is focused on one little boy. And if
the truth is revealed, the consequences will be unimaginable
for the adoptive mother who loves him, the girl who tried
to protect him and the two sisters who hold the key
to all that is hidden…

"Deeply moving and lyrical…it will haunt you…"
—*Company* magazine on *The Weight of Silence*